Praise for Anna Bennett's Wayward Wallflower series:

The Rogue is Back in Town

"Fans of Regency romance authors Eloisa James, Tessa Dare, and Mary Jo Putney will go wild for the final installment of Bennett's Wayward Wallflowers trilogy."
—*Booklist* (starred review)

"Smart and sassy romance . . . simply a joy!"
—*RT Book Reviews* (A Top Pick)

"A standout historical romance novel . . . truly delightful."
—*Romancing the Bookworm*

"Bennett's gift for writing a page-turner of a plot is on full display . . . a solid Regency story of true love."
—*Kirkus Reviews*

"Entertaining . . . [offers] plenty to satisfy Regency fans."
—*Publishers Weekly*

I Dared the Duke

"Sharply drawn characters, clever dialogue, simmering sensuality, and a dash of mystery make this well-crafted Regency thoroughly delightful."   —*Library Journal*

"Readers will enjoy this sassy Regency take on the classic *Beauty and the Beast* tale."   —*Booklist*

"A captivating page-turner that will become a new favorite among romance enthusiasts!"   —*BookPage*

"Will truly win readers' hearts."
        —*RT Book Reviews* (A Top Pick)

"Bennett brings new life to traditional Regency stories and characters."   —*Kirkus Reviews*

"Scrumptious . . . I devoured every word! A hot and wounded hero, a heroine you wish could be your friend in real life, and witty scenes that sparkle with life . . . The Wayward Wallflowers just keep getting better!"
        —Laura Lee Guhrke,
        New York Times bestselling author

My Brown-Eyed Earl

"Heart, humor, and a hot hero. Everything I look for in a great romance novel!"   —Valerie Bowman

"One bliss-giving read . . . witty and whimsical."
        —*USA Today*

"Delightful historical romance."
        —*Night Owl Reviews* (A Top Pick)

"Heartwarming and joyous . . . a delightful read."
        —*RT Book Reviews*

St. Martin's Paperbacks titles
By Anna Bennett

MY BROWN-EYED EARL

I DARED THE DUKE

THE ROGUE IS BACK IN TOWN

FIRST EARL I SEE TONIGHT

First Earl
I See Tonight

ANNA BENNETT

St. Martin's Paperbacks

For anyone who's kept a diary,

especially if it had a lock

that turned out to be entirely decorative.

This is a work of fiction. All of the characters, organizations, and events portrayed in this novel are either products of the author's imagination or are used fictitiously.

FIRST EARL I SEE TONIGHT

Copyright © 2018 by Anna Bennett.
Excerpt from *The Duke is But a Dream* copyright © 2018 by Anna Bennett.

All rights reserved.

For information address St. Martin's Press, 175 Fifth Avenue, New York, NY 10010.

ISBN: 978-1-250-19946-1

Our books may be purchased in bulk for promotional, educational, or business use. Please contact your local bookseller or the Macmillan Corporate and Premium Sales Department at 1-800-221-7945, ext. 5442, or by e-mail at MacmillanSpecialMarkets@macmillan.com.

Printed in the United States of America

St. Martin's Paperbacks edition / November 2018

St. Martin's Paperbacks are published by St. Martin's Press, 175 Fifth Avenue, New York, NY 10010.

10 9 8 7 6 5 4 3 2 1

Chapter 1

Miss Fiona Hartley's etiquette was far from flawless, but even *she* was not in the habit of writing letters to gentlemen who were of no relation to her. And she'd certainly never had occasion to propose marriage in such a letter.

Until now.

Frowning, she sat at her desk and tickled her chin with the tip of the downy quill she held poised above a blank sheet of stationery. Miss Haywinkle's School for Girls had neglected to cover the finer points of proposing to an earl. But then, the headmistress had failed to cover any number of topics that might have proven helpful, such as how to walk down the street wearing a ridiculous bonnet without feeling foolish. Or how to properly hit a cricket ball while encumbered by a gown and two petticoats.

And, regrettably, Miss Haywinkle had never offered the lesson Fiona needed the most: how a shy heiress might discern which of her gentlemen suitors was interested in more than her fortune. Alas, the men of Fiona's acquaintance seemed unable to comprehend that she was a person first and foremost—that she existed wholly independently of her substantial dowry and the vast wealth she stood to one day inherit. Perhaps it was a naïve notion, but she'd always longed to marry a man who genuinely cared for her. Maybe even loved her.

At least now she needn't bother continuing her fruitless search. The dream of a love match had flown out the window yesterday afternoon—with the arrival of a perfectly ordinary-looking letter in the regular post, addressed to her.

Curious, Fiona had lifted it from the silver salver, admiring the heavy paper and elegant script. But as she'd opened and read it, dread had seeped into her veins.

No one could discover the truth revealed in that letter—not her parents or her dearest friend, Sophie, or the authorities. Most certainly not her younger sister, Lily.

A shiver stole over Fiona's skin despite the silk shawl draped over her shoulders and the cozy fire burning in her bedchamber's fireplace. The scoundrel who'd sent the horrid note obviously knew she'd sacrifice anything to protect her sister and was demanding an exorbitant amount of money to keep Lily's secret. But procuring such a large sum wasn't easy—even for an heiress.

Papa was out of town and wasn't expected back for at least a week. Even if time weren't of the essence, Fiona didn't dare tell him the shocking news for fear his weak heart would give out. After Papa collapsed in his office last year, his doctor had warned him to avoid undue stress. Fiona had already lost her real mother, and the thought of losing Papa terrified her.

She'd lain awake much of the night, debating what to do, and had reached the only logical conclusion. What she needed was a titled husband—and fast.

The Earl of Ravenport was the perfect candidate. His desperate financial situation was widely rumored, and though he'd once been engaged, his fiancée had called off their marriage a fortnight ago. His lack of fortune and his brooding personality kept most of the matchmaking mamas at bay, which reduced the competition and increased Fiona's odds of success.

He'd come to mind for one other reason as well—on the most humiliating night of her life, the earl had shown her kindness. She'd tripped on the dance floor and landed among the musicians in the orchestra, sending their sheet music flying. Her dance partner had frozen, aghast. Other guests had snickered.

Only Lord Ravenport had stepped forward and offered his hand, effortlessly pulling her to her feet. Somehow, that simple contact—his large gloved hand enveloping hers—had managed to be simultaneously reassuring and thrilling. The brief encounter had meant a great deal to her, and yet she wasn't at all certain that the earl knew her name.

The fact that the earl happened to be handsome was immaterial. Entirely irrelevant, really. But if his devil-may-care smile made Fiona's stomach flutter now and again, she saw no harm in it. She deserved to glean *something* from the deal after all, and what girl wouldn't enjoy having a tall, athletic, ruggedly attractive husband—at least in name? It wasn't as though she intended to give him her heart.

Nevertheless, she'd enjoy sketching him . . . one day. She didn't yet know him well enough to do him justice. Oh, she could recall his physical traits all too easily: the dark hair that spilled across his forehead, the slightly crooked nose, and the boxer's physique. But in spite of his self-assured demeanor, he was more guarded than most— reluctant to reveal who he truly was. She, of all people, respected that.

Fiona tapped a fingernail on her gleaming mahogany desk, determined to forge ahead. How, precisely, did one broach the subject of marriage with a relative stranger?

Shrugging, she dipped the nib of her quill and let the ink flow.

> *Dear Lord Ravenport,*
> *We've not been formally introduced, but you may*
> *remember me from the Millbrook ball, where I*
> *tripped during the cotillion and tumbled headfirst*
> *into the musicians, knocking the violinist clear off*
> *his chair. Would you consider binding yourself to*
> *me in matrimony for the rest of your natural life?*

A bit too honest, perhaps. And too direct. Miss Haywinkle would be utterly appalled by Fiona's lack of decorum. Though the thought of shocking her former headmistress cheered her slightly, the letter would never do. Sighing, she tossed it in the dustbin, withdrew a clean sheet from the desk drawer, and began writing anew.

She took the most polite and businesslike approach she could manage given the rather forward nature of her request.

> *Dear Lord Ravenport,*
> *I am writing to you with a proposal that is*
> *unconventional but quite sincere. After much*
> *deliberation, I've reached the conclusion that that*
> *each of us would benefit greatly if we were to ally*
> *ourselves through marriage. I possess a very large*
> *dowry which I'm certain you would find useful. In*
> *addition, I would promise to be a very*
> *undemanding wife. Indeed, you would be free—*
> *nay, encouraged—to pursue your own interests.*
> *All I would ask in return is that you allow me to*
> *retain a small property with a cottage in Cornwall,*
> *five thousand pounds for my own use, and a*

*reasonable yearly allowance. The stipulated
monies shall be mine to spend as I please without
any explanation or interference.*

*I do have one last requirement. We must wed
within a fortnight. I understand that this may seem
rash, but since our union would merely be one of
convenience, I see no reason to delay. Please
consider my proposal and provide your response
at the first opportunity.*

*Sincerely,
Miss Fiona Hartley*

In the end, she was quite satisfied with the result. And yet her hands trembled as she folded the sheet and melted the sealing wax.

Once sent, the letter could not be retrieved; the words could never be taken back. There was no way to know how Lord Ravenport would react to the deal she'd proposed. He might tell all his friends and make her the laughingstock of the ton, or he might refuse to dignify her proposal with a response. But proposing to him was her best hope of sparing her sister, Lily, untold ridicule and pain. Fiona had no choice but to try.

A knock on her bedchamber door made her jump guiltily. She quickly hid the letter in the folds of her skirt. "Come in," she said, attempting a breezy tone.

Her sprightly maid, Mary, bustled into the room, and Fiona released the breath she'd been holding. "Pardon the interruption, Miss Fiona. Miss Kendall came for a visit. She and Miss Lily are in the drawing room, and they're quite eager for your company."

"Please tell them I'll be down momentarily. I require a few minutes to . . ." *To contemplate the sheer madness of what I am about to do. To come to terms with my future,*

which most notably includes a cold, loveless marriage.
". . . to finish up a bit of correspondence."

The maid set freshly folded linens on the damask-covered bed. "I'll gladly tell them. But your sister is not a particularly patient person. Don't be surprised if she insists on retrieving you herself." Mary cocked an ear to the door and clucked her tongue. "Alas, it sounds as though she and Miss Kendall are heading this way now."

Oh dear. Fiona sprang from her chair and, before she could change her mind, thrust the letter into Mary's hands. "Would you please see that this is delivered immediately? It's quite important," she said, "and requires the utmost discretion."

Before the maid could reply, Lily burst into the room, poor Sophie in tow. Propping her hands on her slim hips, Lily narrowed her eyes at Fiona. "Here you are. Why have you closeted yourself away in your room on this glorious day? Sophie and I had begun to despair of you ever making an appearance, and we've much plotting to do in advance of tonight's ball."

"*Plotting* sounds rather sinister," Sophie said softly. "Perhaps you meant *planning*?"

"No, no, I meant *plotting*." Lily swept the heavy velvet panels away from the window and shot a suspicious look at Fiona and the maid. "Have we interrupted something?"

"Certainly not," Fiona said, a bit too brightly.

Mary whisked the letter behind her back and dipped a quick curtsy as she inched her way toward the bedchamber door. "I'll leave you ladies to your own devices. Be sure to ring if you require anything." She shot Fiona a reassuring smile before scurrying down the hall.

Fiona fought the urge to chase after the maid, seize the letter, and tear it into a thousand pieces. Instead, she greeted her friend with a warm hug and waved a hand at the armchair beside her bed. "What an unexpected pleasure, Sophie. Please, make yourself comfortable while Lily explains the nature of this apparent pre-ball emergency." Fiona arched a brow at her sister. "No, wait. Allow me to guess. You tried on the blue silk this morning only to find the bodice has grown too snug?"

Lily grinned and launched herself toward Fiona's bed, bouncing on the mattress in a most hoyden-like manner. "No, the gown is fine. Care to take another guess?"

Fiona tapped a finger against her lower lip. "You cannot find a hair ribbon in just the shade of sapphire to match your slippers?"

"Wrong again." Lily sat up on the edge of the mattress, and the familiar gleam in her green eyes sent a chill down Fiona's spine. "I realized something during my walk after breakfast. Here we are—the three of us—barely a month into our first season, and despite all we learned while we were away at finishing school, it seems we are woefully unprepared."

Fiona wrapped an arm around the post at the foot of her bed and smiled. "I had a similar thought this morning. But I doubt Miss Haywinkle will agree to reimburse our tuition, if that's what you're thinking."

Sophie smoothed a lock of golden blond hair behind her ear and tilted her head. "I found the headmistress's lessons quite instructive. Perhaps I could have done without the endless French conjugations, but she *did* teach us how to avoid a myriad of social blunders."

"You would have avoided them anyway," Lily said, and Fiona agreed. Sophie possessed a natural grace, was unfailingly polite, and never uttered an unkind word about anyone. "Besides," Lily continued, "I'm not talking about black-and-white matters, like which fork to use during the first course or the correct way to address a dowager duchess. I want to know . . . more important things."

Sophie's brow wrinkled. "What sorts of things?"

Lily leaned her head back and closed her eyes. "I should like to know how it *feels* when the most handsome man in a crowded ballroom looks directly at me."

"As would I." Fiona sighed. "And I'd like to know precisely how it feels when he puts his hand on the small of my back and whispers in my ear." She sat on the arm of Sophie's chair and lightly bumped her friend's shoulder. "What would *you* like to know?"

Sophie shifted uneasily, and her fair cheeks turned pink. "Well, I suppose it would be helpful to know how it would feel . . . that is, the particular sensation of . . . well, being ravished."

"Why, Sophie," Lily cried, "how positively wanton of you! I am impressed."

Sophie covered her face with hands and groaned. "I'm mortified. I don't suppose we could forget I ever said that?"

Fiona slipped an arm around her friend. "Don't be silly. Lily's only teasing. You can tell us anything."

Lily leaped off the bed, impatiently pushing a long, dark curl away from her face. "Yes! These are *precisely* the sorts of things we must know. I'm going to make a list." She plopped herself behind Fiona's desk and began rummaging through the piles of sketches covering the surface, pausing to consider one. "Oh, Fi, this is a brilliant drawing of Lady Everly, and the parrot perched on the branch behind her is genius. That woman is an insatiable gossip."

"Thank you," Fiona said sincerely. "But I wasn't trying to make a statement."

"I know," Lily said with admiration. "And yet your drawings never fail to reveal the truth about people." She shuffled the sketches some more and opened a desk drawer. "Do you have a blank sheet of paper around here?" She peered over the desktop. "Never mind, I shall reuse this one in the dustbin."

"No!" Fiona's heart pounded as she snatched the first draft of her proposal to the earl from Lily's hand and crumpled it in a fist. "This list deserves a new, clean sheet." She quickly located one in her drawer and placed it in front of her sister, who stared at her curiously.

Lily raised her delicate eyebrows, dipped the pen in the ink, and meticulously enumerated all the things they wished to experience during the remainder of their first season. "It's ambitious, to be sure, but I have faith that we shall learn all this . . . and more."

Fiona was not quite as optimistic as her sister. As of this morning, her season was not about finding love, but rather, about securing a husband in the least amount of time possible. The blackmailer had demanded payment within a fortnight, which meant she *must* convince the earl to marry her before then.

Obviously, she did not have the luxury of indulging in a slow, heartfelt, romantic courtship. But surely there were advantages to a betrothal that was perfunctory, businesslike, and practical—even if they escaped her at the moment.

"We are all agreed then?" Lily said, more like she was issuing an edict than asking a question.

Fiona and Sophie nodded and murmured their assent. Resisting Lily was an exercise in futility.

"Excellent," she said, pacing the length of the bedchamber. "Each of us will keep a diary in which we record these things"—she waved the list—"so that we don't forget what it's like to . . . to fall in love."

Sophie shook her head vehemently. "Oh dear. I can't

write such things in a diary. What if my mother were to discover it?"

Lily shrugged. "You can tell her it's mine."

"Mama *knows* my handwriting." Sophie stood and nibbled the tip of a finger. "No, a journal is much too dangerous. Besides, I doubt I'll have anything of significance to record."

"Nonsense," Fiona countered. Oddly enough, her sister's idea had some merit. It was a small way of taking charge of their lives when very little else seemed to be within their control—a most vexing state of affairs. "If you pay attention to your feelings, you will discover little things can be the most meaningful. Sincere compliments, gallant gestures, furtive smiles . . . I think we should give it a try."

"You don't have to write names if you'd rather not," Lily added. "Let the gentlemen remain anonymous if you wish. What we want to capture are the *feelings*."

"But why?" Sophie asked. "Who is our audience? It's not as though we're going to publish our journal entries." She turned a shade paler. "Are we?"

"*No.* The diaries will be for our own edification," Fiona said firmly. She glared at her younger sister sternly. "Perhaps we'll choose to share them with each other. Maybe we'll save them in the bottom of a trunk so that one day, when our own daughters make their debuts, we'll be able to warn them about the unique combination of exhilaration, dread, and hope that's wrapped up in one's first season."

"I suppose there's no harm in taking a few notes," Sophie said, still more than a little skeptical. "With all names excluded."

"Good. It's decided," Lily announced. "We shall begin keeping journals immediately. May tonight's ball provide ample material."

Fiona cringed inwardly. If the Earl of Ravenport made an appearance tonight—as she hoped he would—there'd be no shortage of drama in her corner of the ballroom.

Tamping down a wave of panic, she linked hands with her sister and Sophie, so that the three of them formed a tiny, intimate circle. "To the debutante diaries," she said earnestly. "And to charting our own courses—even if they're different than the ones we'd envisioned."

"Has something happened, Fi?" Sophie's brow knit in concern. "You seem rather preoccupied. You'd tell us if something was wrong, wouldn't you?" Sophie was too perceptive by half, curse it all.

"I fear something *is* wrong." Fiona released her friend's and sister's hands and propped her fists on her hips. "The gown I'd selected for tonight's ball. I've decided it's ghastly. Help me choose another?"

All too happy to assist, Lily strode to the armoire and flung open the doors. "Are we looking for something that Miss Haywinkle would disapprove of?" she called over her shoulder, hopeful.

"Most definitely," Fiona replied. Now that she'd proposed to an earl, a demure white gown seemed far too safe a choice. Besides, she didn't believe in half measures. "Let's try the deep rose silk, shall we?"

She couldn't force Lord Ravenport to marry her, but she *could* make him notice her.

And the sumptuous rose silk was a fine place to start.

Chapter 2

As a rule, David Gray, the Earl of Ravenport, avoided two types of women: those who were alarmingly desperate and those who were stark raving mad. Unfortunately, Miss Fiona Hartley fell squarely into both categories.

He wasn't personally acquainted with the heiress, but he didn't need a formal introduction to know that she was trouble personified. The proposal she'd written him, now tucked into the chest pocket of his jacket, provided irrefutable proof.

Even her father's substantial fortune, amassed by trade, had not gained Miss Hartley's acceptance into London's most elite circles. A regrettable combination of innocence and awkwardness made her an easy target for the gossips who took pleasure in ridiculing a common-born woman who dared to rise above her station.

Gray had problems of his own—a manor house literally crumbling around him, estate finances in complete disarray, and a sweet but doggedly determined grandmother who reminded him daily that he needed an heir.

He wanted no part of Miss Hartley or whatever game she played. For he had no doubt she was playing a game—and that the stakes were perilously high.

Still, he couldn't deny that her letter had piqued his curiosity, at least enough to make him put in a brief appearance at the Northcroft ball tonight. From his relatively secluded spot near the open doors leading to the terrace, he could observe everything: guests streaming into the ballroom, couples twirling on the dance floor, and shrewd matrons casting their matchmaking nets. Thank heaven for the cool breeze at his back—which made him feel less trapped.

George Kirby, Gray's closest friend, sidled up to him and handed him a drink. "If you're not interested in dancing or chatting with other guests, why bother dragging yourself here at all?"

"Good question. I'm already regretting my decision." Gray took a long draw of brandy and tried not to let his gaze linger on Helena, his fiancée—or rather, his *former* fiancée—as she batted her eyes at a duke. But old habits died hard.

Somehow, he always knew precisely where Helena was, who she was with, and the exact shade of the gown she wore. He was attuned to her every move and every emotion—and wished to hell that he weren't.

Kirby scoffed as though he'd read Gray's mind. "It was wise of you to show your face here tonight. You wouldn't want people to think you're avoiding the social whirl, or worse, that you're heartbroken over Lady Helena."

"I don't give a damn what people think," Gray muttered.

But for the record, his heart was *not* broken. It was frozen.

He'd envisioned a future with Helena—had seen it with utter clarity. They'd sneak afternoon naps under the grand old oak on his estate and dance midnight waltzes on his moonlit terrace. Eventually, they'd be blessed with a couple of children who'd run across the fields, a mischievous puppy yapping at their heels.

But when Helena visited the manor house, she'd seen none of those things.

She'd seen only crumbling chimneys, untended gardens, and peeling paint. And shortly thereafter, she'd changed her mind about marriage—and about him.

Kirby clasped Gray's shoulder and shook it like he was trying to wake him from a drunken stupor. "What you need, my friend, is a diversion. Meet me at the club later tonight, and we'll pay a visit to a gambling hell or a brothel—your choice." He poked a conspiratorial elbow in Gray's side. "Both, if you like."

Gray shook his head as he stared at the crowded ballroom. Damned if he'd wager money he didn't have or squander it on sex. Not when he needed every shilling for timber, brick, and marble. "I have plans early tomorrow morning."

Kirby arched a brow. "Working at the Fortress again?" *Fortress* was the sometimes affectionate, sometimes disparaging name Gray had given his manor house—fitting, since it resembled a small medieval castle . . . after a rather devastating battle.

"The list of projects is long," Gray replied. An understatement to be sure. The house's roof leaked, its plaster walls were cracked, and several shutters hung cockeyed off their hinges. But he was determined to return his family's estate to its former glory so that he could make his grandmother proud and maybe bring a smile to her face—before it was too late.

If, one day, the restored grandeur of the Fortress also happened to make Helena regret jilting him . . . all the better.

"You know what they say about all work and no play," Kirby quipped. "It makes you a tedious ass."

"Well, that explains everything," Gray said with a shrug. "But don't let me stop you from enjoying whatever form of debauchery you have planned. I only intend to stay here another hour or so." Just long enough to tell Miss Hartley there was no way in hell he'd marry her—in the most tactful manner possible.

"You're sure you don't want to join me?" Kirby cajoled.

Out of the corner of his eye, Gray spotted Miss Hartley several yards away, wearing a dark pink gown, a bright spot in a sea of frothy white. Oddly, though, it wasn't her dress that set her apart.

Her auburn hair gleamed in the light of the chandeliers, and her smooth skin seemed to glow from within. She wasn't pretty in the classical sense—too many freckles dotted her face and shoulders, and her limbs were too long for her body, not unlike a newborn colt's. But when she turned to speak to her friend, a smile split her face, and for a moment, he forgot to breathe.

Reluctantly, he dragged his attention back to Kirby and nodded. "As soon as I finish my brandy, I'm going to speak to my grandmother and make my excuses." Not precisely the truth, but Miss Hartley had begged for discretion, and he saw no harm in keeping her secret. For now.

"Very well then. I'll see you at the club for dinner tomorrow night," Kirby said pointedly. "Remember what I said about all work . . ." As he backed away, he circled an imaginary rope around his neck, yanked it toward the ceiling, and let his eyes roll back in his head.

Gray scowled at his friend's antics, but maybe Kirby was right. The world wouldn't fall apart if he was a little less serious now and then. The problem was he didn't know how to be any other way.

Slowly, he made his way toward Miss Hartley and her small group, watching her carefully. When she spotted him approaching, she swallowed and blinked twice before turning her gaze on him.

Despite her brazen marriage proposal, good manners prevented him from striking up a conversation, even about something innocuous as the weather. Fortunately, Miss Hartley's circle included his grandmother's friend Lady Callahan, who was all too happy to perform the introductions.

"Lord Ravenport," Lady Callahan intoned, closing her fan with an expert flick of the wrist. "Please, allow me to present my daughter Miss Sophie Kendall and her friends Miss Fiona Hartley and Miss Lily Hartley."

Gray exchanged the expected pleasantries, then turned to Fiona. A halo of loose curls crowned her head, and she worried her plump bottom lip. Her pink gown exposed the long column of her neck and the curve of her shoulders; he could almost see her pulse beating wildly at the base of her throat.

His instincts screamed for him to run right out of the ballroom, and yet his boots remained rooted to the floor. Worse, before he knew what he was doing he'd asked her to dance.

"It would be my pleasure," she stammered, taking his arm.

As he led her to the dance floor he questioned his own good judgment—and not for the first time that day. He'd witnessed Miss Hartley trip and tumble into the orchestra at the Millbrook ball. He'd been dancing with Helena at the time but had paused to help her up.

So much had changed since then.

He had no idea if Miss Hartley's dance partner had been to blame for the incident or whether she was prone to falling, but just to be safe he tightened his hand on her waist. And they began moving to the music.

The first measure had barely played before she asked, "You received my letter?"

"I did," he said noncommittally, twirling her beneath his raised arm.

When she faced him again, she looked him directly in the eye. "What do you think of my . . . offer?" she asked, her voice cracking on the final word.

He tamped down an unexpected pang of sympathy. "I think that we hardly know each other."

"True, but that is easily rectified, is it not?" There it was—an unmistakable hint of desperation. And a sense of urgency that even her letter hadn't conveyed.

"It is," he conceded. "However, I suspect that the more we know each other, the less we'll like each other." Cynical but true in his experience. His parents certainly hadn't grown fonder of each other. Neither had he and Helena.

She winced and looked away before regaining her composure. "Perhaps. But we needn't like each other."

Gray chuckled at that. "I never thought I'd meet someone more jaded than I."

"So, you'll consider my offer?" she pressed.

"I will not," he said firmly. Under different circumstances, her fortune may have tempted him. But she was clearly intent on using him for her own purpose—and he suspected that she'd set her sights on him for reasons beyond his title. After all, there were half a dozen peers in attendance right now who'd leap at the chance to marry a young and unconventionally beautiful heiress.

But he was not one of them.

"It seems rather closed-minded of you to dismiss me summarily," she shot back, displaying a boldness that was borderline rude—and refreshing.

"If I said I'd consider your offer, I'd only be giving you false hope. Delaying the inevitable."

"The inevitable rejection, you mean," she clarified.

"Yes." He was still reeling from the sting of Helena's rebuff and wouldn't wish anyone that sort of pain and humiliation.

"Please," she begged. "I realize that it's highly unusual for a woman to propose marriage—"

"It's unheard of."

"Surely you must be curious—as to why I did it." She looked up at him, her shining blue eyes challenging him to deny the truth of her words.

Gray shrugged. "You have your reasons for making the offer; I have my reasons for declining it."

"Give me the opportunity to explain," she pleaded. "Just a quarter of an hour to make my case. If, after that, you remain unconvinced, I promise I shan't mention it again."

He must be out of his damned mind to consider engaging in further discussion with Miss Hartley. The very last thing he needed was another conniving, self-serving female attempting to interfere with his life. He had opened his mouth to tell her so when someone bumped into his back—hard.

Gray's torso collided with Miss Hartley's chest, and she stumbled two steps before he wrapped an arm around her slender waist, catching her just before she landed on the parquet floor. She gasped and clung to his jacket, her expression an odd mix of relief and mortification.

"Oh dear," she breathed.

Their faces were so close he could see unexpected dark blue flecks in her irises and the individual freckles dotting her nose. "Forgive me," he said.

"For what?"

For what indeed? Steering her into the collision? Gripping her waist too tightly? Or for staring at the swells of her breasts and having decidedly wicked thoughts while he *should* have been shielding her from further embarrassment? Ignoring her question, he asked, "Are you all right?"

"I am." Her cheeks turned a charming shade of pink. She blew out a breath and shot him a shaky smile. "When it comes to dance floor mishaps, I confess I've survived much worse."

Gray looked over his shoulder to see how the other couple fared, surprised to find Helena and her dance partner smiling apologetically.

And the truth struck him. For the last ten minutes, while he'd been dancing with Miss Hartley, he'd been completely, blissfully unaware of Helena and what she was doing. Even more remarkable, he'd forgotten that she was in the room.

"Meet me in Hyde Park tomorrow," he said to Miss Hartley, mentally cursing his own weakness. "I will listen to what you have to say, but don't expect anything to change my mind."

The corners of her mouth curled in a triumphant smile. "Thank you. All I ask is that you allow me the chance to explain the advantages of the arrangement—for us both."

"Forgive me if I remain skeptical," he drawled. "I'll meet you near the footbridge. Three o'clock?"

"You won't regret this," she said earnestly, but the prickling sensation between his shoulder blades suggested he would. In spite of her naïveté and candor—or maybe *because* of those things—Miss Hartley could prove far more dangerous to him than Helena had ever been.

Chapter 3

On Being Rescued* from Imminent Dance Floor Peril

The strength of the arm Lord R. circled around my waist surprised and—I must confess—thrilled me. I was on the verge of falling mid-waltz for the second time in one month when he easily caught me, as if I weighed no more than the quill I write with. I cannot recall a time when I ever felt so safe . . . or so protected.

*I feel compelled to note, however, that rescue would have been entirely unnecessary if Lord R. had not clumsily steered us into the path of another couple. Indeed, I'm not certain it's possible to rescue someone from a calamity of one's own making; however, I shall give Lord R. a modicum of credit for attempting to do so.

And for having such masculine, capable hands.

Fiona was running vexingly late for her meeting with the earl. She prided herself on arriving promptly to appointments, but escaping the house with only her maid for company had been a challenge. When Lily had learned that Fiona planned an outing, she'd wanted to go, too, which meant Fiona had to concoct the excuse that she was shopping for her sister's birthday gift. And since Fiona really *did* need to purchase a gift for Lily, she and her maid, Mary, had stopped by Bond Street on the way to Hyde Park. Fiona quickly selected a pretty green cloak to match her sister's eyes, but the shopkeeper insisted on showing Fiona an endless selection of ribbons, gloves, and caps, delaying her arrival at the park for her very important meeting with the earl.

And now she was a quarter of an hour late. *Gads.*

She spotted the earl walking along a footpath near the Serpentine and hurried to join him, her maid trailing behind, clucking her tongue.

"Lord Ravenport!" Fiona exclaimed. She frowned at the overcast sky as she approached him. "My apologies for keeping you waiting."

He turned toward her, his handsome face chillingly devoid of expression. "I wondered if you'd changed your mind."

"About meeting with you?" she inquired, catching her breath.

"About your offer."

"I haven't," she said quickly. "It still stands. That is, I hope to persuade you to accept." It was imperative that she convince him to marry her. Her sister's reputation *and* happiness depended upon it.

"Then you're fortunate I'm still here. My time is valuable, Miss Hartley. I've more important things to do than to wander around the park making polite conversation with waterfowl." He scowled at a pair of swans gliding across the sparkling water behind him.

"I'm surprised you were capable," she murmured.

"Of communicating with swans?"

"Of polite conversation," she said, smiling sweetly.

He dragged a hand down the side of his face, clearly exasperated—which made two of them. "It's rather bold of you to lecture me on manners when you couldn't be bothered to arrive at our meeting—a meeting *you* insisted upon—at the appointed time."

"I'm afraid it couldn't be helped," she said, genuinely apologetic.

He raised his eyebrows in mock concern. "Did some sort of peril befall you? Did a highwayman accost you? Did your carriage overturn, casting you into a ditch?"

"Nothing so dire," she answered vaguely, while desperately hoping for a change of subject.

"Then perhaps you could tell me why you were detained?"

"I was . . . shopping," she admitted, raising her chin a notch.

"Shopping," he repeated with a smug nod. As if she'd just confirmed a long-held belief that women were inherently frivolous creatures.

"I was detained while buying a gift. Perhaps you've heard of the custom?" she asked dryly.

The corners of his mouth curved into a smile. "I have. It often involves the purchase of a sentimental object that the recipient neither wants nor needs."

"I happen to be an excellent gift giver. But I understand that not everyone appreciates sentimentality." At least if he agreed to marry her she wouldn't have to fret over his birthday and Christmas presents.

"Quite true."

"In any event, I regret the inconvenience I caused you," Fiona said with as much sincerity as she could muster. Given his surliness, her pity was reserved for the swans forced to endure his company while he waited. But she needed to persuade him to marry her, and squabbling was not going to further her cause. "Please, forgive me."

Apparently mollified, he waved an arm at a bench on the banks of the Serpentine. "Shall we sit?"

Fiona cast a glance over her shoulder at her maid, who paced several yards behind them. "I'd prefer to walk, if you don't mind." She inclined her head toward Mary. "It will afford us greater privacy."

"As you wish." He offered his arm, and the hard, solid feel of it beneath her hand instantly reminded her of the previous night.

When they'd danced, and his face had been mere inches from hers.

When he'd caught her, and his eyes had turned dark with something akin to . . . desire.

In the candlelight of the Northcroft ballroom, he'd appeared dark, brooding, and a tad dangerous. But now, in the broad light of day, he looked twice as intimidating— all rough edges, from the shadow of a beard on his chin to the thin scar beneath his right eye.

She swallowed, tamping down a wave of doubt. Outlining her proposal in writing, with the earl at a distance, had been relatively simple. Now that he was here, in the flesh, the idea of discussing marriage was far more daunting.

But she wouldn't be deterred from her mission—she simply *had* to succeed, and she'd come to the park prepared to argue her case.

Fiona waited until Mary was out of earshot, but spoke softly nonetheless. "I shan't waste any more of your time with small talk," she began. "Should you agree to marry me—and I hope that you will—you would obviously acquire my substantial dowry and marriage portion."

"But not all of it, as I understand from your letter. You

wish to retain a small property with a cottage in Cornwall, five thousand pounds for your own use, as well as a reasonable yearly allowance?"

"That is correct." She attempted a light tone, even though she was acutely aware he watched her out of the corner of his eye.

He reached into the chest pocket of his jacket, withdrew her letter, and unfolded it. "'The stipulated monies shall be mine to spend as I please without any explanation or interference,'" he read.

"I hardly think that's unreasonable," she said coolly.

"Five thousand pounds can purchase a large quantity of hats, gloves, and . . . frippery," he drawled, obviously trying to goad her.

"I suppose it could." All Fiona was interested in buying was a man's silence.

"You also say that you must wed within a fortnight."

"Yesterday it was a fortnight. Now it is thirteen days," she corrected.

He stopped and turned to face her. "Why the urgency?"

"I have my reasons, my lord."

"Reasons you do not wish to share?"

She closed her eyes briefly and recalled the terrifying threat in the blackmail letter. "I do not."

"Then my answer remains no—a firm no." He folded the letter and tucked it back into his pocket, then made a small bow as though he was about to leave.

She couldn't let him.

Her mouth turned dry, and her heart raced madly. If the truth about Lily became known, she'd be ruined. The whole family would. "Please understand," she said, reaching for his arm. "I realize that my conditions are somewhat unusual. But this union would be more like a business arrangement than a true marriage. We'd both stand to benefit."

"I can think of only one reason why you would demand the marriage take place so quickly, Miss Hartley."

"It's a personal matter, and I would rather not—"

"You are entitled to your secrets," he intoned, "but forgive me if I refuse to give my name to another man's bastard."

Fiona gasped and narrowed her eyes. Her palm itched to slap the scruff off his cheek, but she refrained. Just barely. "How . . . dare . . . you."

"Come now," he crooned, apparently unaware of how close she was to physical violence. "We're both adults. We know how the world works. The only logical reason you'd demand such a brief engagement is that you are with child."

"That is *not* the only logical reason," Fiona countered. Although she couldn't very well reveal the real one. "I am not expecting a babe—and I would never lie about something like that." She ignored the single cool raindrop that plopped onto her nose.

"So you say." The earl stroked his chin and continued strolling down the pebbled footpath. "But you've yet to explain what *you* stand to gain from the arrangement—aside from your monetary demands."

"Your title," Fiona said simply. "It matters little to me, but my father and stepmother are adamant that I marry a member of the aristocracy, and I should like to please them."

"Surely my title is not the only reason. Why else?" he demanded. "Why *me*?"

Because she needed someone she *respected*. The other eligible bachelors—even the handsome ones—had disqualified themselves for a variety of reasons. One was inexplicably curt when speaking to his mother. Another had been unnecessarily cruel toward his horse. Yet another was so enamored of his own appearance that it was quite impossible to converse with him in any room where a looking glass was present.

But she couldn't confess those things to the earl, so she avoided the question.

"Marrying you would give me a measure of independence." She sighed. "I don't expect you to understand because you're . . . well, a *man,* but I would like the freedom to pursue my own interests."

He tilted his head. "Such as?"

Fiona inhaled deeply. She was reluctant to expose herself to ridicule, but she supposed her future husband deserved to know. "Drawing," she said softly. "I like to sketch . . . people."

"Why?" he asked.

She managed to refrain from rolling her eyes. "Because they're interesting, my lord."

"Truly? The people I know are predictable. Boring."

"Then perhaps you're not looking at them deeply enough. Drawing people helps me peel away their many layers."

He shot her a wicked grin that melted her insides. "I think I understand. You sketch them naked."

"I do not," she said evenly, aware he was baiting her. "But I do try to see past the masks they wear. Sketching people helps me to . . . understand them."

The earl froze and stared at her curiously for the space of several heartbeats—then nodded thoughtfully before continuing along the path. Light rain began to fall, and he looked to the sky. "You don't have a parasol. I should return you to your carriage."

"I'm not worried about a little water," she scoffed. "And I shan't leave until I have your answer."

"Who is next in line?" he asked.

Fiona blinked. "I beg your pardon?"

"If I say no, who do you intend to ask next?" He shrugged impossibly broad shoulders. "You cannot blame me for wanting to know who else you're considering. Other titled gentlemen, I presume. Hopefully none who are old, portly, or without their teeth. I'd prefer to be in good company."

Good heavens. She hadn't seriously considered anyone else—and she didn't care to examine the reasons why. "I've put all my metaphorical eggs into one basket," she said earnestly.

"A very big gamble, Miss Hartley."

"Perhaps—but isn't that always the case with marriages? No prospective bride truly knows whether her betrothed will be a suitable match, and no one can predict what the future will bring. But if you agree to marry me, I can promise you that I will not be an overbearing wife. You will be free to live your life as you please." She tried to make the arrangement sound as appealing as possible, even though the idea of a husband and wife leading separate lives seemed rather sad to her.

"Who else knows of this plan of yours?"

"No one. Only you." She was encouraged by the fact that he was still asking questions, still talking to her—and he hadn't said no for at least five minutes. A gust of wind whipped her skirts around her legs and raindrops fell sideways, pelting her cheeks beneath the brim of her bonnet.

Fiona looked back at her maid, who still followed them dutifully. With one hand Mary held her cap in place, and with the other she clutched the shawl wrapped around her shoulders. "Return to the carriage before you are soaked,"

Fiona called to her. "I shall join you in moment." The maid hesitated only briefly before scurrying toward the road.

Fiona turned her attention back to Lord Ravenport. Droplets trickled from the dark curls that hung over his brow and the shoulders of his midnight blue jacket had turned black from the rain, but she couldn't leave until he agreed to at least consider her proposal. "All I ask is that you—"

Boom. A rumble of thunder shook the ground and the air crackled around them. "That's it," he said, brooking no argument. "We're heading to our carriages. Now." He laced his fingers through hers and dragged her along, each of his long strides equaling at least two of hers. As they hurried back up the path, the skies opened and the rain came down in sheets, making it difficult to see, much less walk. He slung an arm around her shoulders and pulled her to his side in an attempt to shelter her from the wind, and though the rain was cold, his body was deliciously warm and solid.

"This way," he shouted above the roar of the storm. She huddled against him and ran as fast as her skirts would allow. They splashed through puddles and mud, drenching the hem of her gown. When at last they reached the pavement, she was soaked.

He pointed several yards down the road. "There's my carriage."

As they ran toward it, he waved to a liveried footman, who opened the door, allowing the earl to usher her into the dry, blessedly warm cab. The door shut tightly behind them, and they collapsed onto one of the seats, breathless.

"The storm will pass soon. Until it does, you will remain here."

A crack of thunder pealed overhead, and Fiona nodded mutely. She should not be alone in a carriage with the Earl of Ravenport, but since the alternative was standing out-side in the violent storm, bending the rules of propriety seemed prudent.

Though she seriously doubted Miss Haywinkle would agree.

Chapter 4

Rain pounded the roof of the carriage, lending a cozy, intimate feel to the interior. The earl's long legs were sprawled in front of him, and Fiona endeavored not to gawk at the wet buckskin trousers clinging to his thighs.

She was not, however, entirely successful.

To be fair, a certain amount of study was necessary if she were to draw him at some point—and she intended to. Her artist's eye noted the proportions of his hips and thighs, the pronounced contours of his leg muscles, and the slight hollows on the insides of his knees. But as a woman, she noticed him, too—on a whole different level. The heat from his body. The scents of leather and soap. The light stubble on his chin.

Swallowing, she considered moving to the seat opposite him, but they had already soaked the velvet squabs of one bench and she saw no reason to sully the other.

Instead, she resolved to make use of this time to advance her cause. Mustering as much dignity as she could, given her soggy gown and dripping hair, she squared her shoulders and faced the earl. "Now then," she began. "I believe we were discussing the—"

"Stop," he ordered.

Fiona attempted a haughty look. "I beg your pardon?"

"I can't take you seriously in that bonnet. Not while there's a wet feather dangling in front of your face."

Of course, Fiona could see the rogue ostrich plume—she'd been doing her best to ignore it. "How gallant of you to mention it," she said dryly. She pinched the limp feather between her thumb and forefinger and tossed it onto the top of her hat. "There. Satisfied?"

He wrinkled his nose. "Now it looks as though a small, wet rat is napping on the brim." He flashed a grin so genuine that it momentarily disarmed her.

"Yes, well, I'm certain neither one of us represents the pinnacle of fashion at the moment." But despite his rumpled cravat and the wet hair slicked back from his face, he *did*, blast it all. It was hard to imagine him looking more masculine . . . or more attractive.

"I'll help you remove it." He reached for the ties at her chin, then froze. "With your permission?"

Fiona's cheeks heated, but she nodded and loosened the ribbons herself before allowing him to lift the bonnet off her head. A few pins went with the hat, and several long locks of hair fell around her shoulders.

"Much better," he said, his voice a notch deeper and gruffer than before. He tossed the bonnet onto the seat opposite them and crossed his boots at the ankles. "Now I shall be able to listen properly."

Suddenly nervous, she swallowed. "I realize that my letter must have caught you off guard, but now that you've had some time to adjust to the idea of . . . marrying me, I hope you will at least take a few days to think about my proposal—and give it the same consideration that you'd give any other business proposition."

"Business proposition," he repeated, skeptical.

"Yes, my lord," she choked out. "One that shall be mutually advantageous."

He leaned forward and propped his elbows on his knees. "There's more to marriage than a signed contract and a handshake, Miss Hartley."

"I'm well aware of that." She strove to keep her voice cool. "But it needn't be overly complicated."

"I'd argue it's the most complicated thing on earth."

Ignoring the heat in his eyes, she said, "How so?"

He lifted her hand from the seat between them and slid closer, till his knee was touching hers. "Will you allow me to demonstrate?"

She swallowed. "Yes. Of course."

Good heavens. The words were barely out of her mouth before he'd peeled the wet silk gloves off her hands—and stripped off his gloves as well.

First her bonnet, now her gloves . . . she shuddered to think what articles of clothing might go by the wayside next. Shoes? Stockings? Oddly, her belly fluttered at the thought. "What are you doing?"

"I'm proving a point." He cupped her hand in his and used the rough pad of his thumb to trace slow, languorous circles on her palm. Delicious shivers stole over her skin, curling her toes.

"Do you feel that?" he asked—as if he *knew*.

"Hmm?" She blinked up at him. "Feel what?"

His heavy-lidded gaze searched her face, lingered a bit too long on her mouth. "Nothing about this is simple."

"I disagree." Fiona pretended they were discussing the weather. Or needlework. Anything but the feel of his skin on hers. "It's only as complicated as we allow it to be."

"Then let me kiss you."

"Are you mad?" She snatched her hand away—mostly because it was hard to think clearly while he touched her.

"Very well." He sighed, feigning defeat. "You may kiss *me*."

"What?" She knew what he was about. And she was not some naïve maiden he could trick into doing his bidding. She opened her mouth to protest, then stopped. The earl was attempting to scare her off.

But she didn't frighten easily. And her sister's happiness—indeed, her entire future—depended on Fiona's ability to access her dowry money. Quickly.

"If I kiss you, will you agree to consider marrying me?" She ignored the pounding of her heart as she awaited his reply.

Outside, the rain continued to fall, and rivulets of water streamed down the carriage windows. Thunder boomed in the distance.

"I will," he said disbelievingly—as though he'd surprised himself with his answer.

Gads. He'd surprised her, too.

"Very well," Fiona said with significantly more confidence than she felt. But if a kiss was needed to seal their deal, then kiss him she must. She would demonstrate that their relationship did not have to be complicated at all.

She only prayed that she didn't botch it terribly.

Lord help her, she was about to kiss the earl. And she didn't dread the prospect nearly as much as she should have.

Gray sat very still, mostly out of a sense of self-preservation. For Miss Hartley obviously had no idea in hell what she was doing. He'd already discerned that she wasn't the most graceful of creatures. Dancing had not been her forte, and neither, apparently, was seduction.

She coughed, straightened her spine, and flexed her fingers—as though she were preparing to perform on a pianoforte rather than kiss him. Lines of intense concentration creased her forehead as she inched closer and stiffly braced her hands on his shoulders. She stared at his mouth like it was an unpleasant bit of medicine she must ingest for her own good. Or one of Hercules's labors she must endure.

As her face neared his, she squeezed her eyes shut and stretched her neck forward, bumping her nose into his, not once, but twice. Fragrant hair tickled his cheek. An odd noise—the sort a startled cat makes—escaped her throat. Her soft lips might have brushed against his mouth in the process, but the ordeal was so quick that he couldn't be sure.

However, he did know two things.

First, what had just transpired was the sorriest excuse for a kiss in the history of man- and womankind.

Second, Miss Hartley was *not* with child. Because no one who thought that bit of awkwardness qualified as a kiss had ever had a lover. He'd stake his life on it.

"There." She sat back, exhaled, and smiled as though quite pleased with her efforts.

All Gray could think about was her extraordinary courage and gumption. She'd obviously never had a proper kiss before, but she hadn't let that deter her from accepting his dare. The scents of her skin and fresh linen and rain mingled in his head. A damp auburn curl clung to her neck, and he longed to sweep it away so that he could count the freckles there and brush his lips over each one.

What the *devil* was wrong with him? Had it been so long since he'd lain with a woman that a brief, bumbling kiss could knock the wind out of him?

It was supposed to scare her off. Make her realize that the very idea of marrying him was preposterous. But she'd called his bluff *and* raised the stakes.

"I think the rain is slowing," she said a bit too brightly. Just as if that horrific, god-awful kiss had never happened.

Funny, but he was torn between wanting to scrub it from his memory and wanting to replay it over and over in his head. Truly, there'd been nothing remotely seductive about it. And yet his pulse still raced and his cock twitched as though his body hadn't received the message that the kiss had been a catastrophe of near biblical proportions.

"Your carriage isn't very far away," he said. It seemed far safer than commenting on the kiss. "I'll escort you there whenever you like." But part of him hoped she wasn't too eager to leave.

"Thank you," she said primly. "I must go soon, but first I thought we could discuss the next steps."

"Of course," he said, even though he had no idea what she was talking about.

"You should probably call daily over the next few days, so that it appears you're courting me. Flowers would be a nice gesture. You needn't ask my father for an audience just yet."

"Wait." Gray rubbed his temples before looking directly into Miss Hartley's pretty blue eyes. "I have not agreed to a betrothal. I only agreed to *consider* one."

A wounded expression flitted across her face. "I realize that. But, as I've already mentioned, time is of the essence, and you can't properly consider my proposal unless we spend time together. I feel confident that I'll be able to assuage any doubts or reservations you still have."

"I have many, many doubts and reservations, Miss Hartley."

"Then we shouldn't waste another moment," she countered. "You may choose when and where we meet to further our acquaintance; you may choose any activity or pastime that suits you."

He arched a brow. If she had any inkling of his wicked

thoughts, she would not be so foolish as to give him carte blanche. But she was far too innocent to suspect the workings of his mind.

"It's imperative that we reach an agreement soon," she was saying.

Gray heard the desperation in her voice but still didn't understand it. He'd given her little to no encouragement, and yet she seemed determined to wed him.

He had no desire to hurt her feelings, but he . . . well, he was not the husband for her. Besides, he had no time for pretend wooing. He was overseeing half a dozen projects at the Fortress.

The Fortress. It should have occurred to him earlier. When it came to deterring marriages, his manor house had a proven record.

"Very well," he said. "If you are sincere in your wish to become better acquainted, come visit me at my country estate."

She clasped her hands together and beamed. "A house party? That would be lovely!"

Holy hell. "Nothing grand," he said quickly. "I'm currently renovating, so your accommodations will be rustic, to say the least."

"I'm not certain my father will be able to leave behind his mills, but my stepmother and my sister, Lily, will be delighted to accompany me. And I really must insist on inviting Sophie—Lady Callahan's daughter—we've been friends for ages, and I wouldn't dream of excluding her. It's so generous of you to host us all."

Gray snorted. Miss Hartley wouldn't think him generous after she laid eyes on the Fortress. She'd think the house party was a cruel joke designed to discourage her.

Which was the truth, after all.

"Then it's settled," he said firmly. "I'll call tomorrow morning to extend a proper invitation to your stepmother."

"Thank you for thinking of this." She gathered up her soggy bonnet and gloves, preparing to exit the carriage. "I'm eager to see your house and to meet your family and friends."

Once, the sentiment might have warmed him, but Helena had said much the same thing. Then, she'd taken one look at the Fortress and washed her hands of him.

With a modicum of luck, Miss Hartley would do the same.

Chapter 5

On Initiating a Kiss with a Gentleman in a Coach

I cannot say I recommend it. The combination of our soaked clothes and the close quarters inside the carriage made for rather steamy conditions. Even the windows fogged. I do believe I comported myself well, however, given that it was my first kiss with a handsome earl. Or with any gentleman for that matter. (I shall not count our neighbor William, as we were only twelve years of age and acting on a ridiculous dare.)

Indeed, I suspect that Lord R. would be shocked to learn of my lack of experience given the boldness and competency I displayed in the coach. While much ado is made of kissing, I am happy to report that it is not a terribly difficult skill to master. And though it is not at all unpleasant, I did suffer some unexpected symptoms during the encounter. I am certain that the confined space was to blame for my racing heart and somersaulting belly. Hardly surprising since, as I previously stated, conditions were not optimal. Did I mention the smoldering heat?

Fiona contemplated sketching the earl the next afternoon. Even now, nearly twenty-four hours after their meeting in the park, she could easily recall the texture of his hair, the shadow of stubble on his chin, and the guarded expression on his face. She also remembered the feel of his hand on hers and the current that it sent through her body. In fact, she could think of little else.

And that was precisely why she couldn't sketch him yet. There were facets of Lord Ravenport she could not capture on paper with charcoal—the way his eyes flashed cold one moment and hot the next, and the way his mouth could turn from displeasure to interest in a fraction of a second.

The earl was still a mystery to her.

So, Fiona sketched the vicar from memory instead. Rather, she sat in the drawing room and *attempted* to sketch the vicar, while her sister, Lily, ruthlessly interrogated her.

"You say Lord Ravenport requested permission to call on you today." Lily paced in front of the settee where Fiona sat and pretended to be absorbed in drawing the vicar's spectacles.

"Yes," Fiona confirmed, for perhaps the fifth time that morning. She'd informed her family at dinner last night, so the earl's visit wouldn't catch them entirely off guard. Her stepmother had nearly choked on her roast beef, and her sister had dropped her fork at the unexpected—but most welcome—news.

Lily tossed a cascade of dark curls over her shoulder and crossed her arms. "And he made this request during a chance meeting at the park?"

Fiona ignored her sister's skeptical tone. Avoided her shrewd green eyes. "He did," she said breezily. As if this sort of thing transpired every Wednesday afternoon.

Lily tilted her head to one side. "How would you describe the nature of the earl's request? Was it reserved and polite? Or impassioned and heartfelt?"

Good heavens. Fiona frowned at the sketch on her lap and hoped the vicar would forgive the little lie she was about to tell. Because the truth was that the earl had not requested permission to call so much as she had *instructed* him to. "Reserved," she replied. It seemed less of a stretch than *impassioned and heartfelt.*

Lily nodded, assimilating this new piece of information. "Not surprising. He's rather cold, isn't he? I don't imagine Lord Ravenport has a romantic bone in his body."

Cold was not a word Fiona would have used to describe the earl, but her sister's point was well taken. "He tends to be serious," Fiona said. *And stubborn. And exasperating.* But it was too late to set her sights on another potential husband. Besides, she wasn't certain she wanted to.

"You must have made an impression on him at the Northcroft ball," Lily mused.

"Are you referring to the waltz, when I almost succeeded in pulling him to the dance floor on top of me?"

"He's very handsome," Lily countered. "I could think of worse things."

"Lily!"

"Have you been writing about him? In your diary, I mean?"

Fiona glanced at the doorway to make sure their stepmother hadn't suddenly appeared. She'd retreated to her rooms with her lady's maid shortly after breakfast in order to ready herself for the earl's visit. "I have started a journal," Fiona said, "just as I promised."

Lily clasped her hands together, rapturous. "Very good." The gleam in her eyes might have made Fiona nervous if she didn't know Lily would never stoop to snooping through her bedchamber or invading her privacy.

Which was not to say Lily had any qualms about trying to cajole the information out of Fiona, using any and all means at her disposal.

"Did you write about the night at the ball? And the encounter at the park?"

Fiona pressed her lips together and hummed a little tune while she sketched a buckle on the vicar's right shoe.

But Lily was not easily deterred. "Dear diary," she dictated with dramatic relish, "the earl is both a brooding and breathtaking creature. He possesses the face of Adonis and the body of—"

"That's quite enough," Fiona said, holding up a staying hand. "*Your* diary may contain the scribblings of a lovesick schoolgirl, but I can assure you that mine does not." The very idea was preposterous, and may lightning strike her if she ever succumbed to such sappy, sentimental impulses. "And since Lord Ravenport could soon arrive on our doorstep, could we please begin pretending that we are proper young ladies who do not lose their heads over the mere prospect of a gentleman caller?"

"Lord Ravenport is not just *any* gentleman caller," Lily said. "He's dashing and dark—and an *earl*. You may count on Mama making a complete cake of herself the moment he steps foot in the house."

Fiona cringed. "I know. That's why I'm relying on you to help me prove that the entire family's not mad."

Chuckling, Lily circled behind Fiona and peered over her shoulder at the sketchbook on her lap. "Another lovely drawing, Fi." She paused, then said, "Is it just me, or does the good vicar seem to be judging us?"

Fiona looked down at the vicar's kind face and wise eyes, then sighed. "No, it's not just you." It almost seemed the vicar knew what she was about—and did not approve of her keeping secrets and kissing earls in coaches.

Lily laughed. "I'm going to meet Sophie in the park. Would you like to join us?"

"I think I'll stay and finish this portrait. But please give Soph my best—and don't dally too long. I need you here when the earl calls."

"I shan't leave you to face him alone." Lily squeezed Fiona's shoulders affectionately. "I'll return in an hour or so."

"Thank you."

As soon as Lily left, Fiona fetched the blackmail note from the bottom of her bureau drawer. Whenever she began to question the prudence of marrying a man she scarcely knew, she pulled out the letter and reread it, letting the horror of the threat sink into her bones. Her eyes went to the bottom of the first page, which read:

> *Lest you doubt my resolve, I have enclosed an exact copy of the letter which I have written to the London Hearsay. Upon receipt of your payment, I shall destroy the letter and take your family's secret to my grave. You have my word on this. However, if you do not provide the full amount, I shall immediately deliver the letter to the newspaper for publication in their next edition.*

Fiona took a deep breath before shuffling the pages. The blackmailer's letter to the *Hearsay* was written in the kind of titillating, provocative prose that would have every household in London clamoring to buy the issue—unless Fiona prevented it from going to print:

> *Miss Lily Hartley, the younger daughter of a wealthy mill owner, may possess beauty and fortune aplenty, but she also possesses a dark,*

*scandalous secret. She was abandoned by her true
mother when she was but an infant, left on a
doorstep where, but for the grace of God, she
might have easily perished in the cold.*

*The truth is that the woman who gave birth to
Miss Hartley is none other than the proprietress of
Mayfair's most notorious house of ill repute. One
need only gaze upon the fair faces of the debutante
and Madam Serena Labelle to ascertain they are
indeed daughter and mother. However, additional
proof rests in a memento left with the unwanted
babe. Madam Labelle's newborn was found
wearing one bootie embroidered with an L. Inside
the bootie was a note that read: "Please take care
of my darling Lily." The madam kept the other
bootie for herself—so that she might never forget
her perfidy.*

*Miss Hartley would no doubt have preferred to
keep the truth about her lineage a secret, but since
she is on the marriage mart, it seems only fair that
the gentlemen who might otherwise be inclined to
pursue her be in possession of the facts: Tainted
blood runs through her veins.*

*Neither a proper finishing school education nor
a princess's dowry can erase the truth: Miss
Hartley's mother is a whore.*

Fiona wouldn't have believed the story if the blackmailer hadn't mentioned the bootie and the note left inside
it. How many nights had she and Lily lain awake, wondering about her birth mother? In their romantic musings,
Lily's mother had been a royal princess forced to flee her
kingdom. Unable to care for her beloved child, she'd left
Lily with a couple who would dote on her.

Fiona and Lily naïvely believed the banished princess would appear at their door one day, bootie in hand, begging Lily's forgiveness and inviting her to come and live at a palace where she would claim her birthright.

And in Lily and Fiona's imaginations, Lily would respond by saying that she and Fiona were true sisters and simply could not be separated. Lily's long-lost mother would have to be content with having Lily and Fiona live at the palace for six months out of the year, as they intended to remain in London with the Hartleys for the other six.

The embroidered bootie was supposed to have been a clue leading Lily into the arms of a second, loving family.

Instead, it was the evidence that could ruin Lily.

A small, precious keepsake that could destroy them all.

As Gray stood on the Hartleys' doorstep, his hand poised to lower the knocker, he had an eerie sense of déjà vu. One month ago, he'd been calling on Helena and making polite conversation with her family, trying to ingratiate himself.

And he'd loathed every minute of it.

If there was any bright side to being jilted by his fiancée, it was that he no longer had to feign interest in the dozen different varieties of roses that Helena's fussy mother tended in her godforsaken garden. He wasn't obliged to teach Helena's whiny spoiled younger brother how to fence; he needn't smoke stale cigars and make inane small talk with her stodgy father.

Gray's time was his own, and he answered to no one— save his grandmother, for whom he'd gladly lay down his life.

But now he was standing at Miss Hartley's damned front door—all because she'd dared to kiss him.

He had two goals for today's visit. First, to issue an invitation to a house party—one that was intended to disabuse Miss Hartley, once and for all, of her foolish notion of marrying him. And second, to get the hell out of there before any family members or pets could form an attachment to him.

He knocked and presented his card to a butler in a starched jacket. Despite the servant's impassive expression and courteous manners, Gray detected a hint of surprise—a slight flare of the butler's nostrils and a faint widening of his eyes that suggested Miss Hartley and her sister did not have a great many callers.

An unexpected twinge of anger flickered in Gray's chest. What did it matter if Fiona Hartley was not of noble birth, or if her father had made his fortune in trade? Who gave a fig if she fell and made a spectacle of herself at every ball from now till Christmastide? She was infuriating to be sure, but she didn't deserve to be a pariah.

The butler's shoes clicked across pristine marble floors as he led Gray to an opulent drawing room where every furnishing sparkled like new. The gold clock on the wood-carved mantel, the silver vase on the gleaming mahogany table, the crystal droplets on the elegant wall sconces—every carefully selected piece in the room bespoke luxury. Wealth.

And it made Gray break out in a cold sweat. The Hartleys' house was well staffed and appointed with every creature comfort. What would they think of the Fortress—with its drafty windows, shabby furniture, and peeling wallpaper? Only last night, while he'd lain in bed at the manor house, he'd heard mice rustling behind the walls and bats fluttering in the attic. He couldn't imagine so much as a fly being permitted to invade the Hartleys' house.

His mind screamed for him to call off this ridiculous plan, to walk out and never look back. He'd spare himself a great deal of embarrassment and headache.

But then he spotted Miss Hartley sitting on the settee with her feet tucked under her and her slippers tossed on the floor. Sunlight streamed over her shoulder, and her brows were knit in concentration as her charcoal flew over the sketchbook she held in her lap. Absorbed in her work, she seemed unaware of the loose curl that dangled at her temple, or the hitched skirts that revealed a glimpse of her stockinged calf.

She looked so industrious and earnest and . . . vulnerable. He couldn't go back on his word.

But he could gently dissuade her—and refrain from encouraging her.

Her younger sister, whom Gray hadn't even noticed sitting at the pianoforte, cleared her throat in warning just before the butler announced, "The Earl of Ravenport."

Miss Hartley's sketchbook slipped from her lap, and she scrambled to her feet, covering her empty slippers with the hem of her gown. She attempted to wriggle her feet into her shoes as she dipped a curtsy. "My lord," she managed.

He opened his mouth to reply, but Mrs. Hartley stormed into the room behind him, her ample bosom preceding her like the prow of a Viking ship. "Lord Ravenport," she cooed. "It is a great honor to welcome you into our humble home. You grace us with your presence." She placed one hand over her chest and offered him the other.

Bowing over it, he replied, "The pleasure is mine, Mrs. Hartley." *Two goals. Invitation. Escape.*

"You're acquainted with my lovely daughters, Fiona and Lily." As she waved an arm in their direction, her pungent perfume wafted around his head, stinging his eyes. "They're actually my stepdaughters," she continued, "as

I'm sure you've deduced. Though we're sometimes mistaken for sisters."

Gray's gaze flicked to Fiona, who visibly cringed. He inclined his head so he wouldn't have to look at Mrs. Hartley as he replied. "Anyone could be forgiven for the error."

"Where are my manners?" She clucked her tongue. "Please, do make yourself comfortable while I ring for tea."

"I'm afraid I can't stay," he said quickly.

Fiona gasped. "But you've only just arrived."

"Yes. Duty calls," he said, deliberately vague. "I'm sure you understand." But her crestfallen expression suggested she didn't.

"Of course we understand," Mrs. Hartley assured him. "As an earl, you must have a great many responsibilities. We would never presume to keep you from them." She glared at her stepdaughters, silently forbidding them to contradict her.

"I did wish to extend an invitation," Gray said. "I am hosting a small house party at my country estate next week—starting Monday. I would be delighted if you and your family would attend. Your friend Lady Callahan and her daughter are also welcome."

Mrs. Hartley's jaw hung slack. "A house party?" She turned to her stepdaughters and smiled as though she couldn't believe their good fortune. "A house party," she repeated. "At the Earl of Ravenport's country house."

"The accommodations will be somewhat rustic," he warned. "The house is a work in progress. I'm restoring it—mostly for my grandmother's sake. She lived there when she was a girl and remembers the halls and grounds quite fondly."

Why the devil was he sharing private matters with the Hartleys? He clamped his mouth shut before he revealed all the maudlin details. No one needed to know his grand-mother's health—most specifically her eyesight—was failing. Or that the doctor had predicted she'd be blind within two years. Or that Gray was determined to return the house to its former glory while she could still see it.

He'd be damned if her final glimpses of her cherished childhood home would consist of walls marred by cracked mortar and windows darkened with overgrown ivy. She deserved visions of pristine marble, sparkling glass, and manicured lawns. It was the least he could do for her.

Mrs. Hartley's eyes welled as though she was overcome by the mere invitation. "My daughters and I would be hon-ored to attend your house party, Lord Ravenport."

"Excellent. I shall send you the details tomorrow." Time to make his exit. "I look forward to seeing you next week."

"Next week?" Fiona blurted. "That is, I'd hoped we'd have the pleasure of your company before then."

"Fiona!" her stepmother snapped under her breath.

The younger Hartley sister stepped forward, wringing her hands. "Perhaps we will see you in town before the house party. At a ball or soiree. Maybe the opera," she said, grasping.

"I doubt it," Gray replied. Even if he were inclined to attend such functions—which he most definitely was *not*—he was going to need every waking moment just to make the manor house habitable.

He made a curt bow and hazarded one last glance at Fiona—and wished he hadn't.

Her cheeks flushed pink and her eyes flashed her dis-pleasure. She wanted him to publicly court her. She wanted a whirlwind engagement.

But he'd agreed to neither of those things, and she shouldn't expect more from him.

Because he couldn't give it.

If there was one tiny corner of his heart that wasn't frozen, it was reserved for his grandmother. And the sooner Miss Fiona Hartley realized he was a lost cause, the better off she'd be.

Chapter 6

Fiona's stepmother had insisted on having several of Fiona's and Lily's gowns updated in advance of the earl's house party. Mama claimed none of the dresses they owned was fit for such an auspicious occasion, and though she would have dearly loved to order new wardrobes for all of them prior to the house party, alas—time would not permit it. Much to Mama's chagrin, they would have to be content with some clever alterations.

Fiona and Lily had tried in vain to convince Mama that their gowns were perfectly acceptable as they were, causing Mama significant distress. She'd collapsed onto the parlor settee and pressed the back of a hand to her forehead. In a trembling voice she said, "Opportunities like this one don't come along often. We must make the most of them." Then she gave Fiona a sharply pointed look that was easy to interpret: *Don't muff this, because it may be your only shot at marrying well.*

Fiona hardly needed the reminder. She was acutely aware of the importance of the house party—to Lily, her, and her family. Even if her reason for wishing to marry the earl was vastly different from Mama's.

More than anything, her stepmother craved respectability, status, and acceptance. An advantageous match for Fiona would elevate them all in the eyes of the world.

Meanwhile, Fiona was simply trying to save Lily—and the entire family—from being cast into a pit of ruin.

In any event, arguing with Mama about gowns was both pointless and exhausting, so Fiona and Lily found themselves at the modiste's shop for the third straight day since Lord Ravenport's visit.

Two of Madam Dubois's most talented seamstresses had worked around the clock to alter half a dozen dresses for Fiona and Lily. Even Fiona had to admit that some of the gown transformations were extraordinary.

In a corner of the dress shop behind a plush velvet curtain, she slipped a gold silk dress over her head. The seamstress had stripped off the lace trim and replaced it with delicate beading so that even in the dressing area light danced off the tiny crystals, creating a dazzling effect.

Fiona barely recognized the ball gown. Indeed, she barely recognized *herself.*

Mama must have paid Madam Dubois a small fortune for the miracle her dressmakers had worked. In fact, the shopkeeper's bill probably exceeded the amount Fiona needed to pay off the blackmailer.

She fervently wished there were some way she could ask her parents for the money. But Fiona refused to risk upsetting Papa. His father, Fiona's grandfather, had died suddenly of heart failure when Papa was the same age as she. And Papa's doctor constantly cautioned him that he must slow down and avoid undue stress. Fiona had taken it upon herself to protect Papa as much as she could.

Asking Mama was out of the question as well. She'd balk at the very suggestion. Hadn't they already given her everything a young woman could possibly want? What on earth did she intend to use it for? She'd be suspicious—rightfully so. And if she discovered that someone was trying to extort money from Fiona, they'd demand to know the scandalous secret about Lily.

And Fiona was afraid Mama would never look at her sister the same way.

Which would break Fiona's heart. Lily might not be her sister by blood, but they were almost the same age and had grown up together, as close as twins. Nothing could change the way Fiona felt about her sister.

But Mama . . . well, she was a fickle sort. Anyone who jeopardized her tenuous social standing was a liability. She loved Lily—as much as she was capable of loving anyone, Fiona supposed—but if she feared that the truth about Lily might become known, she'd cut her off. Send her away.

Papa was different. Or he had been, once. He'd doted on Fiona and Lily, taking them on picnics or to the park whenever he could. And when he was working, the girls happily spent their days playing beneath his desk, tidying his office, and tagging along as he visited his mills. But then he'd remarried, and his new wife had put her foot down, claiming well-bred young ladies did not engage in such crass pastimes. Mama had been the one who'd insisted Fiona and Lily go away and attend a proper finishing school. It had broken Fiona's heart when she left Papa—and she was fairly certain it had broken his, too.

Now he was rarely at home and deferred to his wife in all family matters. It was almost as if he didn't trust himself to do the right thing when it came to his daughters.

No, Fiona couldn't risk confiding in her parents.

Besides, it was too late to turn back now. She had only ten days before the blackmailer published what he knew in the *London Hearsay*. She simply had to convince Lord

Ravenport to marry her before then, so she could access her marriage settlement and pay the extortionist.

And it vexed her that the earl was not obediently going along with the plan.

She shrugged herself out of the gold silk and thanked the seamstress as she handed her the dress. Yes, the earl had invited her family to the house party, as promised. But he'd done so as though he was under duress, not even deigning to sit and visit awhile before he escaped their drawing room. Would it have killed him to drink a cup of tea? Or to *pretend* to be a little smitten with her?

With the help of the efficient seamstress, Fiona dressed and returned to the main area of the shop where Mama and Lily waited, their expressions anxious. "You'll never guess who just walked by," Lily blurted.

Fiona's belly sank, and she pretended to admire a bolt of cloth on a nearby counter. "Oh?"

"Lord Ravenport!" Mama sang, confirming Fiona's fears. "Fortuitous, is it not? If we leave now, we shall be able to catch him."

"It wouldn't be seemly for us to chase after the earl," Fiona said firmly. "Besides, we shall see him in two days' time—at his house party."

"I don't know," Lily mused. "I should think he'd be pleased to see you. Besides, you could thank him in person."

Gads. "Actually, I've developed a bit of a headache." Fiona pressed a fingertip to her temple for effect. "Trying on six gowns in the space of an hour will do that to a per—"

Mama yanked her by the arm and pulled her toward the door of the shop with enough force to uproot a small tree. "You mustn't be shy. Never fear, we shall make it seem as though our meeting is purely coincidental."

Oh dear. Mama was not known for her subtlety. Fiona prayed that she'd delayed long enough for Lord Ravenport to make his getaway. It wasn't that she was opposed to seeing the earl; she simply wanted to avoid a public meeting until she'd had the chance to privately explain to him what she'd done. Which was to take matters into her own hands.

Lily burst through the shop door onto the pavement outside and surveyed the street. "There he is, talking to a gentleman outside the bootmaker's shop."

"How convenient," Mama said smugly. "Come along, girls. It just so happens that your father is in desperate need of a new pair of hessians."

Gray bid a good day to Kirby and headed toward his carriage parked around the corner from the bootmaker's. He'd taken only a few steps when a shrill voice rang out. "Lord Ravenport."

Reluctantly, he turned toward Mrs. Hartley and plastered some semblance of a smile on his face. He'd been kicking himself ever since he opened his mouth and invited her family to the house party. Now that guests would be descending upon him in only two days, he realized the folly of hosting any event at the Fortress. Even Kirby, who was always game for adventure, thought Gray mad for going through with the plans. His friend had wagered ten pounds that the Hartleys would be in their carriage, heading back to town, within twenty-four hours of arriving at the Fortress.

Which suited Gray just fine.

"Why, I thought it was you." Mrs. Hartley bustled toward him, her daughters in tow. The way the older woman gazed at him, as though he were some sort of hero, made him want a stiff drink. Her younger daughter,

Lily, appeared similarly dreamy eyed, while Fiona looked distinctly . . . unenthused.

Gray made a polite bow. "Good afternoon, ladies."

"We've just come from Madam Dubois's shop. She's the best modiste in all of town, but I'm sure I don't need to tell *you* that." Mrs. Hartley paused and gave him a conspiratorial wink that simultaneously frightened and baffled him. "In any event, we just happened to see you, and good manners dictated that we stop to pay our respects."

Gray nodded amiably and stole a glance at Fiona. The sunlight brought out the deep reds in her hair, and her freckles were more pronounced than usual. She didn't hide beneath a parasol or cake powder on her face, thank God. With a soft breeze rustling the curls at her nape, she looked more like a woodland fairy than a London miss on a shopping excursion.

But she would not meet his gaze. In fact, if there had been a rock nearby she no doubt would have tried to slink under it. *Interesting.*

"I trust you're enjoying your outing, Miss Hartley?"

"Oh yes." She stared at the pavement between their feet, like a demure miss. Which he knew very well she was *not.*

"We were attending to some errands in advance of your house party," the younger sister said, leaping into the awkward silence. "You'd think we were readying ourselves for a voyage to America rather than a week at a manor house," she teased.

"It never hurts to be prepared. Besides, your cabin on a transatlantic voyage would probably be more luxurious than any of my guest chambers."

The women laughed as though he were joking. If only that were true.

Fiona shot him a tight-lipped smile. "Well, we do not

wish to keep you from your own errands, my lord. Do enjoy the rest of the afternoon."

He should have been relieved that she was trying to end their encounter so quickly. Instead, he was oddly annoyed.

"Fiona," Mrs. Hartley said, giving her daughter a subtle elbow jab. "Wasn't there something you wished to say to the earl?"

Fiona's eyebrows rose halfway to her hairline. "Not that I can recall. Shouldn't we be on our way? We wouldn't want to be late for dinner."

The younger sister, Lily, shot Fiona a mildly scolding frown, then beamed at Gray. "The flowers were lovely. Pink roses," she sighed. "Such a romantic choice."

"Flowers," he repeated, glaring at Fiona.

She closed her eyes briefly and swallowed. "Yes. Thank you for sending them. Such a thoughtful gesture. I was remiss not to mention it."

Indeed. He was starting to put the pieces of the puzzle together. Someone—not him—had sent Fiona flowers. Pink roses, to be precise. And she'd led her mother and sister to believe Gray had been the one to send them.

Good grief. He had neither the time nor the tolerance for this sort of nonsense. But he could see the silent plea in Miss Hartley's startling blue eyes and took pity. "No thanks are necessary."

Fiona blew out a long breath, obviously relieved. "We've taken far too much of your time, my lord. We look forward to—"

"The earl is being too modest," Lily protested. "After all, it wasn't merely the flowers."

Gray arched a brow at Fiona. "It wasn't?"

"Lily, we mustn't embarrass Lord Ravenport," Fiona said under her breath, all but begging her sister to drop the subject.

But Gray didn't want to let it rest. If she had an admirer, he deserved to know who the swain was. Not that he objected to Fiona having a suitor. Quite the contrary. If someone else was willing to marry her, maybe he could wipe his hands of the whole business and spare himself a lot of trouble.

"I'm not embarrassed," Gray said. He'd attempted an amiable tone but sounded slightly irritated, even to his own ears. What else had Fiona's beau sent her?

"Nor should you be," Mrs. Hartley said, quick to reassure him. "Your poem was . . ." She closed her eyes and fanned herself with a hand as she searched for the correct adjective. "Moving. Dare I say, *stirring*? All the ladies at my whist game agreed—you have a gift with words."

Gray clenched his jaw to keep himself from uttering words that would send Mrs. Hartley straight to her fainting couch. But it was Fiona who deserved his ire. Oh, he had plenty to say to her. Instead, he replied to her stepmother. "I've never been accused of being a poet, much less a good one."

The younger sister, Lily, shrugged her slim shoulders and smiled mischievously. "Perhaps you never had the proper inspiration before." She inclined her dark head toward Fiona.

"That's enough," Fiona proclaimed. Her cheeks were a vivid pink—the better to match her precious roses. "The poem was intended for me," she said, "and it was meant to be private."

"I know, dear," her stepmother said, contrite. "Forgive me. But some things are simply too delicious not to share. Such as the verse that read: 'Your eyes shine brighter than the stars on a moonless night. No mortal man could help but be blinded by the sight.' It made Mrs. Greenbriar shed a tear right there at the card table. Even the vicar's wife declared it hopelessly romantic. Everyone loves young love. You can't blame us all for being a little swept away."

"Ah . . . yes. The *moonless night* line," he managed. *What the devil?* If word of this spread to the men in his club, he'd never hear the end of it. He had no idea what sort of game Miss Fiona Hartley was playing—attributing some other sap's flowers and poetry to him—but he intended to put a hasty end to it.

He only required a few minutes alone with her in order to discover what she was about, and before he'd fully considered all the ramifications he opened his idiotic mouth. "Miss Hartley, would you care to join me for a drive in the park tomorrow afternoon?"

Fiona gulped. "That sounds . . ."

"Wonderful!" Mrs. Hartley exclaimed. She clasped her hands against her large bosom and bit her bottom lip as though fighting back joyous tears.

God save him.

"Excellent," he said to Fiona, making a slight bow. "I'll come around at five."

She nodded somberly—as if she'd agreed not to a drive in the park, but to twenty lashings in the town square.

As he strode toward his carriage, he heard Mrs. Hartley's loud, suggestive whisper: "Perhaps tomorrow's outing will provide the earl inspiration for a new poem."

Perhaps it would—but damned if he wouldn't be the last to know.

Chapter 7

On Accepting an Invitation to Ride in the Park

Certain milestones in a girl's life are long anticipated and much dreamed about. Some—like attending balls and dancing the waltz—fulfill every lofty expectation, while others fall disappointingly short. Wearing a corset, for example. As a schoolgirl, I was quite desperate to have one. I begged Mama for months before she agreed to purchase a few for me. Now I have a drawerful of the things, and I can't imagine why I was once so eager to be squeezed in and laced up to the point where a deep breath is nigh impossible.

In any event, having a gentleman ask me to join him for a ride in the park was another particularly vivid fantasy. Until yesterday, when Lord R. single-handedly crushed it.

In my naïve imaginings, the invitation went something like this: A handsome gentleman would call on me and pay me pretty compliments. He'd gaze deeply into my eyes, and, with barely controlled passion, beg me to accompany him for a ride. When I accepted, he'd exclaim that he was sure to be the envy of every man in town.

But Lord R.'s request was a pale imitation of the fantasy, more akin to an unfeeling summons than a

romantic invitation. I suppose I have only myself to blame
for conjuring up such fanciful and unrealistic expectations.
   Just like the corset.

"I do *not* write poetry," Lord Ravenport announced, somewhere between annoyed and irate. He shot Fiona a side-
long glance, then returned his attention to the road in front
of them, expertly steering his horses around a parked carriage. The earl's curricle was neither new nor particularly
flashy, but people throughout the park were staring—
presumably at her. And the earl. Together.

With the top down, they were on display for all to see,
and Fiona's nerves were already strung tight. Not because
Lord Ravenport was angry—justifiably so—but because
his thigh inadvertently brushed against her skirts each
time the curricle rolled over the slightest bump. And every
time the earl pulled the reins to the right, his flexed bi-
cep lightly collided with her elbow. She couldn't quite
decide if she dreaded the bumps and turns or eagerly anticipated them. But she suspected the latter.

The skies were a brilliant blue, a rarity for London, but
Lord Ravenport seemed distinctly unappreciative—of the
lovely afternoon, her company, and the world in general.

"I do not write poetry," he repeated, "and I don't read
it. I don't even *believe* in it."

"That's ridiculous," Fiona said. She'd been on the verge
of apologizing for the ruse of him having sent the flowers
and poetry, but she couldn't let such a ludicrous statement
go unchallenged. "You may say you don't believe in uni-
corns or dragons or one-eyed giants. But you cannot deny
the existence of poetry."

"I can," he countered. "I just did. Poetry is nothing more
than a puffed-up collection of words—words that think
they're too good for common, plain-speaking folk."

"Poetry is snobbish?" Fiona asked, incredulous.

The earl nodded. "Absolutely. It was invented by sentimental fools who have nothing better to do than wax on about rubbish like their lover's eyes or lips."

"I see," Fiona said dryly. "Poetry is snobbish *and* superfluous."

He leaned closer and smiled at her, smug. "Precisely."

"Ovid and Homer would be distressed to learn of your poor opinion of them."

"No doubt," he agreed wryly. "Shakespeare would be inconsolable."

Fine. If Lord Ravenport failed to see the value in great works of literary genius, she was not going to waste her breath trying to change his mind. He could remain unenlightened, for all she cared. She needed a husband, not a poet.

She smiled brightly—as though his lack of refinement didn't trouble her in the slightest—and soaked in the scene around her. The path was crowded with phaetons and barouches, pedestrians and onlookers. "The park is quite busy today," she remarked.

"Hell is empty, and all the devils are here," he grumbled.

Fiona narrowed her eyes at him. "Two minutes after renouncing poetry, you have the audacity to quote Shakespeare?"

The earl shot her a wry grin and shrugged. "Even idiots like the Bard stumble upon the occasional gem."

She took a deep breath and resolved to avoid sparring with him. He wasn't scowling at the moment, indicating a marked improvement of mood—and she intended to take advantage of it. "I owe you an apology," she began earnestly. "I shouldn't have led my family to believe that you sent me flowers and wrote me poetry. Please forgive me."

He gave a curt nod and tightened his hands on the reins. "Will you also apologize to your admirer?"

Fiona blinked. "I'm not aware of an admirer."

"*Someone* is making romantic overtures. The flowers, the poem . . ."

Good heavens. Her cheeks flushed. Admitting the truth aloud was going to be nothing short of mortifying. "It's a rather amusing tale, actually."

"If you have a beau, there's no need to hide him. In fact, you should bring him out of the shadows."

The earl's voice had a bitter, hollow quality that made Fiona want to shake him and hug him at the same time. "It's not that simple," she said.

"He obviously has tender feelings for you. If you are determined to wed someone, why not *him*? Why involve me at all?"

For the love of—"There *is* no admirer. No beau," she said. "*I* sent the flowers. *I* wrote the poem . . . to myself."

The earl immediately pulled the curricle to the side of the road beneath the shade of a tree and turned to Fiona. He held the reins in one hand and raked the other through his hair. "You *pretended* to have a suitor?"

"Yes, my lord." She raised her chin defiantly. "I pretended to have *you* as a suitor."

"That is, quite possibly, the saddest thing I have ever heard."

"I don't need your pity." But, heaven help her, she *did* need the earl to marry her, and if a little pity helped her cause . . .

"Why don't you have real suitors?"

Why indeed? "I suppose there are several reasons, but I've no wish to enumerate them. The point is, I shouldn't have involved you in the lie."

"Why did you?" he asked, more curious than angry.

She looked around to make sure no passersby were within earshot and lowered her voice. "I know you haven't agreed to marry me—yet. But in the event that I'm able to persuade you, it's important that our affections seem . . . genuine. Our engagement . . . normal."

"There's nothing *normal* about marrying someone you've known for less than a fortnight, Miss Hartley, and all the flowers and poetry in the world can't make it so." He frowned for a moment, then asked earnestly, "Haven't you ever been in love?"

Fiona swallowed. "I once fancied myself in love with a boy who lived near our country house. I was twelve and thought him very clever. He would fish or practice archery, and I would sketch him. But when his father discovered how much time we were spending together, he forbade William to see me."

"Were you heartbroken?"

"No," she answered honestly. "But I did miss him."

"And there's been no one since?" He stared at her, disbelieving.

"Not really." A few handsome gentlemen had caught her eye, but none had truly captured her interest, much less her heart.

"Well, I'm no expert on the subject of love either, but I do know this: You can't fake it. Look at all the couples strolling by the Serpentine." He waved a hand in the direction of a nearby footpath. "None of them are in love," he said dryly. "Some might be in the throes of temporary infatuation, but most are wishing they were walking with someone else. You can tell by the way they're swiveling their heads, looking around the park for someone better than their partners."

Goodness. Lady Helena must have wounded him deeply—maybe more than he cared to admit to himself.

"That is a rather jaded view, but you may be correct," Fiona conceded. "Perhaps none of those couples is in love. But I disagree that it's impossible to fake affection. My mother and sister believe you are smitten—partly because of the poetry I wrote, but mostly because that's what they *want* to believe. I'm not asking you to play the part of lovesick suitor for the duration of the house party, but perhaps you could scowl a little less? Maybe pay me the occasional compliment? Would that be so very difficult?"

Paying Miss Hartley a compliment wouldn't be difficult at all. Gray could think of half a dozen off the top of his head. She was easy to talk to, and the lilting sound of her voice warmed his blood. She was the opposite of ordinary, and even though he'd thought nothing could surprise him anymore, she did. She was clever and pretty and nice. She smelled good.

No, paying her a compliment would be easy—and misleading.

"I don't want to falsely raise your hopes with flattery," he said regretfully. "The chances of me marrying you are almost nil."

"So, there *is* a chance," she said, triumphant.

"A minuscule chance." God, he felt like an ass. But the sooner she accepted the truth, the better off she'd be. He'd witnessed the devastating effects of a love that had turned sour. He'd seen things no one should have to see. Was it any wonder he wished her to be spared the same fate? "When you arrive at my manor house tomorrow, you'll see. We are from different worlds, you and I."

"You say that as though being from different worlds is a bad thing. Maybe it isn't. All I'm asking is that you open your mind to the possibility we might suit one another."

Gray snorted, slapped his horses' reins, and steered the

curricle back onto the road. Damn, but Miss Hartley was stubborn. "I'm hosting you at the Fortress for a week," he told her. "That will fulfill any obligation I have to you."

"I know you could use the money from my marriage settlement," she said boldly. "And I presume you'll eventually need an heir."

Jesus, she wasn't mincing words. But two could play that game. "I will require an heir. And a spare. But why should I stop there? Perhaps I'll want a wife who's willing to give me a whole houseful of brats." He hazarded a glance at her, pleased to see she'd turned a shade paler.

"I am open to negotiating such matters," she said. "But I suspect you're merely trying to scare me off—and I don't scare easily."

"I'd noticed."

She wrung her hands in her lap. "The trouble is, I have only nine days left in which to marry someone."

An idea dawned. "Does your sense of urgency stem from one of those odd, antiquated clauses in a will? The kind that states you must marry by the time you're a certain age, or the money reverts to the estate?"

"No, nothing like that," she said, forlorn. "It stems from wanting to protect my family. More than that I cannot say."

"I'm sorry I can't help with your predicament, Miss Hartley." But then another thought occurred to him. Maybe he *could* help her—by finding her an eligible beau. Someone *besides* him.

She was beautiful, smart, and kind—and her father was richer than Croesus. She wanted a titled husband, and he knew plenty of bachelors who were peers. Gray was not in the business of matchmaking, but if finding Miss Hartley a real suitor took the pressure off him he wasn't averse to playing Cupid this once.

He'd already roped Kirby into attending the farce of a

house party; what was one or two bachelors more? Gray would ensure that the potential candidates were well-mannered, decent fellows—the kind he wouldn't object to courting his own sister, if he'd had one.

He was congratulating himself on his brilliant idea when the left wheel of his curricle unexpectedly dipped into a rut. Miss Hartley had no time to brace herself. She slid on the bench seat, and the side of her body—from shoulder to hip—collided with his.

Any notion of comparing her to a sister fled.

All rational thought fled.

"Oh my," she breathed as she wriggled against him, trying unsuccessfully to right herself.

Gray gathered the reins in one hand, wrapped his free arm around the nip of her waist, and nudged her upright. "Forgive me. I should have avoided the hole in the road."

"No, no," she said, charmingly flustered as she adjusted her bonnet, which now sat cockeyed on her head. "I should have been more alert. I confess I'm more accustomed to lumbering carriages than spritely curricles. But the change is wonderful," she assured him. "I like feeling the breeze on my face."

Gray smiled at her candor. "You can't fully appreciate the vehicle's speed in a park setting. Once we're in the country, I'll take you for a ride and let the horses—" He stopped, irritated with himself for forgetting, even momentarily, that he mustn't lead Miss Hartley on. He should definitely not be making promises to take her on additional outings when the goal was to be rid of her as soon as possible. "Actually, I'm sure any gentleman at the house party would be happy to drive you through the countryside."

She smiled knowingly, damn it all. "That sounds divine."

Determined to regain control of the conversation—

assuming he ever had it—he announced firmly, "There will be no more poetry. At least none attributed to me."

"Fair enough," she replied with a sigh. "No poetry, no flowers, no love letters. And I do apologize if I embarrassed you."

He shrugged and decided he could afford to be magnanimous. "No harm done. If word of my poetry spreads to my club, I'll tell everyone I was foxed when I wrote it."

"It wasn't *that* bad."

"It was horrid."

She didn't reply but smiled and lifted her face to the sun, letting the ribbons of her bonnet flutter in the wind. They rode in companionable silence for a minute or two; then she turned to him. "May I ask you a question?"

"Of course."

"How do you feel about romantic ballads?"

The back of his neck prickled. "About listening to them or *writing* them?" he asked pointedly.

"Singing them. Perhaps while a young lady of your acquaintance accompanied you on the pianoforte?"

"Miss Hartley . . ."

She blinked innocently. "It's purely a hypothetical question. Although it might be fun."

He turned and shot her a glare that would have made most men tremble in their boots.

She laughed. *Laughed.* The deep-bellied kind that can't be faked. And the way she beamed, brimming with mirth . . . It momentarily stopped his world.

"I was only teasing," she said, giving him a saucy wink. "But let me know if you change your mind about the ballad."

Chapter 8

Gray and his grandmother arrived at the Fortress the next morning a few hours before guests were expected. He'd tried valiantly to dissuade her from attending the house party—not because he didn't want her company, but because he didn't want her to trip over a warped floorboard or freeze in the drafty dining room. She'd insisted on joining him, however, saying it had been far too long since he'd entertained there. Or anywhere.

And when she heard that several young ladies would be spending the week at the house . . . well, Gray doubted the Devil himself could keep her away.

He'd made sure his grandmother's bedchamber was appointed with the best curtains and carpets the Fortress had to offer—which wasn't saying much, unfortunately. He'd instructed her maid to pack several extra blankets, her favorite books, and anything else she required for her comfort.

His grandmother had patted his shoulder and assured him that one didn't live to be her age without being stubborn and hardy.

And she was both. She'd survived a husband who succumbed to scarlet fever; she'd buried a son and daughter-in-law. Gray was a boy of twelve when he lost both

parents, and his grandmother had been the one who con-
soled him, the one who loved him.

She'd helped Gray to survive capsizing waves of grief
and guilt, never letting him see the depths of her own
heartbreak.

And now that he was finally able to return the favor and
take care of her, she was going blind—and there was absolutely nothing he could do to prevent it.

He escorted her to the drawing room, which was the
most habitable space in the house. The furnishings were
shabby, but a few strategically placed paintings covered
holes and cracks in the plaster walls. Gray had already replaced the broken windows, and his housekeeper had
sewn a few colorful silk pillows to make the threadbare
settee and chairs seem more welcoming.

A small fire warmed the seating area, and Gray settled
his grandmother into an armchair near the fireplace. "Shall
I ask your maid to fetch a blanket?" he asked.

"No, my dear boy. Not unless you wish me to expire
from the heat."

"Should I ring for tea?"

She shook her head. "Please sit," she said, waving a
hand at the chair across from her. "Tell me about the Hartley sisters and their friend Miss Kendall. Why did you
invite them? You could have chosen any of the young ladies in London to be your guests."

He arched a brow at her. "Yes, and a great many would
have declined." Including Helena. But he didn't need to tell
his grandmother who he was thinking of. She already
knew.

"Don't be so contrary. Any miss worth her weight in
salt would have been delighted to receive an invitation
from the Earl of Ravenport, but you chose these three.
Why?"

Gray lowered himself into the chair, debating how to best dodge the question. He'd avoided answering at least three times during the coach ride there, and—

Crack. The right back leg of his armchair broke, and Gray flew backward, somersaulting across the drawing room and toppling a small table in the process. *Good grief.*

"Gray!" his grandmother exclaimed. "Are you all right?"

"Fine," he assured her. But in truth, his heart pounded with the fear of what *might* have happened. What if he'd sat his grandmother in the bad chair? She could have hit her head, broken her neck, or worse.

He stood, brushed off the sleeves of his jacket, and went to inspect the faulty chair. The wooden leg had split in two, but it could be easily fixed. He'd add it to the list of necessary house repairs—oh, somewhere near the bottom of the fourth page.

"I'm beginning to think you'll resort to any lengths to avoid answering my questions," his grandmother teased. "Even performing tumbling tricks."

"In case you've forgotten, *you're* the one who directed me to sit." Gray shot her a grin, dropped to the floor, and inspected the legs of the chair she sat in. No sign of any loose or rotten parts. "Your chair appears to be sturdy."

"Pshaw. I'm not worried."

"Well, *I* am. You must take extra care while you're here." He paced in front of the fireplace, making a mental note to check the furniture in her bedchamber later.

"I promise to," she began slyly, "*if* you'll answer my question. Why did you invite these particular young ladies?"

Why indeed? "I invited the Hartley sisters because . . ." *The older one proposed marriage and kissed me in my carriage. And though it's the height of idiocy, I find myself inexplicably attracted to her.* "They seem like they could use a few friends."

His grandmother narrowed her eyes and nodded sagely as she pondered his words. "I see."

"But you'll be able to form your own opinion of the ladies very soon. They'll arrive this afternoon, as will the gentlemen." Gray had invited Kirby and his father, Lord Dunlope, because they both loved to hunt and if there was one amenity that the Fortress could offer—the only amenity, actually—it was an abundance of pheasant and grouse.

Gray had also extended an invitation to Lord Pentham, a friend from his club. The marquess seemed a decent sort. He didn't drink or gamble excessively. Didn't put on airs. Even-keeled and steady, he'd provide a fine counterbalance to Fiona's passionate personality. Perfect husband material.

A far better match for her than Gray.

If Fiona agreed with his assessment—and there was no reason she shouldn't—Gray would no longer be her target and he'd be able to move on with his life. Fixing the Fortress. Doting on his grandmother. Proving himself to Helena and the rest of the world.

He only had to endure seven days of playing host and entertaining.

And given the current shoddy state of his home, it would be a miracle if his guests lasted half that long.

"Thank heaven," Mary said, holding up one of Lily's pink silk slippers. "I feared I'd failed to pack both shoes, but this one was hiding near the bottom of the trunk—beneath the petticoats. 'Twould have been a disaster if it had been left at home."

Fiona chuckled. "Hardly. Mama made certain we have enough shoes to wear a different pair each day."

The maid bustled about the cavernous bedchamber that Fiona and Lily were to share for the duration of the house party, unpacking ball gowns, undergarments, nightgowns, and accessories.

"Why don't you let Lily and me see to the rest of the unpacking?" Fiona suggested. "You can go help Mama get settled." Their stepmother had her own room just down the hall, near the bedchamber Lady Callahan and Sophie shared.

"If you're certain," Mary replied. "She'll be wanting a tincture to calm her nerves."

Long drives always made Mama queasy, and the prospect of living under an earl's roof for a week was as terrifying as it was exciting—although she'd sooner eat her bonnet than admit it.

"Yes, do go," Lily agreed. "And once Mama is resting, you can settle yourself in your quarters."

"Very well." Mary cast a critical eye around the room as she went to the window and pulled back the curtains—revealing a pane with a large crack. "Oh my."

"Did I mention the earl intends to make improvements to the property?" Fiona said brightly. "He's already begun."

Lily scrunched her nose. "I think he should have started with furniture, personally. There aren't enough pieces to properly fill the room. I feel like I'm in a medieval castle. Perhaps we've time for a jousting match before dinner in the banquet hall?" She shrugged her delicate shoulders. "I wouldn't mind meeting a knight in armor—shining or otherwise."

"Granted," Fiona conceded, "it's not quite as elegant as our house in town, but we're terribly spoiled. And these walls must hold so much history. Imagine the tales they could tell."

The maid clucked her tongue and made her way toward the door. "If I hear any walls talking, or see any ghosts floating for that matter, I'll be on the first coach headed home." She paused at the threshold and smiled. "But assuming the house is not occupied by disgruntled spirits, I'll return in plenty of time to help you dress for dinner." With a bob of her capped head, she scurried off.

Lily pulled a sprigged muslin gown from the trunk and handed it to Fiona to hang. One of the armoire doors hung open, but when Fiona attempted to pull open the other it refused to budge, no matter how hard she yanked on the handle.

Arching a brow, Lily said, "I wonder what's hiding in the dark recesses of that wardrobe. Actually, I don't think I want to know."

"The wood is a little warped, that's all," Fiona said. She reached around the stuck door and placed the morning gown on a hook, praying the inside of the armoire wasn't infested with spiders. "Granted, the room is sparsely furnished . . . and lacking the luxuries we're accustomed to. But it does appear to be clean. And it's not as though a little dust or dirt would hurt us. Remember the days when we sat on the floor of Papa's office playing game after game of knucklebones?"

Lily smiled softly and handed Fiona another gown. "And when he'd take us out walking in the rain? We managed to tromp through every puddle, and even though our frocks were splattered with mud, Papa laughed as hard as we did."

"Yes," Fiona said wistfully, sad that she'd all but forgotten the sound of her father's laughter.

"I miss him," Lily said, and Fiona knew she missed

more than his physical presence. She longed for the way things used to be. Before he'd remarried. "I wish he'd been able to come with us."

Fiona did, too. Maybe a few days' respite from his work would have allowed him to truly connect with his daughters—and be the type of father he once was. "Let's write him a letter," she suggested. "We'll tell him all about this sprawling house and the plentiful game and the cigar-smoking gentlemen. Maybe he'll be persuaded to come." But Fiona doubted it, and Lily's wan smile suggested she was equally skeptical.

"We'll make the most of our time here, whether Papa joins us or not," Lily said resolutely. She clutched one of her newly updated gowns to her chest and twirled. "I do hope there'll be dancing one evening."

"I wouldn't count on it." Fiona placed their jewelry on a starkly barren desk, which, in the absence of a proper vanity, would have to serve as a dressing table. Thank heavens they'd tucked a small mirror into their trunk. "The earl was emphatic that we should not expect lavish parties or entertainment."

"What a charming host," Lily said dryly. She hung her gown, then hoisted Fiona's valise onto the large bed where they'd both sleep. She reached in and extracted an armful of books—including Fiona's diary. "Where shall I put these?"

Oh dear. "I'll take them." Fiona hurried over and relieved her sister of the stack, questioning the wisdom of bringing the journal with her. She'd assumed she would have her own bedchamber, and while she trusted Lily not to snoop, she couldn't be too careful—especially since the latest blackmail note was hidden between the diary's pages.

The second note had arrived that morning, shortly before they'd departed London, and Fiona had barely had a chance to read it before joining her sister and Sophie in the carriage. She thought that perhaps if she studied it, she'd find a clue as to who the blackmailer was, or at least a hint as to how he—or she—came to learn the secret about Lily. Fiona had tucked it into the diary before packing it in her valise, hoping she'd have a solitary moment to analyze it during the house party. Now she was not so sure.

Fiona placed the small tower of books on a bedside table—except for the journal, which she whisked behind her skirt. Then she picked up her sketchbook and used it to conceal the diary, sandwiching it between the large drawing pad and her chest.

Lily's bemused expression said she knew precisely what Fiona was hiding.

Only she didn't.

Fiona would let Lily read every page of her diary aloud in the public square before she let her sister see the extortionist's note.

"I was thinking I'd take a walk around the gardens," Fiona said nonchalantly. "Maybe explore the grounds and draw for a bit. Would you like to come?"

Lily smiled knowingly. "You go ahead. I'll check on Mama and visit with Sophie for a little while before dinner. Will you return in time to help with my hair? I've a feeling Mary will have her hands full with Mama."

"Certainly." Fiona slid a pencil behind her ear and threw a shawl around her shoulders. "I won't be more than an hour. Just long enough to check the grounds for knights, ghosts, and fairies."

"Very good. I shall expect a full report." Lily grinned. "Especially about the knights."

Chapter 9

Fiona encountered no one on her way to the garden at the rear of the house, which was just as she'd wished. She required a few moments alone—to reread the latest letter, sketch a bit, and regain her equilibrium before facing the earl at dinner.

She followed a stone path that led to a large semicircular terrace with marble benches around the perimeter. The flagstones were bare, save for a few shaded areas covered with moss. No colorful flowers or sprawling ivy softened the cold hardscape; no fanciful lanterns adorned the bare branches of surrounding trees.

But the garden beyond was everything that the terrace wasn't—wild, alive, intriguing. It was the opposite of a well-manicured English garden. Bushes that refused to be trimmed into clever little shapes. Trellises that bowed under the weight of overgrown vines. Flowers and weeds that hadn't seen pruning shears in at least a decade. Listing, cracked sculptures of cherubs and nymphs peeked through leaves and brush–like spies from some lost civilization.

Fiona loved everything about it. Her fingers itched to capture the scene on paper, so she waded through the long grass, found a large rock to perch on, and flipped to a clean sheet in her sketchbook. She usually preferred to draw portraits, where she could peel away a person's layers and reveal something new, but this garden seemed to pulse and breathe with a personality all its own. Every lush nook hinted at a mysterious history—and a myriad of secrets.

She narrowed her focus to a defunct fountain with an alabaster mermaid holding court at the center. Once, freshwater would have gurgled and flowed around the siren's tail, but now she was forced to content herself with a shallow puddle of rainwater sullied with leaves and twigs. Fiona sketched it all: the encroaching shrubs, the waning light, the chipped plaster. But as she drew the mermaid, she also saw hope—and fierce determination. Fiona channeled those emotions, spilled them onto the page, lost track of time.

And when a long, dark shadow slanted across her sketchbook, she started.

"Miss Hartley."

Fiona recognized the deep, smooth voice even before she looked up at the devilishly handsome face. "Lord Ravenport."

How many hours had she lost? She prayed the earl wasn't part of a search party sent to retrieve her. Suddenly frantic, she looked at the ground near her feet for her journal and found it there, still closed, thank heaven. But she wasn't at all comfortable with the diary and the earl being in the same vicinity. It was rather like storing a tinderbox in a straw house.

"What are you doing out here?" he asked, half-curious, half-accusatory.

She slammed her sketchbook shut. "Just soaking up the raw beauty of your garden. It's lovely."

He snorted at that. *Snorted.* "I'm fully aware of the garden's shortcomings. But please, by all means, feel free to mock me—at least that's one form of entertainment I can offer you during your stay."

"I wasn't mocking you—or your garden, my lord." Miss Hartley shook her head, as though confused. The consummate actress. "I truly like it. In fact, I was sketching your fountain."

Gray maintained a calm exterior, but beneath the surface he seethed. "If our relationship has one thing to recommend it, it's our ability to be frank with one another."

"I completely agree." She sat on a rock like a woodland sprite while the evening breeze blew the soft curls framing her face, making it difficult for him to remain angry. But he was doing his damnedest.

"Then do not insult me by being disingenuous," he said. "You elected to draw a waterless, broken, filthy fountain. Why, exactly? So you could show your sketch to friends in town and snicker at this travesty of a garden?"

"I would never do that." She flushed as though she was offended. Or perhaps guilty.

Stupidly, he'd thought she might be different from Helena. Less shallow. More open-minded. But she'd wasted no time in proving him wrong. "This garden was once fit for a royal palace—my grandmother's pride and joy. It is obviously in dire need of improvement, but I *will* make it beautiful again, even if I have to tear out every living thing by the roots and start from bare soil."

She frowned as she slipped her pencil behind a delicate ear. "You may not see the beauty in this place, but I do. It's different and daring. It doesn't follow the rules."

"That's what happens when shrubs are left to their own devices for two decades or so. They become very rebellious," he said dryly.

She scrambled off the rock and perched a fist on one

hip. "You accuse me of mocking, but *you* are the one who is being snide."

Maybe he was. Might as well add *bitter* and *cynical* to the list. Better to be all those things than a fool. "Fine. I am snide. But you . . . you are going to be late for dinner."

"Dash it all," she muttered to herself. "I knew it. Lily must be worried."

"Allow me to escort you out of the wilderness and back to the house," he said coldly. In spite of her apparent callousness, she tempted him. More than he cared to admit. Even now, he was picturing her with her hair falling around her shoulders and her gown puddled at her feet like some erotic version of Eve. He could easily imagine laying her down on the verdant ground and kissing her, touching her, till they were both breathless with desire.

Instead, he offered her his arm.

"Wait." She swallowed nervously, then let out a long breath. "We'll go in a moment. But first I want you to see my drawing." She flipped open the sketchbook and turned the page toward him.

Gray planned to give it a perfunctory look and make the obligatory response, so they could get the hell out of this godforsaken Eden—before he did something he'd regret for all eternity.

But the picture, with all its bold strokes and subtle shading, its varied textures and dramatic lighting, drew him in. Made it impossible to look away. The mermaid appeared less like stone and more like a living, enchanted creature. She wore a flirtatious, satisfied smile—as if she were queen of the lush, wild paradise that surrounded her.

Gray stared, mesmerized. By the drawing, certainly. But also by all it revealed—about the garden, Fiona . . . even him.

"It's very rough," she said, pulling the sketch pad back. "I don't normally draw landscapes, so it's not my best—"

"I owe you an apology." He reached for the sketchbook and examined the drawing more closely. "I assumed you saw what everyone else sees—an assortment of dead and overgrown plants, choked by weeds. But you saw something different. More. Something even I didn't see."

Her eyes welled. "Thank you. Sometimes the greatest beauty hides in the most unlikely of places."

Gray gazed at the auburn glint of her hair, the thick fringe of her lashes, and the random pattern of freckles dotting her nose. "Indeed."

Before he knew what he was doing, he'd set the sketchbook on the rock and picked a purple flower from the bush beside it. He stood toe to toe with her, holding the blossom between them. "I'd wish I could tell you this is a rare, exotic flower. But it might well be a weed."

She smiled. "Then it is a pretty weed."

"Please accept this unidentified flora specimen as a humble but sincere peace offering."

Her eyes crinkled at the corners, and she nodded as though all was forgiven. "Of course."

When she would have reached for the flower, he shook his head. "Wait. I've a better idea." Gently, he removed the pencil that was tucked behind her ear and replaced it with the blossom. He let his hand linger near the shell of her ear, let his knuckles graze the sweet curve of her neck.

Her lips parted, and her breath hitched; her eyes darkened with desire.

He suddenly felt like he was tumbling headlong down a hill, rolling too fast to stop himself.

Shit. He was going to kiss her.

He took a step toward her, and she toward him. Their

bodies collided—hers pliant, his unyielding. He dipped his head and tipped his forehead to hers, letting them both savor the awareness—and inevitability—of what was to come.

With a sigh, she melted into him. He speared his fingers through her silken hair. His heart galloped, his lips found hers . . . and he was gone.

This kiss was everything the last one had not been. Raw, primal, uncivilized—just like the garden around them.

Gray traced the seam of her lips with his tongue and tasted her as he'd longed to since that first awkward encounter in his carriage. He'd suspected that when it came to passion, she'd be a quick study—and she was. Her tongue eagerly tangled with his; her bare hands wound their way around his neck and caressed his nape, stoking his desire—as if he needed further encouragement.

She tasted sweet, like honeysuckle plucked from a branch. Her scent mingled with the fragrances of the flowers and greenery that surrounded them, like some potent, ancient aphrodisiac. She was a siren, just like the one she'd drawn—an unexpected, dazzling beauty. Even a saint would have succumbed to temptation such as this.

But Gray couldn't. Not when there was no future for them. Instead, he'd content himself with one perfect, utterly enchanting kiss.

Just when he was congratulating himself on regaining a modicum of control, she tentatively, inexpertly, traced a path along his jaw and down his neck, loosening his neckcloth. Daring him to deepen the kiss.

Damn it all. He'd never been one to refuse a dare.

He cradled her head in his hands and slanted his mouth across hers, holding nothing back. He swallowed her soft moans and skimmed his palms down the back of her gown, over the ripe curve of her bottom, pressing her body to his. Letting her feel his arousal.

And *still* she kissed him back—as though she, too, was powerless to stop it.

He wanted to strip off every stitch of their clothing, lay her down right there in the long, fragrant grass, and take her slowly. Make love to her until she cried out in ecstasy.

He reminded himself that she wasn't looking for a *real* marriage. And he sure as hell wasn't.

Gradually, reluctantly, he slowed the kiss. Gently pulled back.

Looking into her dazed eyes, he silently cursed himself. "I find myself apologizing for the second time tonight. I was carried away. Forgive me."

She smoothed a curl behind the ear where the flower had fallen away, then touched a slender fingertip to her swollen lips. "No. That is, there is nothing to forgive."

Gray doubted she'd say that if she'd been privy to the wickedness of his thoughts.

"Thank you," he said sincerely. "For showing me the sketch. I know it wasn't intended for me, but it was a true gift. I've been so blinded by the crumbling bricks and leaky roof that I didn't notice . . ."

"The mermaid?" she asked.

"Right." He shot her a grin. "I didn't see the mermaid."

"Now that you know she's there," she said saucily, "perhaps you'll be inclined to visit her occasionally. Flowers and poetry are optional, of course."

"Do not fret. She's going to have more than her share of admirers. In due time."

Her expression suddenly turned sober. "Unfortunately, my lord, time is a luxury she cannot afford."

"After the kiss we just shared, you may not address me as *my lord.* At least not in private. It's *Ravenport.*" Impulsively, he added, "Or *Gray,* if you prefer. That's what my grandmother calls me."

"Gray," she said, testing it out. "It's a fine name."

"As is *Fiona.*" His voice was gruff to his own ears. "It's a fitting name for a mermaid . . . *and* for a beautiful woman."

"I am not beautiful," Fiona protested. She knew it with the same certainty she knew her gown was green and lemons were tart. Lily and Sophie were beautiful. Whereas she . . . she wasn't *unattractive.* But, rather, interesting looking.

Lord Ravenport—that is, Gray—arched a brow at her. "It seems I'm not the only one who requires a lesson in beauty. If I could draw with half your skill, I'd prove it. But you'll have to trust me on this one. You *are* beautiful, Fiona." He cupped her cheek and brushed his thumb over her lower lip. Slowly. Reverently. "Don't ever forget it."

Fiona nodded, thinking it extremely unlikely she'd forget anything about that moment. For days, he'd done his best to avoid her, giving her the distinct impression that he didn't desire her—but the kiss they'd just shared told her differently. She still reeled from the feel of his lips branding hers, his hands cupping her bottom, his heart pounding beneath her palm.

The earl wanted her. And yet he would not agree to marry her.

"It is gallant of you to compliment me so," Fiona replied. "Perhaps we are more compatible than you previously thought?"

Gray's hand fell away from her face. "I have not changed my mind about your proposal. Although you could now force my hand, if you wished."

She thought about that—and was more tempted than she should have been. But she didn't want him to marry her under duress. "I do not. Still, you cannot blame me for trying to persuade you." Boldly, she reached around his neck and speared her fingers through his thick, longish hair.

He half-chuckled, half-cursed under his breath. His heavy-lidded stare had her belly performing somersaults, and his gaze dropped to her lips. "I'm starting to see just how persuasive you can be, siren. I'm no better than the sailor who steers his ship toward certain doom. I confess there's something about you I find utterly irresis—"

"Fiona?" A worried female voice called from the direction of the terrace. "Are you out here?"

Gads. Lily. Gray stepped away from Fiona like she'd suddenly contracted the plague.

"Yes," she called to her sister, beyond grateful that the thick brush and trees shielded them from Lily's view. "I've been sketching the garden. That is, I *was* sketching. Now I've finished." *Wonderful*—she sounded like a rambling lunatic. "Never mind, we're coming."

Blast it all, had she truly said *we're*? Gray pressed the heel of his hand to his forehead and shot her a pained look. Fiona's cheeks flamed.

After a slight pause, Lily shouted the inevitable question. "Who's with you?"

"It's I—Ravenport," Gray said smoothly. "I found your sister with her sketchbook and was just about to escort her back to the house."

"Oh," Lily said thoughtfully. As if she was starting to piece together the situation. "Thank heaven you found her. I'll let Mama know there's no cause for worry, and I suppose we'll all meet in the drawing room shortly?"

"Yes," Fiona called. "I lost track of time, but we're on

our way. I'm just going to wash up before I join you." She was already scrambling around the rock, scooping up her pencil, the sketchbook, and her—

Good Lord. Where was her diary? Her heart sank, and she dropped to her knees, searching frantically.

Gray waved the journal in front of her face. "Looking for this?" He checked the cover and spine, curious.

"Yes." She snatched it from his hand—a bit more forcefully than she'd intended.

He cocked an eyebrow as he helped her to her feet but didn't press her for more information. "We'll resume our conversation at another time." He glanced around the clearing. "Do you have everything?"

"I believe so." With as much dignity as she could muster, she pulled a stray leaf from her hair and headed for the house.

"Follow me. I'll show you to the back entrance. From there, you can quickly make your way to your bedchamber."

A few minutes later, Fiona was alone in her room, splashing cool water on her cheeks. Mama wouldn't be pleased that she was late for dinner—especially since she considered Fiona's sketching an unladylike pursuit. There was no time to change her gown, but she repaired her hair as best she could, grabbed a delicate shawl, and donned some sparkly earrings, hoping no one noticed she still wore her traveling clothes.

She was about to cross the threshold when she realized she'd left her journal on the bed. She dashed to the armoire, removed her valise, and tossed the diary inside. Just as she was about to stuff the bag under the bed, she remembered the blackmail note. She'd intended to reread it in the garden but never had.

She shrugged to herself. When one was already half an

hour late, what was one minute more? She plucked the journal out of her bag and opened it. . . .

Only the note wasn't there.

She checked inside the back cover. Empty.

Frantic, she flipped through the pages. Held the journal by the spine and shook it.

Dear God. The blackmail letter was gone. She'd managed to lose it somewhere between the house and the garden. A wave of queasiness hit her. Lily mustn't find it before she did.

Fiona's first instinct was to retrace her steps and search among the weeds and rocks in the garden until she found it. But it had grown dark, and everyone awaited her in the drawing room.

All she could do was wait until dawn—and hope no one discovered it before then.

Chapter 10

On Kissing a Gentleman (Revisited)

In a previous entry, I may have inadvertently given the impression that kissing is a rudimentary activity—one that is easily mastered.

I feel obliged to correct the record.

It seems kissing is far more nuanced than I ever imagined. When done properly, it's terribly improper. And wonderful.

So much so that I now understand why otherwise sensible young maidens happily ignore a lifetime of cautionary tales . . .

As it turned out, Fiona needn't have worried that her mother would find fault with her appearance at dinner. Mama was far too distracted by the shabby condition of the dining room. It seemed she couldn't drag her eyes away from the peeling wallpaper near the ceiling—except to stare at the mousehole in the baseboard.

The house's flaws presented a distinct dilemma for Mama. While she would normally find such primitive accommodations intolerable, their host was an *earl*.

Moreover, he was the earl who was, ostensibly at least, wooing her daughter.

Those two extenuating circumstances enabled her to forgive a multitude of sins, but her expression suggested that the less-than-than-luxurious accommodations *were* giving her a bit of indigestion.

Indeed, she seemed to be struggling to follow the thread of the conversation with Lord Dunlope, a viscount seated on her left. When he inquired as to the nature of her husband's business, Mama fumbled her fork and replied, "Oh, it was a pleasant drive indeed. Only three hours or so."

To his credit, the viscount nodded and continued eating his soup as though Mama's nonsensical answer had been nothing short of illuminating.

But the handsomely distinguished gentleman was surely judging Mama on the inside—and Fiona didn't blame him. That evening's dinner was the first time all the house party's guests had been assembled, and it was only natural that all in attendance would take their measure of the others.

Gray sat at the head of the table, of course, but Fiona didn't dare look his way for fear she'd blush to the roots of her hair. Just the memory of his hands on her face and body had her reaching for her wine goblet. And while she couldn't be sure, she was almost certain he was stealing glances at her. She knew from the way her skin tingled and her blood heated.

It was a very good start to the house party—and her campaign to make him her husband.

She might have savored the small victory if she weren't so distressed about losing the blackmail note.

But since there was nothing to be done about it now, Fiona spent most of the meal observing the other guests. Gray's grandmother, the dowager countess, sat to his right, wearing an imminently elegant purple gown with a lace fichu. She'd removed the cap she'd worn earlier in the day, opting to style her hair in a smooth twist that revealed a striking swath of grey in her otherwise dark hair. The sleek silver streak, which began at her crown and wound its way to the knot at her nape, gleamed proudly in the candlelight, as though each shining strand had been earned through daring adventures and exciting exploits.

While the countess was rather reserved during dinner, Fiona was able to reach two conclusions about her. First, that while the elderly woman watched everyone at the table with great interest, she seemed to focus on Fiona, Lily, and Sophie in particular. Second, she absolutely adored her grandson, beaming with pride every time she looked at him.

Fiona liked the countess. Which was a very good thing, because if she was to have any hope of marrying Gray, it was clear she was going to have to win the older woman's approval.

Lord Dunlope, Mr. Kirby's father, occupied the chair between the countess and Mama. The viscount was close to Mama's age and mostly bald, but the look suited him. His mustache was longish and not at all the fashion, but he won Fiona over with his ability to remain polite and impassive in the face of Mama's unorthodox behavior, which was often too direct for refined tastes.

Lady Callahan, Sophie's mother, sat on Gray's left, wearing one of Mama's gowns from last season. Lady Callahan had to have the robin's-egg blue silk taken in extensively to fit her petite frame, but the color complemented her fair complexion perfectly, and she was grateful for the fine dress, given her family's increasingly desperate financial situation. She and her husband, a baron, were pinning their hopes on advantageous matches for their daughters, but so far Sophie's older sister hadn't captured a gentleman's interest. Or perhaps none had captured hers.

In any event, it appeared more and more likely that it would be up to Sophie to save the family from the workhouse. Fiona, Lily, and Sophie all knew this, and yet none had given voice to it, for much the same reason that no one commented on Lord Callahan's tendency to drink too much—there was nothing to be done about it, and discussing the matter only made everyone feel worse.

Fiona was grateful that Lady Callahan and Sophie were able to join them and enjoy a few days' respite from the worry.

Lord Pentham, a friend of Gray's, was seated between Lady Callahan and Sophie. Given the marquess's expensive tailored jacket, charming manners, and solicitous nature, Fiona wondered what he and Gray could possibly have in common. Though both were handsome, Lord Pentham's good looks belonged in formal ballrooms and proper drawing rooms, while Gray's brand of attractiveness was primitive and wild—more suited to dark forests and windswept moors.

But perhaps she wasn't the most objective judge, given her recent encounter with the earl. She did wonder what Lily thought of the marquess . . . and whether they might enjoy a little flirtation during the house party.

Mr. Kirby and Lily sat across the table from Fiona. He sported the fashionably tousled hair and elaborately tied neckcloth that all the young bucks favored. He kept Lily and Fiona entertained with slightly off-color tales about his and Gray's days at Eton.

Fiona was relieved to escape to the drawing room with the ladies after dessert, but as soon as the older women were out of earshot, Lily and Sophie bombarded her with questions.

"Is the earl always so gruff?" Lily asked. She perched on the edge of a threadbare settee. "I thought he was rather surly at dinner."

"He wasn't precisely rude," Sophie mused, "but I had hoped he'd be more solicitous—at least toward you. Did you two have a falling-out?"

"Not at all," Fiona assured them. "He's just rather reserved. Not the demonstrative sort."

Lily arched a dark brow, skeptical. "He wrote you a romantic poem *and* sent gorgeous flowers. There's nothing subtle about that."

Gads. How could she forget that she'd given everyone the false impression that Gray was smitten with her? "He must be preoccupied with his hosting duties, but I take no offense."

Sophie frowned. "You deserve to have an attentive suitor, Fi."

Fiona felt the need to defend him. "He did mention that he'd like to take me for a drive in his curricle."

Lily sniffed. "Perhaps you should decline the invitation. Just so he'll realize that you expect to be properly wooed."

Fiona nodded as though she'd take the advice under consideration. She stood by the fireplace and gazed up at a portrait hanging above the mantel. Unless she was mistaken, the subject was the dowager countess, painted when she was younger—perhaps Fiona's age. Other walls boasted classical paintings and landscapes, but portraits of Gray's mother and father were eerily absent . . . as though they'd never existed.

"My darlings." Mama toddled over to Fiona, Lily, and Sophie, wrapping her arms around them like a mother swan. "How are you faring?" She asked the question as if they'd survived a week in an abandoned cottage with no food. During a snowstorm.

"We're fine, Mama." Fiona patted her arm.

"That's my sweet girl." Her eyes welled. "Keeping a stiff upper lip, as usual. But it's what we all must do—for now. Once you're married to the earl, you'll ensure that this house and the furnishings are brought up to snuff."

Oh dear. Mama was getting ahead of herself. "Actually, I'm not certain that he—"

"In the meantime," Mama continued, "we must act as though the lack of refinement doesn't distress us in the least. If you're able, my dears, I suggest that you appear oblivious to the water stains on the walls or the doors falling off their hinges or . . . on second thought, it's best that we refrain from speaking of such things." She gazed around the drawing room with obvious dismay.

"I doubt the earl expects us to be blind to the house's imperfections," Fiona said. "But I agree we shouldn't harp on them."

"Just think, Fi," Lily mused. "One day, you could be a *countess.*"

"It is within the realm of possibility," Fiona conceded. "I hope that we *all* make excellent matches." The problem was that Lily's chances would evaporate if the blackmailer revealed her secret—one that even Lily was unaware of. No gentleman would court the daughter of a madam.

Fiona thought of the extortion note. Wondered if the evening breeze was blowing it around the garden or across the lawn into the path of another guest. Pressing her fingertips to her forehead, she said, "I'm rather tired. Would it be awfully rude of me to excuse myself?"

"Not at all." Sophie wrapped a slender arm around Fiona's shoulders. "I'll walk you to your bedchamber."

"No, thank you," Fiona quickly replied. "I would rather slip out quietly if you don't mind. Would you make my apologies to the countess and your mother? I'm certain I'll feel better after a good night's rest."

"Of course," Sophie replied. "They'll understand—as will the gentlemen."

Lily gave Fiona an affectionate hug. "Go, rest. When I join you in a couple of hours, I expect you to be tucked in bed, sound asleep."

"Thank you for understanding." Fiona gave Mama a peck on the cheek and rushed upstairs.

But she had no intention of going to bed. Not while the blackmail note was still missing.

She changed her slippers, threw a midnight blue cloak over her gown, and grabbed a lantern before making her way outside.

She'd planned to quickly retrace her steps to the mermaid . . . but everything looked different and unfamiliar in the darkness. Lily would return to the room in an hour or so, and Fiona would likely need more time to conduct her search.

So she went back to her bedchamber and concocted a new plan. She'd wait till the household was asleep before sneaking out to the garden in the wee hours of the morning.

It was terribly risky, but she simply had to try.

Because Fiona would never forgive herself if anyone at the house party learned the truth.

That the woman who'd given birth to Lily and callously left her on the Hartleys' doorstep was London's most infamous madam.

Chapter 11

When Gray returned to his room that night, he poured himself a glass of brandy—his reward for socializing with guests for the better part of the evening. He'd looked for Fiona after dinner. Felt a stab of disappointment when he'd learned that she'd retired for the evening.

Surprising, that. And dangerous.

He still didn't know what game she was playing, but he felt himself being charmed. By her beauty and wit, yes. But more so by her unique brand of thoughtfulness—and the unique lens through which she saw the world.

He couldn't afford to be distracted by her. He needed to remain focused on his goal. Restoring the Fortress to its former glory.

Before his grandmother's world went dark.

Six more days. That's all he needed to endure. Then Fiona would realize her efforts were wasted on him. She'd leave the Fortress forever and focus her attention elsewhere.

They'd both be better off.

But tonight, too restless and agitated to sleep, he carried his brandy out onto the small balcony outside his bedchamber that overlooked the terrace, savoring the silence and solitude.

He leaned a hip against the iron balustrade and took in

the inky starlit sky and the tree line in the distance. He let his gaze drift beyond the semicircular terrace to the garden—dark, wild, and lovely. At least through Fiona's eyes . . . and now his.

The time he'd spent with her near the fountain seemed magical and unreal—as though the mermaid had cast a potent spell over them. He felt a hint of it even now, no doubt a result of the brandy and moonlight.

Perhaps the garden *was* enchanted—but it was far more likely he'd been drunk with lust.

He smiled as he took a sip of his brandy, then froze.

A faint light shone through the thick brush of the garden, and the leaves around it rustled. Maybe a nymph or fairy . . . but most likely a woman, damn it all. Specifically, Fiona.

What the devil was she doing out there alone at this time of night? Holy hell—what if she *wasn't* alone? He had no claim over her, and yet he couldn't deny the jealousy simmering in his gut.

In any event, it was *his* bloody garden, and he intended to investigate anyone who trespassed there—especially after midnight.

He left his drink on a table and strode toward the back staircase, surprisingly eager for a rendezvous with the mermaid.

Fiona was fairly certain she was on the right path . . . but it was difficult to be sure. Untrimmed branches, wayward weeds, and undulating roots encroached on the pebbled path through the garden.

She'd had no difficulty slipping out of the house unnoticed, but she'd left a note on her pillow for Lily. On the off chance that her sister awoke before Fiona returned, she didn't want her to worry.

Fiona estimated that she'd been in the garden an hour or more, and she was only about halfway to the fountain. So far, she'd found three earthworms, two toads, and one guinea. But no blackmail note.

Her legs ached from crouching, but a bit of soreness was a small price to pay if her search was successful. She kept the hood of her cloak drawn over her head and the lantern's flame low as she inched forward, meticulously checking under every bough and in every rock crevice.

She was looking beneath a bush when something jumped out of the shadows, landing on the toe of her slipper. With a little cry, she started and stepped on the hem of her gown, then tumbled backward onto her bottom. She landed on a large stone just as her lantern rolled under a branch and the flame extinguished, bathing Fiona in darkness.

Croak. Ah, toad number three. It hopped into the brush, apparently unharmed, while Fiona would surely have a bruise by morning.

Well, at least it had not been a spider.

Blinking back tears and muffling a curse, Fiona pushed herself to her feet and rubbed the tender spot on her backside while she waited for her eyes to adjust. As she stooped to retrieve the lantern, footsteps sounded behind her. Not the dainty sound of soft slippers gliding over pebbles. More like large hessians crushing them. Panic flooded her veins—until she heard the deep, familiar voice.

"Out for an evening stroll?" *Gray.*

Fiona whirled around to see him—or rather, his silhouette—in the faint moonlight. She'd prepared an excuse in case she was discovered outside, but for the life of her, she couldn't recall it. Not while he was so near.

"I couldn't sleep," she replied. "What about you? Do you routinely patrol the grounds at midnight?"

"No. But I'm beginning to think that I should." He moved a step closer. "Are you all right? I thought I heard you fall."

"I did and I am. Fine, that is."

"I see," he said, obviously skeptical. "What happened to your lantern?"

"I dropped it when the toad landed on my slipper."

"You were attacked by a toad?" With a chuckle, he knelt beside her, reached into the brush, and extracted the lantern. Holding the now bent handle, he examined the metal frame in the moonlight. "Did you bring a tinderbox?"

A chorus of crickets seemed to mock her. "Alas, I did not."

"Then it's a good thing I'm here to escort you back to the house."

She bristled slightly. "I don't require an escort, my lord."

"It's *Gray.* Remember?"

Oh, she remembered all too well. "I'm not quite ready to return to the house, but please, go on without me."

He snorted at that. "No chance in hell."

"Afraid I'll be sacrificed to the minotaur?" she asked dryly.

"No, but I admit the idea has some appeal." He placed his hands on his hips. "What are you really doing out here at this time of night?" She opened her mouth to answer, but he added, "And don't tell me you were going to draw something. Even if there was sufficient light—which there is *not*—you're not carrying your sketch pad."

She scrambled for a plausible excuse and decided on something close to the truth. "I think I dropped something . . . earlier today, when we were together. I was looking for it."

"And you couldn't wait until after sunrise to retrieve it?" he asked, incredulous. "It must be very important."

If he only knew. Shrugging, she said, "I believe I mentioned I was having difficulty sleeping. A walk usually cures my insomnia, so I thought to kill two birds."

Gray raked a hand through his hair. "Fine. What, exactly, are you searching for?"

"An earring," she blurted. *Heavens.* Why couldn't she have said *a bracelet* or *a glove—anything* larger than a chestnut.

"An earring," he repeated. In a tone that made her feel like a simpleton.

"One of a pair that my mother gave me. Not my stepmother, but my real mother." Her voice cracked—not because she was that fine an actress, but because talking about her mother always gave her a lump in her throat and reminded her of all she missed. Cozy nights reading stories in front of the fire, sun-filled days wading in the creek, and laughter.

"The odds of you finding an earring among the pebbles, leaves, and brush in the pitch black of the night are infinitesimal. You *do* realize that?"

Fiona raised her chin. "Granted, the desired outcome is unlikely. That doesn't mean it's not worth trying for." Maybe she wasn't talking about earrings anymore.

He stood frozen for several heartbeats. "I think you are more than a little mad. But if you insist on looking for your earring tonight, I will help you. I'm going to retrieve another lantern, but in the meantime, you must remain here. Don't try to fumble around in the dark—you'll only end up falling headfirst into a bush."

"You don't need to help me," she said. "It's probably a lost cause."

"It's not open for debate," he said smoothly. He reached for her hand and rubbed a thumb over the back of it. In the darkness, the simple caress felt as intimate as a kiss.

Maybe more so. "If you cherish the earring so much that you're willing to crawl through an overgrown garden looking for it, the least I can do is fend off the toads for you."

"Oh." She didn't say anything else for fear her voice would crack again. Something about the matter-of-fact way he responded had warmed her chest. And this time, it wasn't simply desire that was to blame—it was emotion.

Since the day she'd received the blackmail note, she'd felt so alone. There'd been no one Fiona could talk to about the shocking news, no one to share the grave responsibility for Lily's future and her family's well-being.

And now Gray was there, willing to jump in and search the garden for an earring in a garden that resembled a jungle.

Of course, Fiona couldn't confide in him about the blackmail note, but perhaps for tonight she could pretend she had an ally and a partner. She could imagine that someone was at her side, willing to fight off demons and blackmailers. Even toads.

And heaven knew, she needed all the time with the earl she could finagle in order to persuade him to propose. There were worse settings than moonlit gardens.

"I'll return within five minutes," Gray said. "Let me take you to a bench where you can sit safely until I'm back. Unless you'd prefer to come with me?"

"The bench will be fine, thank you."

He led her by the hand to a wrought-iron bench with an arched back that was nestled beneath a trellis just off the path. He set the lantern on the ground and, with his free hand, reached into his pocket for a handkerchief, which he used to dust off the seat. "You'll be safe here." Fiona wasn't sure if he was trying to convince her or himself.

"I shall be on the lookout for minotaurs, in any event,"

she teased as they continued to stand in front of the bench. His hand was so warm and assuring—like he'd never let any trouble befall her. But the contact was more than comforting. His touch was exhilarating, and awareness of him radiated throughout her body, a heady elixir.

Best of all, it seemed Gray was as reluctant to let go as she was.

But since they couldn't stand there all night, Fiona released his hand and tucked herself into the corner of the bench. He made sure she was comfortable, pulling the sides of her cloak around her. "Are you chilled? I could leave you my jacket."

Fiona smiled to herself. No gentleman had ever offered her his coat, and she was tempted to accept in case it turned out to be a once-in-a-lifetime thing. "I'm warm enough. But it is gallant of you to ask."

He gave a curt nod and rubbed the back of his neck. "Very well. I shall return shortly." He took three strides toward the house and turned around. "Promise me you won't do anything foolish while I'm gone."

"I don't plan to move from this spot," she assured him.

"That wasn't exactly a promise, but I suppose it will have to do." He took two steps backward before turning and jogging down the path.

Fiona snuggled into her cloak and let the sounds of the garden soothe her frayed nerves. Perhaps the night could be salvaged after all. When Gray returned with the tinderbox, she could resume her search, ostensibly for the earring . . . but she'd really be looking for the note. And if Gray happened to find it first, she'd snatch it from him before he could read it and rip it to shreds. Or perhaps she'd stick it inside the lantern and let it burn to ash.

In the meantime, she would ignore the voice in her head, which, not coincidentally, sounded remarkably similar to Miss Haywinkle's. It was telling her that proper young ladies didn't have assignations with men in the dead of night. And that those who dared to flout the rules would inevitably receive their due.

One night of illicit pleasure leads to a lifetime of despair, girls. The headmistress had recited the reminder frequently and fervently—almost as though she spoke from personal experience. Ridiculous, since the thought of Miss Haywinkle succumbing to basic urges was unfathomable. In fact, Fiona would have bet her favorite pair of slippers that the headmistress completely lacked basic urges, which she would have deemed unseemly.

Fiona shushed the voice by dwelling on the memory of Gray's warm, large hand holding hers. She recalled the taste of his lips and the deep timbre of his voice and the sweetness of his caress. Perhaps she'd close her eyes for a few moments while she waited for him . . . and dream of the illicit pleasure to come.

"Miss Hartley?"

Fiona jolted awake and gripped the arm of the bench, too petrified to speak. The man who approached her held a lantern in one hand—but he wasn't Gray.

"Forgive me if I startled you. I was sneaking a cheroot on the terrace and heard a noise out here. Are you all right?"

"Lord Pentham?" She placed a hand over her racing heart and squinted past the glow of the lantern at the marquess, surprised that he was the cheroot-sneaking sort. Fiona's first impression had been that he was serious and imminently proper.

"Yes, it is I. I should have identified myself from the start," he said apologetically. He looked around the small clearing. "Are you alone?"

The skin on the back of Fiona's neck prickled. "I am." Although Gray could come traipsing down the path at any moment, making a liar out of her. "I . . . I needed a breath of fresh air. And then I came across this little bench. . . . I must have nodded off."

"I see." Lord Pentham's kindly tone didn't completely mask his skepticism.

"Mama would be livid with me if she knew I ventured out by myself. I would appreciate it if you'd refrain from mentioning to anyone I was here."

"You may count on my utmost discretion," he said sincerely. He hesitated for a second. "I've no wish to intrude on your solitude, but would you mind if I joined you for a minute?"

Fiona swallowed. Not wishing to be rude, she waved a hand at the bench seat beside her. "Of course not—although I should return to the house very soon. My sister will worry when she notices I'm gone."

"I understand." The marquess set his lantern on the ground and settled himself on the bench while keeping a respectable distance. He was strikingly handsome. In fact, if he traded his tailored jacket for a flowing robe he could have passed for a golden-haired angel straight out of a classical painting. "I had planned on speaking with you at breakfast tomorrow morning, but since the opportunity has presented itself, I shall ask you now." He paused and shuffled his feet. Unless Fiona was mistaken, Lord Pentham was nervous.

"Ask me what?" she prodded.

"There's to be an archery contest tomorrow afternoon. I hope to see you there, and I wondered . . . if afterward . . . you might like to accompany me on a drive. To properly see the countryside," he sputtered.

Oh. It was a lovely invitation . . . but issued by the

wrong man. "It's very kind of you to offer, but I'm not yet certain of my plans."

He nodded graciously. "Perhaps another time then. Forgive me if I seem too forward. It's just that I was talking with Ravenport earlier and he suggested that I borrow his curricle."

Fiona blinked. "Did he?"

"He thought you might enjoy an outing, and I confess I jumped at the chance to spend some time in your company."

So, Gray thought to pawn her off on someone else. Wash his hands of her. This whole house party was probably arranged to try to divert her attention from him. "Are you and Lord Ravenport close acquaintances?"

"We know each other from our club. But I shouldn't have presumed to ask—"

"Actually, I am glad you did," she blurted.

"You are?"

She blew out a long breath. "I would be pleased to join you for a drive tomorrow afternoon, Lord Pentham."

"Why, that's excellent," he said, mildly surprised. "I shall look forward to it. But for now, I have taken enough of your time and will leave you to enjoy the peace."

He stood and made a formal bow—as if they were in a brightly lit ballroom instead of a pitch-dark garden—and started to walk back toward the terrace.

"Your lantern," Fiona called out. "You left it here."

"I feel better knowing you have it," he called back. "Good night, Miss Hartley."

She sat on the bench a few minutes more, contemplating her conversation with Lord Pentham and waiting to see if Gray emerged from the shadows—but he didn't. Deflated, she picked up the lantern and followed the path all the way to the fountain, looking for the blackmail note as she went. She didn't find it, but admittedly, she was distracted.

If Gray was attempting to play matchmaker between Lord Pentham and her, perhaps she should let him think that he'd succeeded. Because while she knew very little about desire, she was fairly certain that Gray desired her in spite of himself.

Maybe if he saw Fiona with the marquess, Gray would realize that he cared for her more than he'd admitted to himself.

She desperately hoped so, because she'd started to realize something herself. She'd thought she could be content to marry anyone who met a few basic requirements. That as long as her prospective husband was titled, good-natured, and open-minded, she could make a happy life with him.

Now she knew that wasn't the case at all.

The only person she could imagine marrying was Gray—and that was a dangerous thing. Because if she was going to save Lily and her family from ruin, she needed a gentleman who, unlike Gray, was actually willing to marry her and agree to her terms.

Unfortunately, she had only seven days in which to find him—*and* convince him to say his vows.

Chapter 12

The next morning, Fiona was tempted to plead a headache and skip the archery contest. After she had been roaming the garden for half the night, her head was throbbing and she would have given her favorite parasol for a few more precious hours of sleep, but she refused to let Gray think he'd discouraged her—even if he had.

No. She resolved to attend the contest, if for no other reason than to make him aware of her ire. Not only had he failed to return to her in the garden last night as promised, but he'd also tried to wriggle out of his offer to take her for a drive in his curricle. She did not wish to give him the impression that all was forgiven—because it was not.

She hopped out of bed and pretended to be as excited about the competition as Lily and Sophie were, donning one of her smart new day gowns and allowing Mary to style her hair in a bouquet of curls that cascaded over one shoulder. After all, it never hurt to look one's best when trying to make a gentleman regret his actions.

By the time everyone assembled in the grand foyer and prepared to leave, Fiona couldn't help but be swept up in anticipation of the outing.

She'd attended an archery contest on a previous occasion—at an estate neighboring her father's. The contestants and guests had mingled and enjoyed refreshments served beneath large white tents that had been erected for the event. Footmen were engaged to retrieve the arrows from the target after each round. The fields were neatly mowed, and chairs lined the perimeter so that spectators could view the competition in comfort.

But today's archery contest was turning out to be altogether different.

Everyone set out in high spirits, but the tall grass, damp with dew, proved too daunting for Mama, Lady Callahan, and Gray's grandmother. All three older ladies complained that their half boots were no match for the slippery lawn and had barely walked a stone's throw before they announced their intention to return to the house and sip hot tea by the fire. Lord Dunlope, Mr. Kirby's father, gallantly offered to escort them and was not eager to return himself.

In the end, all that remained of their party were four gentlemen—Gray, Mr. Kirby, Lord Pentham, and his brother, Lord Carter, and three ladies—Lily, Sophie, and Fiona.

Traipsing through the long grass in her silk gown felt like slogging through mud, and by the time Fiona spied the archery target on a hill in the distance her slippers were soaked, her hem was soiled, and she was huffing as though she'd run all the way there.

Gray and Mr. Kirby walked ahead, leading the way and carrying the bows and quivers of arrows, while Lord Pentham and his brother flanked the women and carried a couple of quilts and baskets containing wine, bread, and fruit.

"At last." Lily held a hand level with her bonnet and

squinted into the distance. "Someone, please tell me that target isn't a mirage."

Lord Pentham swiped the sleeve of his jacket across his brow. "Almost there. Would you ladies like to rest a moment before the final leg of our journey?" He set down his basket and braced his hands on his knees, anticipating—and no doubt hoping for—an answer in the affirmative.

"I, for one, am not stopping," Fiona replied. "If I did, I fear I wouldn't be able to move again until sometime tomorrow. Onward."

Sophie eyed the hill with trepidation but valiantly marched alongside Fiona as the sun beat down on them.

By the time they arrived at the top, Gray had already paced off the distance from the target and laid out a pair of bows and two dozen arrows.

Vexingly, he didn't appear winded in the least. "Who wants to go first?" he asked without preamble.

Lord Carter chuckled. "I won't speak for anyone else, but I'm going to need a glass of ale before any further exertions."

Most everyone voiced their agreement, but Fiona stepped forward. "I'm ready."

Lily leaned close to her ear. "Are you sure that's wise? When was the last time you used a bow?"

"A few years ago."

Her sister clucked her tongue in dismay. "Miss Haywinkle's?"

Fiona shrugged. "Perhaps." All the girls at school had received archery instruction so that they could comport themselves admirably in just this sort of situation. Two weeks of lessons had culminated in a competition, in which Fiona placed dead last. Even the youngest student—who was half her age—had easily bested her and spent the rest of the term taunting her.

"This should be interesting." Lily hoisted the quilts and walked toward a lone tree several yards off. "Sophie, help me spread these in that spot of shade. Trust me, we're going to want to be far away once this contest begins."

"That's probably wise," Fiona said to no one in particular. For her, this competition wasn't about winning. It was about showing Gray that she wouldn't be easily manipulated or deterred. She wasn't exactly sure *how* she would accomplish her goal, but perhaps if she was holding a lethal weapon he'd be inclined to take her more seriously.

She scooped a bow off the ground with one hand and plucked an arrow from a quiver with the other. "I suggest you stand back, Lord Ravenport. I will not be responsible for your wounds if my arrow takes an unexpected turn."

Even though every instinct Gray possessed screamed for him to give Fiona a wide berth, he stepped closer to her—so that he could speak without being overheard. "About last night," he began. "I want to apologize."

"For making me promise to remain on a bench and then abandoning me?" She refused to meet his gaze and instead fumbled with the bow.

"When I returned, Pentham was sitting beside you, and I thought it best not to approach."

"So you turned around and went back to bed?" she asked dryly.

"I waited." And watched, to be certain that Pentham behaved like a gentleman. Gray had never known him to be anything but honorable. However, he wasn't taking chances where Fiona was concerned. "When I saw that he was about to leave you, I hurried back to the terrace to pretend I'd strolled outside to smoke a cigar. Then he asked to join me, and I couldn't think of a way to refuse without being rude—or, worse, raising his suspicion. It would have looked very bad if he'd encountered both of us in the garden."

"Agreed. It would have been quite the scandal," she said, not bothering to hide her sarcasm. "Who knows? You might have had to marry me." She uttered a curse at the arrow that slipped from her hands and he bent to retrieve it for her, but she snatched it out of his hands.

"Fiona," he said gently. "You're angry with me."

"My, but your powers of observation are keen."

He glanced over his shoulder at the rest of their party. The other men had followed Fiona's sister and their friend Sophie to the shade, where they poured drinks and sliced apples and wedges of cheese. Satisfied that they were too preoccupied to eavesdrop, he continued. "I deserve your ire, but I also deserve the chance to explain."

"Please do," she said, her smile too sweet. "Did you smoke a whole box of cigars last night? Or perhaps you sailed to the West Indies to fetch another case?" She angled one shoulder toward the target and squinted as if gauging the distance.

"Pentham began telling me a story and wanted to continue it over a drink of brandy. I couldn't politely decline." In truth, Pentham had shared some details about his father and Gray's. Both their fathers had a proclivity for drinking to excess, and Pentham's had died as a result of overindulgence. "By the time I returned to the garden in the wee hours of the morning, you were gone."

"Forgive me. I thought it best not to sleep there," she said dryly.

"I didn't expect you to wait for me." Although he *had* hoped. "I only wanted to be sure that—"

Good God. She was holding the bow upside down. "Here, allow me to help you," he said.

"I don't require your help," she said. "I learned how to use a bow at Miss Haywinkle's."

Gray blinked. "Did you say *Haywinkle's*?"

"Miss Haywinkle's School for Girls." She frowned at the bow. "Although our equipment was slightly different."

He offered her a leather armguard, which she waved away. Gray might have admired her stubbornness if he weren't afraid she'd maim someone—especially herself. Her tongue poked out of the corner of her mouth as she threaded an arrow on the string and tried to level it. But the tip drooped toward the ground as though it were mocking her. Gray caught it out of the air.

"Blast," she said, grabbing it back.

"The point is," he said sincerely, "I wanted to return to you." He'd dreamed of her all night. Imagined what might have happened if they'd spent the night in the garden. Had visions of removing her gown and seeing how her skin looked soaked in moonlight.

"But you were too busy smoking, drinking, and swapping stories with Lord Pentham," she said. "I believe I understand the way of things."

"I would have rather been with you," he said earnestly. "But I also wanted to protect you from scandal. I hope you'll let me make things up to you." When she didn't reply, he said, "Did you find it?"

Her gaze snapped toward his, and her expression turned wary. "Find what?"

"Your earring. The one that belonged to your mother."

"No." She looked away.

"Then I will help you look for it when we return to the house." And maybe start to make amends.

"Please do not bother," she said quickly. "In any event, I am otherwise engaged this afternoon. You may recall asking your friend Lord Pentham to parade me around in your curricle so that you would be spared the trouble."

"I may have suggested it," Gray admitted. And he was already regretting it. He'd casually mentioned the idea to Pentham before they left town—and the marquess certainly hadn't wasted any time in extending an invitation to Fiona. "But that was before . . ."

"Before what?" she demanded. She let the bow drop to her side and looked into his eyes. As though his answer mattered very much.

He lowered his voice. "Before you showed me your sketch. Before I kissed you. Before I started to—"

"How are the preparations coming along?" Kirby called out as he sauntered toward them, damn it all.

"Meet me tonight," Gray said impulsively. "I'll slip you a note at dinner with the time and place."

She opened her mouth as if she'd refuse, then smiled. "Only if you let me sketch you."

Oh hell no. Her pencil revealed far too much. "Fiona, I don't think—"

With a shrug, she faced the target, raised her bow, and pulled back the string.

"Very well," Gray whispered urgently. "Just meet me tonight."

Fiona released the string and smiled as the tip of her arrow planted itself in the ground approximately three paces in front of her. But it didn't matter. She turned toward him, positively triumphant. "Do not make the mistake of disappointing me twice, Lord Ravenport." With that, she thrust the bow at him and marched toward her friends, who were relaxing in the shade.

Kirby sidled up to Gray and tilted his head to mimic the awkward angle in which the arrow protruded from the lawn. "It would appear you've won the first round, my friend."

It might have *appeared* that way, but Gray knew the truth.

Fiona had hit her target—with chillingly frightening precision.

And while he was obviously the loser of this battle, he was already anticipating the moment when he'd be alone with her again.

Chapter 13

On Having a Row

Heretofore, I had not realized it possible for a man to simultaneously be the source of fierce attraction and extreme infuriation. Though I consider myself to be a levelheaded sort, I confess I briefly contemplated sneaking into Lord R.'s bedchamber while he was at breakfast in order to crumble a scone between his sheets or shred all his neckcloths or drop the ends of a rotting onion in his boots—anything to vex him as he had vexed me.

I am happy to report that I refrained in the end, and my restraint was duly rewarded.

Lord R. has agreed to allow me to sketch him, which will require us to meet several times over the course of the next few days . . . starting tonight.

All of which leads me to believe that having the occasional row might not be a bad thing, especially if the gentleman realizes the error of his ways and attempts to make amends—in the form of kisses, caresses, and more. . . .

All through dinner, Gray kept an eye on Pentham as he conversed with Fiona. Nothing the marquess said or did was untoward, but the way he looked at her—like he was completely and utterly smitten—gave Gray the irrational urge to throttle him.

He couldn't blame Pentham for having taken Fiona for a drive across the countryside that afternoon. It *had* been Gray's idea after all. But he didn't care for the way they'd stumbled into the house afterward, laughing and breathless. Her hair had been charmingly windblown, her cheeks flushed, like she was . . . happy. *Damn it all to hell.*

Gray wasn't jealous. Lord knew he had no right to her, no claim. Pentham and Fiona were perfect for each other. And that was the plan, all along—to introduce Fiona to someone else. Someone who might divert her attention from Gray.

But that didn't mean he wanted to watch her fall in love with another man right under his damned nose.

"Is everything all right, my dear boy?" Gray's grandmother reached across the corner of the table and patted his forearm. "You're unusually quiet this evening."

"I'm fine." But she'd always had an uncanny knack for reading him. He swiveled his neck, looking around the dining room at the rotted fireplace mantel, the stained wood floor, and the cracks in the plaster ceiling. "I was making a mental list of the improvements needed in here."

She shot him a sympathetic smile. "As long as the wine and conversation are flowing, your guests will scarcely notice the imperfections."

"But *I* do. Tell me how the room used to look, when you were a young girl. Was there a crystal chandelier? Silver sconces? Intricate molding?"

Her watery eyes turned wistful. "I suppose there were. I remember Christmases with evergreen boughs strewn across the table and mistletoe hanging over the doorway.

The scents of pinecones mingled with roasted partridges, mincemeat pies, and suet pudding. My father—your great-grandfather—sat where you are now, entertaining everyone with fantastical tales. Hours after dinner ended, we'd still be gathered round, laughing and chatting. No one wanted to leave."

Gray twisted the stem of his wineglass, sober. "It will be that way again, Grandmother. I promise."

"Worry less about the house," she said softly. "Devote your attention to your guests. Are the Hartley sisters enjoying themselves?"

Gray shrugged. "The younger one, Lily, won the archery competition today."

"And what of Fiona?"

"She's finding ways to pass the time," he said—a little more bitterly than he'd intended.

"You should take her to the river," his grandmother said. "It's beautiful there. Row her about in the boat."

Gray didn't have the heart to tell her that the boat was probably as seaworthy as a sieve and the pier was missing half of its slats. "I will think about it," he said.

"Sometimes you think too much," she teased.

Gray grunted. The note in his pocket, which he intended to give to Fiona after dinner, was proof to the contrary, but he adored his grandmother too much to contradict her. "You are right—as always."

"I wasn't right when it came to Helena," she whispered. "I thought she was worthy of you, but I was wrong."

"The state of this place would scare anyone off," Gray replied.

"It doesn't scare Miss Fiona Hartley."

Gray smiled wryly and patted his grandmother's thin hand. "Give it a few more days."

* * *

For the second night in a row, Fiona was sneaking out of her bed. Taking care not to disturb Lily, who snored softly beside her, she slipped from beneath the covers and shrugged on her robe. She picked up her sketchbook and a pencil and tiptoed out of the room.

The note that Gray had subtly handed her in the drawing room after dinner was not the romantic missive she'd craved—but they'd already established that he was not a poet. The slip of paper had contained exactly four words: *One o'clock. The library.*

She skulked through the dark corridor and down the staircase, hoping she didn't lose her way. Gray's grandmother, the countess, had briefly pointed out the library during a tour of the house, but she hadn't even opened the door before ushering the group to the next room, leaving Fiona curious.

When she arrived, a faint light glowed from beneath the door. She entered tentatively, gasping at the sight of two-story bookshelves on two walls and floor-to-ceiling windows on a third. No curtains impeded the view of the starry sky, and moonlight spilled across the center of the room cluttered with boxes, sheet-covered furniture, ladders, and tools.

Gray sat on a large white lump, which she assumed was a sofa, his elbows propped on his knees. He was still dressed in his dinner jacket, trousers, and boots, looking heartbreakingly handsome.

So much so that Fiona wished she were wearing something more elegant than her nightgown and robe. Her hair hung down her back in a simple braid and her feet were bare—but she hadn't dared to change or even stop to put on her slippers for fear of waking Lily.

He stood when she entered and blinked at the sight of

her, then rushed over to close the door. "Did you encounter anyone on your way here?"

"No. My sister is sleeping soundly, as is everyone else."

"Good." He dragged a hand down his face. "I shouldn't have asked you to come, but I wanted . . . no, I *needed* to explain."

"Tell me anything you wish," she said. "I'm listening."

Propping his hands on his hips, he glanced around at the ghost-shaped furniture. "Let me find someplace comfortable for you to sit."

"Anywhere will do."

He lifted the corner of one sheet and produced several pillows and cushions, which he stuffed under one arm. "This room isn't fit for entertaining. Hell, it's barely habitable. But I knew we wouldn't be disturbed here."

"It's lovely—and large enough to host a ball."

He grunted. "Trust me, this is hardly the sort of place for a ball—or any celebration." He stalked to a rug near the fireplace and arranged the pillows on the floor. "Will this suffice? I could bring a chair over if you'd prefer."

"This is perfect." She laid aside her sketchbook and settled herself on a plump silk pillow.

"Are you chilled? I could light a fire."

Fiona was about to decline, but she wanted to properly see his face as they talked—and as she drew him. "That would be wonderful."

He crouched in front of the grate and added some kindling before striking the flint. Still staring at the fledgling flame, he said, "I shouldn't admit this, but I hated seeing you with Pentham today."

Fiona's chest squeezed, but she would not make this too easy for him. "You have only yourself to blame."

"I know. I thought you would be better off with someone like him."

"You mean you thought that you could rid yourself of me."

"I suppose there's a little truth in that." He shot her a rueful smile as he lay on his side, propped on one elbow, with his long, muscular legs stretched across the carpet. His cravat was loose, his hair ruffled, and the stubble on his chin darker than normal.

This was who he truly was, beneath the brooding, somber mask. And this was how she would draw him.

"I made a mistake," he continued. "I shouldn't have left you alone in the garden. And I shouldn't have encouraged Pentham to pursue you."

"That's two mistakes," she said with a smile.

Gray inclined his head as if conceding the point.

"But I accept your apology."

"Thank you." His voice, deep and sincere, had her belly performing flips. But he made no move to touch her, showed no indication of wanting to kiss her. Finally, they were alone, and he'd apparently decided to play the part of a gentleman.

She gazed up at the towering bookcases with awe. "Tell me about this room."

A shadow crossed his face. "There's not much to tell."

"Nonsense. What does it mean to you? What are your plans for it?"

"It means nothing to me," he said curtly. "The plan is to strip away everything but the walls and convert it to a music room."

"Oh," she said. It seemed a terrible waste to her, but sensing it was a sore subject, she refrained from voicing her thoughts. Instead, she asked the question she'd been wondering about since she arrived. "Forgive me for being blunt, but how did the Fortress come to be in such a state?"

He didn't respond right away, and Fiona feared she'd

overstepped. But after the space of several heartbeats, he said, "My father inherited the earldom when he was younger than I. He did not take his duties to the estate or his tenants seriously. Since he and my mother preferred to live in town, they closed up this house. Over the course of three decades, it fell into disrepair. Thieves broke in and stole some of the furnishings. Gypsies and other vagrants took shelter here for extended periods. Storm-force winds battered the roof and walls; nature had its way in the garden and fields."

"Thirty years of neglect," she mused. "And now you intend to fix it all."

"Yes," he said simply. Determinedly.

Fiona suspected there was more to the story but didn't press him further. She'd found a chink in his armor—that was enough for tonight. "You invited me and my family here, hoping to scare me away."

He arched a brow. "Is it working?"

"Not in the least." She reclined on her side and stretched out her legs, mirroring his pose.

"Then I shall have to think of another method to scare you off," he said gruffly.

"Do your worst."

He leaned forward as though he intended to kiss her—then froze. "I didn't ask you to meet me here so I could take advantage of you."

"I know."

Reluctantly, he sat up. "I promised you could sketch me, but if you've changed your mind—"

"I have not," she assured him. "I confess I didn't expect you'd be so eager to begin."

"Keeping ourselves occupied would be the prudent thing to do," he said, as though trying to convince himself.

True. But for once, Fiona didn't *feel* like being prudent or proper. She wanted to do something scandalous and impulsive. Something that would make Miss Haywinkle clutch her pearls in abject horror.

The problem was that Fiona was a novice at the game of seduction. Anything she knew about passion she'd learned during her knee-melting kiss with Gray in the garden . . . and from a few risqué paintings she'd spied in houses she'd visited. Some of the images had been so shocking that they'd made her blush with embarrassment—and arousal. She would simply attempt to mimic the sultry, barely dressed creatures depicted in those paintings, and hope that Gray would be overcome by desire.

"Very well. You lie right there, just as you are," Fiona said smoothly, "and I shall prepare to draw you."

With deliberate slowness, she pulled the end of her braid in front of her shoulder and plucked at the ribbon securing it.

"What are you doing?" Gray asked.

"I should think it would be obvious." She tossed the ribbon behind her and, beginning at the bottom of the braid, separated the thick strands of hair. All the while, Gray stared at her fingers—as though he couldn't quite believe what was happening.

"You're letting your hair down," he said tightly.

"Hmm?" She blinked up at him innocently. "Oh yes. I find it helps."

"Really?"

She ran her fingers through her long tresses, erasing the remnants of the braid and easing the tightness at her crown. "I do my best work when I'm comfortable, and I'm determined to sketch you accurately," she improvised.

"Naturally," he said, skeptical. "But I don't think we

should waste any more time. The longer we are here together, the greater the risk of discovery."

"Never fear. I'm almost ready." *Drat.* What would a seductress do? Suddenly inspired, she sat up, gave a luxurious stretch, and reached for the satin sash of her robe.

"Fiona." He spoke her name like it was both a plea *and* a warning.

A warning that she did not intend to heed. She toyed with the end of the silky sash, running it through her fingers as she gazed into Gray's dark eyes. "You *did* say I could sketch you."

"Yes, but—"

"Then you must try to relax." Summoning courage, she took a deep breath, slowly loosened the knot at her waist, and let her robe fall open.

"Jesus," he whispered. He closed his eyes for three seconds, then opened them. "I trust you're comfortable now?"

"Not quite."

Chapter 14

Gray had sworn to himself that he'd restrict tonight's activities to two areas: apologizing and sketching—or rather, sitting patiently while Fiona did the sketching. But his relationship with her grew more complicated by the day.

He'd thought that spending a few days together at the Fortress would prove how wrong they were for each other. Instead, she'd shown him the beauty of this place and persuaded him to share a bit of its history. She'd let him kiss her and kissed him back. She'd driven him half-mad with jealousy and charmed her way into his grandmother's heart.

And those were just a few of the reasons why he couldn't be with her.

She claimed to want a simple marriage—a union that would be convenient and advantageous to them both. But Gray now knew better.

Fiona was not the type of woman who would be content with a distant, if pleasant, relationship. She demanded more than mere affection. She needed a man who would be her partner in the truest sense. A man who was willing to share with her his deepest secrets and dreams.

And Gray couldn't be that man. He'd tried once to give

himself completely, and it had ended disastrously. He'd naïvely thought he could have a marriage different from his parents'—one free from bitterness, jealousy, and middle-of-the-night shouting matches. But he and Helena hadn't even made it to the altar. *Thank God.*

Fiona was different from Helena, but if Gray allowed himself to fall in love with her he'd be setting himself on the same path as his father had. He'd become distracted and weak and vulnerable. And one day, in the grips of despair, he might do something that would jeopardize . . . everything.

That was the reason he was doing his damnedest to resist her. Even now, as she sat across from him in a body-skimming robe, her eyes gleaming in the firelight and her hair tumbling around her shoulders.

The problem was, he would have had to be a bloody saint to resist her—and God knew he was no saint.

A tremulous smile played about her lips as she slipped the silky ivory robe off her shoulders and let it pool on the floor around her knees.

Shit. The nightgown she wore dipped low in the front, revealing the tantalizing swells of her breasts. The sleeves of the garment were nothing more than frills, for God's sake. The flounce at the hem grazed her smooth, slender calves. Best of all, the fine lawn fabric left precious little to the imagination.

Gray sat up and rubbed the back of his neck. Tried not to look at her skin glowing in the firelight or the curve of her hips or the pert tips of her breasts.

She clucked her tongue in mock dismay. "I believe I asked you not to move, my lord."

"You can't expect me to lie there while you—"

"While I *what*? Sketch you? I rather thought that was

the point." She picked up her pad, flipped to a clean sheet, and made a great show of examining the tip of her pencil. "I confess I'd hoped you'd be a better subject."

"What do you really want, Fiona?" His heart was pounding, and he was aroused as hell.

"You know what I want," she said softly. "I've made no secret of it."

"I desire you. But I can't marry you."

Her lower lip trembled slightly, but she quickly composed herself. "Fine. Then let me sketch you—as you promised."

Damn it all. Lying there and watching her work while she was barely dressed was going to be pure torture for him—which, he supposed, was the point.

Scowling, he stretched out again, not even attempting to hide his erection. He wanted her more than he'd ever wanted any woman—and he didn't care if she knew it. It didn't change the way of things.

For a full minute or so, she stared at him, her expression thoughtful and serene. Her pencil hovered over the paper, never touching it. When at last she began to draw, her strokes were bold and graceful, her hand steady and sure. The ruffle of her sleeve slid off a satin smooth shoulder, but she was too absorbed in her sketchbook to notice. The fine muscles in her arms alternately flexed and relaxed as she worked, and her brow furrowed in concentration.

She sat a full yard away, and yet Gray could feel the energy flowing between them as though it were a real, physical thing. While he lay there on his side, propped up on one elbow, she seemed to draw him from the inside out, exploring corners of his soul that he'd boarded up years ago. Of course, she couldn't really know what dark secrets lurked there, but her mere presence warmed him. Maybe even healed him a little.

He'd already learned the power of her sketches and knew that in posing for her he'd be revealing more than he wished.

What he hadn't expected was to gain a glimpse behind *her* façade. Emotions played across her face as she drew—triumph, curiosity, sympathy, and doubt—all plainly there for him to see. No one who watched her draw would believe she was the shy, awkward debutante who'd stumbled into an orchestra. She was passionate, fearless, kind . . . and nigh irresistible.

For nearly an hour, Gray sat watching her, enraptured. Though she never spoke, he read every tilt of her head, felt every shift in her expression. She rocked slightly as she worked, as though swaying to a subtle melody only she could hear. Soft curls framed her heart-shaped face, and when an errant auburn lock fell in front of her eyes she pursed her lips and blew it away. The sleeves of her nightgown inched their way down her arms, exposing more and more of that glorious, luminous skin.

Every so often, her gaze shifted to his face and their eyes met; the connection was electric. Intense. Palpable.

At the moment, her attention seemed focused on his chest and the folds of his neckcloth. When she frowned, he broke the silence. "Are you all right?"

"Your jacket is bunched." She set aside the sketchbook and crawled toward him, reaching for his lapel—oblivious to the fact that she afforded him an excellent view of her breasts. The loose, lacey neckline of her nightgown gaped and grazed the dark pink tips, bringing him to the very brink of his self-control. While her nimble fingers smoothed the wool of his jacket and rearranged the folds of his cravat, her breasts were precisely level with his mouth.

He groaned.

Concerned, she ran her fingers along the edge of his jaw and lifted his chin. "You've been still for an hour. Would you like to take a break?"

Holy hell. The sight of her, so near, wearing so little, was too much to bear.

He grasped her hand and pressed his mouth to her open palm. "I thought I could resist you," he murmured. "But I can't."

With her free hand, she pushed the hair back from his face and cradled his cheek. "As I understand it," she said softly, "the whole point of this house party was to determine if we are compatible."

"No, damn it." He laced his fingers through hers. "The point was to discourage you."

"And yet I'm not discouraged in the least." She swallowed and fingered the silk drawstring at the front of her nightgown. "So why don't we see if we *are* compatible?"

"Fiona, no matter how much I might wish to, I cannot bed you." And sweet Jesus, he wanted to. But he couldn't risk getting her with child. Not if he wasn't going to marry her.

"Then do not bed me." She pulled on one end of the drawstring, exposing the deep valley between her breasts. "I assume there are other activities we may engage in?"

"Yes." He was going to hate himself in the morning, but, by God, if Fiona wanted an introduction to passion, he was the man for the job. He would savor every moment and see to her pleasure if it killed him—which it well might.

He tugged down the front of her flimsy nightgown, leaned forward, and captured a taut nipple in his mouth, alternately sucking and nibbling until she moaned. He backed away, sober and breathless. "You must tell me if you want me to stop. I would not hurt you."

Fiona sat back on her heels. "I know that. It's one of the reasons I chose you." Gazing into his eyes, she eased one arm out of her sleeve, then the other. A nervous smile played about her lips as the fabric slid down her body and pooled around the curve of her hips. She scooted closer and touched her forehead to his. "You told me that you don't believe in flowers or poetry. Do you believe in this?"

Heaven help him, he did. With a growl, he pulled her down beside him and laid her back on the carpet. Cradling her face in his hand, he said, "Yes, siren, I do. *This* is real." And complicated and messy as hell. But he wouldn't think about that now—not while her eyes glowed with unbridled desire. Not while she arched her gloriously naked body toward him.

All the passion they'd kept pent up for the last hour exploded in a flurry of hot kisses, wicked caresses, and blissful sighs. He kissed her like she was the last woman he'd ever know, exploring her mouth with his roving tongue. She did not shy away but met him thrust for thrust and pulled his head closer, as though she'd never have enough of him.

"Gray." The sound of his name on her lips had an intensely intoxicating effect.

He traced a spiral around the tip of one perfect breast. "Hmm?"

"May I . . . make a request?" she asked shyly.

"Anything. Don't hesitate to ask for what you desire."

"Even if it's poetry?" she teased.

He scowled. "I can do better than poetry."

"I was just thinking that I am wearing very little, while you are wearing an awful lot. Would you take off your jacket? And perhaps your waistcoat . . . and shirt?"

Gray had thought it impossible to be more aroused than he already was. *Wrong. So, so wrong.*

He shot her a grin as he yanked off his cravat, wrestled off his jacket, and stripped off his waistcoat and shirt. He wanted to cover her body and feel her skin next to his, with no space between them.

But he lay down next to her, giving her time to acclimate. Tentatively, she reached for him. Her fingertips drifted over his chest, and down . . . across his abdomen near the waistband of his trousers. His skin tingled in the wake of her touch, and he closed his eyes from the sheer bliss of it.

Next thing he knew, she was kissing his neck and tasting him—as he'd tasted her. She nipped at his shoulder as she slipped a hand behind him, lazily tracing a path down his spine.

"In all my life, I've never done anything half so daring as this," she said softly. "And though I'm sure it's wanton of me to admit, I regret nothing. Being with you this way . . . well, I'm sure I've broken at least half a dozen of Miss Haywinkle's rules. But it doesn't *feel* wrong. Does that even make sense?"

"Yes." But in truth, very little about the situation made sense to Gray. He shouldn't be hosting a party in a house that looked like it had barely survived the Middle Ages. He shouldn't be absurdly jealous over a curricle ride. And he most certainly shouldn't risk being alone with Fiona like this. If they were discovered together, they'd be in a coach headed for Gretna Green before dawn. "Sometimes," he continued, "it's enough to feel. To live completely in the moment."

"I doubt Miss Haywinkle would agree," she said, wriggling closer. "But I was not the most apt of students. As you have already deduced, no doubt, based on my horrid archery skills."

"I don't know," he mused, sliding a hand up the inside

of her leg. "You seem like a quick learner to me." With her heavy-lidded eyes and kiss-swollen lips, she was the most sensual woman he'd ever seen. He had to remind himself that all of this was new to her.

The hell of it was, it felt new to him, too.

"I'll have to return to my bedchamber soon," she said. "But we have a little more time. Teach me something new."

Shit. "Very well, siren. Tonight's lesson shall be all about . . . letting go."

Fiona drank in the sight of Gray's bare torso, mesmerized by the way the firelight danced on his skin. She should have asked him to take off his shirt *before* she'd begun sketching so that she could capture the sinewy muscles of his shoulders and the contours of his chest and abdomen on paper. But she doubted she'd ever be able to do them justice.

He moved with the confidence and power of an athlete, and she supposed that the many hours he'd spent repairing the roof, mending fences, and working in the fields had given him a physique far superior to the average earl's.

And yet it wasn't his good looks that had drawn Fiona to him so much as his manner. She'd never met anyone who sparked with such intensity, such drive and determination. It might have frightened her if she didn't know that the source of that flame was a deep and abiding loyalty to his grandmother.

No, Gray didn't frighten her . . . but he did perplex her. She speared her fingers through the curls at his nape as he drew circles on the inside of her thigh, easing his way closer and closer to her entrance. His gaze lingered on her mouth, breasts, and hips, and she basked in the knowledge that he wanted her. Or, at the very least, desired her.

"What, precisely, does this lesson entail?" She sighed

softly as he nuzzled the underside of one breast. "Must I jot down some notes?" she teased. "Memorize a series of steps?"

"It's not that sort of lesson," he said, his words brimming with promise. "All you must do is relax and tell me what feels good."

"I feel certain I can do that."

"Excellent." A warm, strong hand glided over her hip, cupped her bottom, and squeezed—as though he were claiming her as his own.

"Mmm," she murmured. "Very nice."

With a growl, he took her nipple in his mouth and drew it into a tight bud. She arched her back and moaned as desire, raw and hot, spiraled inside her. He tugged on the nightgown still bunched at her waist and slid the soft fabric between her thighs. With slow, steady strokes, he caressed her, stoking her desire. The sensation was lovely, like a feather tantalizing and teasing . . . but it wasn't enough. She wanted more pressure, more friction, just *more*.

As if he knew, Gray pushed aside the nightgown and found her entrance with his fingers. He lifted his gaze to hers, a question in his eyes.

"Yes." She took his face in her hands and kissed him with everything she felt—affection, lust, and something else, which she didn't dare name. He slid a finger inside her, filling her and thrusting in a rhythm that resonated through her body like an echo—except instead of fading away, it grew stronger. More intense. More demanding.

He whispered in her ear. "Move your hips, siren. Take what you want."

Letting passion guide her, she threw one leg over his and moved with him.

He groaned as he slid another finger inside her. "You feel so . . . damned . . . good."

Gray seemed to be everywhere. His warm lips trailed kisses down her neck. His hard chest pressed against her sensitive breasts. His sure fingers stroked her inside and out. Grasping his shoulders, she angled her hips to take him deeper. And the echo became a roar. Starting in her core and radiating through her limbs till she was shimmering. Floating. Free.

She gasped at the raw power of it, cried out in awe. All the while, Gray held her. "Yes, Fiona. So beautiful. So perfect."

And she believed him. He'd uttered the words so fervently that it was impossible to doubt them—or him. She wrapped up the warm, precious sentiment and tucked it into her heart for safekeeping. Snuggling closer, she savored the comforting weight of his arm slung around her waist.

When at last she was capable of moving, she caressed his jaw and brushed a kiss across his lips. "That was a very good lesson. Extremely enlightening." More soberly, she added, "I shall never forget it."

He laced his fingers through hers and planted a reverent kiss on the back of her hand. "Nor shall I."

She curled against his warm body, savoring the intimacy of his skin next to hers. If she succeeded in convincing him to marry her, perhaps every night would feel like this. But it was almost too much to wish for. She'd convinced herself that she'd be content to marry without love. Now . . . well, she wasn't so sure.

But she *was* certain of one thing. If she had to marry someone—and she did—she desperately wanted it to be Gray.

She nuzzled her cheek against his chest and traced a circle around his flat nipple. "I want to please you," she said. "As you pleased me."

His heartbeat tripped beneath her cheek, but when he spoke his voice was full of regret. "I am more tempted than you know. But it wouldn't be wise. You must return to your bedchamber before your sister misses you."

Fiona was not giving up so easily. She traced the top edge of his trousers with her fingertips. "Just a half hour more?"

He sat up abruptly—as though he didn't trust himself to remain there a second longer—and she instantly felt the loss of warmth. Of him.

"I have already taken more liberties than I should have."

"You did not *take* anything," she countered. "I freely gave myself."

He scooped his shirt off the floor and stuffed an arm into the sleeve. "True. But you are still hoping that I'll marry you."

Fiona slipped her nightgown over her head and stood toe to toe with him. "Perhaps. But this is not a scheme to coerce you, if that's what you're thinking."

"I don't believe it is your *intent* to ensnare me. But that doesn't mean it won't happen."

His words cut to the core. She was *not* trying to manipulate him into doing her bidding. What she had in mind was more akin to . . . seduction. Blast it all, the line was admittedly murky. But she couldn't let him shut her out completely. Grasping at a thread of hope, she waved a hand at her sketchbook. "I . . . I haven't finished drawing you yet."

He arched a brow as he shoved his shirttail into his trousers. "That's because we squandered our time on . . . other things."

Her cheeks warmed. "Shall we meet again tomorrow night?"

"I don't think so." He wriggled his shoulders into his jacket, retrieved her robe, and handed it to her. "Give me some time. I shall think of a more suitable place for sketching."

"You don't want to be alone with me."

"It's not a matter of wanting, Fiona. Trust me."

"I do." She picked up her sketchbook and tucked her pencil behind an ear. "I wish you trusted me half as much as I trust you."

He raked a hand through his hair. "If you expect too much from me, you are destined to be disappointed. I guarantee it."

Perhaps she would, but what choice did she have? She needed her dowry to pay off the blackmailer, and she'd come too far to turn back now. "I would rather make the mistake of expecting too much from you than expecting too little."

"Go to your bed and sleep well," he said simply. "I will see you tomorrow."

She would not let him discourage her—not after what they'd just shared. She shot him a serene smile before padding across the library toward the door. Her hand on the knob, she paused and faced him. "Six days," she said. "That's all the time I have left. I will marry *someone* before then, and I hope that someone is you."

Chapter 15

On Secret Assignations

Miss Haywinkle was inordinately fond of reminding her pupils that rules formed the very fabric of a civilized society. She asserted we should be grateful for the myriad strictures that governed our behavior, as they were designed to protect young ladies. She never elaborated on what, precisely, the rules were designed to protect us from, but our vivid adolescent imaginations filled in the blanks. Indeed, she insisted, rules of polite behavior were for our own good.

But I am not so certain.

A midnight rendezvous with a gentleman is, of course, strictly forbidden by the rules. I suppose Miss H. would have said that such a meeting could only result in a proper miss's ruin. A young woman might well suffer the loss of her innocence, and if the gentleman did not agree to marry her afterward, alas, all was lost.

But the headmistress should have also instructed us that some experiences, no matter how illicit, are well worth the risk.

Miss H. said the rules were intended to keep us safe.

But perhaps they were intended to keep us in the dark.

Fiona slept late the next morning and woke only when Mary burst into her room and drew the curtains wide, spilling sunlight across the bed. "Miss Lily sent me to see if you'd taken ill," the maid informed her. "She said she doesn't want to share a bedchamber with you if you've contracted the plague."

Fiona buried her head under the pillow. "Her show of sisterly concern is touching."

"If you want to know the truth, I think she misses you. Everyone is in the drawing room, making plans for the afternoon. I'll help you dress so that you may join them."

"Would it be terribly rude of me to stay in bed all day?"

"I'm afraid you'd be the subject of gossip." Mary held a gown in each hand. "Which one?"

"The sprigged muslin, please." She sat up and stretched.

The maid gasped. "Your hair, Miss Fiona! What happened to your braid?"

Fiona patted her head and felt a bird's nest of curls. "It seems my ribbon's gone missing. Thank heaven you're here to make me presentable."

The maid clucked her tongue. "The state you're in? We'll be lucky to have you downstairs before dinner."

With Mary's help, it actually took Fiona less than a half hour to wash, dress, and style her hair into a pretty twist. She was looking forward to seeing Gray again, but by the time she breezed into the drawing room only the women remained.

Gray's grandmother sat on the settee, flanked by Mama and Lady Callahan. Lily and Sophie were standing beside the pianoforte, paging through sheet music. "Good morning, everyone," Fiona said with a smile.

"There you are, my dear!" Mama exclaimed. "You just missed the gentlemen. They're all preparing to go hunting for the afternoon."

"Apparently, shooting arrows at archery targets yesterday did not satisfy their primitive urge to slay innocent creatures," Lily said dryly. She slid onto the pianoforte bench and played a few bars of a ballad.

"Men will be men," Lady Callahan said, ever philosophical.

"Well then," Fiona said, "we shall have to find something equally exciting to occupy us."

Sophie winced. "Mama suggested I accompany Lily at the pianoforte."

"But it's a beautiful day," Fiona said. "I think we should venture outside."

"Where on earth would we go?" Mama asked—as if they were stranded in the middle of a strange and foreign land.

"We could take a jaunt to the nearby village. Perhaps see some of the local sights and do a bit of shopping?"

"Shopping? Here?" Mama said, aghast. "Whatever would we buy—goats?" She chuckled at the thought.

"A trip to the village is a capital idea," the dowager countess announced. If she took offense at Mama's words, she showed no sign of it. "The baker makes the best gingerbread cakes in the county, and the millinery shop sells lovely bonnets—the simple yet elegant sort one rarely sees in town."

Lily was already putting away the sheet music. "Sounds like the perfect outing to me. I'm going to fetch a shawl. Mama, shall I retrieve yours as well?"

"I don't know." She wrung her hands. "I think I'd prefer to remain here. I'm sure the village is very quaint, but I've no need for bread or bonnets. Besides, my gout has been acting up lately."

"Oh dear," Lady Callahan said, obviously torn. "I think I must stay here to keep my friend company."

"Do not fret," the countess said. "We shall return with enough gingerbread cakes for both of you *and* the gentlemen. Gray can eat a dozen at one sitting." Winking at Fiona, Lily, and Sophie, she said, "I'll send for the coach and we'll leave in a quarter of an hour."

Buoyed at the prospect of exploring the village, Fiona almost forgot her disappointment over not seeing Gray. But he'd said he'd arrange another time and place for her to sketch him—and she knew he'd be true to his word.

Fiona, Lily, and Sophie darted upstairs to gather their reticules, shawls, and gloves. They were heading back to meet the countess when Fiona realized she'd left her bonnet on the bed. "I've forgotten something. I'll meet you in the foyer in two minutes," she said, turning around.

"Hurry," Lily said. "I don't think it's good form to keep a countess waiting."

Fiona retrieved her bonnet in a trice, and when she arrived at the foyer the butler told her the other ladies awaited her in the coach.

"Thank you," she said, a little breathless. He was about to open the front door for her when a male voice sounded behind her.

"Miss Hartley, do you have a moment?"

She turned to find Mr. Kirby dressed in his hunting jacket, looking very dashing—and did her best to hide her disappointment. "Good morning, Mr. Kirby," she said politely. "I'm afraid I am already late in joining the rest of my party. We're heading to the village."

"I understand," he said smoothly. "And I shall soon be leaving with the gentlemen. Perhaps we could speak when we both return? There's a matter I wished to discuss."

"Certainly." She swallowed, wondering if he suspected that she'd been with the earl last night. But perhaps she was jumping to conclusions. Mr. Kirby had seemed rather interested in Lily during the archery competition yesterday; maybe he wished to know if her affections were already engaged. Surely that was it. "I will look for you upon my return so that we may resume our conversation."

"Excellent." He flashed a winning smile and tipped his hat to her. "Enjoy your outing."

Fiona was enchanted by the village. Everywhere their group went, the townspeople asked after the earl, eager to hear of his progress at the Fortress. All were delighted to know that he was entertaining, even on a small scale. And more than a few of the older folk raised their eyebrows upon meeting Fiona, Lily, and Sophie. They clearly hoped the earl was courting one of them and thinking of settling down. Maybe even producing an heir.

The villagers obviously adored the countess as well. The baker insisted on giving her several pies to take home—in addition to the gingerbread cakes—and refused to take the money she offered. All three girls bought bonnets and ribbons at the milliner's, delighting the owner. Fiona was surprised to find a darling little shop where she could purchase some new pencils and sketch paper.

"I hope we'll have room for all our purchases," Fiona teased. "Perhaps we should begin loading them."

"Sophie and I want to take a quick look at the produce cart across the way," Lily said. "We're going to pick up a few items for a picnic tomorrow. Shall we meet you back at the coach?"

"Yes, go on," the countess urged. "Fiona, you may stay with me, and we shall nestle ourselves in the coach where we can sneak a cake before anyone is the wiser."

Fiona helped the older woman into the cab, placed a light blanket across her lap, and sat on the bench opposite her. "I'm so glad you came with us," Fiona said. "I hope all the walking hasn't overtaxed you."

The countess smoothed a silver strand behind her ear, where it glistened in stark contrast to her otherwise dark hair. "Not at all. I enjoy being around young people—especially friends of my grandson's."

Fiona's cheeks warmed. "'Tis a shame the gentlemen had other plans today. I'm sure you would have liked for Lord Ravenport to join us."

"Actually, I'm glad to have the chance to speak with you privately."

Fiona's belly somersaulted. "You are?"

"Mmm." The countess reached into a basket on the seat beside her and withdrew a delectable-looking cake, which she handed to Fiona. She helped herself to another, closing her eyes as she savored the first bite.

Fiona tasted the aromatic gingerbread, letting the frosting and spices mix on her tongue. *Heavenly.*

"My grandson has endured much over the last twenty years," the countess continued. "More than any young man should have to."

"I am sorry," Fiona said, sincere. "He told me a little of the Fortress's history and how it fell into disrepair."

"Did he tell you about his parents?"

"Only that his father did not take his duties seriously, and that his mother preferred to live in town."

The countess's eyes clouded over. "Yes. There is more, of course. There's always more to a person's story."

Fiona swallowed her last bite and perched on the edge of her seat as she waited for the countess to reveal a tidbit of Gray's past—anything that might help her unlock the secrets guarding his heart. "What happened to the former earl and his wife?" Fiona recalled thinking it strange that no portraits of Gray's parents graced the walls, but perhaps he wished to protect them from damage during the renovations.

"That is Gray's story to tell," the countess said. "Be patient with him, and I'm certain he will in due time."

"He is a very private person," Fiona said dryly, thinking she'd just uttered the understatement of the century.

"He has good cause to be wary of others, but if you can manage to wriggle past all his defenses, you will earn his devotion . . . and more."

The problem was that his defenses were the equivalent of towering walls, alligator-infested moats, and a spiked portcullis. "I wish I were half as confident as you."

"He already likes you; anyone could see that. And it's not so difficult to gain his trust. Confide in him. Tell him your greatest fears . . . and perhaps he'll tell you his."

Fiona considered this. Maybe she *should* tell him about the blackmail note. She wouldn't dream of revealing the identity of Lily's birth mother to him, but at least Fiona could explain what she intended to use her dowry money for. "Thank you. I will think about it."

The countess smiled and smoothed the blanket on her lap. "Did he tell you *why* he is so driven to return the Fortress to its former glory?"

"I assumed it was a matter of pride and duty."

"I suppose pride plays a part. He would, no doubt, like to show Lady Helena that she was foolish to jilt him."

Fiona winced at the mention of his former fiancée. It hurt to think that Gray might still long for Helena. Last night, as he held Fiona, had he been thinking of Helena . . . wishing he were with her instead?

"Do not be dismayed, my dear," the countess continued. "Helena is not the real reason he feels such urgency."

"I suppose I must wait for him to tell me his true motivation?"

"No," the countess said, chuckling. "For this is *my* story to tell. Gray is going to such great lengths for me. I recently learned that my eyesight is failing. Before long I shall lose my sight completely."

Fiona impulsively reached for the countess's hand and squeezed it. "Oh no. I'm so sorry. I didn't know."

"Of course you didn't. Gray inherited his penchant for privacy from me. Others will learn of my diagnosis soon enough, but for now, I'm cherishing every colorful blossom, every radiant sunset. I'm memorizing the faces of the ones I love." She stared at Fiona earnestly for several long moments. "And the ones whom I will surely come to love."

Fiona didn't pause to examine the countess's words. "Is there nothing that can be done for you?"

"I'm afraid not. But I consider myself blessed. To have a grandson who would go to such lengths for me—just because he believes it will make me happy."

"Will it please you, seeing the Fortress restored?"

"I have told Gray countless times that I will be happy as long as *he* is happy. But he is determined to see the renovations completed posthaste—as if doing so will recreate the days of my youth."

"He loves you," Fiona breathed. "That is all the reason he needs."

"Yes." The countess dabbed the corner of her eye with a fingertip. "I tell you all of this so you will know he has a good heart . . . and so that you will have a care with it."

"Oh, I would never—"

Fiona had been about to tell the countess that Gray was far more likely to break her heart than she was to break his. She hadn't even considered the possibility that she might wound him.

But then the door to the coach swung open and Lily and Sophie climbed in and sat on Fiona's seat, swinging a sack of fruits for tomorrow's picnic and exclaiming over the delightful smell emanating from the basket of baked goods.

"Sophie and I were talking just now," Lily said excitedly. "And we have a wonderful idea."

"By all means," the countess said. "Please share."

Sophie clasped her hands while Lily bounced on the seat. "We should have a ball!" Lily cried. "The villagers we met today have been so kind and welcoming. Wouldn't it be grand to host a celebration in their honor?"

Oh dear. As mere guests of the earl, it was not their place to suggest balls or any other entertainments. Miss Haywinkle would suffer an apoplexy if she knew one of her former pupils had been so bold. Fiona opened her mouth to say so, but the countess cut her off.

"A ball," the older woman said thoughtfully. "I am wholly in favor of it."

"We know it's not much notice," Sophie said, "but it could be a simple affair, and we would gladly help with the preparations."

Goodness. Fiona could just imagine Gray's reaction. "Isn't the ballroom undergoing improvements? Lord Ravenport might prefer to wait until after the renovations are complete before hosting such a large event."

"Allow me to worry about informing Gray. I feel certain I shall be able to persuade him." The countess passed the basket of cakes to Sophie and Lily. "You girls must try one."

While they indulged, plans were made.

"The last night of the house party would be best," Lily mused.

Sophie nodded her agreement. "We can decorate with greenery and wildflowers."

"And we'll enlist the local musicians to play," the countess said. "It will be a festive affair."

Fiona smiled weakly. "Perhaps we should check with the earl before becoming too carried away."

The countess leaned across the coach and patted Fiona's knee. "Do not fret, my dear. This ball is *going* to happen—with or without my grandson's blessing."

Chapter 16

Upon returning to the Fortress, Fiona was so anxious to see Gray that she almost forgot she was supposed to meet with Mr. Kirby. She was on her way to her bedchamber to change for dinner when he intercepted her at the bottom of the staircase.

"Miss Hartley. I trust you enjoyed your excursion to the village?"

"Very much. And how was the hunting?" She craned her neck a bit to see if Gray happened to be nearby.

"The grouse are plentiful—and after our feeble efforts, I've no doubt they'll remain so."

"Then it was a good day for the grouse," Fiona said with a smile. "I have a few minutes before I must prepare for dinner. Would you like to talk now?"

Mr. Kirby glanced over his shoulder and stepped closer. "It's a matter that requires discretion. I wonder if we could speak someplace more private?"

Alarm bells sounded in Fiona's head. "I'm not certain that's wise."

"Forgive me—I didn't mean to suggest anything untoward." He shot her an apologetic smile. "It's a rather delicate subject, however."

Fiona quickly weighed her options, and curiosity won out over prudence. "The terrace then?" They could talk there without being overheard but could still be seen from certain vantage points in the garden and from within the house.

"That would be fine," he said gratefully. "I promise not to take too much of your time."

While they strolled toward the terrace in companionable silence, Fiona prayed that her earlier suspicion was correct—that Mr. Kirby merely wished to reveal an interest in Lily, or perhaps Sophie.

He ushered Fiona toward a bench in the corner of the patio, and she hesitated only briefly before sitting. She'd give him ten minutes—no more.

"I'm not quite certain how to begin, but you seem like the sort of person who appreciates forthrightness."

"I do," she confirmed, even as a sense of unease slid down her spine.

"Very well. I happened to find something which I believe is yours."

No. God, please, no. She tried to keep her voice light. "Oh? I don't believe I've lost anything."

Mr. Kirby reached into his pocket and withdrew a folded paper. It was wrinkled and mud splattered, but she recognized it instantly—the blackmail note.

He handed it to her, and she accepted it with trembling fingers. "You read it?" It was half question, half accusation.

"I confess I did." He bowed his head as though contrite. "It caught my eye on the way back from the archery competition yesterday, and I slipped it in my jacket pocket. I didn't realize the letter was yours until I opened it and read the salutation."

"I see." Fiona's mind raced with questions. How much had the note revealed? And what did Mr. Kirby intend to do with the information?

"I should have stopped reading immediately once I realized it was yours; I know that. But I read the first sentence . . . and became concerned."

Fiona's head throbbed, and her heart pounded. Through her carelessness, she'd jeopardized everything. Frantic, she opened the letter and scanned the scrawling penmanship. Some of the words overlapped due to the writer's rather ornate lowercase *f,* but the threat was all too clear. She re-read the missive, assessing just how much Mr. Kirby now knew:

> *Dear Miss Hartley,*
> *This note serves as a reminder that the clock is ticking. If you wish to spare your sister and family untold humiliation, you will adhere to the instructions set forth in my initial message.*
> *Deliver the money at the designated time and place—or all of London will know the salacious truth about your sister's parentage.*
>
> *Any attempt to involve the authorities would, of course, result in the immediate publication of the sordid truth in the London Hearsay.*
>
> *Do not cross me, Miss Hartley, and do not test me, unless you wish to see your entire family suffer the disastrous consequences.*

She closed her eyes for moment, debating what to say. Thank heaven the note had not specifically mentioned that Lily's mother was London's most infamous madam. Nor had it given any details about when or where the money was to be paid. But it was damning enough. She stuffed it into her reticule, praying she didn't burst into tears.

When she could bring herself to speak, she faced Mr. Kirby. "As you can imagine, this is a very private matter. I would appreciate it if you would keep the contents of the note to yourself."

"Miss Hartley," he said sincerely, "I promise you I will not breathe a word of this—I swear it on my life."

"Thank you," Fiona replied, even though she was distinctly uneasy. All she knew of Mr. Kirby was that he was Gray's closest friend. Now that he'd discovered the letter, she had no choice but to trust him.

He steepled his fingers and pressed them to his chin. "I know it is none of my business, but I am worried about you."

"You needn't be," Fiona assured him. "I've devised a plan to handle the matter." Granted, the plan wasn't working very well at the moment, but she had faith that Gray would come around. He simply had to.

"Blackmail is a serious thing," Mr. Kirby said, his slightly patronizing tone grating her nerves.

"It is. And while I appreciate your concern, I would prefer that you not dwell on my predicament. In fact, if it's at all possible, I wish you would forget it entirely."

"Forgive me," he said sincerely. "I did not mean to be presumptuous. I'm sure you've thoroughly considered your options and will decide upon the correct course of action."

She swallowed the knot in her throat and tamped down a wave of self-doubt. "Thank you for understanding."

"Well then." He planted his palms on his knees and took a deep breath. "I don't suppose there's anything left to discuss—except for this: If you should need assistance of any kind, you mustn't hesitate to ask me."

"I don't think I shall—"

He held up a hand. "I know. And I admire your independent nature. Miss Lily is fortunate to have a sister like you. I only extend the offer because, like you, I am fiercely loyal to my family. I would do anything to protect them."

Fiona considered this for a moment. "Even paying off a blackmailer?"

"That is a difficult question to answer. I am not privy to the truth about Lily's parents—and I do not wish to be," he added quickly. "But my response to a blackmailer would depend on how hurtful the truth would be, should it become widely known."

Suppressing a shudder, Fiona stared at the cold slate beneath her slippers. The truth would destroy her sister's chances of making a good match and cast a pall over the entire family.

Mr. Kirby continued, his voice sympathetic. "Common wisdom says that giving in to a blackmailer's demands doesn't erase the threat. There is always the possibility that the scoundrel will ask for more."

"So, you would not pay the money?"

He crossed his arms. "I'd like to think that I wouldn't. But the truth is, when it comes to safeguarding the people we love . . . we don't always act rationally. I suspect I'd do what I had to do. And in the case of your sister, perhaps a little more time is all she needs."

"What do you mean?"

"She will no doubt marry soon. Once she is happily settled, the power of the threat will diminish."

"Yes," Fiona said. "That is a bolstering thought."

"I am glad." Impulsively, he reached for her hand and squeezed it. "My offer to help stands. Even if you simply wish for someone to talk to, please do not hesitate—whether we are here or back in London, you must feel free to call on me."

"I appreciate that." She withdrew her hand and stood, signaling that the conversation was over. "I must go. Thank you again for keeping this in the strictest of confidences."

Mr. Kirby stood and bowed. "You are most welcome, Miss Hartley. Your fortitude in the face of such adversity is admirable. Indeed, it is but one of the many things I admire about you."

Good heavens. The unexpected compliment made Fiona flush from her neck to the roots of her hair. And since she could think of nothing witty or charming to say in response, she resorted to her normal course of action in these situations—which was to slink away as quickly as possible.

Gray watched the scene on the terrace from the balcony outside his bedchamber. He couldn't make out what Kirby and Fiona were saying to each other, but three things were utterly clear.

First, Kirby had given Fiona a note and she'd been visibly affected by the contents. Even from the balcony, Gray could see her shining eyes and trembling hands, damn it all. Maybe Kirby had written a sappy poem or showered her with compliments. Whatever the letter contained had moved her—as Gray had been unable, nay, unwilling, to.

Second, Kirby had held her hand—the Devil take him. He'd done so as if it were the most natural thing in the world, and Fiona had allowed it. Gray desperately wanted to believe that she was simply stunned. Caught off guard. But there was a level of intimacy between them that was evident in their whispered confidences and meaningful glances.

And third, the way Kirby looked at Fiona betrayed his feelings for her. There was no denying it; he was smitten. Kirby may not have even realized it yet, but sometime over the last few days he had apparently crossed over the line of mild flirtation and was now veering perilously close to the level of lovesick foolishness.

And Gray had no one but himself to blame.

For the second time in as many days, he had the Neanderthal-like impulse to punch a plaster wall—and probably would have, if it wouldn't have added one more repair to the mile-long list.

First Pentham, now Kirby. Next thing Gray knew, Carter would be nipping at Fiona's heels.

Gray stormed back into his bedchamber and paced the length of the room.

Reminded himself that Fiona had proposed to *him*.

Had chosen *him* to introduce her to pleasure.

And wanted to spend more time with *him* in private.

Perhaps he'd been too quick to dismiss the idea of marrying Fiona. He desired her, and she desired him. He needed money for the Fortress, and she was an heiress with a huge dowry.

Best of all, if they became engaged Gray would no longer have to witness other men falling all over themselves to court her.

He'd be honest with her and tell her that he had no intention of falling in love. Ever. That he wasn't capable of it.

But that if she could abide a marriage of convenience, perhaps he would go along with her plan. He'd even arrange for them to exchange their vows within the week, or on whatever timeline she dictated, under one condition.

That she be completely honest with him.

There would be no secrets, no half-truths, no lies, in their relationship. He would not be played for a fool. Again.

As he dressed for dinner, he debated when to tell her the news—and decided that it could wait until tomorrow morning. He'd thought of the perfect setting to tell her, a rustic but charming spot. They'd have a few hours to themselves before most of the household awoke, plenty of time for her to sketch and for them to discuss a future life together.

And if she wished to continue her lessons in passion, by God, *he* would be the one to indulge her.

Chapter 17

"Where are you going?" Lily moaned and covered her head with a pillow.

"I want to sketch the sun coming up over the hills," Fiona whispered. "Go back to sleep and I'll see you later—at breakfast."

"You're mad," her sister grumbled. As an afterthought she added, "Be careful."

Fiona dressed quickly and quietly, leaving her hair in a single thick braid, then grabbed her sketchbook and pencil. Lily was already snoring softly by the time she slipped out of their bedchamber.

Last night after dinner, Gray had asked Fiona to meet him at the mermaid fountain just before sunrise—and there'd been something different in his manner. He'd seemed more purposeful and serious than usual, as if he was on a mission. One that involved her.

The golden glow of the early morning sun gilded every leaf and pebble as she walked through the garden, and though her fingers itched to capture the glorious scene on paper, she walked on, toward their meeting spot.

She rounded a bend in the path to find Gray already there, prowling to and fro in front of the fountain. With his broad shoulders and longish hair, he appeared more dashing pirate than refined gentleman. The shadow of a beard darkened his jaw, and his hair was charmingly disheveled, as though he'd just tumbled out of bed—which he no doubt had.

When he spotted her, he shot her a wicked grin. "Miss Hartley," he drawled. "You made it. I was afraid that you might prefer the coziness of your bed to my company."

The seductively deep timbre of his voice already had her body thrumming. "It was a rather close call," she fibbed. "But I am here." She looked around the small clearing, her practiced eye taking note of the shadows and considering the best angle from which to draw him. "The garden looks so different at this time of day."

"It does." His gaze roved over the lush landscape surrounding them. "But we're not staying here. Come. I have a surprise for you."

He held out a hand, and she took it, lacing her fingers through his. Neither of them had bothered to don gloves, so their bare palms melded with a delicious warmth. Without saying a word, they walked across the lawn, damp with dew, all the way to the edge of the woods. Gray led her toward a narrow path that wound around a mixture of mature trees, saplings, hollowed logs, and brush, making her grateful she'd worn her boots.

"I apologize for the long walk," he said. "But it's not much farther."

Fiona smiled up at him without saying what she was thinking—that the walk hadn't seemed long at all. That she was delighted to have an excuse to hold his hand.

They reached the crest of a hill and paused to take in the view. "There it is," he said, pointing a short distance away. Nestled in the valley beneath them was a tiny stone cottage with a proud, stout chimney and green shutters that seemed to smile. "It used to belong to the groundskeeper, but—as you may have guessed from the current state of the grounds—he hasn't been here for decades."

"It's lovely," she said, though she was a bit apprehensive about the condition of the interior.

"I'm glad you like it." He helped her navigate the steep and slippery hill, then escorted her to an arched wooden door before fishing a key from his pocket. "Here we are." The door creaked open, and Gray waved an arm toward the inside. "After you."

Fiona inched her way into the cottage and looked around the small living area. Sunlight streamed through unadorned windows on opposite walls, revealing a small table and a pair of mismatched wooden chairs on one side of the room, and a basket of thick quilts and pillows near the fireplace. A round braided wool rug covered most of the floorboards, which were freshly swept.

"It's perfect—our own private portrait studio. And you sent someone in advance to prepare it for us," she said, pleased he'd thought of it.

"Actually, I saw to it myself."

As he knelt before the fireplace and lit the kindling in the grate, she took note of the small thoughtful touches—a bowl of fruit on the table, candles on the mantel, a vase of wildflowers on a windowsill—with renewed appreciation. She had the sudden and fierce urge to throw her arms around his neck, but she refrained.

He was quieter than usual—which was truly saying something—and he hadn't looked at her since they entered the cottage. "Has something changed since yesterday?" she probed. "You seem . . . different."

He continued to stare into the fireplace at the flames that were just beginning to lick at a huge log. "I saw you with Kirby last night."

Drat. She scrambled for an explanation and decided to

stick to a version of the truth. "Yes. He found a note that belonged to me and wished to return it."

"I realize it's none of my business, but it seems you have captured his affections," he said flatly.

"I don't think Mr. Kirby is interested in me. He was simply offering . . ." She'd been on the verge of saying *comfort,* but that would have sparked a host of unanswerable questions. ". . . his friendship."

Gray stood and paced before the fire. "I have no claim to you. And I certainly have no right to object to any attachment you form with another gentleman, and yet . . ."

Hope sprouted in her chest. "Yes?"

"I confess I am opposed to the idea."

"I see." She lowered herself onto one of the chairs, waiting for him to elaborate, to convey the depths of his feelings for her. To tell her that the sight of her with Mr. Kirby had driven him half out of his mind with jealousy and that he wanted her for his own. Forever.

"A little over a week ago, you said you wished to marry me."

"Yes." She held her breath.

"Do you still wish it?" he asked soberly.

She didn't hesitate. "I do."

"I can't believe I'm saying this . . . but I am seriously considering agreeing to this scheme."

Fiona's heart fluttered. "That's . . . that's wonderful." Perhaps he could have been a bit more gracious about it, but she knew better than to expect him to recite poetry or profess his love. The only thing that mattered was that he was coming around. She could save Lily and her family from ruin—and still reach for her own happiness.

"I will marry you," he said, "but there's something you should know."

"Whatever it is, it won't change my mind." She wished

he'd stop wearing a hole in the rug and come to her. He didn't have to kneel before her or bare his soul, but he might at least hold her hand again.

He gazed at her, his expression tortured. "I can't ever love you."

She shook her head, thinking she hadn't heard him properly. "Pardon? I don't understand."

"I like you well enough, and I desire you—far more than I should—but I cannot love you."

Her belly twisted uncomfortably. "Love isn't something we can conjure in an instant. It will no doubt take time, but I'm certain that as we become better acquainted, we'll—"

"No," he said firmly. "It will never happen. Not with me."

"Why not?" she asked, even though she was more than a little afraid of the answer. Maybe he thought her too common or forward or outspoken. Maybe he was still in love with Helena.

"I am not capable," he said simply. "I tried once and got it all wrong. I was a fool to think I could marry for love. After all, my own parents claimed to be passionately in love and that ended . . . disastrously. I don't even know what real love looks like."

Her heart ached for him. "Then I will show you."

At last, he came to the table and sat in the chair opposite her. But instead of taking her hands, he crossed his arms. "There are some things you can't teach, Fiona, and if you think that you will change me, you are certain to be disappointed."

"How can you be so sure?"

"It's not in my nature. You wouldn't expect a sheep to fly or a fish to crawl . . . and you shouldn't expect me to be the husband of your dreams."

"But you *will* be my husband?"

"There are a few particulars we must discuss."

Good heavens. This was not the proposal she'd imagined in her youthful fantasies. For one thing, she'd never thought *she'd* be the one to propose. And she never dreamed her intended would have a list of stipulations. Still, she couldn't help but be encouraged that he'd uttered the word *husband.* "Please, go on."

He grabbed an orange out of the bowl and tossed it from hand to hand as if he were discussing the dinner menu rather than the rest of their lives. "I will marry you quickly, as you requested—even if we must go to Gretna Green."

Her eyes fluttered shut in relief. "Thank you. But I'm hopeful we can procure a special license. I feel certain my parents will be happy to supply the Archbishop with a handsome donation."

He arched a brow. "Fine. I will leave the arrangements to you."

She nodded, not quite believing this was happening. "What else?"

His heavy-lidded gaze snapped to hers. "You will bear me an heir."

The air seemed to rush out of her lungs, but she managed to reply, "I will try." She'd always hoped for a few children—who could grow up to be as close as she and Lily were. "But, assuming I do conceive, there is the possibility that we'll have girls."

He fumbled the orange momentarily but quickly composed himself. "Obviously, there are no guarantees, but we will make a valiant effort."

Fiona knew admittedly little of passion but had already deduced that, with Gray, the marriage bed would be no hardship. "I have no objections to that," she replied. "And I'm pleased to hear that your expectations are realistic."

She fought back the sadness at the edges of her joy. She felt as though they were negotiating a business deal, which was what she had intended—initially. Somewhere along the way, however, she'd begun to yearn for more. Boldly, she reached out and clasped his wrist. "I realize that this has happened quickly, but I promise I'll try to make you happy."

He looked rather stunned—as though he hadn't even considered the possibility of his own happiness. "You needn't worry about me. You should protect your own interests. Our hasty marriage will raise eyebrows. You must be prepared for cruel gossip. People will say that I'm marrying you for your fortune—or to spite Helena."

"Are you? Marrying me for those reasons?"

He had the good grace to look contrite. "I won't deny they've played a part in my decision. But there are other factors, too."

She winced. "Such as?"

"As I said, I desire you."

Her cheeks warmed. "Yes, I believe we've established that. But is there anything else?"

With a shrug, he said, "You are talented and kind. I enjoy your company."

Well. It might not have been the most romantic of proposals. Indeed, she wasn't at all certain it qualified as an actual proposal, but it was *something*—and many marriages had been built on less.

She sighed and pulled back her hand. "Have you any other conditions?"

"Yes. You must promise that you'll be honest with me. No deception. No secrets."

"I assume that you will abide by the same terms?" she challenged.

He hesitated for the space of three heartbeats. "I will

be honest and forthcoming—concerning any matters that relate to our marriage."

Fiona narrowed her eyes, aware he was hedging. But since the qualifier worked to her advantage, she didn't argue. The truth about Lily's birth mother and the blackmailer had nothing to do with Gray. Well, perhaps it had a *little* to do with him, but the fewer people who knew, the better. And nothing was more important than keeping Lily's secret safe. "Very well."

"I think we should wait a day or two before making our intentions known. I want you to be certain you can live with my terms."

"I don't require time," she protested. "Marrying you was *my* idea, if you recall."

"I do. But now you know me better. You've seen my country house and know there's next to nothing left in my coffers. You know that I abhor poetry and sentimentality and that there's a block of ice where my heart should be. Carefully consider all those facts, and, if you still want to marry me . . . we'll see it done."

He tossed the orange straight up into the air and tracked it with his eyes, preparing to catch it—but Fiona snatched it out of the air.

And was rewarded with his full attention. "I'm not going to change my mind," she said evenly, "but if it will make you feel more at ease, we can wait to announce our betrothal."

She reminded herself that Helena had called off their engagement and that he was understandably reluctant to subject himself to that sort of humiliation again. A couple of days made little difference in the big scheme of things. As long as Fiona could access her dowry in time to pay off her blackmailer, she would be content.

Satisfied, if not elated, she plopped the orange into the

bowl and leaned back in her chair. "I told you this would be easy."

He shot her a tight smile. "You did."

Why did everything seem so suddenly awkward now that they were engaged, albeit secretly? Shouldn't they have been embracing or kissing each other to celebrate this milestone? Instead, the air between them had grown chilly. The cottage that had seemed so cozy when they'd first entered seemed rather lonely and barren.

Gray stood stiffly and planted his hands on his hips. "Now then. We have at least an hour before we must return for breakfast, and I promised that you could finish your sketch. Would you like to continue?"

So, this was to be the way of it. If he had his druthers, they'd continue as they had been, amicable and coolly detached, never truly breaking down the barriers between them. But Fiona had already discovered the chink in his armor—the hidden entrance into his soul: her sketching. And he was unwittingly playing right into her hand.

"Yes. I am eager to finish your portrait." She looked around the cottage. "Shall we spread a quilt on the floor in front of the fire and work there?"

"You are the artist," he said. "I am merely the subject, at your service." With that, he strode to the large basket and layered two fluffy quilts as she'd requested. "Here are a few pillows. I hope you'll be comfortable enough to work."

"I'm certain I will be." Fiona grabbed her sketch pad and settled herself while he assumed the same charmingly nonchalant and wickedly languorous pose he had during their last session. Just the sight of him reclining next to her made her breath hitch. She reached for the pencil behind her ear and prayed that whatever magic her drawing had managed to conjure before could be summoned again.

She decided to begin by sketching his hand—the same large, warm hand that had enveloped hers as they'd walked through the mist earlier that morning. Now he rested it casually in front of his taut abdomen. A dusting of hair peeked from beneath his sleeve near his wrist. The back of his hand was several shades darker than her own, and his veins were visible just beneath his skin. Unlike most gentlemen, he wore no signet ring or jewels—no jewelry at all. Long, strong fingers tapered to short nails, and three knuckles were red and scabbed over as though he'd scraped them while working. Or fighting. But she would not ask about it—not now, at any rate.

For she was too absorbed in the task before her.

She did not study his hand in artistic terms. She wasn't thinking about texture and shadows and color and light. Rather, she was remembering how his hand had *felt*.

When he'd placed a blossom behind her ear that first night in the garden.

When he'd tenderly brushed the hair away from her face before kissing her.

When he'd caressed her, bringing her exquisite pleasure.

That was the hand she needed to capture on paper. Somehow, she needed to show the strength and gentleness, the calluses and the warmth.

Swept up by a swirl of memories, she almost forgot she was drawing. Her chest flushed as she recalled how he'd slid that hand beneath her nightgown. Her skin tingled as though he touched her now, his fingers skimming the insides of her thighs, teasing her with light brushes. A sure and steady pulsing began at her core. Her breathing grew heavy.

To her surprise, his did, too. He swallowed and looked at her with . . . longing. Not affection, precisely, but something close to it. One thing was certain—there was nothing cool in his demeanor now. His gaze was molten, and though at least a yard separated them, she could feel the heat emanating from his body and creating a current that traveled through hers.

"Fiona," he breathed. It was an apology and a plea.

She blinked up at him, and the pencil fell from her fingers.

He crawled toward her slowly, searching her face.

Without hesitation, she set aside her sketchbook, met him halfway, and answered the question in his eyes. "Yes."

Chapter 18

Gray cursed his own weakness. He'd managed to discuss the particulars of his and Fiona's betrothal with cool detachment. He'd refused to give in to the temptation to hold her and kiss her. He'd thought he was capable of maintaining a modicum of control.

He was dead wrong.

The moment she'd begun drawing, his control began to slip away. The way she observed him was intensely intimate. Sensual. Almost erotic.

Still, he'd refrained from giving in to the impulse to gather her in his arms and pick up where they'd left off that night in the library. He'd resisted her . . . until it became glaringly clear that her desire mirrored his own. The darkening of her eyes, the rapid rise and fall of her chest, and the parting of her lips had been his downfall.

When he couldn't bear to be apart from her for another second, he went to her, desperate to taste her lips and caress her skin.

He stopped, scarcely a breath away. "This is madness."

Her gaze dropped to his mouth, and they collided in a kiss that was raw and primal. His tongue plundered her mouth as she grasped at his clothes. He speared his hands through her hair as she pressed her body to his.

"When you draw, I'm pulled to you like the tide." He pressed his lips against her neck. "You wield that pencil like an enchanted wand."

Amused, she pulled away and arched a sardonic brow. "You accuse me of being a witch?"

He laid her back on the quilt and gazed into her eyes. "I'm under your spell."

"Then I fear I am under the same spell. Surely no witch worth her weight in toads would cast a spell on herself, though. So I think we have disproved that theory."

"Is it always like this when you draw?" He had to know.

Her brow furrowed. "What do you mean?"

"The connection we feel. Is it always there—between you and your subject?"

She propped herself up on an elbow and traced the curve of his jaw with a featherlight touch. "The pull we feel is not due to my sketching. It's there because you let me in. You let me see beyond the brooding earl who trusts no one, beyond the man who is obsessed with improving his house."

"That's all I am," he said flatly. "If you see anything beyond that, then it's a figment of your imagination."

"I will tell you what I see." She cupped his cheek, and every instinct screamed for him to turn away—lest she see too much. Instead, he kept his face stony and braced himself. "I see a man whose primary goal in life is to dote on his grandmother and ensure her happiness. A man who thought to prepare this cottage with fruit and wildflowers and quilts. A man who introduced me to pleasure and refused to take his own in order to protect me."

She ran a fingertip across his lower lip and lightly dragged it down, teasing him. Stoking the fire that already burned for her. "To answer your question, I don't feel this way with anyone but you. I never have. And I daresay I never will."

Shit. She was uttering everything his godforsaken heart wanted to hear. Hell, she probably *believed* what she was saying. But that didn't mean it was true. "You are too young, too inexperienced, to know your own heart."

"No. I am courageous enough to see what is written there. It tells me I belong with you." She pulled his head down for a brief but soul-melting kiss. "What is your heart telling *you*?"

Nothing he trusted, damn it all.

"It doesn't matter. What I know is this: The thought of you with another man—whether it's Pentham or Kirby— makes me want to fight a bloody duel." Her beautiful eyes clouded with confusion, so he sought to explain. "*I* want to be the one who keeps you safe . . . who makes you sigh . . . who makes you smile."

Her expression turned soft. Seductive. "If that is true, make me yours. Here. Now."

His whole body tensed. He'd fantasized about making love to her, of course, but all of this—it felt like a dream. "Are you certain?"

Her eyes gleamed, and the corner of her mouth curled. "We will be wed within the week." With nimble fingers, she loosened his cravat and caressed his neck. "Why should we deny ourselves?"

Gray was hard-pressed to think of a reason. His heart pounded, and he was so aroused that he wasn't sure he could form a sentence. "I . . . don't want to hurt you."

She frowned slightly. "Physically, or . . . ?"

"Neither." God help him, he'd never forgive himself if he did.

"Do you want to know what hurts me the most? When

you are detached and cold and indifferent. You keep telling me that you're not a poet. You cannot find the words to tell me how you feel about me. So *show* me. Now."

The words had barely left her mouth before he pressed his lips to hers. He tugged at the laces of her gown, desperate to remove the layers between them. "No clothes," he growled. "I want to see you."

She shoved his jacket off his shoulders. Unbuttoned his waistcoat. Pulled the tail of his shirt out of his trousers.

He slid the ribbon from her hair. Pushed her bodice down her body. Unlaced her corset.

When he sat and began to take off a boot, she jumped up. "Let me."

Wearing nothing but her shift and stockings, she grabbed on to a heel and yanked off one boot, then the other, laughing as she stumbled backward.

But when he stood and pulled her hips toward his, neither of them was laughing. He reached for the hem of her shift, lifted it over her head, and tossed it onto the floor. When she slid her fingers inside the top of his trousers, he stripped them off as well.

As they stood toe to toe in front of the fire, he hesitated, savoring that last, perfect moment of anticipation. God, she was beautiful. Her skin glistened; her eyes sparkled. He drank in the sight of her breasts and hips. Her long, graceful limbs. The way she stood before him—proud and vulnerable at the same time.

And Lord help him, he was going to make her his.

Their bodies crashed together, and the sensation of her skin against his nearly undid him.

This . . . *this* he understood. This was not poetry or ballads or romance. This was pure passion. Lust. Satisfying a physical need, nothing more.

Because it *couldn't* be more.

* * *

Gray laid her down in front of the fire. The quilt was soft beneath her, his body hard above her.

"I'm going to taste every inch of you," he promised. He started with her lips and kissed his way down her neck, across her breasts, and over her hips, growling when little moans of pleasure escaped her throat. The slight scruff of his beard against her breasts and belly delighted and aroused her.

He responded to every shift of her body, every sigh, every whimper. It almost seemed as if he was studying what she liked best. Committing it to memory.

She speared her fingers through his thick hair as he cruised down her body and spread her legs. Every intimate touch was new to her, glorious and intense.

"Gray," she gasped. "What are you . . . ? *Oh*. . . ."

His mouth was *there*—precisely at the center of the pleasure swirling inside her. She gave herself up to it and to him. Her whole body, from the roots of her hair to the tips of her toes, ached for him. Surrendered to him. With every wicked lick and moan, he brought her closer to the precipice, imprinting himself on her heart and her soul.

Slowly, steadily, she spiraled higher, till there was nowhere left to go. Her climax blossomed slowly—gloriously so—and hard. Her back arched, and every coiled muscle in her body released, catapulting her over the edge. Pleasure shimmered through her, carrying her across a starlit sky.

Gray lay beside her and pulled her close, planting a kiss on her forehead. She placed her palm over his heart and felt it beating as fast as her own. Looked down at the hard length of him and moistened her lips.

"Don't," he said.

"What?"

"Don't do that."

"But you just—"

He cut her off with a kiss, fierce and raw. Boldly, she reached between them and curled her fingers around his shaft. He jerked and groaned at her touch, then placed a hand over hers, showing her how to stroke him.

She reveled at the hitch of his breath and his muffled curse, delighted that she wielded such power. Her tongue tangled with his as she did her best to sweetly torture him.

"Damn it, Fiona," he blurted. "I need you."

"You say that as if it's a curse."

"Maybe it is. But God help me, I don't care." He propped himself on an elbow and looked earnestly into her eyes. "Do you want me to stop?"

She shook her head. "Please, don't. I need you, too."

His eyes never left hers as he positioned himself between her legs and slowly, steadily filled her. The dark hair that spilled across his forehead coupled with the stubble on his chin made him look slightly dangerous. Eminently masculine. "Are you all right?"

In answer, she twined her arms around his neck. Her body stretched to accommodate him as he slowly thrust deeper. A sheen covered his chest, and his powerful muscles flexed with barely contained restraint. He touched his forehead to hers and moaned. "I wanted this to last, but I can't—"

"Do not worry," she assured him, brushing the hair away from his face and kissing his temple. She wanted to tell him that she loved this side of him—this small chink in the armor of her brooding, reserved earl. But since she couldn't quite form the words, she wrapped her legs around his.

He moved his hips faster, in a rhythm that stoked her desire and made her sigh with pleasure. This closeness was what she'd wanted. What she'd craved. All his walls were broken down, his defenses stripped away. And he was binding himself to her—at least physically.

She raked her nails lightly down his chest, and he thrust harder. Faster. Until he was almost shaking with need. He was pulsing, barreling toward his release, when he suddenly growled and left her—rolling away and spilling his seed on the quilt.

For several seconds, she lay there, thinking about what their joining had meant to her, wondering what it had meant to him. And knowing she'd never be able to summarize it in a diary entry.

Suddenly chilled and confused, she curled into his back and waited for his breathing to slow. Waited for him to say something. Anything.

Without facing her, he asked, "Are you all right?"

"Yes." She thought so, at least.

"Good." He sat up and held his head in his hands, as though chastening himself, then stalked around the small room, gathering up their clothes. He tossed her shift, gown, and stockings onto the quilt beside her and quickly pulled on his trousers. "I don't have a washbasin here," he said, apologetic.

Fiona shimmied into her chemise. "I'm fine," she said— even though she felt perilously close to tears. She hadn't expected him to profess his love for her, but she'd imagined that after she gave herself to him he'd be . . . warmer. Which proved precisely how little she understood about such matters.

"I don't mean to hurry you, but if we want to make it back to the house before your mother and my grandmother wake, we should go."

"Of course." As she dressed and braided her hair, he banked the fire.

"I'll return later to clean up," he said.

She sidled up to him and rested her cheek against his shoulder. "Perhaps I could come with you and we could talk some more. Make plans."

He stiffened slightly—almost imperceptibly. "You needn't worry that I'll go back on my word. I'll marry you, as I said I would. But I don't want to risk damaging your reputation before then."

"I see." She supposed she should be grateful that he was concerned with protecting her name, but it felt like he was shutting her out once again. "I just thought it might be nice if we had the opportunity to discuss our future." She should tell him about the blackmail notes, so that they could enter into their engagement without secrets between them.

"Soon." He picked up her sketchbook and slipped her pencil behind her ear—a small, affectionate gesture that gave her hope.

As they quickly left the cottage and walked through the woods in silence, she told herself she had no cause to be unhappy. Things were falling into place far better than she could have imagined when she'd first written to the Earl of Ravenport, proposing marriage.

The problem was that now he wasn't simply the Earl of Ravenport—he was Gray.

And she wanted more than a marriage with him. She wanted his *love*.

Less than an hour later, Gray had washed, shaved, and joined some of his guests in the dining room. He murmured greetings to Fiona's mother and Lady Callahan, who were already seated at the table, and planted a kiss on his grandmother's cheek before filling his plate at the sideboard. He kept an eye on the doorway, looking for Fiona. God, he'd been an ass—and he hated himself for it. But not nearly as much as he would have hated himself if he'd given her false hope that he could be a doting, loving husband.

"You missed the other gentlemen," Mrs. Hartley was saying. "They decided to try their hand at fishing this morning."

He poured himself coffee and reached for his newspaper. "Excellent. Maybe we'll have something to eat at luncheon today."

"So droll," his grandmother tittered. "I say, Gray. You're looking hale and hearty today. Very fit."

Warning shots sounded in his head. He knew his grandmother, and she was warming up to something—he'd stake his life on it. "And you, Grandmother, are lovely, as always. Why do you have a twinkle in your eye this morning?"

"I'm delighted you asked." She turned to Fiona's mother and gave her a conspiratorial smile. "Would you like to share the good news?"

Gray took a scalding sip of coffee and braced himself.

Mrs. Hartley pressed a fluttering hand to her chest, then picked up a letter from the table and waved it in the air. "I've received word from my husband. Unbeknownst to me, my daughters wrote to him shortly after we arrived here, beseeching him to join us, and he has agreed. He shan't stay long, as he won't arrive until Saturday—the day before we are to leave."

Aware that his grandmother was studying his reaction, Gray schooled his expression. "I look forward to meeting him." He congratulated himself on refraining from grumbling. An extra guest for one night wasn't a burden—and it would save him from having to call on Mr. Hartley in London to ask for Fiona's hand.

Assuming she didn't change her mind before then.

He shouldn't have taken her on the floor of a cottage. Jesus, it had been her first time, and she deserved better—a feather mattress, silk sheets, candlelight. He'd wanted it to be good for her, but it had been over in the blink of an eye, and now she probably thought him no better than a rutting boar.

". . . and we thought it would be a wonderful way to end the week's festivities," his grandmother said. "Gray?"

He snapped to attention. "Forgive me. You were saying?"

Her teacup paused midway to her mouth and she arched a thin, dark brow. "I was telling you about our plans for the ball, this Saturday evening."

Holy hell. "A ball, here?" he asked, incredulous. "This house is in no condition for a ball."

His grandmother shrugged her slender shoulders. "We'll hang some greenery, keep the champagne flowing, and provide dancing music. Our guests will be enjoying themselves far too much to worry about a little peeling wallpaper."

"Guests?" He dragged a hand through his hair. "Who would we invite?"

"Why, people from the village, of course. They are delighted to hear that you're improving the Fortress, and even happier to hear you're entertaining."

"I don't mean to disappoint, Grandmother, but there's no time to prepare for a ball. We'd need food, drink, musicians . . . and Saturday is only two days away."

She waved a dismissive hand. "Leave all of that to Mrs. Hartley, Lady Callahan, and me. We will see to the invitations, and the young ladies will take care of decorations. Planning is half the fun, you know." She clasped her hands, and her eyes turned wistful. "A ball. It will be such a festive affair, just like the ones your grandfather and I used to host."

Damn it. She knew it was impossible for him to deny her. "Fine. But we'll keep it simple. Nothing too grand or ostentatious." Because they couldn't afford anything lavish. In truth, they couldn't afford anything at all.

Although he supposed all that would change soon. Once he married Fiona.

"I understand, dear," his grandmother said meekly. But she didn't fool him for a second. She was too excited over the prospect of a ball to rein in the plans. And if it pleased her to throw herself into the preparations, he couldn't object.

He wondered what his grandmother would say once he and Fiona announced their engagement. From the time Gray was in leading strings, he'd known it was his duty to marry and marry well.

Fiona wasn't from an old and respected family, but her fortune more than made up for her lack of noble blood. She'd grow into her role as countess—assuming she didn't have a change of heart before they took their vows.

But if they did make it to the altar, Gray would be able to throw himself into the renovations completely. He'd convince Fiona to stay at his house in London, where she'd no doubt be more comfortable—and closer to her family. He'd remain at the Fortress—and focus on making it something his grandmother could be proud of. Something she could remember in the days after her world went black.

Chapter 19

On the Perils of Passion

Any girl who sits in drawing rooms and attends to the inevitable gossip learns the dangers of succumbing to the amorous advances of a dashing gentleman. A compromised young lady might find herself featured in the scandal sheets or shipped off to the country to live with a spinster aunt. While the gentleman who seduced her is lauded for his virility, her reputation is destroyed beyond repair.

But there is yet another peril—one that even wise matrons often fail to mention. It occurs when the young woman's feelings run deeper than the gentleman's. After giving herself to him, she may fancy herself in love with him.

A dangerous thing indeed.

"I know you've been sneaking out to meet Lord Ravenport," Lily said matter-of-factly as she rummaged through her portmanteau looking for a bonnet later that morning.

Fiona sat on the edge of the bed, trying to ignore the sudden pounding of her heart. She hated lying to Lily, but she simply couldn't confess everything, so she settled on the half-truth. "I know it's not proper for us to spend time alone together, but I've been sketching him."

Lily arched a brow. Her eyes flicked to the table where Fiona's sketchbook sat. "May I see?"

"Not yet," Fiona replied quickly, for the sketch revealed far too much. "I haven't quite finished."

Lily arched a brow, sat beside Fiona, and squeezed her hand. "Listen. I don't give a fig about Miss Haywinkle's rules. But I don't want to see you hurt."

"I know. Thank you. I care for him and think he . . . well, I think we are compatible."

"Compatible," Lily repeated with a hint of distaste. "I like the earl, but he's rather . . . cold. He didn't write the poetry, did he?"

Blast. "No."

"Oh, Fi, you're so kind and smart and talented. You could charm any gentleman you set your sights on. Why would you choose the one man who has a heart of stone?"

An excellent question. "It's not stone. . . . I think he's been hurt."

"Ah, yes." Lily rolled her eyes. "Lady Helena jilted him."

The mere mention of Helena's name twisted Fiona's belly in knots. "Yes, but I think there's more. The countess hinted as much but wouldn't elaborate."

"Well, it seems to me that love shouldn't be so difficult. The beginning of a relationship should be exciting and thrilling. Every encounter should leave you breathless and giddy—not sad and melancholy."

"I'm not sad," Fiona protested, but the words rang hollow. Her relationship with Gray was complicated. There'd been no time for the usual stages of flirtation, courting, or even engagement. But she'd never doubted that he desired her, and now they'd agreed to bind themselves to each other. Perhaps, over time, he'd return her feelings.

"You have at least one other admirer, you know," Lily said smoothly. "Lord Pentham steals glances at you every chance he has. And the looks he's sending your way could melt butter in January. He's exceedingly handsome."

Fiona nodded. Lord Pentham always appeared as though he were ready to sit for a portrait. Jacket pressed, face closely shaven, not a hair out of place. But he didn't possess the same brand of slightly wild, masculine appeal as Gray—not even close.

"I have set my cap for Lord Ravenport." A mild understatement after this morning's tryst. "And I'm hoping to have some time to speak to him privately at the picnic this afternoon," she added meaningfully.

Lily threw up her hands and flounced back on the bed. "Fine. I shall do my best to keep the others—especially Lord Pentham—occupied. Just promise me that you'll be careful where the earl is concerned. I believe he's what Miss Haywinkle would refer to as a scoundrel."

"I think I could be happy with him." Fiona wasn't sure if she was trying to convince Lily or herself.

"If you are happy, then I shall be happy also," Lily said—not entirely convincing. "I wonder what Papa will think of the earl."

Fiona did, too. "I confess I'm surprised—but delighted—that Papa agreed to come."

"Maybe now that we've succeeding in coaxing him away from work and the bustle of London for a couple of days, he'll take the opportunity to relax."

"I hope so," Fiona said. But she knew they both longed for more than that. They wanted him to be the father he'd been years ago—the one who'd laughed at their antics and hugged them before bed. The one who'd loved them even when they weren't terribly proper or prim.

They wanted their old Papa back.

"Where's Ravenport?" Lord Pentham asked, voicing the same question Fiona had.

Everyone who was planning to attend the picnic had gathered in the entry hall. Footmen bustled to and fro, hauling baskets of food from the kitchen and gathering an assortment of blankets and quilts.

"He said we should go on without him," Mr. Kirby announced. "He's repairing some fences on the east side of the estate and plans to join us once he's finished."

Fiona's heart sank, but Lord Carter chuckled. "Ravenport doesn't know the meaning of the word *leisure*. What about the countess and the other ladies—will they be joining us?"

"I'm afraid not," Sophie piped up. "The countess, Mrs. Hartley, and my mother have elected to remain here and see to the ball invitations."

"Better them than us," Lord Carter replied with a shudder. "Well then, I suppose this is our entire party. Shall we set out?"

There was a general murmur of agreement, so Fiona painted on a smile as they filed out the door. She would have an opportunity to talk with Gray soon enough. Till then, there was naught she could do but enjoy the company, the food, and the sunshine.

Mr. Kirby led the way, explaining that the half-hour walk, mostly uphill, would be well worth the effort. Still, Fiona was grateful she didn't have to lug one of the heavy baskets up the steep path—she carried only her sketchbook and a small bag of pencils and pastels.

Lord Pentham fell into step beside her, making friendly conversation. Perhaps he flirted occasionally, but if he was sending any of the butter-melting glances that her sister had mentioned, Fiona didn't notice them. She was too pre-occupied with looking for Gray.

"He'll be here shortly," Lord Pentham said.

Fiona blinked guiltily. "I beg your pardon?"

"Ravenport. He won't miss the opportunity to spend some time in your company—especially since he knows others will be vying for your attention."

"Forgive me. I'll admit to being distracted for a variety of reasons. I feel obliged to point out, however, that I've never been the sort of woman gentlemen flock to."

"Perhaps you weren't before now." Lord Pentham shot her a grin. "Look, we've arrived."

A copse of trees at the top of the hill provided a shady spot where they could spread the blankets and partake of the food and wine. Nearby, large, ancient stones protruded from the ground in a half circle, practically begging to be explored.

Mr. Kirby pointed at them and spoke to the group. "Anyone who's daring enough to climb one of the taller rocks will be rewarded with a view of the estate, the village, and beyond."

Lord Pentham set his basket in the shade and gestured toward Fiona's sketchbook. "Sounds like the perfect inspi-ration for an artist. Maybe after luncheon I could help you scale the rocks?"

"Actually, I'm not very hungry." And she was eager to see the view. "I think I shall try my hand at climbing now."

"Of course," Lord Pentham said gallantly. "Allow me to hold your sketchbook for you—it will be easier for you to navigate the crooks and crevices if your hands are free."

Fiona hesitated. Her sketchbook was almost as private as her diary. Anyone who saw the sketch of Gray would know that they'd been spending time together . . . alone. But Lord Pentham was right; it would be nearly impossible for her to pull herself to the top of the rocks while she held her book. "Very well. But no peeking inside—some of the drawings are still works in progress, and I'm not ready to share them."

Lord Pentham solemnly raised a hand. "Promise." His face cracked into a smile as he tucked the book under one arm and walked with her to the foot of the rocks. They surveyed the stones from all sides, determining which footholds would provide the easiest path to the top before Fiona wedged the toe of her boot in a crevice and started hauling herself up one of the larger stones.

She scrambled to the top of the rock, sat on the warm, flat surface, and gaped at the breathtaking view. Fluffy white sheep dotted verdant hills; low stone walls wound through the valley; red wildflowers swayed in the breeze. A majestic blue and pink sky presided over the entire scene, lending a radiant glow to everything below.

Fiona's hands itched to sketch all of it . . . for the person she suspected would love it the most. Not her father or Lily or Sophie or even Gray—but the dowager countess. Perhaps she'd seen the countryside from this very spot as a girl. She couldn't climb the rocks any longer, but Fiona could bring the view to her—and she prayed she would do it justice.

She crawled to the edge of the rock where Lord Pentham waited. "I'll take my sketchbook now. Thank you for carrying it."

"My pleasure." The marquess watched as she removed the small reticule that hung from her wrist and emptied a few pencils and pastels onto the stone beside her. "I don't suppose you like company while you draw?" he asked doubtfully.

That depended—on whether the person was Gray. But Fiona answered as diplomatically as she could. "I'm afraid I'm poor company while I work. It seems I can't carry on a conversation and move my pencil at the same time."

"I'm sure you're being too modest, but I understand. As much as I'd love to watch you sketch, I will leave you in peace. But if you should require anything, or if you want to go back down, please call out—I'll remain close enough to hear you."

"That's very thoughtful," Fiona said, meaning it.

"Oh, I almost forgot." He reached inside his chest pocket and produced a small cylinder-shaped metal object. "It's a telescope—in case you want a closer view of the sheep." He winked as he handed it to her.

Oddly touched, she twisted one end of the cylinder and pulled it open. As she held the smaller lens to her eye, she felt like a sailor in a crow's nest atop a mast. "This is amazing."

"I'm glad you like it," Lord Pentham said. "Enjoy yourself."

As he nimbly descended the rock, Fiona wondered what was wrong with her. Why couldn't she have proposed to someone like the marquess—someone who was attentive and polite and . . . *interested*? Lily had been right. Falling in love with Gray was akin to tossing her heart off the edge of a cliff. Sure, the feeling was thrilling and heady, but her heart was going to shatter into a million bits.

With a sigh, she picked up her pencil and closed her eyes. Somehow, she had to capture the simple bliss of a warm breeze, the earthy scents of soil and grass, the soothing sounds of birdsong and rustling leaves. For the countess's sake.

Fiona took a deep breath and let her pencil glide over the paper. Slowly, steadily, the rolling hills, the clumps of trees, and the quaint cottages took shape—and came to life on the paper. She used the pastels to achieve the perfect azure sky and the puffy pink clouds as well as the lush green of the pastures and the scarlet wildflowers.

It wasn't a bold, imposing landscape one might expect in a gentleman's library. It was soft and welcoming and humble—like the countess herself.

As usual, Fiona lost track of time as she worked. Lord Pentham climbed up at one point to check on her, and she requested another hour or so. But she knew it was almost time to quit when her bottom started to ache. Besides, the wide brim of her bonnet couldn't completely shield her face from the sun, and she could almost feel the freckles popping out on her nose.

Her picture wasn't perfect, but it was one of her better drawings, and she was certain it would please the countess. And since her belly was rumbling—a not-so-subtle reminder that she hadn't yet eaten today—it was time to put her pencils away. She slipped them into her reticule and picked up the telescope for one last look at the sheep drifting across the fields like fluffy bits of cotton—

And spotted Gray . . . without his shirt. The dark mop of his hair hung low over his brow, and his trousers grazed his hips, stretching across his buttocks.

As she watched, he pulled one of the nails clamped between his lips and bent down to repair the bottom rail of a fence. The muscles in his back flexed and rippled as he swung a hammer three times, connecting with the wood, before repeating.

His hair was damp from his exertions, and a fine sheen covered his tanned skin. His horse grazed nearby, but Fiona was too mesmerized by Gray to spare more than a glance at the gelding.

Gray was beautiful to watch—she could not deny that. But it was more than his physical prowess and dark good looks that captivated her. Anyone who saw him like this would instantly know how passionate he was about his land and his house. Determination was evident in every swing of his hammer.

And thanks to the countess, Fiona now knew that his motivation for repairing the house—or at least part of it— was to bring joy to his grandmother. A fact that touched Fiona even more deeply.

She watched Gray through the telescope as he expertly replaced several more fence rails. Sighed when he threw his tools in a bag and stuffed his arms back into his shirt and shrugged on a jacket.

"Miss Hartley?"

She fumbled the telescope and turned at the sound of a man's voice, expecting Lord Pentham—but it wasn't the marquess. "Mr. Kirby," she said breathlessly. "I was just preparing to rejoin the picnic."

He gestured toward the telescope. "Bird-watching?"

"Sheep," she choked out. "Mostly. What have I missed down below?"

"Your sister, Miss Kendall, and your maid have gone in search of greenery and flowers they can use to deck the ballroom. Lord Pentham and I have been drinking the ale. Lord Carter is snoring, and I cannot blame him, as we were out fishing rather early this morning. How is your sketch progressing?"

"Quite well. In fact, as I mentioned, I was thinking that I really should return to ground level and attempt to be sociable." She snapped the telescope closed and tucked her sketchbook under one arm, preparing to descend.

Mr. Kirby hesitated. "I wondered if I might steal a moment of your time while we are here. Alone."

A slight shiver stole over her skin. "I suppose one minute more couldn't hurt," she said, keeping her tone light. "But since Mama will despair over every new freckle on my face, I must insist we keep it brief."

"Understood." Mr. Kirby lumbered up onto the rock and sat beside her, resting his elbows on bent knees. "I confess I cannot stop thinking about the blackmail note. Now that I'm aware of the threat you are facing, I am having difficulty pretending that I am unaware."

"Then you must try harder," Fiona insisted. "The more you dwell on the matter, the more likely you are to inadvertently reveal my dilemma to others. And that would be disastrous."

"I know." He dragged a hand down his face in a tortured fashion. "I just feel like I should be helping you in some way. It doesn't seem right for you to face this on your own."

"I am not facing it on my own." Almost immediately, she wished she could take back the words. She wasn't ready to discuss Gray or the imminent announcement of their engagement yet.

"So, you have confided in someone else?"

"I meant that I have the support of my family," she improvised. "You needn't worry about me."

"You have decided to pay the scoundrel, then?"

Fiona quickly debated the pros and cons of telling Mr. Kirby her intentions. "I have." *There.* Perhaps now he would be able to put the whole affair out of his mind.

He nodded thoughtfully. "You are fortunate that your family can provide the money."

"Yes." She saw no need to elaborate on her plans. Or

reveal that she had no intention of asking her family for the money.

"It boils my blood to think that someone is capable of such depravity," he muttered.

"I beg you to forget about the whole thing. Surely the reason you are dwelling on it now it that we are constantly in each other's company. But the house party will be over in two more days, and then you will be able to put it behind you—as I hope to be able to do." She smiled and clutched her sketchbook to her chest, signaling the end of the conversation. "I do hope there's a sandwich left down there. I confess I'm famished."

"Of course you are," Mr. Kirby said, apologetic. "Allow me to carry your sketchbook down."

"Thank you." She handed him her drawing pad, tamping down the slight panic that threatened whenever she entrusted it to someone else.

"It's probably best if I go first and guide you from below, pointing out the best footholds and crevices to cling to."

"Very well." She waited as he easily swung his body off the side of the rock and made his way to the ground.

"Take your time," he said.

She crawled backward to the edge of the rock, cursing her skirts. Climbing would be exponentially easier if she were able to wear trousers. As it was, she had to worry about catching her foot in her hem *and* breaking her neck. *Grand.*

"You're doing fine," he called from below. "Move your bottom foot a bit to the right. There—that's it."

She might have been grateful for the encouragement if Mr. Kirby didn't sound as though he were speaking to a child. Clinging to the stone with a white-knuckled grip, she ventured a look at the ground. She'd made it halfway down the rock, which was heartening. If she should fall from this height, she *probably* wouldn't die. A broken bone or two certainly wasn't the worst thing that could happen to a person.

"You know, I think I can manage on my own from here," she called to Mr. Kirby. "I'd prefer it if you'd wait for me at the picnic blanket."

"Are you certain?" he asked doubtfully.

"Quite," she said through clenched teeth.

True, Fiona was borderline famous for falling on perfectly level ground, and the current situation was ripe for disaster. But if she took her time, there was no reason in the world she shouldn't be able to navigate the last few—

Out of nowhere, a horse whinnied and hooves beat the ground. "What the *devil* is going on here?" a deep voice demanded. Gray.

Fiona looked over her shoulder. He'd already dismounted and was rushing toward the rock, scowling. "Good afternoon, Lord Ravenport." She tried for a cheerful tone—as though it were perfectly normal to converse while clinging to a boulder.

"Don't move," he ordered. "I'm coming up there."

"There's no need. I only have a little . . . farther . . . *oh*. . . ." A wave of dizziness assaulted her. She groaned as her fingers slipped from the rock and she fell backward. *Blast.*

Chapter 20

Fiona's back slammed into a solid wall—or rather, Gray's chest. His arms wrapped around her waist, but he didn't completely break her fall. They both hit the ground with a sick, jarring thud. On impact, her teeth clattered and the breath rushed out of her body, leaving her choking and desperate for air.

"Fi!" Lily shouted, her voice frantic. Fiona's eyes fluttered open as her sister ran over and dropped to her knees beside her. "Can you hear me?"

She could. Only her mouth wouldn't form a response. She felt like she was underwater—unable to breathe and unable to scream for help. Panic rose up inside her and tears threatened.

Gray cradled her head in his lap and looked into her eyes. "Listen to me," he said calmly. "You are fine."

No, she really, truly wasn't. Her bonnet ties were choking her. She was suffocating, and she would have told him so, if she could make a sound. She turned in to him, clutching at his jacket, willing him to understand.

He held her shoulders and spoke as though only the two of them were there. "It feels like you can't inhale, right? And it hurts. I know . . . and I'm sorry." As though he'd read her mind, he loosened the ties of her bonnet and tugged it off her head. But she *still* couldn't take a breath. "Just listen to the sound of my voice. I'm going to begin counting, and before I reach ten, I promise you're going to start breathing normally.

Oh God. That seemed like an eternity. But she nodded, eager for him to begin.

"One. Two. Three. Close your eyes and inhale."

She squirmed, writhing in pain.

"Four. Five. Six. Try to relax."

Her eyes burned and her throat ached, but she nodded. And tried.

"Seven. Eight. *Breathe*," he said encouragingly—and she did.

But her whole body ached. She rolled onto her side, gasping and sputtering, sucking in air as fast as she could.

"That's it," he soothed. "You're going to be fine." But Fiona noticed a tinge of relief in his voice—as though perhaps he hadn't been as sure as he'd originally sounded.

"Good heavens." Lily squeezed her hand. "Fiona, you gave me such a fright! Where does it hurt?"

"Everywhere," she croaked.

"Poor dear. We must return you to the house and summon a doctor."

"No," Fiona protested. "Give me a moment. I don't think anything is broken."

"You landed awkwardly," Lily said.

"It wasn't . . . my most graceful moment."

"Forgive me," her sister pleaded. "I only meant that it looked as though you turned your ankle."

Without hesitating, Gray shifted down to her feet, loosened the laces of one boot, and checked her ankle, holding it securely while gently rotating her foot. "How does this feel?"

Fiona was glad her mother was not there to witness an

eligible bachelor caressing her leg, no matter how well-intentioned his actions. She shrugged. "It doesn't hurt."

Gray reached beneath her skirt for the other ankle and repeated—sending a jolt of pain up her leg.

"Owww," she whimpered.

"Probably a sprain. We'll have Dr. Hopewell from the village examine it."

Sophie stepped forward and handed her a glass of lemonade. "Drink," she ordered.

Fiona gulped down a few swallows to appease her friend.

"You must be parched after all the walking we did. And you haven't eaten anything either," Sophie chided.

"What?" Gray frowned. "Kirby, bring Miss Hartley a sandwich."

Oh, for the love of—"I don't require a sandwich." Well, she did, but she had no wish to eat it while everyone looked on. "I would like my sketchbook, though."

"Certainly," Mr. Kirby piped up. "Here you are." He handed the pad to her with a flourish, and Fiona relaxed a little as she clutched it to her chest.

"Thank you."

Gray grunted. If Fiona didn't know better, she might have suspected he was jealous—of her sketchbook. "You'll be returning to the Fortress on horseback," he said. "With me."

Excellent. And just when she thought she'd suffered all the humiliation she could stand for one afternoon. "I don't ride," she confessed. The few attempts she'd made at riding had ended with her covered in mud, bruises, or both.

"You will today," he said firmly. With that, he stood and carefully pulled her to her feet. Or foot, actually. The one that wasn't throbbing and puffing up like a popover muffin.

"I don't wish to be difficult," she said. "It's just that after falling once this afternoon, I'm not eager to repeat the experience."

Gray wrapped an arm securely around her waist and leaned close to her ear. "You cannot walk back to the house, and I cannot carry you the entire way."

"What about a wagon?" she asked, desperate.

"The hill is too steep. Horseback is safer—trust me. We'll go slowly. I won't let anything happen to you."

She wanted to believe Gray. She *did*. Even if he underestimated the likelihood of calamity striking when she was near. "Very well."

The words had barely left her mouth before he scooped her into his arms, stalked over to his horse, and deposited her in the saddle. For the second time that day, she found the ground was much too far away for her liking. She clung to the horn of the saddle with one hand and held her sketchbook with the other, praying she didn't slide off before they even started moving.

But a moment later, Gray stepped onto the stirrup, slung a leg over the horse, and settled himself behind her. His torso was a hard and solid buffer, and the arm he wrapped around her waist made her feel wonderfully safe.

"Fiona, this is Mercutio. Mercutio—Fiona."

"Wait. You, the infamous naysayer of poetry, named your horse after a Shakespearean character?"

"I cannot help it if the name suits him." Gray clucked his tongue twice, and Mercutio began ambling down the hill.

Gray refrained from speaking for the first several minutes of their ride—because he didn't want to say anything he'd regret.

Two things had raised his ire when he arrived at the picnic spot. First, Fiona had placed herself in peril. And when he imagined what danger could have befallen her, he went a little mad.

Second, Kirby had been directly beneath her—as if he'd been up on the rock with her. As if *he* were going to be the one to save her. And he'd also been holding her sketchbook, which made Gray wonder if Fiona had been sketching his best friend.

The worst part was, Gray knew damn well he had no right to be angry with Fiona—on either count. She was a grown woman, and if she wanted to risk life and limb climbing a godforsaken rock, that was her prerogative. And if she wanted to sketch Kirby, Gray had no valid reason to object. Hell, he should be glad that Kirby and Fiona seemed to get on so well. Kirby was his best friend, and she was going to be his . . . his wife.

Of course, the plan had been for them to have a marriage that was uncomplicated and civil. Perhaps more than just in name, but certainly less than a love match.

Because Gray couldn't promise anything more. And he had to make Fiona understand that before she entered into a union that was destined to be a disappointment.

But it was difficult to remember the precise terms of their agreement while she was leaning into his chest and resting her head on his shoulder. When they'd begun riding down the hill, she was coiled tight as a spring, but now her body melted into his. Even through her skirts and his trousers, he could feel her lithe legs brushing against his thighs. The citrusy scent of her hair tickled his nose, and the even rhythm of her breathing soothed his frayed nerves.

She ventured a glance at him—almost as though she

suspected he'd be in a foul mood. He supposed he couldn't blame her. "Thank you," she said.

"I wish I'd been able to stop you from falling."

She laughed at that. "You might as well try to stop a hen from pecking. Or a bull from charging. Shall I go on?"

"No, I understand." He felt his face crack into a smile. "But I wish I'd been able to spare you the pain at least."

"You helped me more than you realize. I was completely panicked. Convinced I'd taken my last breath. And you made me believe that I would be all right. So . . . thank you," she repeated.

He held her a little closer and nuzzled the top of her head. "You are most welcome. But I must insist on sending for the doctor when we arrive at the Fortress."

In response, she heaved a deep sigh. "Very well."

Inclining his head toward the sketchbook, he asked, "Did you draw someone's portrait today?"

"Hmm? Oh no. That is, I was drawing, but not a portrait. Would you like to see?"

"Certainly." But as she started to flip open her pad, he said, "Wait. Let me steer Mercutio into the shade so I can have a proper look."

Once they were out of the sun, she swiveled toward him and offered him her open sketchbook. "What do you think?"

Gray blinked at the scene on the paper, then closed his eyes, letting waves of memories crash over him.

Summers when he and Kirby had pretended the rock was their pirate ship.

The day after his father died, when Gray had gone there to escape the house and the smell of death.

And most recently, the evening when he'd taken Helena there, intent on showing her the moon suspended in the sky and stars twinkling over the valley. But instead of seeing the beauty of it all, she'd turned to him and told him their engagement was off.

"You don't like it," Fiona said, sounding crestfallen.

He opened his eyes and shook his head. "That's not true. I love everything about it." He examined it more closely, noticing a tiny bird's nest in a tree, a warm orange glow in the valley, and the perfect harmony of it all. On the horizon, the silhouette of the Fortress stood proudly. None of the cracks or imperfections were visible from Fiona's perspective. She saw its grandeur—and everything it could be.

She had captured his estate from the best possible angle. But it wasn't because she wished to flatter him or literally paint a rosy picture. She'd drawn it that way because that's how she saw it.

"I'm glad you like it," she said, her relief obvious. "I made it for the countess. But if you would like, I could draw another for you."

"You made this for my grandmother?"

"Yes. I know how much she loves this place, and . . ." She blew out a long breath before continuing. "She told me about her condition and how she's losing her sight. I'm so sorry, Gray."

"She told you?" he asked, stunned. "She's very private. I didn't think she'd mentioned it to anyone."

"We had a moment alone on the day we went shopping in the village. She is an amazing woman."

"Yes, she is."

"When I climbed the rock this morning and saw the glorious view, I knew she would love it. And since she cannot climb up the rock—although I daresay she might have fared better than I did—I thought I could bring the view to her. Perhaps it will give her some comfort."

"She will adore it." And she'd adore Fiona for thinking of it. Truth was, he suspected Fiona had already wriggled her way into his grandmother's heart.

And if he wasn't careful, she'd wriggle her way into his as well.

She held the drawing at arm's length and tilted her head as though examining it with a critical eye. "I shall have it framed when we return to London and present it to the countess as soon as it's ready."

Before he could stop himself, he cradled her face in his hands. "That's the nicest gift anyone's ever given me."

Her cheeks pinkened. "Forgive me, but did you miss the part where I mentioned it's for your grandmother?"

"No. That's why it's the best gift. Nothing makes me happier than seeing my grandmother happy."

Nodding, she smiled. "She said as much."

"She wants me to take you to the river. Row you around in the boat."

"Do *you* want to take me there?"

"Yes." More than he should. And not just to please his grandmother. Now that he and Fiona had lain together, he couldn't stop thinking about her. No amount of sawing, hammering, or mindless labor could make him forget the taste of her lips or the feel of her skin. He wanted her again.

"The river sounds lovely, but we haven't much time left before we return to town. Tomorrow's our last free day. Papa arrives Saturday, and we'll all be preparing for the ball that evening."

"Then we will go to the river tomorrow—assuming the doctor permits you to leave your bed." He would show her the swimming hole where he and Kirby used to splash and play, naked as the day they were born. He'd show her the rope swing suspended from the sturdy branch of an elm on the water's edge—the one that could launch you to the deepest part of the river or deposit you ruthlessly in the mud. He'd show Fiona the bright spot in his childhood. Perhaps the only one.

"Tomorrow," she repeated. "I shall look forward to it. Though I doubt Mama will allow me to go without Lily or Mary—my maid." Her beautiful eyes glowed with regret.

"I wouldn't dream of whisking you away without a proper chaperone." Chuckling, he corrected himself. "Actually, I *would* if I thought I could get away with it." His mind was already devising a plan to steal her away for a few moments. "At the risk of stating the obvious, we are lacking a chaperone right now."

"I confess that fact did not escape me," she said in a slightly husky tone that set his blood on fire. She dropped her gaze to his mouth and leaned in, till no more than an inch separated their lips. "Aren't you going to kiss me?"

With a growl, he covered her mouth with his. He slid a hand over her bottom, pulling her closer. Her free hand wound around his neck, and her tongue tangled with his. God, he'd missed her. And this taste only made him want her more.

When he'd seen her dangling from the rock, his heart had raced with a potent combination of panic and fear.

But now his heart raced for an entirely different reason. Fiona was talented and thoughtful and beautiful beyond measure . . . and she seemed to want him. Not just for his title, but for *him*.

Maybe the idea of them marrying wasn't so mad after all. He might enjoy making her happy. And just being with her made his damned days a little brighter.

He wanted to pull her onto his lap and slide a hand beneath her skirts, but a rational voice in the corner of his mind whispered that she was injured and that he was supposed to be taking her home and summoning the doctor.

Not seducing her on the back of a horse.

Damn it all to hell.

Beneath them, Mercutio shifted and whinnied, causing Fiona to clutch at Gray's jacket. "I have you," he assured her while tightening his grasp on the reins. "But I think Mercutio is telling me that I should take you home."

She sighed petulantly. "He fancies himself a chaperone?"

"He wants to take care of you. As do I."

"Then I suppose I cannot be cross with him," she said with a smile.

Gray made sure she was secure in the saddle before he steered the horse back onto the path. Tomorrow at the river they'd have time to discuss their plans . . . and their future.

For now, he would savor the chance to hold her close and imagine that this feeling of contentment might not be as fleeting as he feared.

Chapter 21

On the Secret to Capturing a Gentleman's Attention

From time to time, Miss Haywinkle would pause in the middle of a lesson and send the younger girls to the dormitories. She'd proceed to share a bit of information that might prove useful to those of us on the brink of entering the marriage mart. Lily, Sophie, and I would eagerly await the nuggets of wisdom that would surely spill forth from Miss H.'s lips.

On one such occasion, she bid us to gather closely, as she refused to utter the words in a voice louder than a whisper. "Gentlemen have a great number of responsibilities and can be frightfully busy," she said. "And that is why, as resourceful young ladies, you may sometimes be forced to employ . . . unusual methods in order to be noticed."

"Applying lip rouge?" Lily asked, most serious.

Miss H. pressed a hand to her chest, aghast. "Heavens no, Miss Hartley—not unless you wish to be mistaken for a lightskirt."

"Please go on," Sophie begged the headmistress.

"Well," Miss H. said dramatically, "one particularly effective method involves wearing high-heeled boots while walking on wet or uneven ground . . . so that you may fall.

If all goes as planned, you will successfully turn your ankle."

When Miss H. noted the confusion on our faces, she elaborated. *"A gentleman likes to feel useful, you see. If you turn an ankle, you give him the opportunity to rescue you. To be a veritable knight in shining armor."*

"But a turned ankle is painful." I felt compelled to point this out, having experienced more than my fair share. "It also prevents one from dancing and walking. And it looks ghastly. Last time I turned my ankle, it swelled to the size of a grapefruit."

"A grapefruit, indeed. Sometimes I despair of you girls ever finding husbands," Miss H. muttered to herself.

Later that night, as Lily, Sophie, and I lay in our beds, we resolved never to do anything so daft as intentionally spraining an ankle.

We also vowed to procure a pot of lip rouge at the first opportunity.

"It's only a minor sprain." Dr. Hopewell smiled as he snapped his bag closed. "If your ankle hurts or becomes noticeably swollen, stay in bed. Otherwise, I see no reason you shouldn't enjoy the rest of your stay here."

"Thank you," Fiona replied, immensely relieved. She'd had no intention of spending the last few days of the house party cloistered in her bedchamber, regardless of the good doctor's orders, but now she could enjoy herself without feeling guilty.

"I spoke to Lord Ravenport on my way up. He seemed very concerned about you."

"Then I will be sure to put his mind at ease," she replied. Her chest warmed at the thought of Gray fretting over her. He claimed to be cold and unfeeling, but perhaps he was changing. She liked to think so.

The doctor made a perfunctory bow and headed toward the door—just as Lily and Sophie burst into the room.

"Please don't say you've broken your leg!" Lily cried.

"Nothing so dire," Dr. Hopewell assured her. "But I shall leave it to my patient to explain. Good day, ladies."

Sophie and Lily rushed to Fiona's bedside. Her sister grabbed her by the shoulders and looked her up and down as though making sure she was still intact. "You didn't fall off the horse?" Lily asked.

"No. I managed to make it all the way from our picnic spot to my bedchamber without ever touching the ground— with Lord Ravenport's help."

Lily's eyes went wide. "Wait. The earl *carried* you to your bed?"

Fiona flushed at the memory but attempted a breezy tone. "Yes."

Clearly uncomfortable with the talk of earls and beds, Sophie cleared her throat. "We've been so worried about you, Fi. How are you feeling?"

"Wonderful." Fiona grinned. "Never better. Dr. Hopewell says it's a little sprain—nothing to be concerned about. I've no restrictions whatsoever."

"Thank heaven!" Sophie exclaimed.

But Lily frowned. "Oh dear."

Fiona chuckled and poked her sister in the arm. "It troubles you that I'm not injured?"

"Mama is going to be disappointed. You know how she adores a bit of drama. When we left her in the drawing room just now, she was beside herself—pacing, crying, and waving her handkerchief about."

"Oh no." Fiona threw off the covers and sat upright. "I'll go to her at once and inform her I'm fine."

"No, no." Lily pushed her back onto the mattress. "If you walk in there as though nothing is wrong, you'll spoil all her fun."

"But nothing *is* wrong," Fiona pointed out.

"Come now. Surely *something* is wrong," Lily cajoled. "A bruise, a bump . . . a scratch?" she asked hopefully.

Fiona considered this a moment. "I *am* rather famished."

Sophie leaped to her feet. "I'll ask for a tray to be sent up."

Lily tapped a finger against her chin. "Yes, that's good. We'll say that nothing is broken, but you're too weak and sore to move. That should make Mama happy."

"But Gray and I—that is, the earl and I have plans to go to the river tomorrow. If Mama thinks I'm unwell, she'll never allow me to go." Fiona shot Sophie a pleading look.

"Perhaps we can say that you're rather tired after today's excitement, but that you expect a good night's rest will restore you," Sophie suggested.

"Perfect." Fiona could always count on Sophie.

Lily propped her hands on her hips and arched a dark brow. "*Gray* invited you to the river, did he?"

"Don't make it sound so scandalous. Mary shall accompany me. You both may come, too, if you like."

Sophie frowned. "I don't know—"

"We'd love to!" Lily piped up. "And we really should be there. Somehow, you've managed to survive climbing rocks and riding a horse. We cannot anticipate that boating will go as smoothly."

A knock at the door startled all three of them.

"Your mother?" Sophie asked.

"No," Fiona and Lily said in unison. Mama never knocked.

"Come in," Fiona called.

A maid pushed open the door and rolled an elegant tea cart across the worn Aubusson carpet. "The earl instructed us to bring up a late luncheon for you, Miss Hartley. There's tea, sandwiches, fruit, and a variety of sweets. Just ring if you'd like anything else." She bobbed her capped head politely before leaving.

"How thoughtful," Sophie said with a sigh.

One look at the food made Fiona's stomach growl. "Am I permitted to leave my bed in order to eat?" she asked dryly.

"Stay there," Lily ordered. "I'll prepare a plate for you."

"And I shall go to the drawing room to inform everyone that you are expected to make a full recovery." Casting a glance at Lily, Sophie added, "After sufficient rest and pampering."

"Wait," Fiona said. "I meant to ask—how did the two of you enjoy the picnic?"

Lily grinned. "Soph spent a great deal of time conversing with Mr. Kirby."

Sophie shrugged shyly. "He's very charming, is he not?"

"He is," Fiona agreed. "Perhaps he could join us at the river tomorrow, too."

"Would it be forward of me to suggest it?" Sophie asked, worried.

"Of course not," Fiona said—even though she wasn't at all certain of the etiquette in these matters. "If you see him in the drawing room, be sure to mention it."

Sophie's eyes sparkled as she left the bedchamber, and once she was out of earshot Lily remarked, "As much as I like Mr. Kirby, I'm not certain he's the right match for our Soph."

"Why not?" Fiona took the plate her sister offered and bit into a chicken sandwich that tasted like a slice of heaven.

"I can't quite put my finger on the reason. I simply feel she deserves better."

Fiona considered this, then asked, "Have you changed your opinion of Lord Ravenport?"

Lily popped a grape into her mouth and tilted her head. "I saw a side of him today that I had not seen before. When you fell from the rock, he was frantic—every bit as worried as I was. And afterward he was attentive and kind and . . . gallant."

"I'm glad you think so," Fiona mused. "Because I'm going to marry him."

Lily coughed, nearly choking on the grape. "The earl has proposed?"

"If all goes well, we will announce our engagement before we return to London," Fiona said, rather proud of herself for deftly dodging her sister's question.

The color drained from Lily's face, and she slowly sank onto the bed beside Fiona. "You . . . engaged? That is, I knew it was only a matter of time, but I confess I'm not quite prepared to share you yet."

Her sister's tearful expression erased any smidgen of doubt Fiona might have harbored about marrying Gray and using her dowry money to pay off the blackmailer. If there was one person in the entire world whom Fiona could rely on, that person was Lily.

And Fiona couldn't let her sister's chance for a happy future be destroyed by scandal.

"You are my sister," Fiona said, squeezing her hand. "And I love you dearly. Nothing on this earth could weaken the bond between us."

"Not even a dashing new husband who happens to be an earl?" Lily whimpered.

Fiona set down her plate and gave her sister a proper hug. "Don't be daft. I'll need you more than ever. I've no idea how a countess is supposed to behave."

"Just follow your heart, like you always have. You won't go wrong. And promise me that you won't change too much."

"I promise." Fiona planted a kiss on the top of her sister's head.

"Have you been writing in your journal?" Lily asked. "Because one day, I shall demand to know all the juicy details of this courtship."

"I've been making a few notes," Fiona said vaguely. "One day, *many* years from now, when we're old and gray, we'll swap stories and laugh at how naïve we were."

"I hope I have some stories of my own to tell." Lily sniffled into Fiona's shoulder.

"You *shall*. I daresay, your stories will be the best."

"I understand you're taking Miss Fiona Hartley to the river today." Gray's grandmother smiled at him over the rim of her teacup. "It is a rare and gratifying thing when you heed my advice."

She and Gray had the entire breakfast buffet to themselves. He shoveled a forkful of egg into his mouth and washed it down with a swallow of scalding coffee. "Stubbornness is a trait I inherited from you. But I always listen to your advice—and value it."

"Then indulge me by allowing me to give you one piece more." She reached across the corner of the table and affectionately squeezed his forearm. "Talk to Fiona. Tell her what transpired here. Trust her to understand."

His fork froze halfway to his mouth, and he slowly lowered the utensil onto his plate. "What makes you so sure I can trust her?" He'd intended for the question to sound casual, but the hitch in his voice betrayed his doubts about her feelings—and his doubts about himself.

"My dear boy," she said softly. "Some young ladies have lived such sheltered lives that any bit of unpleasantness sends them fleeing for the hills."

"Like Helena." It was more a statement than a question.

His grandmother made a face as though her tea were bitter. "Precisely."

"And you think Fiona's different?"

"I *know* she is. And you know it, too. She's faced trials and tribulations of her own, but despite those hardships, her sweet and generous nature has endured. She's made of stronger stuff than Helena . . . but do you want to know the real reason I adore her?"

He nodded mutely.

"Because there's a softness in your eyes when you look at her. A tenderness I haven't seen there since you were a boy. She brings out a side of you that has been buried for too long."

"I have responsibilities now," he said with a shrug. "There's little time for frolicking in the fields and swimming in the river."

"You have time for both the work *and* the fun," she said, somber. "Take the advice of someone who now treasures every glimpse of blue sky and every fiery red sunset. Frolicking is good for your soul, and you're *never* too old for it."

Gray took her hand and pressed a kiss to the back of it. "Not long ago, Kirby told me the same thing—only much less eloquently. I believe he cautioned me about turning into a tedious ass."

"Ah, well," his grandmother said diplomatically, "that's because Kirby specializes in frolicking."

"Did someone take my name in vain?" Kirby strode into the dining room, a wide grin splitting his face. "Never mind, I don't want to know." He plucked an apple from the fruit bowl on the sideboard and bit into it with gusto. "What time do we depart for the river today?"

Gray arched a brow. "Who told you I was going to the river?"

"Miss Kendall invited me last night. Pentham and Carter, too. Do you think we can persuade the ladies to go wading?"

Wonderful. Apparently, half the bloody world was going to accompany him and Fiona to the river.

But he'd find a way to talk with her . . . and perhaps steal her away for a few moments.

Gray snorted. "If anyone can persuade the ladies to shed their slippers, squish their toes in the mud, and generally ignore rules of propriety, it's you, my friend."

Kirby smoothed the lapels of his jacket and grinned, inordinately pleased. "Why, thank you."

"I have some work to do before we go to the river, so excuse me. I shall see you both later." Gray rose and pecked his grandmother on the cheek before heading to his study.

In two days, the house party would be over, and, if he was honest with himself, he wanted to savor every moment he could with Fiona. The irony of the situation didn't escape him—after all, the whole purpose of hosting the house party had been to drive her away.

Instead, he was on the brink of asking her father for her hand in marriage—and, for once in his life, feeling wholly, uncharacteristically, inexplicably . . . optimistic.

Chapter 22

On Being Carried to Bed

If, by some chance, my dear, darling sister, Lily, were ever to snoop through my personal effects, discover my journal, and flip through these intensely private pages, I have no doubt the title of this particular entry would catch her eye and cause her to begin reading precisely here.

But despite the admittedly salacious-sounding heading, my sister is destined to be disappointed (at least in this instance), for I am pleased to report that Lord R. was a perfect gentleman. Given the circumstances, he could not have behaved more decorously.

I shall happily elaborate.

You see, I had turned my ankle and was not yet aware of the extent of my injuries. The earl insisted on carrying me up the front steps of the house and two flights of stairs to my bedchamber, where I was to await the doctor.

Despite the considerable effort this must have taken, Lord R. never complained or displayed any obvious signs of exertion—besides the somewhat accelerated rise and fall of his chest. An exceedingly hard, well-muscled chest, which I only observed because of the necessary and not at all untoward contact of our bodies.

For the sake of clarity, I should explain that my right side was pressed against his chest. With every step he took, my hip bounced lightly against his taut abdomen. The neckline of my gown, while not immodest, revealed a bit more than was seemly—but I daresay the earl did not mind. He wrapped one strong arm around my back and the other beneath my bottom. Some might consider this scandalous; however, in a medical emergency, one does what one must.

I confess that his lips were quite close to my ear, and I could feel his breath upon my cheek. And as he angled me through the door and crossed the threshold of my bedchamber, he stared at my mouth.

But then he gently, tenderly, laid me on top of the counterpane. There may have been a second or two when he seemed oddly reluctant to let go of me. Or a moment when his eyes went dark with desire. I might have briefly imagined circling a hand around his neck and pulling his mouth to mine for a kiss.

But, alas, nothing of the sort happened.

Why, then, am I so disappointed?

Prior to that afternoon, Fiona had never ridden in the back of a wagon. Mama probably would have been horrified at the thought of riding in a conveyance that was also routinely used to transport hens, sheep, and even—heaven forfend—pigs.

But Gray had ensured that the bed of the wagon was clean and the sides were sturdy. He'd fashioned low benches lengthwise along the sides using bags of grain that he'd covered with quilts.

Fiona and Lily sat across from Sophie and Mary, and each time the wagon rumbled over a bump in the road or dipped in and out of a rut, they all clutched the wooden slats behind them and laughed with glee.

Mr. Kirby drove the wagon, and Lord Carter sat beside him, while Gray and Lord Pentham flanked the wagon on horseback. Fiona supposed they were there to make sure no one fell out—or at least to scoop up anyone who did.

When they all arrived at the riverbank, Gray and Lord Pentham dismounted and helped each of the women hop off the back of the wagon. When it was Fiona's turn to alight, Lord Pentham happened to be closest to her, but Gray shouldered his way in front. He circled his hands around her waist, helping her float to the ground with miraculous grace.

Gray craned his head to look behind her, in the wagon. "Where is your sketchbook?" he asked.

"I left it in my bedchamber," she said.

"Ah. You don't want to risk it getting wet. I don't blame you."

The mere thought of her sketchbook falling into the water made her shudder, but that wasn't the only reason she'd left it at the Fortress. "I didn't want to be distracted today," she admitted. "Or encumbered by pencils and pastels."

His smile made her belly flip. "How does your ankle feel?" he asked.

"Much better. I'm afraid the only thing I bruised yesterday was my pride."

"That's too bad." His forehead creased. "I don't suppose you could pretend your ankle was still sore?"

"Why would I do that?"

"Just play along," he whispered.

Addressing the entire party, Gray said, "I'm pleased to

have you all here today. Kirby and I spent the bulk of our childhood here on the banks of this river—"

"And a good portion *in* it," Mr. Kirby interjected.

Gray nodded as if to concede the point. "We are eager to show you its humble entertainments. We would encourage you to relax, explore, and enjoy to your hearts' content. To that end, Kirby has agreed to lead a walk along the river, pointing out some of our favorite spots. Meanwhile, I shall escort Miss Hartley in the rowboat—to spare her tender ankle."

Mary was at Fiona's side in an instant. "I shall accompany you, miss."

Gray winced. "It's a very small boat." He pointed at the tiny vessel behind him, which did not look entirely seaworthy in Fiona's inexpert opinion. "Besides," he continued, "it would be difficult for me to row and maneuver the boat with two passengers."

The maid bit her lip. "I'm supposed to be acting as Miss Hartley's chaperone."

"And so you shall," Gray said soothingly. "From the shore. We won't be far away. And while your commitment to your duties is to be commended, I do hope that you will enjoy yourself during this outing, too."

Mary blushed at the compliment. "Very well."

Fiona rolled her eyes. That was ridiculously easy. All it had taken was a smidgen of charm from the earl.

The maid offered Fiona her parasol. "You'll be wanting this."

"Thank you, Mary, but I shall be fine without it."

The maid looked skeptical but did not object. "Please be careful. Especially since you're not able to . . . that is, since you don't . . ."

The earl turned to Fiona and arched a brow. "You don't swim?"

"Perhaps it's escaped your notice, but I'm not the most coordinated of creatures."

"Well then," he said, nonchalant. "I shall do my best to keep you from falling overboard."

Mary let out a chirp of dismay. "Miss Fiona has already endured one fall, and that gown . . ." She gestured toward the pink silk. "One plunge into the river water and it would be ruined."

Fiona snorted indelicately. "I've no intention of leaving the boat. Shall we be on our way?"

Gray smiled and held her arm firmly as he helped her down a steep embankment toward a narrow strip of beach. The boat sat lopsided on the shore, half in the water and half out.

"I normally keep the boat tied to the pier in the summer, but last time I walked to the end of the dock I found that several of the boards had rotted, and I didn't want to risk you falling through," he admitted.

"How very thoughtful," she said wryly. "However, suddenly I find myself less concerned with the structural soundness of the pier and more concerned with the fitness of this little gondola of yours."

"It's a rowboat."

She cast a critical eye over the peeling paint inside and outside of the boat. Some of the weathered wood looked rather suspect. "I assume you've carefully inspected the boards that comprise this . . . this wherry?"

"I have."

She swallowed. "And there aren't any rotted planks or other defects that we should worry about?"

"The hull is watertight," he assured her. "The only way your slippers would become wet is if a wave splashed over the side. Or if the boat capsized."

"Wonderful," Fiona announced. "The fate of my

favorite pair of slippers depends on your ability to keep us afloat."

Before she'd even finished her sentence, Gray easily lifted her by the waist and hoisted her over the side of the boat. She stood between two narrow benches and peered over the water side warily. The boat lurched a little as Gray released her, and she wondered if it was possible to be seasick while the boat still rested on the sand.

"Sit on that bench," Gray said smoothly. "I placed a cushion there to make you comfortable—and to spare your dress."

"Thank you." She cautiously sat and clutched both sides of the boat while he gave it a shove and waded into the water behind it. "Your boots!" she exclaimed.

"They're old." Bracing both arms on the stern, he nimbly pulled himself out of the water and deposited himself on the bench opposite her—rocking the boat like a diabolical cradle.

Fiona shrieked and held on for dear life.

The crowd on the shore gasped and craned their necks as though they feared she'd plopped headfirst into the water.

Gray leaned close and placed a soothing hand over her white knuckles. "Easy. We'll stop rocking soon, and as long as you don't try to stand, it will be a smooth ride from here on out. Promise."

She barked a laugh. "Rest assured, the last thing I want to do is risk standing on this primitive . . . dinghy."

"Rowboat." He grinned and picked up an oar from the floor as if making his point. "Try to enjoy yourself, Fiona. I'll do the work. All you must do is sit back and enjoy the fresh air, the view—and the excellent company."

She let out a long breath and slowly raised her head to

gaze at the shore where Lily and Sophie waved enthusiastically. "Be careful!" Lily called out. "And have fun."

Fiona would have waved back if it didn't require her to let go of the side of the boat. So instead, she simply shouted back, "I will!"

Slowly, her grip relaxed. Her heartbeat returned to normal. And she had to admit that she was already enjoying the view—not of the lush trees and wildflowers along the shore, but of the handsome man who sat across from her. The sun glinted off his dark hair, and a light breeze rustled the wayward strands that spilled across his forehead. His long, muscular legs were sprawled on either side of her hers, and even through his buckskin trousers, she could observe the subtle flexing of his thighs when he shifted positions. The fine wool of his jacket stretched tightly across his shoulders each time he pulled the oars through the water.

His powerful, effortless strokes mesmerized her. Truly. She would have been content to sit there and stare at him rowing, even if he steered the boat right off the edge of a waterfall.

She'd always found him attractive, but today he was different. Almost irresistible.

She tried to put her finger on what had changed. Perhaps it was his uncharacteristically carefree smile or his charming manner. The tight lines around his mouth had vanished, and the scowl he usually wore hadn't surfaced all morning. He seemed a decade younger, and whatever had wrought the change, Fiona welcomed it.

This relaxed version of Gray would make broaching the subject of the blackmail note with him—which she *would* do today—a bit easier. She waited until he had steered the boat to the middle of the river and the laughter of the people onshore blended with the gentle lapping of water against the hull and the croaks of toads in the distance.

"I'm glad to have a few moments alone with you," she began.

"Oh?" He arched a brow, as though thoroughly intrigued. "What do you have in mind, siren?"

Her cheeks flushed. "Nothing like that."

"Are you certain?"

"Yes," she lied. Heaven help her, she wasn't certain of anything when he spoke in that wickedly seductive manner.

"How disappointing." His heavy-lidded stare made her skin tingle deliciously.

Pretending to be immune to his charms, she said, "I wanted to talk with you."

He rested the handles of the oars across his lap. "I wanted to talk with you, too. You first, though."

Fiona had rehearsed the words she'd planned to say earlier that morning—and couldn't recall any of them now. But it didn't matter. All she had to do was tell Gray the truth. Despite all his usual brooding and gruffness, he was a reasonable person. He would understand.

She gulped past the knot lodged in her throat. "Do you recall the letter I sent when I proposed to you?"

"Vaguely," he teased.

"And after you read it, you pressed me to tell you the reasons I wanted to marry you."

Gray went very still, and his expression turned somber. "Yes."

"And do you remember the reasons I gave you?"

"I believe you mentioned my title," he said dryly. "And wanting access to your marriage portion as well as a measure of independence." He scratched the back of his neck. "What's all this about?"

"I did my best to answer truthfully at the time, but I barely knew you then."

"So those weren't the real reasons you proposed marriage?"

"No, they were." She swallowed nervously. "They *are*. But there's another, very specific reason that I didn't mention before."

Wariness and, perhaps, disappointment flickered in his eyes. "I'm listening."

"A few weeks ago, I received a blackmail note. Someone—I don't know who—is threatening to expose a scandal regarding a member of my family unless I pay them a substantial amount of money."

For several moments, he sat staring at her, his expression grim, and she began to wonder if he'd heard her.

"So you intend to pay off the blackmailer with your dowry money? Jesus, Fiona. You should have told me."

"I know. I wanted to. At first, I thought I should handle it on my own—that the fewer people who knew about it, the better. But then I realized that if the scandal became widely known, your reputation would suffer, too—because of your association with my family. It wasn't fair to keep you in the dark about it."

"That's not why I'm angry." He dragged his hands down the sides of his face. "You should have told me so that I could find the fiend who's threatening you. We've been wasting precious time here at a bloody house party while the villain is likely plotting his next move in London."

Fiona bit her lip. She hadn't anticipated Gray's reaction. And though it warmed her heart to know he was ready to slay an evil dragon on her behalf, something else he said niggled at her. "Do you truly think the house party has been a waste of time?" She recalled kissing him in the garden, sketching him in the library, and making love to him in the cottage. It had been the most glorious, enlightening, and exciting week of her life.

And Gray had called it a waste.

"You've been focused on securing a husband—namely, me—when we should have poured all our efforts into identifying and stopping the blackmailer. Then you wouldn't have had to marry me at all."

Oh God. She should have seen this coming. Now that Gray knew the sordid details—well, some of them—he was having second thoughts about marrying her. Her belly dropped, and her skin turned clammy. "I suppose that's true, but I . . . that is, I . . ." She groaned.

"Fiona?" He dropped to his knees in front of her and held her cheeks in his palms, forcing her to look at him. "What's wrong?"

"If you don't wish to marry me, I understand," she choked out. She couldn't bear it if he resented her for the rest of their lives. "I'll find another way to deal with the blackmailer—and protect my family."

"It's too late for that," he growled. "You gave yourself to me. If you think I'm going to let you marry someone else, you must be mad."

Chapter 23

Gray swore under his breath. Jesus, he was making a mess of things. Everything he said was coming out wrong. Had he really just forbidden her to marry anyone else?

Fiona swiped at a tear that trickled down her cheek. "I don't *want* to marry someone else."

Gray sat back on his heels and took a deep breath. "But you would if you had to?"

"I will do what I must to protect my family's name."

"Even if it means binding yourself to someone you don't love." Hell, he wasn't sure what had made him say that. He was the last person on earth who should be spouting lectures on the importance of love. "What, exactly, did the blackmailer threaten to reveal?"

She raised her chin and looked into his eyes. "I would rather not say."

He flinched. "It must be quite scandalous if you're willing to sacrifice your happiness to keep the information secret."

"As I said, I will do what I must."

"A few days from now, we will be married. And yet you won't confide in me. Why not?" He already knew the answer but wanted to hear her say it aloud—if only to confirm that he wasn't the only one who had a difficult time with trust.

"Because it's not my story to tell." She paused, then added, "A few days ago, your grandmother told me the same thing—in a very different context. The point is, if the secret was about me, I'd be at liberty to share it with whomever I pleased—and I *would* tell you. But it's not about me."

Interesting.

"Lily?" he guessed.

Her shoulders slumped. "Yes. But you must believe me when I say she is *completely* innocent of wrongdoing. The potential scandal is not of her making . . . but it would almost certainly result in her downfall."

Gray considered this as he paddled around a fallen tree and they floated farther down the river. "And yet *you* are the one being blackmailed?"

"Yes." She hesitated briefly. "Though the salacious information concerns Lily, she is entirely unaware of the facts and circumstances—which she would no doubt find devastating. The blackmailer must have known I would go to great lengths to spare my sister from both the public humiliation and personal anguish this knowledge would cause her."

He respected what Fiona had said, and yet he couldn't help wanting to protect *her*.

Couldn't help wanting to throttle the villain who would threaten her family.

"I won't press you to reveal the information about Lily, but perhaps you could tell me the particulars about the blackmail itself—how much the blackmailer is demanding and when and where he expects to collect payment. I'd like to see a sample of the handwriting and whatever parts of the letter you can share—to examine it for any potential clues as to the blackmailer's identity."

"I've received two notes. I suppose I could show parts of them to you." She worried her bottom lip. "But you should know that I've made up my mind. Even if we were to discover who he is, I intend to pay him for his silence."

Gray could think of other, more effective, ways of silencing a man but kept them to himself. "Are you certain the claim he's made is true?"

"He has physical proof—evidence I was able to independently verify."

He nodded. His grandmother was right. Fiona was smart *and* strong. Not to mention strikingly beautiful.

"I'm glad you told me about this." He reached out and brushed his thumb across the satin skin of her cheek. "I admire you for wanting to protect your sister, and I will help you. But most of all, I intend to protect you. I don't want you meeting shady characters in seedy alleys or placing yourself in peril. If something happened to you . . ." He couldn't bring himself to finish the sentence.

"Thank you for understanding—and caring," she said. "But nothing will happen to me."

As he slowly dragged his thumb across her lips, she captured the tip of it in her mouth and teased him with a kiss that was warm, wet . . . and arousing as hell.

Shit. If they'd been anywhere besides a rickety boat, he'd have pulled her onto the ground and kissed her till she moaned with desire. Pleasured her until she cried out in bliss. A rowboat was hardly the ideal place for seduction . . .

But Gray had never been one to shy away from a challenge.

He set his oars down and shrugged off his jacket. "Forgive me—it's easier to row without this."

"I don't mind. In fact, I think I might find it easier to enjoy the view without my bonnet." Deliberately, she tugged on the ribbons beneath her chin, slowly slid her fingers down the lengths of silk, and removed the straw hat, revealing a glorious mass of auburn curls pinned at her crown.

"That is an improvement," he agreed. "But I confess you are too far away for my liking."

"I recall you giving me strict orders not to move from this bench," she countered.

"As captain of this vessel, I am constantly assessing the conditions and deem it safe for you to join me"—he sat on the floor of the boat between the benches—"here."

She shot a skeptical glance at the small space. "Where would I . . . that is, how would I . . . ?"

"Remember how you sat against me while we rode Mercutio?" He spread his jacket in front of him and grinned.

Her eyes widened. "Oh." A telltale blush spread over her cheeks and down her neck. "Are you certain that's wise?"

"No one's around. And I miss you."

A shy smile played about her lips. "I miss you, too. Promise me that this won't result in mayhem?"

"Such as?"

"Oh, I don't know." She waved her arms, exasperated. "Running aground? Drifting into enemy waters? Encountering pirates?"

"Promise." In one swift move, he pulled her down and turned her around so that she sat between his thighs, her back pressed to his chest. Her soft bottom squirmed against his growing erection, and her legs, like his, were bent at the knees.

He bowed his head to the graceful column of her neck and kissed her beneath her ear before tracing the shell with his tongue. God, she tasted good. And being with her felt so, so right.

He kissed her temple, her eyelid, the side of her nose, and the corner of her mouth, greedily claiming all of her. His.

Tracing a path along her neckline with his fingertips, he caressed the swells of her breasts and the smooth skin of her shoulders. She leaned her head back, giving him greater access and a glorious view. With every breath she took, her breasts strained against her corset and bodice, but he didn't dare unlace her gown on a boat—much as he would have liked to.

Instead, he cupped the mounds in his palms, lightly circling the tips till she moaned. When she arched her back, he increased the pressure, rubbing the tight peaks through the layers of silk.

She reached behind her and wound an arm around his neck. "Don't stop."

God, she was amazing. He listened, attuned to every blissful cry and whimper. He watched her eyes flutter shut with satisfaction and her body tremble with desire.

And he committed it all to memory.

The woods were dense around this part of the river, and the lazy current carried the boat so slowly that it felt as though they were standing still. The landscape crawled past them at a tortoise's pace, as if it, too, wanted to savor every moment of the ride.

"Yes," she breathed, parting her legs farther and wriggling her delectable backside against him.

Gray slid a hand under the hem of Fiona's skirt, skimming his palm over her knee and down the inside of her thigh, above her thin silk stockings. He teased the soft, taut skin at the top of her legs with featherlight strokes, venturing closer and closer to the apex of her legs and the spot that would bring her pleasure.

When at last he touched the folds at her entrance, she was damp and swollen.

Surely he'd died and gone to heaven.

Because in the real world, beautiful, talented heiresses did not give themselves to men like him—men with ornery dispositions who lacked fortunes. Men who were utterly incapable of love.

And they most certainly did not give themselves to men like him while floating downstream in rickety rowboats.

Gray kissed a path from Fiona's temple, down the side of her neck, and over the curve of her shoulder, alternately sucking and nibbling, leaving her skin tingling in his wake. With one hand, he caressed her breast, rubbing its tight bud until her body shimmered with delicious warmth. With the other hand, he touched her intimately, finding the center of her pleasure and stroking her, inside and out.

While it wasn't the same as making love with him, she had to admit it was rather spectacular. She relaxed completely against his chest, giving herself over to the aimless drifting and gentle rocking of the boat—as well as the sensations he stirred in her body and heart.

Because she had no doubt her heart was wholly his.

She'd told him about the blackmail, and he hadn't abandoned her. He still wanted her—or *desired* her, at least—and did not intend to go back on their deal. Surely that demonstrated some level of commitment or affection or . . .

Whatever it was, it was enough for now.

The rustling leaves above, the lapping water below, and buzzing insects around her slowly faded from her consciousness till all that remained was Gray.

His impossibly hard body cradling hers.

His wicked touch fanning her desire.

His scorching mouth cruising over her skin.

His gruff voice seducing her with every ragged whisper. "Come for me, Fi. Right here, just like this. I need to feel you come apart in my arms. Need to see your beautiful, perfect release. Need to know you're mine."

Oh God. Her traitorous body obeyed his orders as though he was a sorcerer with the power to command her. For an interminable moment, she held her breath, waiting as the pleasure spiraled higher and brighter.

Desire thundered in her ears as she balanced on the edge of a waterfall. Currents churned around her, dizzying in their intensity. She tumbled over the edge, weightless, pulsing with light and heat and . . . something unspeakably wonderful. Something that felt a lot like love.

Gray held her tightly and took her mouth in a hungry, yet tender, kiss. She clung to him as she slowly surfaced, sated and pleasantly dazed.

He seemed in no hurry to move, so she resolved to savor the closeness for as long as it lasted.

At last, he said, "I have a confession."

"I'll wager it's not as shocking as mine was," she jested. "It's rather hard to outdo the threat of blackmail."

He chuckled wryly and laced his fingers through hers. "True, but you shouldn't underestimate my ability to shock you."

"Thank you for understanding about my secret," she said sincerely. "Whatever your confession is, I shall try to be equally understanding."

"Good. Because we ran aground a quarter of an hour ago and haven't moved since."

"Gray!" She righted her skirts and scrambled onto the bench, looking for signs the boat was taking on water. "Are we going to sink?"

"Not likely. We're sitting on a mudbank in approximately two feet of water."

"But we're . . . stranded?" She placed a palm over her

belly, wishing she'd thought to eat a bit more at breakfast that morning. She was already feeling peckish, and heaven knew how long they'd be stuck there.

"Only temporarily." Grinning, he hoisted himself onto the bench, then slung his legs over the side of the boat and splashed, boots first, into the river. "Hold on."

Fiona barely had time to grasp the bench before he lowered his shoulder against the hull and shoved repeatedly. The boat lurched an inch or two each time before one strong heave finally dislodged it. Gray chased the boat into deeper water and was quickly submerged to his waist.

She panicked briefly at the thought that she might float away without him, but he lunged for the side and managed to climb in, spraying her with water in the process.

"Forgive me," he said, looking distinctly unapologetic.

She shrugged and smiled. "A few water droplets never hurt anyone, and running aground is one more notable detail in a day I shall never forget." She could hardly wait to write about her adventure in her journal and was already considering possible titles for the entry.

"A River Tryst?" No.

"Wickedness on the Waves?" Eh.

"Ravished on the Rowboat?" Not bad.

"Fiona." Gray sat across from her, deftly pulling his oars through the water.

"Hmm?"

His mouth curled into an amused smile. "You are all right then?"

"I am." More than all right. She was happy.

"Good, because there's so much more I want to show you."

She arched a brow at that, making him chuckle.

"Along the river, that is. We will meet up with the rest of the party a bit later to enjoy a late luncheon. But in the meantime, I have you all to myself, and I don't intend to waste a second."

Her heart bounced with joy. She'd been so afraid to tell him about the blackmail, but he'd been even more understanding than she could have hoped. And when he'd held her and kissed her and touched her . . . there was a tenderness in him that made her believe the happiness could last. Beyond today, next week . . . even next year.

"I don't want to waste any time either," she said. "Show me everything you love about this place."

For the space of several heartbeats, he gazed at her—with an intensity that made her flush. At last, he said, "Very well. Our first stop will be the infamous rope swing."

Fiona laughed nervously. "I assume you mean that we will be viewing said swing from afar. Perhaps admiring it as we float by in this vessel—which I've grown rather fond of, by the way."

"That all depends," he said slyly, "on whether or not you are the sort of person who's inclined to accept a dare."

Chapter 24

Gray must be mad. Daring her to ride a rope swing was preposterous.

Fiona cleared her throat and prepared to take a stand. "Perhaps you've forgotten I'm rather prone to mishaps."

"You don't say." He shot her a wicked smirk.

"As a result, I avoid risky behavior."

"Not always," Gray replied, thoughtful. "You wrote to me out of the blue and asked me to marry you. Some would call that risky."

She tilted her head, conceding the point. "Most would call it desperate."

"You did it for your sister. I'd call that bold. And brave."

She laughed. "Hardly. Lily is the courageous one. I prefer to hide behind my sketchbook, observing the world from a safe distance."

"Perhaps you do at times. But you do not give yourself enough credit. You took a risk coming here with me today. And I'm very glad you did."

"I am, too . . . but a swing is a different matter entirely, especially since I suspect this is not the sort of swing that sensible nannies would approve of."

He snorted. "I should say not." As he laid the oars across

his lap, he looked up at a spot behind her in the trees. "But don't take my word for it . . . see for yourself."

Fiona glanced over her shoulder and searched among the branches of the tallest tree on the riverbank. At first, all she saw were leaves, but then she spied a long, worn rope dangling above the water. Just the sight of it made the hairs on her arms stand up straight. "That hardly qualifies as a swing. It's nothing more than fraying twine with a knot at the bottom."

Gray shrugged. "At one time there was a wooden disk at the end that we used as a seat. But it rotted off years ago."

"Of course it did." The light-headed feeling returned.

"Kirby and I never replaced it, since the knot works just as well."

"Goodness." She fanned herself lightly with her hand. "I can just imagine you and Mr. Kirby swinging through the forest like Robin Hood."

He chuckled as he rowed toward the shore, closer to the swing. "This spot was our escape."

"Your escape from what?" she asked.

Gray leveled his gaze at her. "From everything."

"Forgive me for prying," Fiona began, "but what was so hard about being the only son of an earl? Did you have a difficult relationship with your parents?"

"No," Gray said honestly. "They had a difficult relationship with each other. I adored them both, but it seemed they were always fighting."

"So, you were left to your own devices?"

He nodded. "My grandmother did her best to guide me, but she usually had her hands full trying to rein in my parents, who had no interest in performing their duties as earl and countess—much less father and mother. When they weren't busy fighting, they were bouncing from one decadent house party to another. Gambling and drinking to excess . . ." He thought it best not to mention the orgies and opium. "I'm sure you can imagine."

She gazed at him with sympathy. "It must have been hard on a young lad."

"I was happy enough. Kirby spent every summer here, and the two of us had the run of the estate." Gray paddled toward the shore, hopped out of the boat, and pulled it onto the narrow strip of beach. He held his arms out to Fiona and gave her an encouraging wink, smiling when she stood on wobbly legs and allowed him to carry her onto the sand.

He helped her climb onto a large boulder, then grabbed the end of the rope swing and scrambled onto the rock beside her.

"Gray," she said earnestly. "I will *not* swing on that rope. Not on a dare. Not on a wager. Not even if you bribed me with ten thousand pounds."

"Rather closed-minded of you," he teased.

She swallowed, hard. "In this instance, yes. To be clear, if I was being chased through the woods by a wild boar and that rope swing was my only means of escaping the beast, I *still* wouldn't avail myself of it."

"I begin to understand the depths of your disdain for rope swings." He grinned at her and took her hand. "But there are no wild boars here, and I would never force you to try something that you didn't want to."

She exhaled and closed her eyes briefly. "Thank you. My skin turned clammy at the mere sight of the thing. However, I think it's very sweet that you and Mr. Kirby spent so many carefree hours here as boys. You must tell me how it worked. Did you launch yourself from this rock?"

"Sometimes. But we'd usually climb one of the trees

and jump from there. The higher the perch, the more exciting the ride. It's the closest thing to flying I've ever experienced." Gray rose to his feet next to Fiona and tugged on the old rope, letting it hold some of his weight.

"Well, you know how it turned out for poor Icarus. We mortals would do better to keep our feet on the ground."

"The trick is letting go at the right time. Release too early or too late and you end up spraining an ankle on the riverbank. But if your timing is perfect, you splash into the deepest part of the river like a cannonball."

"That sounds terrifying and delightful at the same time."

"I suppose we had our share of injuries, but, oddly enough, I remember those fondly, too."

"It's no wonder you and Mr. Kirby have such a bond. You were much like brothers."

Gray stared straight up, to where the other end of the rope was wound around a thick branch. It had taken him and Kirby days to work up the nerve to climb that high. And once they managed to reach that lofty bough, they weren't sure they'd ever make it back down. But somehow, they had. "Kirby and I may not have the same blood running through our veins, but I consider him my brother. Besides my grandmother, he's the only family I have."

Fiona leaned back on her palms and looked up at him. "I know how you feel. Lily and I do not share the same birth parents; my mother and father adopted her when she was an infant. I was only a toddler myself, and I cannot remember a time when we weren't together. She's my sister in every sense of the word. When I think of what my life might have been like without her, I feel sad—almost hollow."

"Then you truly understand," Gray said. But he had yet to share the worst day of his childhood. He was still circling around the edges, trying to determine the best way to approach it. There was no way to describe that day's events without reliving the horror and anger and utter sorrow. Perhaps that was the reason he hadn't spoken of it—ever.

He'd planned to keep that memory behind a locked door for the rest of his life. But he was going to tell Fiona. If she was going to marry him, she *deserved* to know just how damaged he was. And if there was a tiny part of her that naïvely believed she could change him . . . or teach him how to love . . . well, his pathetic tale would disabuse her of that notion, once and for all.

"You said you can't imagine your life without your sister. Have you ever done the reverse? That is, have you ever tried to picture how your life might be different if one bad thing had *not* happened?"

"All the time," she replied quickly. "I imagine how different life would be if my mother hadn't died. We would have had tea parties in the nursery every afternoon and countless picnics in the park. My father would never have remarried or grown so distant. He would still tease Lily and me about meeting fairies on the road home. He'd still sing ballads at the pianoforte with us, even though none of us can properly carry a tune. Lily and I certainly wouldn't have gone away to school at Miss Haywinkle's. Maybe my mother would have come here, to your house party, and become fast friends with your grandmother. I'd like to think so."

"So would I." Before he could stop himself, he added, "And what would she think about you marrying an earl who's bitter and jaded?"

Fiona's auburn hair gleamed in the sunlight, and her freckles seemed to wink at him. "I was only a girl when she died, so she never shared her wisdom regarding which types of gentlemen make the best husbands. But I do remember this about my mother: When I was happy, she was happy, too. And since being with you makes me happy, I can only surmise that she'd adore you."

Gray snorted, but damn it all if the sentiment didn't melt a corner of his frigid heart. "I'm sorry she never saw the woman you've become. How talented you are. How beautiful and kind."

Fiona reached up and tugged on his hand. "Sit," she said. "Please."

He let the frayed rope slip from his hands and settled himself beside her on the rock. "Is the sun too intense for you here? I could fetch your bonnet from the boat, or we could move to a shadier spot."

She turned toward him and tilted her head, thoughtful, and he knew there could be no more procrastinating, no more hiding. "It's your turn," she said softly. "How would your life be different if one bad thing had not happened to you?"

Shit. "It's hard to say, exactly. But I'll tell you the one bad thing and let you draw your own conclusions."

Her eyes glowed with encouragement, nudging him forward and promising understanding.

"It was the summer I turned twelve. Kirby and I were home from school, and we had the run of the estate. Every day was an adventure, full of fishing, riding, hunting, swimming . . ."

"And swinging?" she asked with an amused smile.

"Naturally. On this particular day, my parents were having a nasty row, so Kirby and I escaped to the stables with a few apples as treats for the horses. I was brushing down my father's favorite stallion when a footman tore across the lawn toward us, waving his arms wildly. He called my name and said my parents wished to see me at once. In the library."

Gray could still hear the panicked tremor in the servant's voice, could still see the ghostly pallor of his face. But mostly Gray remembered the way his own feet had felt full of lead, even as he'd raced back toward the house, Kirby in tow. He'd known it wasn't a normal type of summons. His parents weren't going to inquire about his school marks or scold him for leaving muddy boot tracks in the front hall.

"When I opened the door to the library, I found my father pacing beside his desk, holding a dueling pistol to his head."

Her face turned pale. "My God, Gray. No."

He swallowed, seeing it all again in his mind, clear as the day it happened. His gut twisted, but he focused on the gentle pressure of Fiona's hand.

"My mother sat in the desk chair, shakily holding a drink. Wine sloshed over the rim of her glass, staining the carpet." He closed his eyes briefly and saw the limp strands of hair that hung around his mother's ashen face. Two bright spots of rouge on her cheeks looked oddly out of place—like someone spreading a picnic blanket during a rainstorm. "She spied me in the doorway and told me to stay there. When I asked what was happening, she said my father was trying to control her—by threatening to take his own life.'"

"Oh no." Fiona squeezed his hand. "That's . . . that's horrible."

It was. God-awful. But Gray had started telling the story and was now bound to finish it. "My father's jacket was dark with perspiration and his wild eyes bulged in their sockets. He spun toward me and recklessly waved the pistol at my mother. I thought my heart would pound out of my chest and started to run toward her, but she yelled for me to stay. My father laughed—a horrible, ugly sound. He told me that my mother had whored herself out to half of London and didn't deserve to call herself the Countess of Ravenport."

"Gray," Fiona whispered. "I'm sorry."

"She dropped her drink, launched herself at my father, and beat her hands on his chest, screaming that he was every bit as depraved as she was. The next thing I knew, they were both sobbing and clinging to each other, rocking back and forth. My mother promised it wouldn't happen again, but my father grew even more agitated, and his fingers clenched the pistol's handle."

Gray swiped a sleeve across his brow and fought back a wave of nausea. Fiona slipped her arm behind him and leaned her head on his shoulder. "Do you want to pause for a moment? Maybe find a shady spot to rest?"

"No." He had to finish the sordid tale—now, before he lost his nerve. He needed to expel it like the poison it was, expose it to daylight.

"I was going to fetch help," he choked out. "I was going to find my grandmother, a servant—anyone who might be able to talk some sense into my parents. But when I started to leave, my mother let out a bloodcurdling scream. She begged me not to go. Said as long as I was there my father wouldn't hurt himself—or her. But he laughed at that. My mother pleaded with him. Warned him that he'd scar me—his heir—forever."

Fiona looked up at Gray then, her lovely face awash with dismay. "Please tell me he didn't."

Gray swallowed and nodded. "He shot himself while I stood there watching. I shall spare you the rest of the details." Like the shock of seeing his father stare directly at him as he rammed the barrel into his mouth. Like the bone-jarring crack of the gun exploding.

Fiona didn't need to know about the blood splattered on the ceiling and on his own shirt and face. She didn't need to know about his mother's unearthly screams as she crumpled to the floor, cradling what was left of his father's head in her lap.

But he'd told Fiona enough.

Enough to convey just how warped his family had been.

Enough to explain why he wasn't capable of loving anyone.

And probably more than enough to scare her off.

The hell of it was, he'd finally realized he didn't *want* to scare her off.

Lord knew he didn't deserve her, but that didn't stop him from wanting her. For his. For always.

Chapter 25

Fiona slid her palm across Gray's chest and rested her hand over his heart. "I'm sorry. No one should have to witness such a thing. Most especially not a twelve-year-old boy."

For a while they said nothing. Only the water lapping against the rocks and the breeze rustling the leaves softened the silence.

At last, he said, "You asked how my life would be different if not for that one bad thing, and now you know. I wouldn't have inherited an earldom before I was a man. I wouldn't have watched my mother dull her grief with opium and drink, slowly wasting away before my eyes. I wouldn't be tormented by guilt because I didn't stop my father."

"No." She held his handsome, anguished face in her hands and forced him to meet her gaze. "*No.* It was *not* your fault. Your parents should never have involved you that day. They made you a pawn in their twisted relationship. But you were a *boy.* And it sounds as though your father was beyond help."

Gray shrugged. "Maybe he was."

A painful knot lodged in her throat, and a tear slid down her cheek. She simply *had* to make him understand. His happiness—and perhaps hers—depended on it. "Not maybe," she countered. "You *must* believe me, as someone who is able to view the situation objectively, when I say that what happened to your father was *not* your doing. You could not have prevented it, and if you'd attempted to, either you or your mother—maybe both of you—could have become victims, too. And that would have been doubly tragic. Trust me on this, Gray."

He turned his face into her palm and kissed it, then took both her hands in his. "I'm trying. To trust. But it doesn't come easy . . . and now you know why."

Her chest squeezed at the thought of all he'd lost. His father and mother, his childhood—and his faith in all others. "I'm not like them," she said earnestly. "I would never hurt you. You must believe me."

"I know you don't want to hurt me. Just as I would never want to hurt you."

Fiona flinched. Because she understood what he couldn't quite bring himself to say—that no matter how good their intentions, they were probably going to wind up hurting each other eventually.

But she'd already known that he was scarred and cynical. Convincing him that love was worth the risk was going to take more than one afternoon, and she was willing to invest the time. As long as it took. Besides, he'd begun opening up to her, which had to be a very good sign.

Unable to speak, she brushed her lips across his in a whisper-soft kiss and was rewarded with a weak but genuine smile.

"The point is," he continued, "that day changed everything about my life. Except for one thing—Kirby."

"He helped you through a tragic time. It's no wonder you're so close."

Gray nodded. "The blood . . . it splattered on him, too. Literally and figuratively. And as far as I know, he never told a soul. I didn't swear him to secrecy or beg for his silence. But he realized the scandal such gossip would have created for my family—and the shame it would have brought upon me. Kirby was my best friend before that ugly day, and he kept me from going mad in the days and weeks afterward. He's remained a steadfast, loyal friend throughout the years."

"I'm glad he was there for you—and that he still is. But he's not the only one who cares for you. There's your grandmother, of course . . . and me."

He reached for the strand of hair that had blown across her face and tucked it behind an ear. "I didn't tell you about my father's suicide to gain your sympathy. Only to explain why I'm . . . the way I am. And why this place is special to me."

She rested her head on his shoulder and looked up at the swing. "I think I understand. This is where you could be a boy—even after that day."

"That same evening, while the servants hung black crepe over the windows, Kirby and I escaped here. It was the first time we summoned the courage to jump from the highest branch. I plunged into the river, letting the water wash away the blood—and the horrible images in my head." He shrugged. "Oddly enough, it helped."

She nodded, touched by his honesty. "Thank you for confiding in me. For trusting me with the truth." While she adored the physical intimacy she had with Gray, this was different. Deeper.

It gave her hope that, in spite of all his scars, she could heal him—and perhaps help him love again.

"I suppose we should rejoin the rest of our party." He sighed, regretful.

"Yes, Mary will be looking for me—as will Lily and Sophie."

Gray turned to her then, his dark eyes brimming with longing and affection. Spearing his fingers through her hair, he took her mouth in a sweet but knee-melting kiss. And her heart swelled with joy.

Because it seemed to her that this kiss was more than just a kiss. It was a promise—to try to move beyond the past and face the future together.

When, at last, they reluctantly parted, Gray helped her climb down from the rock and back into the boat.

She sat across from him, mesmerized by the smooth, powerful motion of his shoulders and arms as he rowed their boat down the river. She could already hear the faint sounds of conversation and laughter drifting toward them from the shore where they'd meet up with the rest of the group and enjoy a picnic luncheon before returning to the Fortress.

When they were still several yards from the shore, Gray suddenly lifted the oars out of the water and rested them on the sides of the boat. "I'll speak to your father when he arrives tomorrow. And if it pleases you, I thought we could announce our engagement at the ball tomorrow night."

Fiona's belly fluttered. She impulsively leaned forward, circled a hand around Gray's neck, and kissed him. "That would make me very happy."

Even now, she felt like dancing. Not on the boat, of course, because she'd topple into the river and ruin one of her favorite gowns. But joy bubbled up inside her nonetheless.

Because at times like this, when Gray was so thoughtful and attentive and kind, she could almost imagine that they'd had the usual, genuine sort of courtship. The kind where the dashing gentleman pursues the beautiful young lady and attempts to win her favor. And she could almost imagine that despite the odds, she might somehow manage to save her sister from an awful scandal *and* end up with her very own fairy-tale romance.

It *could* happen. And what better place for a bit of fairy-tale magic than a ball?

On the Reasons We Adore Balls (a Concise List)

1. *The gowns. Slipping into a gorgeous—and slightly daring—gown can make a girl feel like the heroine of her own gothic novel: dazzling, bold, and beautiful.*
2. *The dancing. Every dance from the quadrille to the waltz offers chances for romance: a blush-inducing compliment, a heated gaze, or a lingering touch.*
3. *The champagne. The festive atmosphere encourages every guest to set aside worries and join in the revelry . . . and to indulge one's naughtier side.*
4. *The candlelight. Everything is lovelier beneath ballroom chandeliers. Paste jewelry sparkles like diamonds; lawn fabric shines like silk. Bathed in the glow of candlelight, even a hopeless wallflower can become the belle of the ball.*
5. *The possibilities. When the conditions are just right, even the most unlikely of scenarios may come to pass. Scandal can be averted, rifts can be mended . . . and love can blossom.*

"I can't believe Papa arrives today!" Lily bolted upright in bed, vexingly chipper, given that it was scarcely eight o'clock in the morning. "There's so much to be done. I told the countess I'd help her arrange the flowers today, and I thought I'd venture into the village to find a small gift for

Papa. Maybe a new pipe or smart new hat—what do you think?"

Fiona reluctantly lifted the pillow off her head, rolled onto her back, and pushed the wisps of hair away from her face. "I think it's dreadfully early to be discussing such things . . . but I'm sure Papa would adore either—as long as it was coming from you."

Lily bounded out of bed and yanked open the doors of the armoire. "I know it's silly, but I can't help hoping that some little gesture or snippet of conversation might jar him out of the stupor he's been in. That he might pull us into a fierce hug and kiss our foreheads and tell us how much he's missed us. Not just since we left to come here to the earl's house party, but since he pulled away from us . . . and became so distant."

Fiona sat up and shot her sister a sympathetic smile. "I know. And I'm glad to hear you haven't given up on him, because neither have I. Underneath the brusqueness, he's still the papa we love and adore. Surely the change of scenery will be good for him."

"Would you like to join me and Soph for breakfast and a quick trip to the village?"

"Thank you, but I think I'll spend an hour or two sketching this morning before Papa arrives and all the preparations and festivities begin in earnest. I'll look for you and Sophie in the ballroom this afternoon, and the three of us can assist with the decorations—which reminds me, I wanted to show you something." Fiona slid out of bed, grabbed her sketchbook, and joined her sister near the armoire. "Last night, Sophie and I worked on some drawings of the ballroom, as we envision it. Have a look."

Lily blinked at the rough images as Fiona flipped the pages. "Fi," she said softly, "you are brilliant. I hope you realize that."

"The ideas are all Sophie's. I simply put them on paper."

"There's nothing simple about it," Lily said. "I hadn't thought it possible to be more eager for this evening, but now I am. I can't wait to see the ballroom transformed."

"I'm eager, too," Fiona admitted. "Now pick a day gown and I'll help you dress. No need to ring for Mary."

Lily laid a finger alongside her cheek, thoughtful. "I shall choose the grey. Can you guess why?"

"Because it will provide the greatest contrast with the stunning red silk you plan to wear tonight?"

"Precisely," she replied, eyes twinkling. "You see? We *did* learn some useful tidbits at Miss Haywinkle's."

Shortly after breakfast, Fiona escaped to the garden with her sketchbook. Amidst the untrimmed shrubs and sprawling vines, she sat on a bench near the mermaid fountain and opened her drawing pad to the portrait of Gray.

He may not have been there in the flesh, posing for her as he had before, but during the hours she'd spent with him on the boat yesterday she'd made plenty of mental images—and she intended to incorporate the most important elements into her sketch today. Not physical traits like scars or dimples or the shape of his face but, rather, intangible things: the humor in his eyes as he'd teased her about the swing; the juxtaposition of his virile self-confidence and unexpected vulnerability; the way he'd smiled at her—as though she understood a joke only the two of them were privy to.

As usual, she lost track of the minutes, but by midday she slowly emerged from her creative haze, especially satisfied.

At last, she'd finished her sketch of Gray.

And it was the best she'd ever drawn.

It captured the most important things about him—the essence of who he was. Yes, he was still a powerful, brooding earl. But he was also a wounded boy and a devoted grandson and a loyal friend. He was a passionate, considerate lover and one of the hardest-working people she knew.

And she loved him.

Anyone who looked at the sketch would realize that truth in an instant.

Which was why, despite the encouraging developments of recent days, she was not yet ready to share the portrait with anyone—and most especially not Gray.

When the time was right, she'd show him the portrait and tell him how she felt.

Until then, she would close up her sketchbook and wait—allowing time for his feelings to catch up with hers. For she had to believe they would.

Delighted with the day's efforts, Fiona made her way back to the house and passed through to the drawing room, where she found Mama, Lady Callahan, and the countess taking tea.

"There you are!" Mama said with a *tsk*. "Fiddling with your drawings when you should be resting up before the ball."

"I'm not tired, Mama. Has Papa arrived yet?"

"No, but I expect him soon," she answered breezily.

Fiona could have twirled from sheer happiness. "I think I shall go help Lily and Sophie in the ballroom."

"How many guests are we anticipating tonight?" Lady Callahan asked.

"An excellent question," the countess remarked. "We received a few more replies late yesterday afternoon. Fiona, my dear, before you go, would you fetch the list for me? It's over there—on the escritoire."

"Certainly." Fiona found a large sheet of paper filled with names written in various hands on top of the desk and brought it to the elderly woman. "Shall I tally the number of guests who've accepted?"

The countess shot her a grateful smile. "Please."

Fiona was scanning the list from top to bottom, keeping a mental count of affirmative replies, when an unusual but vaguely familiar flourish caught her eye. The lowercase *f* in Lord and Lady Heflin's name had a distinctive, ornate loop where it dipped below the other letters that reminded her a little of—

Dear God.

Her fingers went numb and the paper trembled in her hand. The handwriting on the list . . . It was the same as on the blackmail notes.

"Well, how many are coming?" Mama prodded.

"I . . . I lost count." Fiona clutched the back of the sofa for support and blinked hard. Perhaps she'd only imagined the writing was the same. Surely any number of people formed their *f*'s in the same way. Didn't they?

Please, please, let this be an odd coincidence.

Because the idea for the ball had only come about during the house party.

Which meant that it was quite possible whoever wrote Lord and Lady Heflin's names on the list was staying at the Fortress—and that the blackmailer was *there,* under the very same roof as Fiona and Lily.

Chapter 26

"Forgive me," Fiona sputtered. "I must have sat in the sun a bit too long." She fanned herself with the paper, then forced herself to look at the list of guests again, quickly counting the names with a check beside them. "Fifty-eight, not including those of us staying here."

"I shall tell the staff to prepare for seventy," the countess said. "A grand number for our celebration."

Fiona nodded in agreement, even though she only half-listened. She simply *had* to find out who had written that distinctive *f.* "Are you certain the list is current?" she asked the countess. "Perhaps a few more replies straggled in today?"

"I don't believe so. Giddings would have delivered them to me with the post."

"Is it possible that someone forgot to record a reply?" Fiona fished shamelessly. "I myself only wrote down a half-dozen names. And I recognize Lily's and Sophie's handwriting on another dozen or so. Who else has been tasked with adding guests to the list?"

The countess frowned slightly. "Oh, well, I pressed various people into service. I would have seen to it myself, but my eyesight isn't what it used to be. I prevailed upon whoever was nearby when I received a reply."

Fiona arched a brow. "Even the gentlemen?" She pretended to be impressed; in truth, she was still struggling to come to terms with what she'd seen. The scoundrel who was threatening Lily and blackmailing Fiona could very well have been hiding in plain sight all week long.

"Oh yes—the gentlemen, too. Gray wrote a few names for me."

"Gray? That is, the earl?" Fiona gulped. She refused to believe it could be him.

"Indeed," the countess said proudly. "And, at various times, the other young men. Lord Pentham, Lord Carter . . ." She tilted her head, thoughtful. "Even Mr. Kirby."

Fiona's mouth turned dry as cotton. "You don't say."

"As I recall, they were all eager to help—excellent sports."

"I am glad to hear it." Fiona waved the guest list in the air. "I'll leave this on the escritoire, where it will be ready in case any last-minute additions are required. I'm off to the ballroom, but Mama, would you please send for me when Papa arrives?"

"If you insist. I, for one, think your time would be better spent resting and preparing yourself for the ball."

"Please, Mama."

She heaved a long-suffering sigh. "Very well."

As Fiona left the drawing room, she was already making plans to return—with the blackmail note. She needed to see it and the guest list side by side in order to be certain that the handwriting was the same, but the sick feeling in her belly told her what she didn't want to accept—that the blackmailer was someone she knew and trusted.

At least there was a silver lining to the discovery. She'd woken that morning thinking that the blackmailer could be anyone in London.

But if the writing matched, she was much closer to identifying the villain. In fact, the number of suspects would be whittled down to three: Lord Pentham, Lord Carter, and—though she hated to even entertain the thought—the person Gray considered a brother. Kirby.

Gray walked from the stables toward the house with an uncharacteristic spring in his step. If someone had told him one week ago that he'd not only be hosting a ball at the Fortress but that he'd also actually be looking *forward* to it, Gray would have informed that person that they were completely and unequivocally mad.

But because of Fiona, everything had changed. *He'd* changed.

Instead of grumbling about the expense of the ball and fixating on all of the house's imperfections and dreading the prospect of making polite conversation with people he scarcely knew, he was dreaming about dancing with Fiona.

And imagining her standing by his side, smiling up at him as he announced their engagement to all the guests.

He was also plotting ways to steal a few moments with her at some point during the evening. Maybe after the guests left and before the servants awoke.

Fortunately, one way or another, they'd be married very soon. Perhaps her father would procure a special license; maybe they'd elope to Gretna Green. Gray didn't much care how or where they were married—only that Fiona would soon be his.

He entered the house and was heading for his bedchamber to change when he spotted her ahead of him on the staircase, making his heart beat double-time. She held her sketchbook under one arm and wore a soft blue gown that brought out the fiery hue of her hair. "Fiona," he called, bounding up the stairs two at a time, like an eager puppy.

She turned and waited for him on the landing. "Gray."

He gently tapped the pencil tucked behind her ear. "You've been drawing this morning, I see. Anything special?"

She tightened her grip on her sketchbook. "Yes, actually. But I'm not quite ready to share it. Soon."

Ignoring the twinge in his chest, he shot her an understanding smile. "I was out riding this morning, but I came in to wash up and make myself look respectable before your father arrives."

"That's very sweet."

He sidled closer and grazed a hand over her hip. "My current thoughts are *not* sweet. They could best be described as *wicked*."

She laid a palm on his chest and smiled shyly. "I confess I'm rather fond of the combination—sweet and wicked."

"Then it is a good thing you can supply the sweetness. I can provide the wickedness. In spades." He glanced over his shoulder to make sure they were alone before circling a hand around her wrist, pulling her close, and brushing his lips over hers.

He loved the way her eyes instantly took on a sleepy, dreamy look and all the tension seemed to drain out of her body.

But something was different about her today. Faint lines showed on her forehead, and she seemed vaguely distracted. "Are you anxious about my meeting with your father?" he asked. "I promise you I shall be on my best behavior."

She traced a fingertip along his jaw. "I'm not worried about that. My father is an excellent judge of character. I've no doubt he'll like you."

"Is something else worrying you?" he asked. "I know

the threat of blackmail must weigh heavy, but now you needn't face it alone. As soon as we have a moment in private, I'll examine the letters for clues and devise a plan—a counterpunch that will rid you of the bully once and for all. I'll protect you and your family. I swear."

"Thank you." The lines on her forehead softened. "I just want to put the whole thing behind me. To forget it ever happened."

Gray wrapped her in his arms. "I know." But he didn't say what he was truly thinking—that unless and until they confronted the blackmailer, they'd never be completely free of the threat. "I hate that some greedy, opportunistic bastard is trying to take advantage of you . . . and yet, if it wasn't for him, I wouldn't be with you right now."

She wound a hand behind his neck and leaned into him, arching a brow when his erection pressed against her belly. "Then I suppose I should thank him."

"I miss you," he growled. "Come to my room tonight."

"I will try. But for now, I shall leave you with this token of my affection." She pulled his head down and took his mouth in a molten kiss—primal, demanding, and full of promise.

It was all he could do not to drag her into the nearest room, lift her skirts, and bury himself in her till they both were drunk with pleasure . . . but since her father was expected any moment, he refrained.

When he could speak, he cupped her cheek and brushed a thumb over her lips. "That was an excellent token. Much better than a starched handkerchief or a silk ribbon."

"Something to remember me by." She pulled away slowly. Seductively. "Until tonight."

"Until tonight," he repeated, wondering how in God's name he'd gotten so damned lucky.

* * *

When Fiona walked into the ballroom a half hour later, the sight of it nearly took her breath away, for it seemed as though the outdoors had been brought inside and the once-plain rectangular room had been transformed into a fairy garden.

Greenery adorned all four walls. Leafy boughs, creeping vines, and colorful blossoms wound around windows and doorways, creating a lush, fragrant cocoon. Gold and silver ribbons tied the trimmings together and lent a delightful shimmer everywhere one looked.

It was unique and tasteful and gorgeous—a reflection of the young woman who'd designed it. "Soph!" Fiona cried. "This is amazing. Even for you." Her friend had always had a talent for harnessing nature's beauty and making plants do her bidding. Somehow, she'd used common flora from the Fortress's grounds and garden—perhaps even weeds—to create a dreamlike setting.

Sophie pushed a wisp of blond hair behind her ear, crossed her arms, and turned slowly in the center of the room, surveying her work. "We couldn't have managed it without the drawings you provided. It did turn out rather well."

"*Rather well*?" Lily snorted. "It's a masterpiece! The countess will swoon when she sees what you've done."

"She's been so gracious to all of us," Sophie said. "I hope she likes it."

Fiona wrapped an arm around her friend's slender shoulders and gave her an affectionate squeeze. "She'll love it. Have you two left anything for me to do, or am I entirely superfluous?"

"The servants have already set out all the candles and trimmed the wicks. They're hanging lanterns out on the terrace now in hopes that the clouds will part and the rain will hold off. All that remains to be done is for us to dress and do our hair."

"That's Soph's kind way of saying you're entirely superfluous," Lily teased. "Why don't you go upstairs and rest for a bit? I've a feeling tonight's ball could be especially momentous for you."

Fiona stooped and picked a few leftover boughs off the floor, careful to avoid Lily's knowing gaze. "Why would you say that?"

"No reason," her sister replied, all innocence. "Except that the earl is obviously smitten, as are you, and since the ball is the culmination of his house party, it would be the perfect time to—"

"You know," Fiona interrupted, "I think you're right. A short nap would be just the thing. I'll take these outside and meet you both upstairs in time to dress before dinner."

Lily chuckled. "I can't wait to see you in your gown. You're going to be the princess of the ball."

Chapter 27

On Falling in Love

I once thought romantic love required poetry, dancing, flowers, and gifts. I naïvely believed Miss Haywinkle when she said that the depth of a gentleman's feelings could be measured by the number of times he calls on a lady or asks her to waltz or joins her for chaperoned walks in the park.

But sometimes love is measured in altogether different ways—like shared secrets and understanding smiles and reassuring touches. The kind that happen spontaneously on a sultry summer day while you're floating down the river in a rowboat.

And after such a day, you somehow know deep in your heart that you'll never be quite the same again.

A few hours later as Fiona stared at her reflection in the small mirror propped on the desk in her bedchamber, she *did* feel like a princess. Her turquoise gown was the prettiest she owned, and Mary had coaxed her wavy tresses into a fetching bouquet of curls that cascaded down her nape.

"You look beautiful, Fi." Lily rested her elfish chin on

Fiona's shoulder and met her gaze in the looking glass. "Lord Ravenport will find himself completely under your spell—if he isn't already."

"You look lovely, too," Fiona said. The two faces staring back at her were so very different—from the shades of their skin to the colors of their eyes to the shapes of their mouths. And yet the impish, slightly conspiratorial expressions on both faces were striking similar, leaving no doubt that they were sisters in the truest sense of the word. "I think I shall have to sketch us one day—just like this."

"Please do," Lily said with a grin. "I don't think my hair has ever looked quite this good, and I doubt it shall ever again."

Behind them, the bedchamber door burst open, and the pair spun around to find Mama bustling into the room. Mary trailed behind her, one hairpin clamped between her lips and another in her hand as she valiantly attempted to tame an unruly lock of Mama's hair into submission.

"That will do," Mama snapped at the maid before drawing a long breath and facing her stepdaughters. Against her bosom she clutched a small wooden chest with roses carved on the sides.

"You look rather flushed, Mama," Fiona said. "Are you feeling well?"

"Quite." But her stepmother's hands trembled as she rotated the box and presented it to Fiona, who stood and took the chest.

"What's this?"

"Open it. You'll see." When Fiona hesitated, Mama sighed impatiently. "Go on."

Swallowing, Fiona lifted the hinged lid and peered inside. Nestled on a bed of black velvet, a necklace of diamond-encrusted sapphires sparkled, brilliant as moonlight on a turbulent sea.

Stunning.

Breathtaking.

And painfully familiar.

Lily gasped and pressed a hand to her mouth, while unbidden tears sprang to Fiona's eyes. "Our mother's necklace."

"To be precise, *your* mother's necklace," Mama corrected.

Fiona shook her head firmly and met Lily's troubled gaze. "She was *our* mother," Fiona repeated. To Lily she said, "Never doubt it."

"It's the necklace she's wearing in our portrait," Lily said with a sniffle. She referred to the painting that Papa had commissioned only months before their mother took ill—the one that hung in their drawing room at home. Fiona and Lily had seen it almost every day of their lives for the last decade or so, and it was the strongest physical connection they had to her.

In the painting, their mother reclined on a chaise while Fiona and Lily, each dressed in a lacey white frock, perched on tufted stools in front of her.

Lily could still recall the hours they'd posed for the artist. He must have asked their mother a dozen times to look at *him* instead of her daughters before giving up and painting what he must have seen before him: the loving, affectionate, and proud gaze of a mother who was utterly devoted to her daughters—*both* of them.

"Was she wearing the necklace in that portrait?" Mama asked coolly. "I confess I hadn't noticed. You'll find a pair of matching earrings in the box as well."

Fiona placed the chest on the desk and carefully withdrew the necklace, surprised at its weight. The gold felt warm against her palm, and the gems seemed to glow from within.

The last time she'd seen the necklace in person, it had graced her mother's neck. After she died, Fiona assumed her father stowed the jewels away, someplace safe. Someplace where he wouldn't have to see the vivid blue of the sapphires, which seemed to perfectly match the color of his beloved's eyes.

Lily reached into the chest, withdrew the earrings, and held them by the candle, where light danced off the dangling sapphires. "I'd wondered where these were but never asked Papa for fear of making him sad."

Mama cleared her throat. "Yes. Well, your father entrusted the jewels to me, asking that I give them to you when the time seemed right. Now that Fiona has captured the attention of an earl, I believe she's won the right to wear them."

Fiona tamped down a wave of anger. "Our mother's jewels aren't a prize to be won. They're one of our last connections to her. *That's* the reason we shall cherish them."

Mama blinked. "I had expected you to show a bit more gratitude and grace, Fiona. These sorts of unseemly outbursts are *precisely* why you are not yet wed. I suggest you wear the necklace and earrings tonight—they may help you outshine any competition for the earl's affections."

Fiona simultaneously bit her tongue and prayed for patience. Arguing with Mama was futile, and this evening was too important to spoil with squabbling. Besides, she and Lily now had a treasured piece of their mother that they could hold close to their hearts.

"I shall wear the necklace tonight," Fiona said. "Lily, you must wear the earrings."

"No," Lily demurred. "You should wear them, too. They're meant to be a set."

"You and I are meant to be a set," Fiona said, matter-of-fact. "Put on the earrings, and then you may help me with this necklace clasp."

Mama threw up her hands. "Suit yourselves. Your father recently arrived and is dressing for dinner now. We shall see you in the drawing room in a quarter of an hour—don't be late."

A short time later, as Fiona and the other house party guests seated themselves around the dinner table, she fingered the stones at her throat, hoping that they'd give her the courage to face whatever challenges the night might hold.

Papa, who was seated on Fiona's left, patted her hand and told her how much he'd missed her and Lily during the past week. Though he'd arrived at the Fortress later than expected, he'd come, just as he'd said he would. And unlike Mama, he didn't bat an eye at the shabby condition of the house. Accustomed to productive mills and functional offices, he valued efficiency above all else. Creaky floorboards and threadbare curtains were hardly cause for dismay, thank goodness—because the Fortress had flaws aplenty.

Gray sat at the head of the table, breathtakingly handsome in a midnight blue jacket and azure waistcoat. He played the part of amiable host to perfection, making cordial conversation with his grandmother and all the guests, but throughout the meal his gaze never strayed far from Fiona.

Everything about the evening would have been perfect—if one of the men sitting at the table wasn't trying to blackmail her. She would not rest easy until the threat to Lily was eliminated. And now she was a bit closer to determining who the villain might be.

She'd managed to return to the drawing room with the blackmail note that afternoon and confirmed that the handwriting matched that on the guest list. Which meant that the scoundrel could only be Lord Pentham, Lord Carter, or Mr. Kirby.

Across the table, Lord Pentham listened raptly as Lily recounted the details of the archery contest for Papa's benefit, laughing at her embellishments. Mr. Kirby complimented Mama's violet ball gown, thus earning her eternal devotion. Lord Carter and Mr. Kirby's father, Lord Dunlope, were embroiled in a passionate discussion about the most superior breeds of racehorses.

None of the three younger men looked the part of the villain—there wasn't a greasy mustache, paunch belly, or sinister glare among them. These were gentlemen she'd played charades with; gentlemen she'd shared stories with. And yet one of them had ruthlessly uncovered the salacious truth about Lily's birth mother—and had sunk to wielding that information like a weapon.

Fortunately, the blackmailer couldn't know what Fiona had discovered, so she planned to use the few remaining hours of the house party to her advantage.

Shortly after the dessert course, Gray quietly addressed Papa. "Mr. Hartley, I wondered if we might have a word in my study before the ball begins?"

Papa turned to Fiona with a hopeful, questioning glance, and she shot him a reassuring smile. He sat up a little taller as he replied, "Certainly, Ravenport."

Her chest squeezed at the sight of the two men—both at the center of her world—walking out of the dining room, shoulder to shoulder. The rest of the guests, including the gentlemen, went through to the drawing room, giving Fiona the opportunity she was hoping for.

She withdrew a small stack of note cards from her reticule and approached Sophie and Lord Carter, who were admiring a large landscape painting beside the pianoforte.

"It's a lovely garden," Soph was saying. "Perfect proportions, beautiful colors, and interesting focal points."

"Perhaps," Fiona said smoothly, "but rather ordinary compared to the gardens you've designed."

Lord Carter arched a dark brow. "I'm impressed."

"Wait till you see the ballroom," Fiona said. "Forgive me for interrupting, but I've a favor to ask, and I hope you'll indulge me." She looked over her shoulder, making sure the countess wasn't within earshot.

"Of course," Sophie replied. "Anything you need."

Fiona explained, hoping her voice didn't betray her nervousness. "I have a sketch of the estate I plan to give Lady Ravenport—as a small token of thanks for hosting us this week. She's made no secret of the fact that she adores the company of young people and the earl's friends in particular, so I thought it might be nice if each of the guests wrote her a brief note. I'll collect them all to include with the framed sketch when I give it to her."

Sophie clasped her hands. "What a thoughtful idea! I'd be happy to pen a note to the countess."

"As would I." If Lord Carter found the request suspicious, he gave no indication of it.

"Thank you. I knew I could count on you." Fiona handed each of them a small card. "I apologize for the short notice, but if you could return the card to me before we leave tomorrow, I'd be much obliged. You needn't write more than a line or two." She wished she could add *and it would be ever so helpful if you could include a lowercase f somewhere in there,* but she was already pressing her luck. She simply had to trust that some distinguishing trait in the handwriting samples would provide evidence of a match.

"I shall compose something tonight," Sophie promised.

Lord Carter tucked the card in his breast pocket and

patted it. "I shall return this to you at breakfast tomorrow." In a conspiratorial whisper he added, "Provided I'm not too hungover to remember."

Sophie smiled serenely. "Then perhaps you should see to the task tonight."

"If I do, will you dance with me?"

Sophie tilted her head, thoughtful. "Yes."

Fiona laughed and squeezed her friend's shoulders. "Thanks, Soph." For her sake, Fiona sincerely hoped Lord Carter wasn't the scoundrel behind the blackmail letters.

She scanned the drawing room and spotted Lord Pentham on the settee, conversing with Lily as she poured tea. Fiona glided over, handed each of them a card, and quietly repeated her request for notes addressed to the countess.

"Happy to oblige," said the marquess. "And if I don't have the chance to write it before departing tomorrow, I'll simply have my secretary send it over to you once we're back in town."

"No," Fiona blurted. She couldn't wait that long. Besides, she needed to be certain the handwriting was Lord Pentham's—and not his secretary's. "I'd prefer to collect the cards here, if possible."

Lily shrugged. "What's the difference?"

"Well," Fiona improvised, "the notes will likely be more heartfelt and meaningful if they're written now— before the memories of this week have had the chance to fade."

"That's very sentimental of you," Lily said, vaguely suspicious.

"It makes perfect sense to me." Pentham made a polite bow. "Consider it done, Miss Hartley."

"Thank you." Fiona exhaled in relief and furtively

waved the remaining cards. "Now if you'll excuse me, I'm off to press a few others into service."

But the only person she truly needed to speak with was Mr. Kirby. He stood alone at the sideboard pouring himself a brandy, and though it was an excellent time to approach him, Fiona's feet felt like they were made of stone.

Summoning all her courage, she pasted on a smile and walked over. "Good evening, Mr. Kirby. I wondered if I might—"

"Ah, Miss Hartley," he said cordially, setting down the decanter. "I'm glad for a moment to speak with you privately."

The hairs on the back of her neck prickled. "Indeed?"

"I wanted to reiterate my offer to assist you in any way I can with the difficult issue you're facing." He took a step toward her and lowered his voice. "The one that I recently learned of through the note."

"That's very kind of you, but I—"

"Please know that while I am not privy to all the facts, I understand that this is an intensely personal and delicate situation. If you were to accept my help, I would employ the utmost discretion."

"Thank you, but I believe I have the matter well in hand."

"Do you?" Mr. Kirby scratched the side of his head, thoughtful. "I don't mean to pry, and I certainly don't wish to frighten you, but blackmail is a nasty business, rife with danger. I don't like it."

Fiona's hands turned clammy. Mr. Kirby seemed so sincere and concerned. In return, she was treating him like a suspect. "I don't like it either," she confessed. But at least she now had Gray on her side. She opened her mouth to tell Mr. Kirby he needn't worry on her account, but he spoke first.

"What sort of cad would have the gall to demand that a proper young lady skulk through the park in the middle of the night and leave money in a tree? It boils my blood."

"I plan to take precautions." But even as Fiona spoke the words, an alarm sounded in her head. Because the blackmail letter that Mr. Kirby had found made no mention of a late-night rendezvous. Or a park. Or a hollowed-out tree.

Dear God. She'd discovered her blackmailer. And he was the very last person in the world she wished it to be.

"Good. One can't be too careful." Mr. Kirby swirled the brandy in his glass and took a sip. "I hope the ordeal is behind you soon—and that you never hear from the scoundrel again."

Fiona's heart pounded, fueled by a potent combination of fury and fear. "But it's you. *You* are the scoundrel, are you not? I never revealed the details about the blackmailer's instructions."

In the blink of an eye, Mr. Kirby's expression slid from concerned to alarmed to menacing. "You must be overwrought, Miss Hartley. Delusional. If you'll recall, I've been trying to assist you," he said through gritted teeth. "I merely guessed at the particulars of the blackmailer's instructions—which are rather clichéd, when you think on it."

Fiona glanced over her shoulder. Mama, the countess, and Lady Callahan sipped claret near the fireplace, while Sophie and Lily mingled with the gentlemen across the room. Surely no harm would come to her in such a genteel setting—but she shivered nonetheless.

She'd exposed Mr. Kirby. Backed him into a corner.

And a tingling at the base of her spine told her he was more dangerous than ever. Still, this was no time to back down.

"I'd already deduced the blackmailer was present at this house party," Fiona said. "You've simply confirmed what I didn't want to believe—that Gray's oldest and closest friend would stoop to such treachery. What perplexes me is *why*. Why would you do it?"

"I've a gambling habit to support." Kirby snorted. "Your family has money to spare."

She raised her chin and crossed her arms to keep her hands from trembling. "When Gray learns what you did he's going to be livid."

Mr. Kirby snarled and took a step closer. "He's *not* going to learn the truth," he ground out, his tone lethal.

"He most certainly will." Fiona ignored the panic rising in her chest. "If he were in this room, I'd tell him right now."

Mr. Kirby shot her a terrifyingly smug smile. "That would be a mistake."

"Do you imagine for one second that he'll take your side? He's the man I intend to marry. And he deserves to know what sort of person you are, even if the news will crush him."

"It would," he said evenly. "But there's something that would devastate him even more—should it become widely known. An unpleasant incident that could be dredged up. A sordid bit of information that could put all of Gray's property, including the Fortress, in jeopardy."

Fiona swallowed. "What are you talking about?"

"His father's suicide, of course. I witnessed it with my own eyes. Felt his blood splatter on my skin. I've never mentioned it because of the obvious legal implications—property forfeit to the Crown, et cetera. Besides, I thought it best to spare Gray and his dear grandmother the shame and heartache of having the old earl's body exhumed and buried at a crossroads with a stake through his heart."

"You . . ." Fiona clenched her fists till her nails dug into her palms. "You are a hateful, opportunistic, self-centered scoundrel. And you won't manipulate me. I don't believe you'd betray Gray that way. You're bluffing."

"That's where you're wrong, sweeting." Mr. Kirby's eyes turned cold and empty. "You see, I've nothing to lose. I borrowed some money from a rather unscrupulous gentleman who will send his henchmen after me if I don't repay him—soon. I've seen what happens to other fellows who've neglected to make their payments on time, and let's just say there's an excellent chance I would not survive the late penalty."

"Surely you have a better option than blackmail," said Fiona, making one last valiant attempt at reason.

"I don't, actually. That's why I must insist that you end your relationship with Gray and provide the money I demanded in exchange for my silence. If you don't leave the money when and where I've instructed, the *London Hearsay* will have not one, but two, extremely salacious stories in its next edition. Headlines mentioning whores and suicides invariably sell lots of papers. There's nothing the ton loves better than a spectacular fall from grace."

Fiona's knees wobbled. "I *can't* break off my engagement to Gray."

Mr. Kirby sipped his brandy, seemingly unperturbed. "Then I hope he'll be able to forgive you for allowing the scandal about his father to surface—and for placing the Fortress in jeopardy."

Heaven help her, Mr. Kirby was heartless. But perhaps she could appeal to his practical side. "I need my dowry money if I'm to have any hope of paying you off."

"You seem like a resourceful girl," he said snidely. "You'll think of another way to come up with the funds." His gaze flickered over her throat, turning hungry at the sight of her mother's jewels.

She fought back a wave of nausea. "I will try." What choice did she have? "But you must swear to me that you'll never reveal what you know—about my sister *or* Gray's father."

"I would not take pleasure in destroying either your sister or Gray, Miss Hartley. But I will if necessary. If you want this nightmare to end, simply deliver the money to me as I've requested—and stay the hell away from Gray." He threw back the rest of his brandy, set his snifter on the sideboard, and adjusted the cuffs of his jacket. "Do try and enjoy tonight's ball. We wouldn't want Gray or the others to suspect that anything's amiss."

Fiona managed a nod. She desperately wanted to flee the room and put some distance between her and Mr. Kirby before she did something rash like slap his face or smash a decanter over his head.

But the truth was she already knew in her heart what she must do. What she *would* do.

If the only way to save Lily and Gray was to pay off Mr. Kirby and end her relationship with Gray, then she would do both those things.

Even if it meant giving up her mother's necklace.

Even if it meant breaking Gray's heart—and her own.

She'd thought she'd have a lifetime to love Gray, but it turned out she had only one more night.

One night . . . to say good-bye.

Chapter 28

Fiona's father was not what Gray had expected. Though Hartley had silver at his temples and stood several inches shorter than Gray, he appeared strong enough to hold his own in any pub brawl. Unlike his wife, he seemed wholly unconcerned with impressing anyone, and he spoke plainly and directly.

Which Gray respected.

He welcomed the older man into his study and offered him a seat in the leather armchair beside the fireplace. Suddenly feeling like a lad of eighteen, Gray loosened his cravat and rolled his shoulders. Forced himself to relax. "Care for a drink?"

Hartley nodded as he settled himself into the chair. He cast an eye about the study, no doubt taking in the dusty bookshelves and faded carpets. "You don't seem like the sort of man who spends a lot of time behind his desk."

Unsure whether the statement was meant to be a criticism or compliment, Gray shrugged. "I prefer to work outside, even if it means getting my hands dirty. But I don't neglect my duties as an earl." He splashed brandy into a pair of snifters.

"Glad to hear it." Hartley took the glass that Gray

offered and sipped thoughtfully. "I wasn't sure why my daughters were so eager to have me join them here," he began. "But after seeing Fiona at dinner, I think I know."

Gray's chest squeezed at the mention of her. "Oh?"

"I would have had to be blind not to notice the way she looked at you—and the way you looked at her. I confess the sight filled me with both delight and dread."

Gray sank into the armchair across from Hartley and looked at him earnestly. "I understand your ambivalence. You do not know me well, and you want the best for your daughter. But I care for her greatly and very much want to marry her." It was such a relief to say the words—to have his intentions out in the open. "I promise to take care of Fiona and do everything in my power to make her happy. I'd like to humbly ask for your blessing."

Hartley said nothing but continued to stare at Gray expectantly. As if he was waiting for Gray to say more.

When the prolonged silence grew uncomfortable, Gray added, "She would become a countess, of course, a title with a host of responsibilities, but she'd still have plenty of time for sketching and enjoying the company of family and friends. We'd spend most of the year in London, and you and your family would be welcome there as well as here at the Fortress—whenever you please."

Hartley shot him a wistful smile. "*Why* do you want to marry Fiona?"

Gray set his snifter on the table beside him and leaned forward. "Because she's kind, talented, beautiful . . ."

"And?" Hartley prodded.

Fiona's father wasn't going to let Gray off easily, damn it, and Gray didn't blame him. But for him, talking about emotions was like speaking in a foreign tongue. The best he could do was focus on the way Fiona made him feel and hope his sentences were coherent.

Gray stood and paced the length of the study as he spoke. "She challenges me to see the world in a different— more thoughtful—way."

"Go on," Hartley said.

"She smiles and a cold, dreary room feels like a sunny summer day. And though she has an adorable tendency to stumble and trip on occasion, she possesses unexpected grace in little things."

"Like?"

Gray stroked his chin, thoughtful. "Like the tender way she dotes on an elderly woman . . . and the courageous way she faces her fears." Hell, he'd said more than he intended— all of it true. But there was something else he hadn't said. Hadn't even realized until that very moment.

He loved her.

He hadn't thought it possible. Hadn't thought himself capable. But over the course of the last two weeks, something deep inside him had changed.

The frozen tundra that was his heart had melted— because of Fiona.

Hartley cleared his throat, and his eyes grew suspiciously shiny. "She's special, my Fiona. Made of strong stuff. We were all heartbroken when her mother died, but Fiona took it particularly hard, crying herself to sleep every night for at least a year. Then one morning at breakfast she said to me, 'Papa, I dreamed of Mother last night. She told me that I mustn't cry anymore. She said I must be brave and take care of you and Lily . . . so that's what I intend to do.'"

"That sounds like Fiona," Gray mused. "Selfless and determined."

"I've tried to give her the best of everything, to do what was best for her and Lily, even when that required me to step back a bit and let her stepmother take the reins. Look-ing back, I fear that, more often than not, I let Fiona down."

"With all respect, sir, you judge yourself too harshly. I happen to know she adores you."

Hartley inhaled deeply and shook his head as if to clear it. "If she does, it's in spite of my myriad mistakes. The point is, Fiona deserves to be happy and cherished. She deserves to be *loved*."

"I couldn't agree more, sir."

"I want the world for my daughter, and she, apparently, wants *you*. I will give you my blessing under this one con-dition: You swear that you will have a care with her heart."

Gray exhaled, relieved. "I swear. You have my word." He stood and extended his arm for a handshake, surprised when the older man embraced him and patted him on the back gruffly instead.

"Your life is about to change in the best possible ways, Ravenport. If anyone can brighten up this dark, musty castle, Fiona can. You'd be a fool to underestimate her."

Gray clasped Hartley's shoulder and looked him in the eye. "If there's one thing I've learned about Fiona, it's to never, ever bet against her."

By the time Fiona slipped into the ballroom, men and women dressed in their finery had already started stream-ing in, craning their necks and exclaiming over the unique and delightful decorations adorning the walls. Gray and his grandmother were stationed by the room's main entrance, graciously greeting their guests—mostly villagers and neighbors from nearby estates—as they entered.

The atmosphere was everything a ball should be: fes-tive, merry, and a little magical.

It was also precisely the opposite of what Fiona felt inside. But there was no one she could confide in. No one could know the secrets Mr. Kirby had threatened to reveal—or that he'd threatened her at all. Determined to make the most of her last night at the Fortress, she'd pinched her cheeks and smoothed her hair before entering the ballroom through the terrace doors.

"There you are!" Mama exclaimed, looping an arm through Fiona's and pulling her into the throng. "I was just about to send Lily in search of you. I spoke with your father briefly—he told me the good news about Ravenport. Just imagine—my daughter, the countess." She fanned her face with one hand as though shooing away impending tears of joy.

"Please, Mama, do not raise your hopes prematurely." Fiona felt like her heart was cracking open. "Nothing is official. No announcement has been made."

And no announcement *would* be made. As soon as she had an opportunity to pull Gray aside, she'd tell him she wasn't ready to make their betrothal public. She wasn't certain what reason she'd give for her sudden reluctance after she'd shamelessly pursued him, constantly reminding him that time was of the essence.

But she'd think of something.

"My dear," Mama said, incredulous. "Do not be daft. Lord Ravenport has asked for your hand. This is a most encouraging development, an undeniably auspicious occasion, an exceedingly—"

"Hasn't Sophie done a remarkable job with the decorations?" Fiona interrupted, desperate for a change of subject. "I wouldn't be surprised if a fairy or sprite mistook the ballroom for her very own enchanted forest."

Mama gave her a sharp look. "You'll not spoil this evening for me, Fiona. This is the moment we've been work-ing toward. All those years at Miss Haywinkle's, the endless strategizing, the kowtowing to people who con-sider themselves our betters—"

"But I never—"

Mama yanked Fiona's arm back so that she turned, and they stood toe to toe. "This isn't only about you."

Her stepmother was right. It wasn't. It was about Lily and Papa and Gray, too. Fiona had to do what was right for all of them. But since a tiff with Mama was the last thing she needed, she took a conciliatory tone. "You're right, of course, and I won't forget it. I suppose I'm simply a bit nervous. But I do think it best to rein in our excite-ment and remain outwardly cool."

Mama raised her brows. "Very well. You have managed to string the earl along this far. Now that the finish line is in sight, see that you don't botch it."

Fiona prickled at the implication that she'd been ma-nipulating Gray but bit her tongue. "Yes, Mama." She was about to excuse herself in order to seek out Lily and Sophie when her stepmother sucked in her cheeks and nar-rowed her eyes.

"*Who* is that woman?"

Fiona followed the direction of Mama's wary gaze to the ballroom's main entrance where a beautiful young lady gracefully extended her hand to Gray. He bowed over it and looked up at her with barely concealed curiosity—and as he did, a sick, uneasy sensation slithered up Fiona's spine.

"I believe that's Lady Helena," she breathed, "to whom Lord Ravenport was once engaged."

"What is she doing *here*?" asked Mama, echoing the question in Fiona's head.

"Forgive me for intruding upon your conversation." Lady Callahan scurried toward them, dragging her gaze away from the earl and Lady Helena. Indeed, it seemed half the ballroom was fixated on the pair, amazed that the woman who'd scorned Gray not a month earlier now waltzed into his ball as though she were an esteemed guest of honor. "I overheard you asking about Lady Helena. I'm told her uncle owns a neighboring estate. When he inquired as to whether his relatives might accompany him tonight, the countess politely agreed. But I'm sure she never dreamed the woman who jilted her grandson would have the audacity to make an appearance."

"And yet here she is," whispered Fiona.

"Never fear," Mama said, in a rare attempt to bolster her. "You outshine her in every respect. Her dress and jewelry cannot compare to yours."

Perhaps not, but Helena didn't need those adornments to shine. She wore a simple, elegant gown of white silk with silver embroidery on the sleeves and at the hem—the kind of gown that enhanced one's beauty instead of competing with it. But it wasn't her flawless complexion or golden curls that inspired envy in Fiona. Rather, it was her confidence and grace. Fiona would bet her favorite pearl earrings that Helena had never been so gauche as to fall off a rock or trip over her own feet in a public venue.

Helena had been born and bred as a proper lady, endowed with a natural elegance that could never be replicated in someone like Fiona—despite all Miss Haywinkle's valiant attempts.

Fiona swallowed the bitter taste in her throat, reminding herself that none of it mattered. After Mr. Kirby's latest threat, she couldn't marry Gray anyway.

For once, she was grateful that he hadn't fallen head over heels in love with her as she had with him. It would make it easier to deliver the news that she couldn't wed him. He'd no doubt be shocked and a bit hurt, but he'd recover.

Long, long before Fiona would.

Chapter 29

Receiving lines were one of the great many reasons Gray was opposed to hosting balls. He'd shaken more hands and made more polite conversation in the last hour than he had in the entire last year. All he wanted to do was find Fiona and tell her about the meeting with her father.

He'd been considering what Hartley said—about wanting what was best for Fiona and feeling as though he'd failed her. It seemed her father regretted the distance that had grown between him and his daughters as much as Fiona did. Perhaps if Fiona confided in him about the blackmail, they could work together to prevent a scandal . . . and in doing so start to mend the rift.

Gray knew that would make her happy—and, more than anything, he wanted her to be happy.

He also wanted her to know that she didn't have to marry him to protect her sister. He would help Fiona regardless. So would her father.

She shouldn't make the decision to marry Gray out of sheer desperation. She had options.

To be clear, Gray wanted her to *know* she had options—and choose to marry him anyway.

He'd been contemplating the best way to explain his feelings to Fiona when Helena made her entrance, looking like a Roman goddess who'd graciously deigned to join some lesser mortals at their quaint version of a ball.

He wanted her gone.

"Good evening, Gray."

Keenly aware that his grandmother, who stood on his left, listened to every word he uttered, he inclined his head. "Lady Helena."

"I hope my presence here isn't unwelcome."

"I confess it's rather baffling."

She cast her gaze downward, her dark lashes fluttering over her cheeks. "I realized that I owe you an apology."

He arched a skeptical brow. "And you thought the best time and place to deliver it was in the midst of a ball I'm hosting?"

She had the good grace to look contrite. "I was curious to see how you'd managed it—and what improvements you'd made." She stared at the transformed ballroom with undisguised appreciation. "It's lovely. This house has more potential than I realized."

Once, he would have given anything to hear her say those words.

Now . . . he didn't give a damn what she thought. He wished her no malice, but he no longer cared to impress her. No longer sought her approval.

And he definitely didn't want her interfering with his plans. "Now that we've satisfied your curiosity, I see no reason—"

He was about to say *for you to stay,* but his grandmother gently squeezed his forearm, reminding him of his manners, damn it all.

"I see no reason why you shouldn't enjoy the rest of your evening," he improvised.

Helena shot him a distinctively sultry look. "I hope to," she said, before turning her attention to his grandmother, who was polite but reserved—a sure sign that she did not hold the younger woman in high regard. But Helena seemed unperturbed by the cool reception as she walked toward the center of the room like this ball was her coronation.

At least most of the guests had arrived and Gray was now free to seek out Fiona. He escorted his grandmother to a chair beneath a decorative trellis—part of Sophie's fanciful design—where some of the other matrons sat, looking out over the dance floor. "Would you care for a drink, Grandmother?"

"No, my dear boy. I shall be fine. Go enjoy yourself." Her eyes twinkled. "I suggest you start by dancing with Fiona."

"That is the plan." He planted a kiss on her soft cheek and easily spotted Fiona, a vision in her blue-green gown, talking with some of the villagers on the other side of the room.

He'd taken exactly two steps in her direction when someone seized him by the elbow.

"There you are." Kirby handed Gray a glass of brandy, which only partially made up for the annoyance Gray felt at being intercepted on his way to Fiona. "There's something I wanted to ask you."

Gray rubbed the back of his neck. "By all means. But make it quick—I'm looking for someone."

"It's about Fiona Hartley."

Kirby suddenly had Gray's full attention. "What about her?"

"Have you noticed her behaving strangely?"

Gray blinked at his friend. "What do you mean?"

Kirby's forehead wrinkled as though he were perplexed. "I spoke with her after dinner tonight, and she seemed . . . nervous. Almost as if she were plotting something."

"You're being paranoid. Perhaps she was preoccupied with the ball. She, Lily, and Sophie have worked tirelessly preparing this place."

"Maybe that's it." Kirby waved his glass in the direction of the dance floor. "Is she the one you're looking for?"

"Yes, damn it. And now she's waltzing with Carter." Gray muttered a curse and decided he might as well do his duty as host. "I'm going to ask the vicar's daughter to dance. You might try playing the part of the gentleman, too."

Kirby snorted. "What's the fun in that?"

"Suit yourself," Gray said with a shrug. "Just stay out of trouble."

Determined to take his own advice, Gray located his partner and made his way to the dance floor. He caught Fiona's eye a few times as she turned, wishing *he* were the one holding her hand and touching the small of her back. Now that he'd defined exactly what it was he felt for her, he could hardly wait to tell her.

But when the set was over, he was obliged to escort the vicar's daughter back to her mother, and by the time he found Fiona, she was dancing with the baker.

He'd begun to despair of ever claiming a dance with her, but at the end of the second set he spotted her speaking with his grandmother before scurrying from the room.

At last, he had a chance to catch up with her—away from the crowd. Damned if he'd let that golden opportunity go to waste.

When Fiona entered the countess's bedchamber, rain pelted the windows and wind rattled the panes. She closed the curtains and found the countess's lorgnette on her dressing table, precisely where the older woman had told her it would be. She took a moment to check her own reflection, somewhat shocked to see that the angst she felt inside wasn't plain on her face. She was grateful for the chance to escape the ballroom for a short while, so she could cease pretending that everything was fine. But there was no time to soak her handkerchief with tears.

Fiona had to give the lorgnette to the countess and then find a way to speak with Gray.

Hoping to avoid as many people as possible, she took the back stairs and made her way down a corridor that led to the ballroom. Most of the rooms along the hallway were closed off, but one door hung slightly ajar, and as she passed it she heard a man whisper her name.

A chill skittered up the back of her neck. The last thing she needed was another confrontation with Mr. Kirby.

"Fiona," the voice said again. "It's me—Gray." He poked his head out of the doorway and shot her a smile that melted her knees. How on earth was she ever going to summon the strength to tell him she couldn't marry him?

"Gray? What are you doing in there?"

He glanced up and down the hall. "Waiting for you."

She waved the lorgnette in front of her. "I . . . ah, I have to give this to your grandmother."

"I'll see to it." He darted out the door and took the glasses from her. "Will you wait for me inside? I shall return in no less than two minutes."

"You once made me a similar promise," she teased. "I seem to recall spending half the night in your garden. Alone."

He stepped closer and slid a hand over her hip, making her belly flutter. "I won't fail you this time."

"I'll wait." She did need to speak to him. "But please hurry."

"Lock the door and don't open it till I knock," he said, before striding toward the ballroom.

Fiona stepped inside the small, windowless room and locked the door before looking around. A lone candle flickered on a small table, and she picked it up to better inspect her surroundings. The room was scarcely bigger than a closet, and she doubted she could take four steps in any direction. The shelves that covered one entire wall contained baskets of yellowed linens, dusty china, and chipped glassware. The wooden table in the center of the room was taller than average, as though it had been used for ironing tablecloths and such. A utilitarian chair was tucked into the corner, but Fiona was too anxious to sit.

Instead, she carefully set the candle back on the table and paced as best she could in the cramped space.

Before long, a knock sounded at the door. "It's Gray."

Thank God. She opened the door and he rushed in, his broad shoulders and considerable height instantly filling the room. He locked the door, turned to her, and pulled her into his arms. Like he couldn't wait to hold her. Like he'd . . . missed her.

Her breath hitched in her throat because she'd missed him, too. And because now that he was here, she didn't want to say good-bye.

He cradled her face in his hands and took her mouth in a kiss that was impatient, hungry, and hot. His hips pressed against hers, and her bottom bumped into the table, almost toppling the candle.

He caught it in one hand and swiftly propped it on a high shelf where it cast a soft glow over the room. "God, Fiona. It seems like I've been waiting forever to touch you. To taste you."

"I've been eager to see you, too." She paused to swallow the painful knot in her throat.

"Listen," he said earnestly, "I didn't invite Helena, and I don't want her here. If I could send her away without making a scene I would."

His words were a balm to Fiona's soul. Even if there was no future for her and Gray, she needed to believe that what they'd shared over the last few weeks was real. "That's sweet of you to say, but it doesn't matter."

"You're right," he said smoothly. Her heart squeezed in her chest as he backed her up against the table again, lifting her a few inches so that her bottom rested on the edge. "It doesn't matter who's in that bloody ballroom. The prince himself could make an appearance and I wouldn't give a damn. As far as I'm concerned, tonight is all about *you*. Starting. Right. Now."

Sweet Jesus. She should end it here, before his kisses rendered her completely incapable of coherent thought. Before she lost the resolve to tell him what she must. But his mouth was on hers and his hands were everywhere—caressing her neck, cupping her breasts, stroking between her legs.

Yes, she should most definitely put a halt to this. Instead, she was spearing her fingers through his hair, wrapping her legs around his, and kissing him with wild abandon.

Would it be so wrong to surrender—and savor her last night with him?

Perhaps it was greedy of her, but she wanted one more precious memory to tuck away. One more chance to feel adored and cherished and loved.

"You're so beautiful." He dragged his mouth down her neck, kissing every inch of her exposed skin. "All through dinner, as I watched you across the table, I imagined stripping this gown off you. Making you mine."

Good heavens. "We're taking enough chances as it is," she said, her voice breathless to her own ears. "I can't remove my gown."

Gray growled. "Fair enough. We'll work around it. For now."

Fiona gulped as he bent and raised the hem of her gown and shift, exposing her legs all the way up to her thighs. He wrapped an arm around her waist and effortlessly lifted her off the table, hiked her dress around her waist, and gently set her down again. Only, this time her bottom rested on the smooth wood of the table.

A wicked gleam lit his eyes and he knelt before her, making her heart flutter. "Ever since that morning in the cottage, I've been wanting to do this again."

He parted her thighs and tasted her, tentative at first. But soon his tongue grew bolder, his mouth more insistent. She arched her back, leaning into him, and he moaned in approval—which sent delicious vibrations through her body. Suddenly, her bodice felt tight and her legs felt weak. As if he knew, he lifted her knees over his shoulders and gripped her hips, steadying her.

Here was the man she loved, kneeling before her, completely and selflessly devoting himself to the task of pleasing her. He'd claimed he couldn't love her, but this . . . well, if it wasn't love, it was an excellent imitation.

With every wicked flick of his tongue and every sensual caress, he coaxed her closer. She let her head fall back and gave herself up to the pure, potent pleasure that coiled inside her, crying out as her release came.

Sweet little waves still pulsed through her as Gray stood and looked at her solemnly. "I swear to you that I will never, ever tire of that."

His admission made her smile, even as it broke her

heart. When she was certain her legs would support her, she eased herself off the table and pressed her body to his. "There's something I must tell you, Gray."

He cradled her head in his hand and brushed a finger over her bottom lip. "May I tell you something first? Please?"

His earnest gaze and the hitch in his voice made it impossible to deny him. "Of course."

"I realized something earlier tonight. Our engagement might have started out as a business arrangement, but sometime after you kissed me and before you sketched the Fortress, it became much, much more."

Dear God. These were the words she'd been dying to hear. But the timing was all wrong. It was too late for her and Gray. "I care for you, too," she began. "And when I wrote that letter proposing to you, I never dreamed that things would turn out like this."

"Nor did I." Gray picked her up and spun her around in the center of the tiny closet—as if he could barely contain his joy. "I love you, Fiona Hartley. I didn't think I was capable, but the last two weeks have changed me. *You've* changed me."

Tears stung her eyes. "Truly?"

He nodded. "I've been in a stupor for the last two decades. Living without really living, if that makes sense. Now I've started to see things the way *you* see them—full of possibility and hope."

"That's the most beautiful thing anyone's said to me." Fiona swallowed the huge lump in her throat.

"I couldn't wait to tell you," he said, caressing her cheek. "But now you may tell me what's on your mind. You said you wanted to talk."

"I do," she said. But she couldn't break off their engagement only moments after he'd bared his soul to her. And selfishly, she wanted this night with him. She needed a taste of what might have been if fate had been kinder to them both. "But it can wait."

She unbuttoned his waistcoat and the front of his trousers, wishing she had the slightest clue as to what she was doing. But what she lacked in experience she would simply have to make up for with determination.

Letting instinct be her guide, she pushed Gray back so that he sat on the edge of the table. With uncharacteristic daring, she circled her fingers around his erection and stroked, pleased to hear him moan in response. When she would have knelt, he stopped her.

"Wait. Don't spoil your gown." He grabbed the back of the wooden chair and placed it behind her. When she sat and scooted the chair between his sprawled legs, she found she was at the perfect height for . . . well, for doing what she was about to do.

Boldly, she brushed her lips up and down his shaft. He seemed to approve, so she tried swirling her tongue around the top. When he muttered a curse, she took him in her mouth and sucked.

"God, Fiona." He gripped the edge of the table, his knuckles white. "You'll be the death of me."

Encouraged, she took her cues from him. Every groan, gasp, and muscle flex helped her discern what he liked. Knowing she could give him such pleasure thrilled her.

This night was but another thread in the intimate tapestry they'd woven. Another wall she'd broken down. Another memory.

"Fiona," he said hoarsely. "Please, stop."

She sat up, momentarily wondering if she'd done something wrong, but he quickly pulled her to her feet and kissed her . . . almost reverently.

"I need you," he said. "Now."

She slid her fingers through the curls at his nape. "I am yours," she said simply. And it was true. Even if she couldn't marry him, she would always be his. He would always have her heart.

"You are amazing." He touched his forehead to hers. "And I am the luckiest man in the world."

Fiona refused to cry. It would spoil everything, and she would not allow their final evening together to turn into some maudlin scene. So she kissed him.

He steered her toward the table and gently spun her so that his chest was to her back. She rested her palms on the table and glanced at him over her shoulder. He pulled her skirts up again, but this time he bunched the fabric on the table in front of her.

She felt exceedingly wanton, but Gray's growl of appreciation alleviated any embarrassment.

When he caressed the insides of her thighs, just above the tops of her stockings, the tips of her breasts tightened into hard little buds.

When he trailed hot kisses down the side of her neck, desire pooled in her belly.

And when he stroked the folds at her entrance and eased a finger inside her, she moaned with pleasure.

A sweet, insistent pulsing began at her core and radiated through her body. "Gray. I want you."

He kissed her beneath her ear and nipped at her lobe. Glided his hands over her hips and gently lifted them so that she stood on the tips of her toes. Positioned himself at her entrance and slowly thrust.

"Oh. My." He inched deeper and deeper, filling her and moving in a rhythm that made her dizzy with desire.

"Good?" he asked.

"Yes," she said breathlessly. *So good.* Pleasantly light-headed, she focused only on her connection with Gray. She moved in time with him, matching his pace, meeting him thrust for thrust. She listened to his breathing and the low moans that escaped his throat. She basked in the knowledge that in this moment he was hers. Completely and utterly. Hers.

"Come for me, Fiona."

"Again?" She hadn't realized it was possible, but then she *did* feel a delicious sort of tingling inside, and the pulsing beckoned—like a gift begging to be unwrapped.

He slid a hand around her front and dipped it between her legs, expertly locating the center of her desire. "I have every faith in you, siren. Just think wicked thoughts."

That much was easy—in fact, Miss Haywinkle would have suffered a bout of apoplexy if she had any inkling of what Fiona was thinking.

Because she was thinking about Gray's callused hands, roving over her naked skin.

She was thinking about his tongue, tasting and sucking until she'd cried out in bliss.

She was thinking about his wicked fingers, and the pleasure he could bring her just by—

"*Oh.*"

Her climax blossomed like a perfect sunrise—slow, sweet, and warm. Exquisite sensations echoed through her core, pulling Gray closer, deeper. Tendrils of pleasure unfurled through her body and stretched through her limbs.

Just as she crested, he did, too. He groaned as he came, and she felt his release inside her, a potent mix of raw power and sultry heat. All the while, he held her close and whispered her name.

When at last he was spent, he leaned forward, resting

on top of her. She savored the comforting weight of his body and the way he nuzzled the back of her neck—like a puppy craving affection. "Are you all right?" he asked, with a tenderness that made her eyes burn.

"Yes. But there's—"

"Wait. Let me find something to clean you up." He left her briefly and returned with a soft linen napkin, which he gently pressed between her legs, wiping away his seed. "There, that's better." He carefully pulled her skirts down, then grabbed another napkin off the shelf to clean himself.

As he stuffed his shirttail back into his trousers and buttoned up, he grinned at her like she'd given him . . . the world. "That was amazing." He stepped closer and cradled her head in his hands. "*You* are amazing. And I cannot wait to announce our engagement tonight."

Oh no. She could feel the tears coming, and already her throat was closing up. "About that—"

Boom. A deafening crash was followed by the clinking of shattered glass. Screams erupted.

And the commotion came from the direction of the ballroom.

Gray cocked his head. "What the hell—" He grabbed the door handle. "I must go. Stay here for a while at least. Don't return to the ballroom till we know it's safe. I'll find you as soon as I can." He pressed his lips to hers in a short but soulful kiss before releasing her.

"I love you, Gray." The words had tumbled out of her mouth, and while they were true, she shouldn't have said them. Because they couldn't be together after tonight. She couldn't be the reason he lost everything he owned or the reason his family's name was dragged through the mud.

"I love you, too." He shot her a look so warm and genuine and happy that her chest felt like it was cracking open. Then he bolted into the corridor.

She held back tears as the door clicked shut behind him.

Chapter 30

Gray sprinted out of the linen closet and headed down the corridor toward the ballroom, almost too terrified to imagine what had caused the earthshaking boom.

What if a chandelier had crashed down upon the guests? Or a large chunk of the plaster ceiling had dropped on their heads? *Sweet Lucifer.*

His gut clenched. He had to find his grandmother, had to make sure she was all right.

He jogged into the ballroom through the side entrance, relieved to see the chandeliers still hanging and the ceiling intact—but the far side of the room was in a shamble.

It looked as though someone had used a large tree as a battering ram on the French doors that led to the terrace. Thick, leafy boughs protruded through the panes, and splintered wood littered the parquet floor. Wind whipped through the room, blowing soggy sheet music everywhere. Most of the guests had gathered around the rubble.

Gray started to maneuver his way to the front where he saw Kirby. "Is anyone hurt?" he shouted.

"A few cuts and scratches, but nothing serious as far as I can tell." Kirby stood between the tree and the crowd, arms outstretched to keep people back from the sharp glass and broken beams. "I haven't inspected the terrace yet."

"The countess?" Gray asked. He'd already spotted Fiona's family and the rest of the house party guests in the throng. "Has anyone seen her?"

"I spoke with her a few minutes ago," Mrs. Hartley said. "Just before I heard an awful crack. My hair stood on end, and then the tree came right into the ballroom." She sobbed into her handkerchief, hysterical.

"My grandmother," he said slowly. "Where was she?"

"Right over there, beneath the decorative trellis." Mrs. Hartley waved in the direction of the rubble. "But after the crash, it was complete chaos. Glass raining down. People running everywhere. Armageddon, I tell you."

Gray dragged a hand down his face and addressed the crowd. "Please check that everyone in your party is accounted for. Then carefully make your way to the drawing room."

The guests gingerly walked over the shards of glass, wet leaves, bits of tree bark. As they milled about, Gray located Dr. Hopewell. "Would you tend to the cuts and bruises?"

"Of course."

"Kirby, will you lead everyone out of here? Ask the staff to bring towels and tea for the guests. I'll meet you in the drawing room as soon as I find my grandmother."

His friend clasped his shoulder and gave him a reassuring nod. "Certainly. I pray she's safe."

Gray hopped onto the trunk of the fallen tree and shimmied toward the exposed roots until debris from the broken doorframe prevented him from going farther. Craning his neck, he looked out onto the terrace. "Is anyone out there?"

His only answer was a steady rain punctuated by distant thunder.

He scanned the rubble around the tree, looking for a way onto the terrace. On the floor, in a corner where the

French doors had been, he spotted an opening big enough for him to crawl through. He jumped down, dropped to his stomach, and used his elbows to drag his body through the tight space.

"Grandmother?" Part of him wanted to hear her respond because it would mean she was conscious—and alive. But mostly he prayed she was nowhere near this mess. Mrs. Hartley said she'd been sitting by the doors before the tree crashed into the room, but maybe she'd had enough warning to get out of the way.

He squeezed his hips and legs through the opening, then scrambled to his feet. "Grandmother," he called again. "Is anyone out here?"

He grabbed a lantern hanging from the exterior wall overlooking the terrace and checked beneath every branch of the fallen tree. The weight of the trunk had crushed one of the marble benches on the terrace, but thankfully there was no sign of anyone hurt or trapped. Rain quickly soaked through Gray's jacket and shirt as he examined the base of the tree located just beyond the stone patio. Charred and jagged, it jutted from the ground like a miniature angry volcano. On the border of the terrace and the lawn was a hole ten times the size of a man's hat—a calling card left by the lightning strike.

Gray exhaled in relief. His grandmother wasn't out there—and she hadn't been crushed by the tree. Miraculously, no one had been. He hoped that he'd find his grandmother inside, wrapped in a shawl and sipping a cup of warm tea. Or in her chambers, tucked into bed by her maid. Anywhere, really—as long as she was safe.

Rather than crawl back into the ballroom, he walked outside the house toward the drawing room. Pentham spotted him from inside and unlocked the French doors. "I just sent Carter looking for you. The countess is here—she's fine. Her maid whisked her from the ballroom as soon as the wind began rattling the windows."

"Thank God." Gray wound his way through the packed room to his grandmother's chair beside the fire and wrapped her in a fierce hug. "You are all right?"

"Of course I am, dear boy. Why wouldn't I be?"

"I don't know—because the ballroom's been reduced to rubble?" He pressed a kiss to the back of her hand. "You gave me a scare."

"No one sustained more than a scratch." She gestured around the room at the guests squeezed onto every sofa, settee, and chair, happily sipping their drinks and chatting. "And thanks to the tree falling, they'll be talking about our ball for decades."

"I suppose that's true." His grandmother always found a silver lining.

"You're soaked. You should change before you catch your death of a cold," she said with a *tsk*. She narrowed her eyes. "*And* you should have the doctor examine that hand—you're bleeding."

"I'm fine," he assured her. He looked around the room for Fiona, hoping she wasn't still waiting in the linen closet.

As if his grandmother knew exactly what he was about, she said slyly, "Fiona is over there, comforting some of the matrons from the village."

He followed the direction of his grandmother's gaze and spotted her in a far corner of the room. With her fiery red hair and turquoise gown, she was a vision, bold and beautiful.

She circulated among the older guests, offering them small sandwiches, scones, and biscuits from the platter she held. She paused to talk with a plump white-haired woman seated on the pianoforte bench, momentarily setting down the platter to offer the woman her shawl. When the older woman appeared to protest, Fiona insisted she take it, smiling as she wrapped the fine silk around her shoulders.

Gray was riveted to her every move. She may have considered herself awkward and accident-prone, but he disagreed. To him, she was grace personified. Kind and thoughtful, she had a gift for putting others—including him—at ease.

Tonight's ball was supposed to have been a special occasion for her, the celebration of their engagement. All of that had changed with a bolt of lightning.

But maybe it didn't have to.

He stretched his neck above the crowd, trying to attract Fiona's attention. As though she felt his gaze on her, she looked up at him, and their eyes met.

Hers flashed with relief and affection and then . . . something sadder. Perhaps regret.

She must have been dismayed by the way the evening had turned out, and he didn't blame her. But he intended to remedy the situation immediately.

He hopped onto a small footstool so that he stood a couple of heads above everyone else. "Ladies and gentlemen," he called above the din, "may I have your attention?"

The crowd quickly quieted, and everyone turned toward him expectantly.

"First of all, I want to apologize for the scare we had tonight. I'm happy to report that no one was seriously hurt. I appreciate your cooperation and your understanding more than you know. I especially want to thank my friend Kirby—who I've always been able to count on—for helping to keep everyone calm in the aftermath."

Several of the guests raised their glasses. "Hear, hear!"

Gray inclined his head as he toasted Kirby, who, in turn, waved away the praise.

After a smattering of applause, Gray continued. "As

many of you know, the Fortress—and this entire estate—
has been largely neglected for many years. There have
been no balls, no dinner parties, no celebrations of any
kind. But I'm hoping to change all that . . . starting
tonight."

Gasps of anticipation filled the room, and several of the
ladies tittered in delight.

Gray wished he'd rehearsed the announcement a
little—for Fiona's sake. He didn't have a fancy engagement
ring or flowers to give her, but he'd suspected what she
really wanted was a romantic gesture. Something that
required him to step outside of the comfortable role of
cynical, brooding earl—and express what she meant to
him.

With poetry. Bad poetry. It was going to be humiliating. Kirby would mock him for the rest of his godforsaken
life. But if it made Fiona happy, it would be worth it.

Swallowing his nervousness, he pulled a rumpled
paper from his breast pocket, and unfolded it.

"I am the furthest thing from a poet, but earlier today I
wrote a few lines for someone special." He looked back at
the corner where he'd last seen Fiona, but she wasn't there.
Surely she was somewhere in the crowd—maybe with her
sister or his grandmother. Where else could she have gone?

And then he spied her standing by the door, her expression wistful. His heart swelled, and he forged ahead.

> *"Her beauty is so great no mermaid can compare.*
> *To challenge her in archery I would not dare.*
> *And whether we travel by horse or by boat,*
> *Her company keeps my troubled soul afloat."*

God, this was an abomination. He stared at his paper
and prepared to deliver the final couplet.

"With her, my future I intend to plan,
Forever striving to be a better man."

Several of the ladies sighed. More than a few gentlemen snickered.

Gray brushed it off, stuffed the poem back in his pocket, and continued. "Tonight's ball was intended to be a celebration—and a chance for me to share some news." He glanced back up at the doorway to find Fiona . . . only she wasn't there.

"Who is she, Ravenport?" Carter shouted. "Don't keep us all in suspense!"

Gray scanned the drawing room but didn't see Fiona anywhere, damn it. Maybe she'd taken ill. Maybe she'd been appalled by his attempt at poetry. "I'd hoped to make an announcement tonight," he said, "but it turns out the timing's not quite right."

"Of course it is, my darling."

Holy hell. Helena tossed a cascade of curls over her shoulder and wound her way through the crowded drawing room. Before he knew what she was about, she'd tugged him off the stool and was standing at his side, hooking her arm through his.

"No," he warned under his breath. "You misunderstand."

As though she hadn't heard him, she smiled broadly and addressed the crowd. "It's the perfect time to announce that we have realized we are indeed meant to be together. Our engagement is officially resumed, and I couldn't be happier."

"No," Gray repeated firmly. But the guests were already exclaiming over the news, cheering, and toasting the couple of the hour. He pulled away from Helena, but it was too late. Fiona's father stormed out of the drawing room, scowling. Mrs. Hartley clutched Lily's arm for support and fanned herself vigorously. His grandmother slumped in her chair, looking like she'd aged a decade in the last five minutes.

How the *devil* had events spiraled so out of control?

As women swarmed around Helena, eager to offer her their congratulations, Gray jumped back onto the stool. "Your attention, everyone." Slowly the buzz of chatter died down, and the crowd faced him once more. "Lady Helena and I are *not* engaged."

Gasps of shock and confusion filled the room.

"The poem was intended for another—Miss Fiona Hartley—but she seems to have . . . disappeared." He'd bared his soul, poured out his heart, and after everything they'd shared that evening, she'd left him.

He'd been so sure that Fiona was different. That she was courageous enough to weather any storm they might face. But it had only taken one storm—a literal storm—to send her running. And for the life of him, he couldn't understand why.

Though he wanted nothing more than to go in search of her and the answers to all the questions swirling in his head, he suspected she needed time and space. All he could do was mitigate the damage—and end the evening before things could get worse.

"I suspect that Miss Hartley, like many of you, may have felt overwhelmed by the events of the night—an understandable reaction after the near tragedy we experienced in the ballroom. All things considered, it seems prudent that we bring the evening to a close. I shall make my coach available to anyone who requires a ride back to the village. We'll have the rest of your carriages brought round as well, and my footmen will stand ready with umbrellas to escort you to your conveyances."

Somewhat reluctantly, the guests set down their drinks and began to say their good-byes. As Gray circulated throughout the room, offering apologies for having to cut short the festivities, Helena confronted him, blue eyes flashing with indignation.

"You've made a monumental mistake," she said icily. "I was willing to save your pride *and* take you back. I would have married you in spite of your empty coffers and this crumbling excuse for a house. Now you've destroyed any chance we had at reconciling."

"I've no interest in reconciling—and you shouldn't have assumed I did. You shouldn't have come tonight, Helena."

"In hindsight, I wish I had not. You don't deserve me. The gauche rich girl with the complete lack of breeding is a much better match for you. But perhaps she is having second thoughts as well? You're handsome enough that many women would be willing to look past your financial woes, Ravenport. What's harder to accept is the coldness in your heart. It's going to take more than a few lines of horrid poetry to convince a woman you're capable of love."

"You're right," he said thoughtfully. "Except for the part about Fiona—you couldn't be more wrong about her. She's smart, kind, and loyal. And while she may not be of noble birth, she *is* a lady—and one of the most generous, self-less people I know."

"How very touching," Helena said dryly. "You should have used some of that material in your poem instead of the bit about the mermaid."

"Kirby," Gray called. His friend ambled over and arched a brow. "Would you be so good as to escort Lady Helena to her uncle's carriage?"

"It would be my pleasure." Kirby offered his arm, and Helena took it stiffly. As they walked from the room, Helena called over her shoulder—one final, parting shot.

"Whatever haunts you can't be fixed with plaster and wood and nails. I'm not certain it can be fixed at all."

"That's nonsense, you know." Gray turned to find his grandmother standing at his side. "Anything can be fixed if you're willing to put in the work."

He slipped an around her shoulders. "I know . . . and thank you. The evening didn't turn out as I'd hoped." It was the understatement of the century.

He grandmother shrugged. "Perhaps it can be salvaged. Whatever you do, don't give up on her."

"Don't worry—I won't." And he prayed she hadn't given up on him. "Will you be all right for a few moments? I want to talk with Lily." He could trust her to give Fiona a message.

"Go. It's time for me to retire, and my maid will attend to me." She patted his hand affectionately. "I shall see you in the morning, my dear boy."

Gray pressed a kiss to her cheek and went to Lily, who sat at the pianoforte. Her fingers lightly danced across the keys, playing a sad but soulful melody.

"That's pretty," he said. "What's the song?"

"Something I made up." She stopped playing and looked at him. There was no censure in her gaze or in her voice, but he felt guilty just the same. "I don't know exactly what's going on between you and my sister, but I do know she looked troubled when she left the drawing room a few minutes ago."

"Yes. I'm sorry if I upset her," he said earnestly. "I need the chance to make things right."

"I'm not the one you should be talking to."

"I know. And I'm in desperate need of your help. Will you give Fiona a message for me?"

Chapter 31

Lily stood at the foot of the bed she and Fiona had shared for the duration of the house party, ticking off each part of Gray's message on her fingers. "He said that he wants to apologize for whatever distresses you and he must speak with you in person. He requested that you please meet him at the arranged time and place. I'm certain he would have come to you now if he could. But he's ensuring all the guests make it home safely."

Fiona nodded, pretending that her heart wasn't shattering into tiny pieces. "Anything else?"

Lily gave her a sympathetic smile. "No, but he seemed quite sincere. Do you intend to hear him out?"

In answer, Fiona strode to the armoire, pulled out her portmanteau, and tossed it onto the bed.

"Fi?" Lily stared at her curiously. "We can pack after breakfast tomorrow. You should try to sleep—"

"Papa and I are leaving tonight." Fiona yanked open the bag and stuffed her brush, jewelry, and robe inside. "As soon as the coach and horses can be readied."

Lily blinked, incredulous. "What? In the middle of the night? Why not leave first thing in the morning?"

"I can't really explain, except to say that it's impossible for me to spend one more night here." If she did, she wouldn't be able to resist running into Gray's arms. And then she'd be tempted to tell him about Kirby . . . and she couldn't. Gray stood to lose too much.

Lily sank onto the bed. Fiona continued to jam stockings and other items into her portmanteau, not really seeing or caring what she packed. She wasn't even going to change out of her ball gown before she departed. Every minute she spent under Gray's roof was a minute in which her resolve might falter. She couldn't risk it.

Especially not after the poem.

It was god-awful—and she'd adored every sentimental, bumbling word.

"Is Lady Helena the cause of your distress?" Lily asked. "She obviously came here hoping to stir up trouble but only succeeded in make a spectacle of herself. The earl seemed unfazed by her antics."

Oh God. "What antics?"

"After you left the drawing room, she announced that she and Lord Ravenport had reconciled and were once again betrothed."

"No wonder Papa was so irate," Fiona murmured. He'd intercepted her on the way to her bedchamber, taken one look at her tearstained face, and vowed to tear Gray from limb to limb. That's when she'd begged him to take her away from the Fortress immediately. And like the doting father he'd once been, he agreed.

"The earl publicly denied Helena's claim," Lily said. "He sent her away."

"That's good, I suppose." Fiona shook her head and checked the clock on her bedside table. She was to meet Papa in front of the house in ten minutes. "But Lady Helena is not the reason I'm upset."

Lily took Fiona's hand and squeezed it surprisingly hard. "I don't know what the earl said or did, but if he hurt you, I swear I'll make him pay, Fi. You have shown him nothing but kindness and understanding, and if he has taken advantage of you, I'll . . ." Her lovely face twisted into a grimace. "I'll find a way to make his life a living hell."

Heavens, her little sister could be terrifying. "Please don't," she said through grateful tears. The fact that Lily was willing to charge into battle for Fiona only reinforced her decision to pay off Kirby. She had to protect her sister—and Gray—at all costs. "He hasn't hurt me. I thought we could be happy together . . . but I've recently learned that's impossible." A sob escaped her throat. "I must go. Will you and Mary bring the rest of my things tomorrow?"

"Of course. Don't give it a second thought. I'm going to walk you downstairs to meet Papa." Lily wrapped a shawl around Fiona's shoulders and insisted on carrying her bag. "I'll depart with Mama tomorrow morning and see you at home in the afternoon."

Fiona walked quickly through the front hall, keeping her head down and praying she didn't encounter Gray. "We'll talk more when you are home."

"Promise you won't do anything drastic before then," Lily said.

"Like what?"

"Like cut off your gorgeous hair or burn your ball gown or join a convent."

Lily always knew how to make her smile. "Promise."

When they descended the front steps, the carriage was already waiting, and Papa stood beside the driver, shouting instructions to him. Upon seeing Fiona, he hurried to her side, ushered her into the cab, and planted a quick kiss good-bye on Lily's forehead.

A moment later, their carriage rumbled down Gray's

drive, which was riddled with puddles and ruts. Fiona ignored the curses Papa uttered at every teeth-rattling lurch of the coach and stared at the Fortress as it grew smaller through the back window.

When she'd arrived at the house party a mere week ago, she'd hoped to be engaged by week's end, secure in the knowledge that she'd have the money she needed to pay off the blackmailer.

Now she was leaving with nothing.

No fiancé.

No money.

No plan.

Just bittersweet memories of her time with Gray—and tantalizing glimpses of what might have been.

Gray paced the floor of his bedchamber waiting for Fiona, certain she'd come to him. He trusted Lily to give her his message, and after everything that he and Fiona had shared that evening she wouldn't stay away. They'd been as close as two people could be—and not just physically.

She'd told him she loved him.

Yes, he'd botched things by leaving immediately after their lovemaking. And then Helena had created a spectacle.

But he'd make it up to Fiona, starting tonight. He'd show her how he felt about her. Make her believe.

But with every hour that passed, more doubts crept into his head.

Something wasn't quite right.

Maybe she was cross with him for some other reason. Or perhaps circumstances had made it impossible to sneak out of her bedchamber. Maybe she'd been so exhausted after the events of the night that she'd fallen asleep.

Any one of those reasons was perfectly logical.

But a niggling suspicion told him something else was to blame.

He waited impatiently in his room, staring at the clock as the hour hand cruised past the two and then the three. Sometime around four o'clock, he ventured into the corridor and skulked through the darkness, daring to pause outside Fiona's room. Sorely tempted to knock on her door, he refrained—only because she shared the room with her sister.

Throughout the wee hours of the morning and right up till sunrise, he played the scene in the linen closet over and over in his mind, wishing he hadn't run off.

But all he could do was try to make amends before Fiona left later today.

At the first light of day, he washed and dressed without his valet, who was no doubt still abed, and went downstairs to wait for her.

Pentham and his brother were the first to come down for breakfast, eager to be on their way back to town.

"No one can accuse you of hosting a dull party." Carter winked as he shook Gray's hand.

"It was an enjoyable week," Pentham added. "Plenty of excitement and excellent company."

Kirby and his father were the next to join Gray downstairs—and the next to leave. As they said their farewells outside, Lord Dunlope slapped Gray on the back. "I know how much you want to restore this house, and your heart is in the right place. But sometimes one must cut one's losses . . . and move on." He shot Gray a regretful, slightly pitying, smile. "Take good care of the countess."

Gray bit his tongue as he shook the older man's hand. While Dunlope clambered into the coach, Kirby rolled his eyes. "Forgive my father. He lacks vision. He would rather count the money in his safe twenty times over than spend it on creature comforts or—God forbid—sheer enjoyment."

Gray snorted. "Thanks for your help this week. At least I know I can count on you."

"Always, my friend." Kirby gave him a mock salute before climbing into the carriage and riding down the drive.

Gray walked back through the front door, relieved to hear women's voices filling the front hall. Mrs. Hartley and Lady Callahan were dressed in their traveling clothes. Lily and Sophie, too.

But there was no sign of Fiona or her father.

"Good morning, all." Gray greeted them in the foyer, using every ounce of self-restraint to refrain from demanding to know where Fiona was. "I didn't see you at breakfast this morning."

"We had trays brought to our rooms." Mrs. Hartley didn't look at him as she tugged on her gloves. "We are still quite fatigued, which is hardly a surprise after the traumatic and, dare I say, disappointing night we endured."

Ouch. Gray turned to Lily. "I trust your sister is well. She hasn't taken ill, has she?"

Lily shook her head, her expression one part wary, one part sympathetic. "She was fine when last I saw her. She and my father departed late last night—or rather, early this morning. They're probably already in London by now."

Shit. How had Fiona managed to leave without him knowing? How could he have let her go before making things right? He rubbed his forehead, trying to quell the panic that rose up in him.

"I'd hoped to talk with her before she departed," he said.

"I did relay your message," Lily assured him, unwittingly twisting the knife. Fiona had known he was desperate to see her—but had packed up and left anyway.

The truth was he couldn't blame her. He'd had plenty of chances to commit to her before last night—in the library, at the cottage, and on the rowboat. He'd wasted every bloody one of them.

Mrs. Hartley gave a haughty sniff as she and Lady Callahan walked past him, her lady's maid in tow. "Come along, Lily. I'm eager to return to the comforts of home."

Lily dutifully followed her mother but paused in front of Gray. "If you truly care for Fiona, you'll give her some time to sort out her feelings."

He nodded gratefully, but the problem was, Fiona didn't have time.

If she didn't pay off the blackmailer in two days, Lily—and their whole family—would be disgraced.

And there was no way in hell Gray was going to let that happen.

Chapter 32

"What are you doing?" Lily stood in the doorway of Fiona's spacious bedchamber in their London town house.

"Hmm?" Fiona glanced up from her jewelry box, frozen like a thief caught red-handed. She shoved her mother's beloved necklace into the box and slammed the lid. "I was just unpacking some items from the house party." They'd returned to London only yesterday, but it felt like a week since she'd seen Gray. She missed him—and doubted the ache in her chest would ever really go away.

"I'm here if you want to talk about anything, Fi," Lily offered.

"I know. I'm sorry I've been a bit distant lately. I'm afraid I need to sort through some things on my own."

Lily shot her a wan smile. "Lord Ravenport returned to London yesterday, too. There's a new note from him downstairs if you're curious. Next to the first one he sent."

Fiona *was* curious. Intensely. But she didn't dare read them, lest she be tempted to meet with him and resume their relationship—a relationship that could go nowhere. "I'll reply to the earl later," she said vaguely.

Her priority was finding a way to pay Mr. Kirby. Her mother's necklace was the most valuable thing she possessed. And though it would break Fiona's heart to part with it, she had no doubt her mother would have understood. She wasn't sure what excuse she'd give Lily for the disappearance of the necklace, which belonged to her as well. Perhaps Fiona could say it had been lost or stolen. She hated lying, but giving up the necklace was the only way to protect her sister—and Gray.

"Who are you drawing today?" Lily gestured toward Fiona's desk, littered with papers, pencils, and pastels.

Not who, but *what*. She'd been sketching the necklace. So that years from now she'd be able to recall exactly what it looked like.

"Nothing of import." Fiona rubbed her forehead. "But I'm glad you're here. I need my sketchbook and diary. I've felt completely lost without them."

Lily frowned. "Why would I have them?"

Sweet Jesus. Panic clawed at Fiona's insides. "Because Mary unpacked our trunk from the Fortress and I didn't see either the journal or my sketchbook. I assumed you'd hidden them somewhere in your things. Please, say you did."

Lily's face turned ghostly white. "I didn't."

Fiona's belly lurched. "Lily, this isn't funny. If anyone were to read my journal . . ." *Oh God.* If *Gray* read it . . . she'd wither up and die on the spot.

"I know." Lily paced, spearing her fingers into the twist at the back of her head. "But I didn't see the diary or the sketch pad when we were packing yesterday morning. I figured you'd brought them with you."

Fiona's hand flew to her mouth—and then she remembered. "Sweet heaven. I left them under the mattress in our room on the night of the ball . . . and forgot all about them."

"Then they're probably still there," Lily reasoned. "You could ask the earl to have a member of his staff locate them and deliver them directly to you."

"Yes. Of course." Fiona clung to the hope that they hadn't been discovered. Because if Gray read her diary she'd never be able to face him again. She'd have no choice but to live out the rest of her life in a remote village where sheep outnumbered people one hundred to one. Or to join a convent.

"There's another letter for you downstairs as well—I don't know who it's from."

The hairs on the backs of Fiona's arms stood on end. The note could be from anyone—their cousin, the countess, or a friend from Miss Haywinkle's. But with just one day until the extortion money was due, she suspected the unmarked note was from her blackmailer—Mr. Kirby.

A nervous laugh bubbled out of Fiona's throat. "I'm sure it's from an old acquaintance."

Lily's eyes twinkled mischievously. "Or a secret admirer. I'm leaving for Sophie's in a few minutes. Will you join us for tea?"

"I'm rather tired. I think I'll lie down for a bit."

Lily arched a delicate brow. "Are you feeling ill?"

"Not at all." Fiona glanced in the mirror above her vanity and smoothed a curl behind her ear, hoping she'd sounded convincing.

"Very well. I wish you luck securing the return of your journal and sketch pad. Please let me know if I can help . . . with anything."

"Thank you." For some ridiculous reason, Fiona felt on the verge of tears, so she busied herself with straightening the items on her dressing table. "I shall see you at dinner."

As soon as Lily left her bedchamber, Fiona returned to the jewelry box, removed her mother's necklace, and held it to her cheek. Perhaps it was her imagination, but the necklace seemed imbued with her mother's scent. Somehow, her sketch had to capture that delicate floral fragrance—the essence of her mother. And there was no time to waste.

A half hour later, Fiona sat in Papa's carriage across from Mary. While the maid stared out the window, humming happily, Fiona opened the mysterious letter that had been waiting for her on a silver salver in the front hall. One look at the handwriting confirmed her fears—the note was from Mr. Kirby.

> *Dear Miss Hartley,*
> *Do not forget what's at stake: your sister's future, your family's reputation, and everything Gray owns—including the Fortress. If you stay away from Gray and deliver the money as directed, all will be well.*
> *If you do not, the gossip-loving readers of the Hearsay will be in for a most salacious treat—the sort that will be on their lips from now till Christmas.*
> *I look forward to concluding our business tomorrow night. Then we both shall be able to put this unsavory episode behind us.*

Perhaps Mr. Kirby would move on, but Fiona wouldn't. She'd never forgive him for the hateful words he'd threatened to publish. The ones that haunted her, day and night: *Miss Hartley's mother is a whore.*

Fiona's fingers curled into fists. She wanted to throttle Mr. Kirby. No, worse. She wanted to—

"Are you well, Miss Fiona?" Mary's forehead creased in concern. "You're frowning."

"I shall be fine." She took a deep breath and shoved the letter into the bottom of her reticule. "As soon as I take care of an important but rather unpleasant piece of business."

When the carriage rolled to a stop, the maid peered outside and frowned. "Unpleasant business," she repeated. "At the park? Are you meeting someone?"

"Not today. Today I simply wish to . . . walk." And find the tree where she would have to leave her mother's treasured necklace in the hopes of silencing a vile, greedy man.

Two hours later, Fiona stood outside Papa's study, heart hammering in her chest.

After she saw the tree where she was supposed to leave her mother's jewels, Fiona's skin had turned clammy and her stomach had churned. Her whole body seemed to reject the idea of parting with the necklace, but she had no other choice.

Unless Papa would lend her the money—without demanding the reason she needed it.

As much as she longed to confide in him, she couldn't tell him about Lily's birth mother. The news would be too much for his weak heart to take.

Fiona raised her fist to knock on the door.

"Your father left this morning."

"Mama." Startled, Fiona spun around. Her stepmother stood in the hallway behind her, scowling slightly, as if she disapproved of finding Fiona here. "When do you expect him to return?"

"In a few days, I should think. He's visiting some of the mills again. Why did you wish to see him?"

Fiona's stomach sank. He wasn't going to be back soon enough to help her, and there wasn't enough time to deliver a message to him.

She thought about the horrid letter she'd stuffed into her reticule.

"Mama, I need to ask you something."

She arched an imperious brow. "What is it? Does it have to do with Lord Ravenport? Because after the debacle at his house party, I think it best to avoid further contact with him."

The mention of Gray made Fiona's chest ache. "I promise this has nothing to do with the earl. I wanted to ask a favor—a rather large one, actually. I wondered if you and Papa would lend me some money."

Mama waved a dismissive hand. "If you wish to purchase fripperies, drawing supplies, or what have you, you may do so. Simply bill them to your father."

"The money isn't for those types of expenditures," Fiona said vaguely. "I need a large sum."

When Fiona revealed the amount, Mama pressed a hand to her chest, incredulous. "Your father and I have provided you with everything a young lady could possibly want. Why on earth would you need that much money?"

Fiona closed her eyes briefly. "I cannot say."

"Then I cannot give it to you." Mama gave an indelicate snort, then narrowed her eyes. "Have you been gambling, Fiona?"

"No," she replied quickly. "Nothing like that, but it *is* important. If it wasn't, I would never ask."

Mama spun on her heel and began to walk down the corridor. "This is what comes from spoiling you girls. Instead of appreciating all you've been given, you demand more."

Fiona followed her, prepared to beg. "You're right. I'm terribly fortunate. You and Papa have been generous to a fault. But I'm asking you to trust me. I shall pay you back as soon as I'm able."

Unable to hide her mirth, Mama cackled. "And where,

precisely, do you plan to find the money? Do not tell me that you intend to sell those little scribblings you call portraits." She strode into the drawing room and proceeded to recline on the settee, pressing the back of her hand to her forehead. "No daughter of mine is going to humiliate this family by hiring herself out as a portraitist. And frankly, Fiona, I doubt anyone would pay a shilling for your sketches."

Fiona ignored the sting of her stepmother's words. "I thought that once I was wed, I could use my marriage portion to pay you back."

"Truly? I feel obliged to point out that suitors are not exactly lined up outside our door." Mama's words were cruel, if accurate. "But that is beside the point. If you will not reveal what you intend to use the money for, I must assume that you are involved with something unsavory at best—perhaps even illegal." She moaned and closed her eyes. "Summon my maid. Tell her I need a compress—and perhaps a tincture."

"Of course." There was no point in pleading her case further.

Mama wasn't going to lend her the money. Papa was out of town. There was absolutely no chance of Fiona marrying before tomorrow.

Leaving her with exactly one option—she must hand over her mother's necklace to Kirby.

In the meantime, she rang for Mama's maid, helped her stepmother to her bedchamber, and retreated to her own room to think.

Perhaps she couldn't solve the blackmail dilemma tonight, but she *could* try to get her journal and sketchbook back—and grant Gray some closure. She sat at her desk and composed a note to him so brief, so businesslike, that he'd never guess she'd started over three times. He'd never know how may tears she'd swiped away as she wrote it or how desperately she missed him every minute of the day.

And, God willing, he'd never know what she'd sacrificed to protect him.

Chapter 33

Dear Lord Ravenport,
Upon my return to London, I discovered I
inadvertently left behind my sketchbook and
personal journal at your country house. Both
items can be found under the mattress in the room
where I stayed, and I would appreciate it if you
could see that they are located and returned
directly to me. I trust that you will respect my
privacy in this matter.

I regret the necessity of my hasty departure
from the Fortress, but circumstances have
changed. I realize now that my proposal was
ill-advised. I think it best for us to avoid each
other for the foreseeable future.

Most sincerely,
Miss F. Hartley

Gray read Fiona's letter again, baffled. *What* circumstances had changed? They'd spent time together, begun to care for each other, and made love. She'd said she'd loved him. And then she'd run away. None of it made sense.

He sat alone in the study at his London town house,

pondering not only the letter but also every encounter between Fiona and him.

She'd enclosed the two letters he'd written to her—both unopened. And he had the distinct impression that she wouldn't have written to him at all if she hadn't left her sketchbook and journal at the Fortress.

But over the last couple of days, he'd had plenty of time to think. He'd talked to his grandmother and, more important, listened to his godforsaken heart.

And he was dead certain about a couple of things.

First, what he and Fiona had shared was real. As real as the armchair he sat in, as solid as the massive mahogany desktop he propped his boots on. The connection between them was *not* a figment of his imagination. True, it may have started out thin and tenuous—like a single strand of a spider's web. But with every encounter, conversation, and kiss, their connection had grown stronger till it was as thick and durable as the rope of his boyhood swing—frayed a little on the outside, but in no danger of breaking.

Second, Fiona had earned and deserved his trust. The fact that his parents had failed him miserably and Helena had callously betrayed him had absolutely nothing to do with Fiona. They'd been weak and consumed with their own problems. But Fiona wasn't like them. He'd witnessed her compassion toward his grandmother, her loyalty toward her family, and her kindness toward complete strangers.

If she was running away and shutting him out, she must have a good reason—and he suspected it stemmed from the blackmail. Even before she'd pulled away from him, she'd been reluctant to share the details of the threat to her sister and her family.

She'd been patient with him as he learned to trust again. Every time he'd pushed her away, she'd coaxed him back.

Now he needed to be patient with her. He needed to convince her that she could tell him anything. That whatever the secret was, whatever the danger, he would stand by her and protect her. Nothing was going to scare him off.

The question was, how the hell was he supposed to convince her that he loved her when she'd asked him to keep his distance? And how could he protect her from the blackmailer?

A knock at the study door interrupted his thoughts, and a glance at the clock told him it was nearly time for dinner. "Come in."

His butler entered the room holding a large brown parcel balanced on the palm of one hand. "This was delivered from the staff at the Fortress."

"I'll take it, Burns. Thank you."

He knew without opening the package that it was Fiona's sketchbook and journal. A conscientious maid must have discovered the items in Fiona's bedchamber and taken the initiative to send them here.

Gray laid the parcel on his desk and carefully unwrapped it, eager to touch the sketchbook that was so much a part of Fiona. Maybe he'd find her pencil—the same one she loved to tuck behind her ear—sandwiched between a couple of drawings.

A small leather-bound journal rested on top of the sketchbook. There was nothing especially remarkable about it on the outside, but he imagined the pages were filled with Fiona's hopes, fears, dreams . . . maybe even a few sentences about him. Though his fingers itched to flip open the cover and peek at what she'd written inside, he refrained.

He desperately wanted to know her private thoughts . . . but only when she was ready to share them herself. And he was confident that someday soon she would.

With a sigh, he set the journal on the corner of his desk and turned his attention to the sketch pad.

He admired each of Fiona's drawings, lingering over a few: the mermaid in the garden, the view from the top of his favorite rock, her portrait of him. It was impossible to separate the beauty of her pictures from her own beauty. Her unique, refreshing, incisive view of the world.

Almost every page conjured memories of the time they'd spent together at the Fortress—and made him miss her more.

Nestled between a couple of pages in the back of her book, he found a small sketch of two hands, one large, the other smaller, crossed at the wrists. Palms pressed together, the fingers loosely entwined, they were the hands of lovers—easy, tender, intimate.

His and Fiona's hands.

He stared at them, transported to the morning they'd spent together in the cottage.

"My lord?"

Startled, Gray turned quickly, knocking over Fiona's journal. It landed on the wooden floor with a thud, and the butler moved to pick it up.

"I have it, Burns." Gray scooped up the journal and a folded note that had fallen out of it.

"Forgive me for interrupting, my lord. Dinner is served, and the countess awaits your company."

"Thank you. I shall join her in a minute."

As the butler nodded and left, Gray turned the folded note over in his hand. There was something familiar about it, and he wondered if it was the same one that Kirby had found at the Fortress. The blackmail note.

Too curious to resist, he opened and read it—every sinister word.

Every thinly veiled threat made his blood boil; every brazen demand made his fists clench.

Something else about the note troubled him also . . . but he couldn't quite place his finger on it.

He would read it again after dinner, before wrapping up Fiona's things and having all her possessions delivered to her.

All her possessions, that is, but the one he needed to win her back.

Fiona clutched her heavy silk purse tightly against her waist as she walked through Hyde Park that evening, grateful for the clouds and drizzle that had kept the usual crowds at home. Yesterday's excursion to the park had been a trial run so that she could locate the precise spot in the park where she was to deliver the necklace. While the instructions had been very specific, she'd worried she might have difficulty finding the tallest tree on the south side of the Serpentine—which happened to have a hole near the base of its trunk. But she'd found the tree in the exact spot Mr. Kirby had described in his blackmail note.

She was supposed to arrive at the park after dark, wait for a moment when no one was about, and place the money deep in the hollow where it couldn't easily be seen. She was to leave the park immediately afterward, understanding that any attempt to trap him would result in the publication of the letter in the *London Hearsay*.

She planned to follow the directions to the letter except that in place of the money she would be leaving her mother's treasured sapphire necklace. He couldn't possibly object to the substitution, however, for the jewels were worth twice the amount he'd demanded.

Fiona had expected to be nervous, but she hadn't expected to be nearly paralyzed with fear. Her feet did not want to move, and her tongue felt thick as she turned and spoke to Mary. "Wait here, please. I'm going to walk to the river and back to see if I dropped my fan somewhere in the grass yesterday. Then we may return home."

The maid gave Fiona a curious look but bobbed her capped head. "Do hurry, Miss Fiona. Your gown is already half-soaked from the rain."

But Fiona barely felt the droplets on her face as she scurried toward the designated tree. She reached the tree, stooped near the base, and carefully placed the silk pouch in the hollow. No one passing by would notice it, especially not in the darkness.

Exhaling, she stood and said a fervent prayer that all would be well.

But the rumble of thunder that echoed through the silence was a decidedly bad omen. As she walked back to the coach, she couldn't help feeling like she'd left a part of her soul behind in the base of that tree.

Chapter 34

On Denying One's Heart

I think of him as I go through my day, longing to see his face and hear his voice. Aching to hold his hand and kiss his lips. But mostly, knowing in my head that I've chosen the right course.

I detest the thought that he might be hurting and missing me, too. But I suspect that while his heart may be temporarily bruised, he'll soon recover. And why shouldn't he? Ours was hardly the usual sort of courtship. Instead of romantic waltzes, hothouse flowers, and glittering ballrooms, we had dance floor mishaps, overgrown gardens, and fallen trees.

Gray will, no doubt, be eager to put this awkward chapter behind him, and our time together will soon become a distant memory.

But I will never, ever, forget him. The way he protected me from toads and recited adorably bad poetry and whispered my name like a prayer.

I will never forget him.

Fiona closed her journal with a sigh. Foolishly, she'd thought that perhaps Gray would insist on returning it and her sketchbook in person, but no—a footman had dropped them off. Then she'd looked to see if Gray had tucked a note inside the cover of her journal or included a personal memento such as a pressed flower or a handkerchief or . . . something. But he had not.

Who could blame him after she'd run away and returned the letters he'd written her? But a stubborn corner of her heart had wanted to believe that he wouldn't give up on her so easily. That he'd fight for her—and find a way for them to be together.

But it was high time she accepted the truth. Gray was not a knight in shining armor, and she was certainly no princess. Not everyone was destined for a happy ending, and she'd been more fortunate than most—at least she'd known the bliss of loving someone fully. With her body, soul, and heart.

She tucked her journal in the desk drawer and closed it with a slam that was both satisfying and symbolic. This chapter of her life was over, but Lily was safe. And in the years to come, she'd find joy in watching her sister fall in love and marry and have babies.

All the wonders that Fiona might have shared with Gray—if things had been different.

Gray's greatcoat kept him dry despite the drenching rain. More important, it allowed him to blend into the darkness and move behind the trees and shrubs in Hyde Park unseen. He'd been tracking Kirby all night, praying that his suspicions were wrong. Hoping that his best friend would never resort to blackmailing an innocent young woman—the same woman Gray loved.

Hell, he felt guilty for even entertaining the thought. But the handwriting on the threatening note he'd found in Fiona's journal was eerily similar to his friend's. And if

Gray's worst fear was true, it would help explain why Fiona had run away. Why she was shutting him out.

He knew Kirby gambled too much and played too deep. But then, lots of men did. Gray even knew about Kirby's longtime lover—a woman several years his senior who wasn't the sort he could bring home to dinner with the family.

Gray cared about none of that. Kirby had stood by his side through the worst of times. He was honorable at his core.

Which was why it made no sense that Kirby had taken a hackney cab to Hyde Park well after midnight and now skulked across the rain-soaked grass like a common footpad.

Gray pulled the brim of his hat low across his brow and followed twenty yards behind, hiding in the shadows.

Then Kirby stopped. He crouched beside a tree, felt around the base of it, and reached inside the trunk. As he stood, he stuffed a small object inside his jacket. He glanced over each shoulder before walking in the direction of the road.

Gray's stomach churned. Maybe it was only a coincidence that on the very same day Fiona was supposed to pay off the blackmailer Kirby was lurking around the park in the dead of night, retrieving objects from secret locations.

Gray whispered a curse. Half of him clung to the belief that there was some other explanation. That he should go home and forget what he'd seen.

But the other half had to know the truth. This was his chance to confront Kirby, and if Gray was wrong—as he hoped he was—he trusted Kirby to understand.

Before Gray could change his mind, he darted out of the woods. "Kirby!"

Without turning around, his friend broke into a run.

"Wait!" Gray took off after him, the heels of his boots churning up the soggy earth.

But Kirby didn't stop. He ran like the hounds of hell nipped at his heels.

So Gray ran, too. "Kirby, I know it's you!" he shouted. "Face me like a man."

Kirby didn't. He made for the road at breakneck speed—until he hit a patch of mud. His feet slipped out from under him and his body sailed forward. He landed facedown on the ground, and as he scrambled to regain his footing Gray hauled him up by his collar, turned him around, and looked into his eyes.

"What are you doing here?" Gray demanded.

"Walking." If Kirby was aiming for a jocular tone, he missed the mark. He sounded panicked—and guilty.

Gray gave him a shake. "Walking in the rain after midnight?"

"Jesus, Gray. It's hardly a crime." Kirby shoved off Gray's chest. "You scared the hell out of me, by the way. I thought you were the chap I owe money to."

"Are you in some sort of trouble?"

"Aren't I always?" Kirby swiped the sleeve of his jacket across his forehead and scooped his hat off the ground. "I borrowed some blunt to pay a gambling debt. But I've figured out a way to pay it back. I'm taking care of it."

Gray's blood turned to ice. "Where are you getting the money?"

Kirby looked away. "My father. He's not pleased with me, but he agreed to help me one last time. He doesn't want the moneylender's thugs to break my nose—only because it would be substantially harder for me to snare a wealthy bride with a disfigured face."

Gray wanted to believe the story. Desperately. "What's inside your chest pocket?" he asked flatly.

Kirby shrugged. "What are you talking about?"

Cold rain dripped off Gray's hair and trickled down the back of his neck. "You stuffed something into your jacket. A few minutes ago. A bag or pouch that was left in a tree."

"I dropped my pocket watch. Right here, see?" He reached inside his jacket and produced the brass timepiece on the center of his palm. Barking a laugh, he asked, "Did you think a kindly gnome left me some gold coins?"

"No. I thought Fiona did."

"Fion— Are you referring to Miss Hartley?" Kirby asked, incredulous.

"I want to see what else is in your jacket."

"Don't be ridiculous, Gray. You're smitten, aren't you? Maybe she's been putting strange ideas in your head, but don't turn against me. *I'm* the one you can trust. We've been friends for two decades, and you've known her for what—two weeks?"

"Yes." Two weeks. And she already knew him better than anyone, save his grandmother. "If you have nothing to hide, show me what's in your jacket."

Kirby snorted. "Sod off. I don't need to prove myself to you." When he turned to walk away, Gray clamped a hand on his shoulder, spun him around, and reached into his jacket.

"What the hell are you doing?" Kirby struggled to pull free of Gray's grasp.

But Gray easily located the lump concealed in Kirby's chest pocket and withdrew a small silk pouch. He shook it, surprised to find the contents didn't clink like coins.

Kirby held up his palms in surrender. "Fine. You've discovered my secret," he sputtered. "I bought a necklace for

Serena. I realize it's far too extravagant, but you know what it's like to care deeply for someone. You want to give her the world."

"I do know what it's like." Gray loosened the ties on the pouch and spilled the necklace into his hand. Even in the rain-muted moonlight, the sapphires glowed in his palm. Disbelief, hurt, and rage warred within him. "This necklace is Fiona's. It once belonged to her mother. And she would never willingly part with it."

"It's merely a reproduction," Kirby said. "Paste jewels."

Gray carefully placed the necklace in his pocket. "You blackmailed her." The accusation echoed through the night air.

"She has money and jewels to spare," Kirby spat. "She wouldn't have missed that trinket."

The words were barely out of his mouth before Gray plowed his fist into Kirby's jaw.

"You bastard." Kirby wiped the blood that trickled from his mouth. "I've been nothing but loyal to you."

"Loyal? You don't know the meaning of the word. You threatened the woman I love. You would have destroyed her entire family. You're contemptible and pathetic. And you are *not* my friend. I would challenge you to a duel, but I find myself too eager to dispense justice." Gray swung again, connecting solidly with Kirby's nose.

His face contorted in pain and anger, Kirby launched himself at Gray, fist cocked.

But Gray deflected the punch with his forearm and pummeled Kirby in the ribs till he crumpled to the ground, dragging Gray into the mud with him.

Gray flipped Kirby over and pinned his shoulders to the ground. He squirmed and kicked and strained, whimpering as blood gushed from his nose.

Perhaps he'd learned his lesson.

But the moment Gray released him, Kirby rolled away, reached into his boot, and sprang to his feet, brandishing a knife.

Shit. Gray hadn't thought to arm himself before he began tracking Kirby. Warily, he stood and circled his new foe. "Let us settle this like men, then. Men of honor."

"Honor is overrated, my friend. We will settle this right here. Right now. May the most resourceful man win." Kirby lunged at Gray, but he jumped back before the knife's blade could graze him.

In that instant, Gray realized the staunch friendship he'd had with Kirby had been an illusion—like a castle façade with nothing substantial behind it. Yes, he'd kept Gray company and kept his secrets—but only because it had been in his best interests to do so.

Gray shrugged off his coat and tossed it to the ground. "I dare you to try that again."

Kirby twirled the knife in his hand, and the blade glinted, sending a chill over Gray's shoulders. Kirby's gaze flicked to Gray's coat, puddled on the grass. "Let me take the necklace. I'll leave town before morning and you'll never hear from me again."

Gray stepped forward. "I like the sound of that. All but the part about the necklace. It's Fiona's. I intend to return it to her."

"How noble of you," Kirby said snidely. "But perhaps it's only a ploy to get her in your bed. Again."

Blood thundered in Gray's ears, but he refused to take the bait. "Don't be a coward. Accept my challenge. Try to cut me again and see what happens."

For several seconds, they stared at each other in silence punctuated only by the pattering of rain. Then Kirby's body slumped, and his arms dropped to his sides. "Fine. You win. I'll leave town. Without the necklace. Just let me collect my things and say good-bye to my father."

Gray swallowed. He hadn't expected Kirby to accept his terms so easily. "I want you gone before dawn."

"I understand." Kirby hung his head and turned to go.

Gray stooped to pick up his jacket—and saw Kirby charging at him once more, teeth bared and knife flailing.

But this time Gray was ready. He grabbed Kirby's arm, twisted it behind his back, and pulled up hard. *Crack.*

Kirby dropped to his knees. The knife fell from his limp hand. His howls echoed through the park like the wailings of a tortured soul from the spirit realm.

Misery personified. And Kirby deserved every wretched second of it.

"Unless you wish me to haul your ass to the authorities and accuse you of theft, you will do exactly as I say." Gray shoved Kirby's face into the mud and pressed his boot heel in the center of his back. "Do you understand?"

"Yes." Kirby whimpered like a spoiled child.

"Good. First you will answer some questions. And do not even *think* of lying to me."

The day Fiona had been dreading for over a fortnight had arrived, and she would have given anything to jump back into bed and pull the covers over her head. But she forced herself to dress, make her way downstairs, and join Mama and Lily at the breakfast table.

Mama speared a hunk of ham with her fork and addressed Fiona from across the table. "Why are you so morose again this morning? You're looking far too pale and thin of late—you must eat."

The thought of food made Fiona queasy, but she buttered a slice of toast to appease Mama.

"I think you look lovely, as always," Lily piped up. "But perhaps a bit tired. Did you have a restless night?"

"I . . . ah . . . suppose I did." Fiona had lain awake debating whether she should prepare her sister for the possibility that unpleasant news about her might appear in the gossip pages this morning. But that would only make her intensely curious. She'd given Mr. Kirby the necklace, which was worth more than he'd demanded. But she hadn't followed his instructions to the letter, and he was the sort of horrible person who might relish the opportunity to ruin a young woman and her family—just for sport.

Lily reached over and rubbed Fiona's shoulder, her expression full of sympathy. "The Dillingham ball tonight will be a festive affair. Perhaps that will cheer you."

"Yes, I'm certain it will." Fiona had already planned to develop a horrid headache—the kind that would require her to remain in bed all evening. She couldn't risk running into Gray, not while her wounds were so raw.

"Has the post arrived yet this morning?" Lily asked.

Fiona suppressed a shudder. "Why? Are you expecting a letter?"

"No, just the *Hearsay*." Lily's eyes gleamed with excitement, and she glanced at the breakfast room doorway. "Excellent! Here it is now."

Dear God. As her sister eagerly took the paper from the butler, Fiona tamped down a wave of nausea. "Actually, I wondered if I might have a look first—"

But it was too late. Lily had already set down her teacup and was turning to the gossip column.

Fiona gripped the arms of her chair and studied her sister's face, bracing for the worst.

Lily arched a brow as she scanned the page in front of her. "Oh my."

Fiona's fingers turned to ice.

"What?" Mama demanded. "Don't keep us in suspense."

"There's a paragraph on Lady Helena," Lily said. "It seems she's become engaged to Lord Potsbridge."

"The viscount?" Mama coughed, nearly choking on her eggs. "Why, he's nearly three times her age, and rather sickly, if I recall."

"Yes, although I understand his gout is improving," Lily said diplomatically.

Fiona exhaled. Perhaps everything *would* be all right. Lily was reading the *Hearsay* and the world hadn't come crumbling down around them. Fiona leaned back in her chair, daring to hope that, for now, the nightmare was over.

"Dear God," Lily intoned.

Fear clawed at Fiona's heart. "What is it?"

The color drained from Lily's face, and she swallowed. "I can't believe it."

No, no, no. Lily shouldn't be learning the truth like this. Fiona grabbed the newspaper out of her sister's hands and threw it onto the floor. "I'm sorry. I thought I could keep it out of the gossip pages."

"For the love of— Fiona Hartley, what are you doing?" Mama demanded.

Lily searched Fiona's face. "You *knew* he was going to do this?" She still looked stunned—as if she didn't know whether to scream or laugh or cry.

"I knew it was a possibility, but I thought I could stop him."

"Why would you want to?"

Fiona blinked. "Because I . . . because you . . ." Something wasn't adding up, blast it all. She scooped the paper off the floor, opened it to the gossip column, and—

Sweet Jesus. There, in the middle of the page, was her sketch. The one of her and Gray's entwined hands.

The words below read:

F., You have my trust, my heart, and my soul. I love you. Please, marry me. G.

"It's one of your sketches," Lily breathed. "I'd recognize your work anywhere."

Fiona nodded.

Mama sputtered her tea. "One of your drawings is in the *paper*?" Fiona couldn't tell if she was dismayed or proud.

"Lord Ravenport must have submitted it," Fiona said.

"Along with a brief note." Lily nudged Fiona's shoulder. "Read it to Mama."

Fiona did, and Lily sighed dreamily. "So romantic."

"I don't know," Mama said. "I find it rather less inspired than his earlier poetry."

Perhaps, but Fiona couldn't have loved it more. "I need to see him."

"You mustn't appear too desperate or anxious," Mama chided. "Wear your best morning gown and have Mary style your—"

The butler appeared in the doorway again, clearing his throat. "Forgive the interruption, but Lord Ravenport is here. I told him you were still breaking your fast and that you preferred to receive callers later in the after—"

Fiona carefully folded the paper and clutched it to her chest. "I must speak with him. Please, Mama—may we have a few minutes alone?"

She frowned at first, but then her face softened. "If you want to give the earl a second chance, I have no objection."

"He's giving me a second chance, too." Fiona set her napkin on the table, sprang from her chair, and hugged her stepmother. "Thank you."

"Wait," Lily said. "Does this mean you're going to say yes?"

Fiona winked on her way out the door. "Actually, *he's* the one saying yes. I proposed to him first."

"Lord save me!" Mama cried, but Fiona had already hiked the hem of her gown and was running toward the drawing room in a manner that would surely give Miss Haywinkle a fit of the vapors.

Fiona found him sitting with his back to her and his elbows propped on his knees. His dark hair curled a little around his collar, and his broad shoulders spanned half the sofa. His midnight blue jacket hugged his muscled arms and trim waist.

One day she would sketch him just like this, looking determined and thoughtful and more handsome than any man should. "Gray."

He stood and strode toward her, his long legs eating up the distance between them in a few strides, but he stopped just short of touching her. "Fiona. God, I've missed you."

Her throat felt thick. "I've missed you, too."

"I know about Kirby," he said. The pain in his voice cut through her chest.

"How?"

"I read the blackmail note and thought it might be his handwriting. Hoped it wasn't. But I followed him to the park and saw him pick up your necklace. I'm sorry." He reached into his pocket, pulled out her silk pouch, and handed it to her.

She loosened the pouch's drawstrings and took out the necklace. In the morning light, it sparkled brightly, reminding Fiona of her mother's smile. She looked up at the portrait that hung over the fireplace and saw the same jewels adorning her mother's slender neck. "I didn't realize how much I wanted this piece of my mother—how badly I needed it—until it was gone. Thank you for returning it to me." Tears spilled down Fiona's cheeks.

Gray pulled her close and kissed the top of her head, but panic flooded her veins again. "Wait. You don't understand. He's written a letter—an awful, ugly letter to the *London Hearsay*. This necklace was the only thing preventing him from publishing it."

"You have nothing to fear from Kirby," he said earnestly. "Not anymore. Let's sit down and I'll tell you everything."

They settled themselves on the sofa and Gray took her hand, as if it were the most natural thing in the world—and it was. A weight lifted off her chest, and she breathed easier than she had in weeks.

"Kirby will never threaten you or Lily or your family again."

Fiona shook her head, disbelieving. "You should see the letter he penned to the *Hearsay*. It is ruthless and cold—almost gleeful about destroying my sister's reputation."

"I know, because I read it. Just before I burned it." He met her gaze. "I'm sorry for everything he put you through. But the nightmare is over. You have nothing to fear from him. If he dares to show his face in town again, he will face me at dawn. And he's far too spineless to risk a duel."

Fiona frowned, still confused. "How did he know about Lily's past?"

Gray pressed a tender kiss to the back of her hand. "Kirby learned about Lily's birth mother from the madam herself. He's been in a relationship with Serena Labelle for two years. She's considerably older than he is, but he claims to be in love with her." Gray shrugged. "Maybe he is."

Fiona looked down at their entwined hands. Regardless of what Kirby had done, she hated the thought that the bond between lifelong friends was irreparably severed. "You've lost your best friend."

"No, I haven't. *You* are my best friend—and more. You're everything to me."

"I owe you an apology, too," Fiona said. "I shouldn't have left the Fortress without saying good-bye. I figured out that the blackmailer was Kirby, but I couldn't tell you. He threatened to expose your father's suicide, and I feared you would lose everything. So, I did the cowardly thing and left without explanation. I thought you'd eventually forget about me."

For the space of several heartbeats, Gray said nothing, but when he did, his voice was full of anguish. "Did you really think that?"

She nodded and felt her eyes brim with tears again.

Gray dropped to his knees in front of the sofa and looked up at her, pleading. "God, Fiona. You're the most unforgettable woman I've ever met. I knew after our first dance that you were going to turn my life upside down, and you have—in the best possible way. You're beautiful and passionate and talented beyond belief."

She smiled at that. "I assume you're referring to my archery skills?"

"Your talents extend to many, many areas." His wicked grin left her slightly breathless. "The point is, you captured my heart from the start, and I didn't tell you because I was afraid."

"Afraid of what?"

"That you wouldn't feel the same. Or that you'd discover you could do better than a bitter, impoverished earl. But damn it, I *should* have told you how I felt long before the night of the ball, and I'm telling you now: I love you, Fiona. I wish I had more to offer you, but everything I do have is yours—my life, my heart, my soul. And God help me, I'll spend the rest of my days trying to be the man you deserve."

Breathless with wonder, she cradled his face in her hands. "I love you, too. When I first proposed it was out of desperation, but now . . . Now I can't imagine my life without you."

"Oh no." His devilish smile made her knees go weak. "You're not going to beat me to the punch again. This time it's my turn." He cleared his throat and held both her hands. "Miss Fiona Hartley, you showed me what it means to love . . . through your small kindnesses and great sacrifices, through your heartfelt tears and dazzling smiles. I want us to share all those things and more. Make me the luckiest man alive. Say you'll marry me."

Warmth blossomed in her chest and filled her heart. "Of course I'll marry you. I don't even mind if I must write myself poems and send myself flowers," she teased. "Because you're my partner in all the ways that truly matter."

She'd barely finished her sentence before he pulled her head toward his and took her mouth in a kiss so tender and deep that she felt it from the roots of her hair to the tips of her toes. God, she ached for him.

He joined her on the sofa and trailed kisses up the column of her neck. "Now that the threat of blackmail had been eliminated, I suppose you'd prefer a longer, traditional engagement." He traced the shell of her ear with a fingertip. "A reading of the banns and such."

"Oh, I don't know," she murmured happily. "Gretna Green has much to recommend it at the moment."

Chapter 35

"Your father would have had an apoplexy if you'd eloped," Mama said to Fiona. She contentedly sipped her tea in the drawing room at the Fortress where she, the countess, Lily, and Fiona had gathered to plan the wedding celebration.

"Are you *certain* you wish to have the breakfast here?" her stepmother asked. "They're still repairing the damage from the tree, and the garden is rather . . . wild." Fiona had to give Mama credit—she was *trying* to be diplomatic.

"I'm certain." It seemed impossible to Fiona that only a fortnight ago Gray had proposed. Fiona had persuaded Mama and Lily to return to the Fortress so they might make arrangements for the wedding at the village church.

But truthfully, Fiona was less interested in selecting the flowers and menu items than she was in stealing a few private moments with Gray. "The terrace will be cleared off soon, and I don't mind that the garden is a bit untamed. It feels rather exotic that way."

Mama clucked her tongue. "Exotic indeed." But she could tolerate a few weeds if it meant her daughter would be a countess.

"Shall we invite Miss Haywinkle to the wedding?" Lily teased. She sat at the desk, quill poised above the guest list.

"I think not," Fiona said with a shudder. "She'd spoil the fun."

"I'll not have anyone counting how many glasses of champagne I've tipped." The countess's eyes twinkled. "I've been waiting for this day for far too long."

So had Fiona. Her heart felt light enough to fly away. "I brought a small gift for you," she told the older woman. She retrieved the framed landscape she'd hidden behind the settee and placed it on the countess's lap.

She raised her lorgnette and studied the sketch for several moments. Her watery gaze lingered on the pink clouds streaking across the sky, the lush fields stretching toward the horizon, and the proud Fortress holding court at the center of it all. "It's magnificent," she said, her voice suspiciously raspy. "And the view from atop the rock is just as I remember it from decades ago. I can't tell you how much it pleases me to know you see it the same way."

Fiona hugged the countess's soft shoulders. "I'm glad you like it."

"It is beautiful," Lily sighed. "I should add it's not easy living in the shadow of such a talented older sister."

"Your day is coming," the countess predicted. "Probably sooner than you think."

"I hope so," Lily replied. "Have you decided where you'll hang your picture?"

The countess paused to consider the question. "The library, I think. As a symbol that we can keep the best parts of our past and let go of the rest. I'm so glad you convinced Gray to keep the shelves and books. It's going to be a lovely, peaceful place when it's finished."

Fiona smiled. "I hope so."

"This looks like a momentous gathering." Gray strode into the room wearing the sort of wicked grin that never failed to make Fiona's belly flutter. "Deciding the fates of kings and nations, are you?"

"You're not far off." His grandmother beamed at him.

He reached for Fiona's hand, pressed a kiss to the back, and addressed the room at large. "May I borrow my betrothed for a moment?"

"Of course," everyone chimed, giving one another sly looks.

Fiona's breath hitched as Gray led her from the room. "You rescued me from a heated debate over the merits of lilies versus tulips."

"I love nothing more than rescuing you." He stopped in the hallway, pressed her back to the wall, and kissed her till her toes curled in her slippers. "Have I mentioned yet this morning how amazing you are?"

"Twice," she said. "And the day is still young."

"There's something else I want to ask you while we're alone."

"This sounds promising." She leaned into him. "Go on."

"I received a letter from my contact at the *London Hearsay* yesterday. Apparently, the reaction to your sketch was extraordinary. Letters from readers have been pouring in ever since it appeared in the paper. They loved the passion and the mystery behind your drawing and have been demanding to know who the couple are."

"That's sweet," Fiona said. "Our little secret."

"What would you say if I told you the *Hearsay* wants more of your drawings?"

She blinked at him, incredulous. "Truly?"

"To feature in a weekly column. One of your sketches and a few romantic lines accompanying it every Saturday. You can remain anonymous if you like. And they're willing to pay you handsomely."

Her drawings. Published. Happiness bubbled up inside

her, and she threw her arms around his taut waist. "That would be incredible, but *you* penned the romantic verse. Are you willing to become a professional poet?"

"Not bloody likely. I've retired for good. You'll have to find someone else to fill the role. Someone with charm and wit to spare."

Excitement sparked in Fiona's chest. "I think I know the perfect person."

The next afternoon, Fiona stood atop a flat rock overlooking the river—holding the rope swing.

"I've reconsidered." Her knees knocked together uncontrollably, and coarse fibers itched against her sweaty palms.

This was a horrid idea. She hadn't been in her right mind when she'd agreed. Gray's slow kisses and tender caresses had drugged her till she scarcely knew what she was saying, and now she found herself standing on a cliff—fine, perhaps it was more of a gently sloping embankment—wearing nothing but her chemise, about to risk life and limb as she hurled herself into the river below. *Blast.*

Gray was grinning as he treaded water a few yards below her, his broad bare shoulders glistening in the summer sun. "Just hold on and jump," he called to her. "Release the rope when you're directly over me, and I'll catch you."

"Excellent. I'll succeed in breaking both our necks," she said dryly.

"No, you won't. Trust me."

She took a deep breath. Yes, she *did* trust him. And now she was going to prove it once and for all. Before she could change her mind, she clutched the rope, stepped off the rock—and sailed through the air.

Her hair whipped around her shoulders, and her chemise billowed as she floated over the river. It was the most exhilarating, glorious feeling she could imagine—almost.

A second later, she remembered to release the rope. She plunged into the water, right into Gray's strong arms.

"I did it!" she cried, clinging to him for dear life. Perhaps she hadn't glided over the water like a swan. Her toes had dragged awkwardly across the surface and she'd flopped on her belly for the landing, but she'd taken a leap of faith . . . and survived.

"I'm proud of you," Gray murmured, warming her inside.

Still breathless, she wrapped her legs around his narrow hips and touched her forehead to his. "I hope you enjoyed that little spectacle, because one swing on the rope was quite enough for me. There shan't be a repeat performance—ever."

"Not ever?" He arched a dark brow. "What if an army of spiders surrounded you and the swing was your only means of escape?"

She shuddered. "If spiders attacked me, I'd faint before I could jump."

A wicked gleam lit his eyes. "What if I blackmailed you?"

She blinked at him, incredulous. "What could you possibly blackmail me with?"

"A letter," he drawled. "A letter in which you made a rather bold—some would say scandalous—proposal."

"Gray!" She splashed him in the face.

"I could send it to the *London Hearsay*," he said, grinning.

"You wouldn't!"

"Miss Haywinkle will be so disappointed." He shook his head in mock dismay.

Fiona shrugged. "I suppose it would be a bit humiliating, but I shall never regret writing that letter."

"Good. Because I cherish it. And I cherish you." He spun her in circles, as though they were waltzing through the water. Only thankfully, there was no orchestra to bump into, and no way Gray would let her fall.

"I was thinking I'd like to do a little sketching while we're here," she said.

"Anything you want."

"Even if it requires you to pose without your shirt?"

He responded with a chuckle so deep she felt it in her toes. "I'm certain you'll find a way to persuade me, siren."

She was feeling rather confident of it, too. And as they splashed toward the shore, kissing and laughing, Fiona knew this sketch of Gray would surpass anything she'd drawn before.

Perhaps she would send a copy to Miss Haywinkle.

She'd wager the headmistress would find it quite, *quite* instructive.

Author's Note

Thanks so much for reading Fiona and Gray's story—I hope you enjoyed it! I loved writing this book, and Fiona's diary entries were especially fun. They reminded me of my own diary-writing days and the unique thrill (and risk!) that comes from writing down such personal thoughts.

My very first diary, a pink and white notebook with a lock, was filled with secret crushes, middle school drama, and the gloriously awkward details of my first real kiss. Predictably, my brothers discovered where I hid the notebook and picked the lock. You can guess how mortified I was when they memorized and recited a few passages at Thanksgiving dinner. Trust me, diaries provide the best blackmail material.

I kept another journal in college during a semester in London. Long before the days of camera phones (ahem), I tried my hand at sketching the places I visited—ancient castles, awe-inspiring cathedrals, and lush gardens. I wrote about seeing the Rocky Horror Picture Show play in Bath and having a few too many pints at the university pub.

Now, flipping through those pages helps me remember the semester through my twenty-something eyes.

In a small way, these diaries served as the inspiration for Fiona's. And if you've ever kept a journal, you know just how powerful they can be. In diaries, we reveal the secrets we wouldn't dare tell our best friends. We relive life's poignant moments—the ones that crushed our souls and the ones that made our hearts sing. Most of all, we make sense of the world and tell our own truth, in the moment, the best we can.

And that's why I can't wait for you to read the next Debutante Diaries story, THE DUKE IS BUT A DREAM. You'll see that Lily is taking the diaries to a whole new level—by sharing them with all of London. Of course, this doesn't sit well with a certain disapproving duke, and that's precisely where the adventure begins . . .

As always, happy reading!

Anna Bennett

Read on for an excerpt from
The Duke is But a Dream, the
next charming novel in the
Debutante Diaries series, available
soon from St. Martin's Paperbacks!

The Debutante's Revenge: Issue #12
If she wishes, every young woman on the marriage
mart should experience a romantic kiss before she is be-
trothed. She should know the sensation of a man's lips
brushing against hers and the pressure of his hand at the
small of her back. And if she should desire to deepen the
kiss to include the tangling of tongues or caressing of
skin, there is no harm in it—as long as she may trust the
gentleman involved.
A man wouldn't dream of committing himself to a
woman for the rest of his life without experiencing a taste
of passion. Why, then, should a woman?

Miss Lily Hartley carefully observed her older sister's
expression as she read the paragraphs Lily had drafted
that morning for their wildly popular weekly column in
The London Hearsay. Noting Fiona's widened eyes and
arched brow, Lily braced herself.

Her sister lifted her gaze from the paper and swept an
auburn curl behind her ear. "You truly believe this?"

Lily plucked a silk pillow off the settee in her sister's
drawing room and hugged it to her chest. "Absolutely. It's

only fair, Fi. Why must there be different rules for men and women?"

"*Have* you kissed someone?" Fiona help up the paper tentatively. "Like this?" Lily didn't detect a trace of censure in her sister's voice—but she *did* hear a touch of worry.

Lily sighed, deflating. "Much to my chagrin, no." She found it tragically ironic that the anonymous author of *The Debutante's Revenge*, the column that had scandalized matchmaking mamas and chaperones throughout London with its salacious advice and provocative drawings, had never been properly ravished.

Fiona blew out a long breath. "That's good."

"Good?" Lily asked, incredulous.

"I don't want to see you hurt."

"I know." But perhaps Fi wasn't aware that Lily was already hurting. Over the last few months, she'd watched wistfully as her sister fell in love and married a handsome earl who adored her. Lily couldn't have been happier for Fiona, but she missed having her at home. Everyone said Lily's turn was coming, but so far, no Prince Charming had appeared on *her* horizon.

At least she and her sister would be together for the next fortnight. Fiona's husband, Gray, was traveling to Scotland to conduct some business, and Fi had invited Lily to stay with her while he was gone.

Lily walked to the desk and shuffled through a small pile of Fiona's sketches, each one dreamier than the next. A vignette of a broad-shouldered soldier bowing over a young woman's gracefully extended hand. A man and woman seated on a park bench beneath a parasol, their heads intimately inclined toward one another. The silhouettes of a couple facing each other, their bodies only a breath apart—as though they were on the very brink of a kiss.

Lily brought the last drawing to the settee where Fiona sat and handed it to her. "I didn't think it possible, but you grow more talented with every sketch. We should pair this one with the column I just drafted. It's a perfect match."

"Very well. But perhaps we should temper the advice in the column. What if a naïve young lady read this issue and acted upon it? She could be ruined. Or forced to marry."

Lily frowned. "The column isn't meant to be taken as gospel. Our readers know the advice is on the daring side and a bit tongue-in-cheek, but truth lies at the heart of all we say. We should not shy away from that truth."

Fiona set aside the sketch and pulled Lily into an unexpectedly fierce hug. "You're absolutely right. Someone needs to champion all the shy debutantes and meek wallflowers out there, and I can think of no one better than you." She pressed a kiss to Lily's temple. "And don't worry."

"Please, don't say my time will come." Lily wriggled away from her sister's embrace. "In any event, I'm eager to deliver the column and sketch to the *Hearsay*'s offices." She peered at the elegant clock on the mantel. "It's only an hour until they close—I must leave soon. When I return I'll arrange to have some clothes sent from home. Just think, we'll have two weeks together. We shall stay up late chatting, raid the kitchen for midnight snacks, and lounge about all day."

"It will be lovely," Fiona agreed. "Like old times."

Lily nodded. "Just like it used to be." Except that now Fi had a doting husband and a home of her own. For all Lily knew, Fi was expecting a babe already. The gulf between them seemed to widen daily. "I'm going to change. Are my clothes still in the trunk?"

"Yes." Fiona smirked. "Unless one of the maids mistook them for dust rags."

"Heaven forfend." Lily's disguise was one of her favorite parts of the job.

She, Fiona, and their dear friend Sophie had agreed that no one must discover they were the creative forces behind *The Debutante's Revenge*. Though the column was all the rage, it also had plenty of detractors—aristocrats who found the advice too scandalous, too shocking, and too *true*. Which was why no one could know about the three friends' involvement. One whisper of their connection to the column would destroy their reputations. They had no wish to be cast out of polite society or bring shame upon their families—not before Lily and Sophie had made fine matches. And especially not before they'd had sufficient opportunity to convey all they wished to say to the young, female population of London.

So, each week, Lily took the precaution of donning her disguise prior to delivering the column to the newspaper's offices. The editor assumed she was merely a scrawny messenger boy.

Lily hurried to the guest bedchamber where she slept whenever she visited her sister and brother-in-law's house, closed the door, and opened the trunk at the foot of the bed. Buried deep in a corner of the trunk were an old pair of boy's breeches, a dingy white shirt, and a jacket with patched elbows along with socks, shoes, and a cap.

She unlaced her gown and let the deep green silk slide off her shoulders before removing all of her undergarments and tightly binding her breasts with a long swath of linen. She wriggled her hips into the breeches, which were vexingly snug across her bottom—but that couldn't be helped. A few minutes later, she stood before the full-length mirror and carefully tucked the last long strand of dark hair into her cap.

Her transformation was complete. A lad of fourteen or so stared back at her, smooth-faced and slight of build. As long as she kept her head down and her stride sure, no one would suspect she was a woman, much less the authoress of *The Debutante's Revenge*.

And they *definitely* would not suspect she was Miss Lily Hartley, heiress and sister-in-law of the Earl of Ravenport.

Enjoying the familiar ease and comfort of her breeches, Lily slung the strap of her leather bag across her body and hurried downstairs into the drawing room. "I'm ready to go," she announced, expecting only Fiona.

"Who the devil are you?" Gray demanded. The earl stalked toward Lily and planted his hands on his hips, apparently prepared to defend his bride from any ruffian who dared invade her drawing room.

Lily stepped back, more amused than frightened by his blustering. Her disguise was even better than she'd hoped.

Fiona rushed to Gray's side and laid a calming hand on his arm. "It's only Lily. She's preparing to deliver our column to the *Hearsay.*"

"Lily?" He backed slowly away and tilted his head to see her face beneath the brim of her cap.

"It is I." She pointed her toe, made a theatrical bow, then grinned up at him. "Nice to see you, Gray."

The earl chuckled and dragged a hand through his hair. "Good to know the Hartley sisters are up to their usual tricks. Forgive my outburst. I didn't realize you were planning on staying here till Fiona mentioned it just now."

"Oh? Is it a problem?" They'd never treated her as a

guest in the past, making it clear she was welcome to drop in whenever she chose.

"Not at all," Gray assured her, but Lily sensed something was amiss.

Fiona wrung her hands. "Gray just informed me that he'd hoped to surprise me with a belated honeymoon. He wants to whisk me away to Scotland with him . . . but I've already told him it's out of the question. You and I intended to have a couple of weeks of sisterly bonding, and so we shall."

Lily pasted on a smile so bright that no one would dream her heart was breaking. "A honeymoon? How romantic! Fi, what's this nonsense about not going? You absolutely must. I insist that you march upstairs and pack this instant."

"I'd already instructed her maid to prepare her things." Gray shot an apologetic smile at Fiona. "But I should have checked with her first."

"And spoiled the surprise?" Lily interjected. "Never. I *know* you want to go," Lily said to her sister, "and *I* want you to go as well."

"But you were so looking forward to staying here, and there was a particular matter I wished to discuss."

Lily waved a dismissive hand. "We shall schedule a visit for another time." She paused and searched her sister's face. "Unless the matter is urgent?"

"No." Fiona worried her lip. "You're certain you don't mind?"

"Not at all," Lily said, impressively convincing.

"What about *The Debutante's Revenge*? We'll need columns for the next two weeks, and Sophie is staying in Cornwall with her aunt. She won't be able to help."

"Leave it to me." Lily strode to the desk, collected Fiona's sketches, and carefully placed them in her bag.

"You've already drawn beautiful illustrations. I'll simply write articles to accompany them. It shan't be a problem."

"You see," Gray said, pressing his lips to the back of Fiona's hand. "Everything is settled. If we leave now, we can make it to a charming little inn before nightfall."

Fiona shot Lily an imploring look, so she fought back the tiniest twinge of resentment and smiled widely. "*Go*," she said encouragingly.

"Very well." Fiona threw up her hands. "I confess I can't resist the idea of a honeymoon."

"No happy bride in her right mind would," Lily said. "Off with you now."

"Will you explain to Papa and Mama where we've gone?"

Blast. Until that very moment, Lily had forgotten that her father and stepmother left for Bath a few hours earlier. Mama insisted taking the waters would do wonders for Papa's weak heart, even though he'd never looked healthier to Lily. She was supposed to inform her sister that their parents would return in two weeks. But if she told Fiona about their excursion now, she'd cancel her honeymoon in a heartbeat. "Of course," Lily fibbed. "I'll be sure to let them know where you two newlyweds are headed."

Fiona wrapped her in a grateful embrace. "I'll make this up to you," she vowed.

"Another time," Lily murmured, willing herself not to cry.

"Can I be honest with you about something?" Fiona asked.

Lily sniffled. "Certainly."

Grinning, Fiona tweaked the brim of Lily's hat. "I feel like I'm hugging a chimney sweep."

"Interesting," Lily mused. "Perhaps next week's column shall address the subject of dressing as the opposite sex."

Gray grimaced and dragged a hand down his face. "I beg you to exercise restraint."

"Restraint has never been Lily's forte," Fiona said proudly. "It's one of the many reasons I adore her."

Lily laughed. But Fiona's assessment hit the mark. Ever since they'd attended Miss Haywinkle's School for Girls, Lily had been known as the pupil most likely to stretch rules. To push boundaries. Unfortunately, her well-meaning but ever-vigilant family kept her wilder side in check.

But the next two weeks afforded a rare opportunity. While her father and stepmother stayed in Bath and her sister and brother-in-law honeymooned in Scotland, Lily would be left to her own devices. Each side of the family assumed she'd be looked after by the other, and Lily would be free.

Free to venture to places where proper young misses dared not go.

Free to mingle with people from other walks of life.

And, best of all, free to experience the passion she'd only written about.